Then all listened while Elrond in his clear voice spoke of Sauron and the Rings of Power, and their forging in the Second Age of the world long ago. A part of his tale was known to some there, but the full tale to none, and many eyes were turned to Elrond in fear and wonder as he told of the Elven-smiths of Eregion and their friendship with Moria, and their eagerness for knowledge, by which Sauron ensnared them. For in that time he was not yet evil to behold, and they received his aid and grew mighty in craft, whereas he learned all their secrets, and betrayed them, and forged secretly in the Mountain of Fire the One Ring to be their master. But Celebrimbor was aware of him, and hid the Three which he had made; and there was war, and the land was laid waste, and the gate of Moria was shut.

Then through all the years that followed he traced the Ring; but since that history is elsewhere recounted, even as Elrond himself set it down in his books of lore, it is not here recalled. For it is a long tale, full of deeds great and terrible, and briefly though Elrond spoke, the sun rode up the sky, and the morning was passing ere he ceased.

Of Númenor he spoke, its glory and its fall, and the return of the Kings of Men to Middle-earth out of the deeps of the Sea, borne upon the wings of storm.

*The Lord of the Rings: The Fellowship of the Ring*
Book Two, II 'The Council of Elrond'

*Works by J.R.R. Tolkien*

THE HOBBIT
LEAF BY NIGGLE
ON FAIRY-STORIES
FARMER GILES OF HAM
THE HOMECOMING OF BEORHTNOTH
THE LORD OF THE RINGS
THE ADVENTURES OF TOM BOMBADIL
THE ROAD GOES EVER ON (WITH DONALD SWANN)
SMITH OF WOOTTON MAJOR

*Works published posthumously*

SIR GAWAIN AND THE GREEN KNIGHT, PEARL AND SIR ORFEO*
THE FATHER CHRISTMAS LETTERS
THE SILMARILLION*
PICTURES BY J.R.R. TOLKIEN*
UNFINISHED TALES*
THE LETTERS OF J.R.R. TOLKIEN*
FINN AND HENGEST
MR BLISS
THE MONSTERS AND THE CRITICS & OTHER ESSAYS*
ROVERANDOM
THE CHILDREN OF HÚRIN*
THE LEGEND OF SIGURD AND GUDRÚN*
THE FALL OF ARTHUR*
BEOWULF: A TRANSLATION AND COMMENTARY*
THE STORY OF KULLERVO
THE LAY OF AOTROU & ITROUN
BEREN AND LÚTHIEN*
THE FALL OF GONDOLIN*
THE NATURE OF MIDDLE-EARTH

*The History of Middle-earth – by Christopher Tolkien*

I THE BOOK OF LOST TALES, PART ONE
II THE BOOK OF LOST TALES, PART TWO
III THE LAYS OF BELERIAND
IV THE SHAPING OF MIDDLE-EARTH
V THE LOST ROAD AND OTHER WRITINGS
VI THE RETURN OF THE SHADOW
VII THE TREASON OF ISENGARD
VIII THE WAR OF THE RING
IX SAURON DEFEATED
X MORGOTH'S RING
XI THE WAR OF THE JEWELS
XII THE PEOPLES OF MIDDLE-EARTH

* Edited by Christopher Tolkien

# The Fall of Númenor

### and Other Tales from the
### Second Age of Middle-earth

Edited by Brian Sibley
and compiled from *The Lord of the Rings*,
*The Silmarillion, Unfinished Tales*, volumes from
*The History of Middle-earth* by Christopher Tolkien,
and other sources

*With illustrations by*
ALAN LEE

HarperCollins*Publishers*

To the memory of
Priscilla Reuel Tolkien
(1929–2022)
ever a friend to friends
of Middle-earth

HarperCollins*Publishers* Ltd
1 London Bridge Street
London SE1 9GF

HarperCollins*Publishers*
Macken House, 39/40 Mayor Street Upper,
Dublin 1, Ireland, D01 C9W8

www.tolkien.co.uk
www.tolkienestate.com

This paperback edition 2024
4

First published in Great Britain by HarperCollins*Publishers* 2022
Copyright © HarperCollins*Publishers* 2022

# CONTENTS

## CONTENTS

* Maps by Christopher Tolkien

THE WEST OF
**MIDDLE-EARTH**
AT THE END OF
**THE THIRD AGE**

Miles

50    100    150    200

# ABOUT THIS BOOK

*The Fall of Númenor* seeks to present, in a single volume, selections from J.R.R. Tolkien's posthumously published writings about the Second Age of Middle-earth. This book would not have been possible without the extraordinary literary achievements of Christopher Tolkien, who introduced readers of *The Hobbit* and *The Lord of the Rings* to the rich legacy of myth and history from both the Elder Days and Second Age. This he achieved through his long years of dedicated curatorial stewardship: editing, assembling, compiling and providing invaluable commentary to his father's many manuscripts and drafts. It was in the pages of *The Silmarillion, Unfinished Tales,* volumes of *The History of Middle-earth,* and other works, as edited and prepared for publication by Christopher Tolkien, that the story was first told of the Fall of Númenor, the rise of Sauron, the forging of the Rings of Power and the Last Alliance of Elves and Men against the Dark Lord of Mordor.

The intention is not to supplant these works, as each already stands as the definitive presentation of J.R.R. Tolkien's writings, with peerless, insightful commentary and analysis by Christopher Tolkien, but rather to provide extracts from the above – with as few editorial interventions as possible – that illustrate in the author's own words the rich and tumultuous events of the Second Age as summarised by J.R.R. Tolkien in his 'The Tale of Years (Chronology of the Westlands)' that appears as part of Appendix B in *The Lord of the Rings* and which is reproduced at the beginning of this volume. For those wishing to delve deeper into its history, the notes provided at the end of the book, many of which draw upon Christopher Tolkien's own invaluable editorial expertise by reproducing or quoting from his own notes to the original published sources, will aid their explorations as they seek to discover more about the Second Age of Middle-earth. Page references relate in all cases to the first edition of that work, with the exception of *The Lord of the Rings*, where reference is made to the reset edition published in 2004 for the book's fiftieth anniversary.

The selected passages and extracts are arranged following the chronological year order set down in 'The Tale of Years (Chronology of the Westlands)', and are presented in chapters titled to accord with the chronology. This presentation has been augmented by two other sources: the names and dates of the Númenórean Kings given in 'Appendix A: Annals of the Kings and Rulers' – again in *The Lord of the Rings* – and 'The Line of Elros: Kings of Númenor' as found in *Unfinished Tales*, Part Two: 'The Second Age'.

The events of the Second Age as they unfold respectively on Númenor and in Middle-earth are chronicled using material from the following sources.

For Númenórean history: the text of 'Akallabêth' (in *The Silmarillion*); the story of 'Aldarion and Erendis' and the genealogical table 'The earlier generations of the Line of Elros' (in *Unfinished Tales*); and taking into consideration material found in 'The History of the Akallabêth' (*The Peoples of Middle-earth*), 'The Early History of the Legend' and 'The Fall of Númenor' (both in *The Lost Road and Other Writings*) and 'The Drowning of Anadûnê' (in *Sauron Defeated*).

As Christopher Tolkien would have wished, research into his father's writings continues and the text additionally draws upon a further posthumous volume of Tolkien's writings, *The Nature of Middle-earth* (2021) edited by Carl F. Hostetter. These sources are edited so as to tell the history of the establishing of Númenor, its geography and wildlife and the lives of the Númenóreans, additionally including or drawing upon

'A Description of the Island of Númenor' (in *Unfinished Tales*) and, from *The Nature of Middle-earth*, 'The Land and Beasts of Númenor', 'The Lives of the Númenóreans' and 'The Ageing of Númenóreans'. Passages used do not necessarily appear as originally presented in that volume, but in an order best suited to the chronological narrative.

The events that unfold in Middle-earth concurrent with those on Númenor have been selected from the text of 'Of the Rings of Power and the Third Age' (in *The Silmarillion*), 'The History of Galadriel and Celeborn' (in *Unfinished Tales*), and 'Galadriel and Celeborn' (in *The Nature of Middle-earth*).

This volume adheres to the principle established by Christopher Tolkien that the published texts are treated as being the final versions, and in instances where material is included from earlier drafts with variant names, dates and spellings, such variations are amended to conform with those finally adopted. Where he considered words or phrases in his father's handwriting to be uncertain, they are preceded by a question mark.

Editorial interventions are in a smaller font size and indented; explanatory emendations by the editor to introduce passages or within the body of an extract are shown in square brackets. The opening words to passages, where not capitalized in the original, have been silently emended to begin with a capital for ease of reading. Omissions of words within a passage are indicated with an ellipsis.

The book also includes extracts from *The Letters of J. R. R. Tolkien* (1981) edited by Humphrey Carpenter with the assistance of Christopher Tolkien, and incorporates significant passages from *The Lord of the Rings* related to the Second Age, which provide important, relevant material. In some of these, the text has been abridged (with edits indicated by ellipses) or silently rearranged; in all instances end-notes will direct the reader to the relevant passages in the three parts of the work, indicated as '*Fellowship*', '*Towers*' and '*Return*'.

# INTRODUCTION

## THE SAGA OF 'A DARK AGE'

It is a powerfully abiding moment in modern literature: the One Ring – the Dark Lord Sauron's Master Ring of Power, the destruction of which has been the object of an epic quest – falls into the fiery heart of Mount Doom; thus, returning to the inferno in which it was forged, the Ring is, at last, unmade.

Of course, there is much that the author still has to deal with: matters to do with rescue, healing and a coronation, followed by final reckonings and reconciliations, farewells, partings and departures. But the destruction of the Ruling Ring, and with it the fall of Sauron and his dark tower and an end to his millennia-long war of attrition against the Free Peoples of Middle-earth is effectively the climactic moment in J.R.R. Tolkien's *The Lord of the Rings*.

For the author, however, it was an elaborate appendix to a far older tale – or series of tales – with which he had been engaged for many years and towards which his imagination had been working for even longer. As he would write, a few years before *The Lord of the Rings* was published: 'I do not remember a time when I was not building it.'[1]

Through the tireless efforts of the engines of popular culture, *The Lord of the Rings* is now a universally appropriated symbol of the art of myth-making, ranked among the world's centuries-long storehouse of legends, folk- and fairy-tales. But, for Tolkien, the exploits of Bilbo Baggins and the monumental quest of his nephew Frodo, were but part of a far greater story reaching back into a distant past.

J.R.R. Tolkien, writing to his son, Christopher, in November 1944, revealed the extent to which the 'great Romance' with which he was engaged was a continually growing, changing and emerging chronicle. In sending Christopher the latest completed chapters together with an outline for the remainder of the narrative, he commented: 'It will probably work out very differently from this plan when it really gets written, as the thing seems to write itself once I get going, as if the truth comes out then, only imperfectly glimpsed in the preliminary sketch.'[2]

This approach to creative writing stemmed from Tolkien being both an acknowledged scholar and, at the same time, an admitted amateur practitioner of the novelist's craft. Although professionally and passionately rooted in research and trained in the comprehension and use of words, he was constantly – and to his genuine surprise and delight – buffeted and redirected by the freewheeling, liberating inspiration of the creative imagination. The result was *The Lord of the Rings*: a uniquely conceived and executed masterpiece of fantasy literature that was an ambitious 'sequel' to his earlier and more modest tale, *The Hobbit*.

Initially, Tolkien's readers were only aware of the book itself, not its forensically, even obsessively, constructed foundation that was the disciplined labour of an academic mind. Only later, and gradually, did the public become aware of the vast, labyrinthine structure of linguistics, chronologies, genealogies and histories underpinning the epic (yet intimate and particular) narrative of the War of the Ring. Part of that foundation was a work-in-progress known as 'The Silmarillion', an intricate mosaic of imaginative writings constituting the prehistory of *The Lord of the Rings* and the genesis of the Middle-earth legendarium.

In 1951, Tolkien was seeking a publisher who was willing to not only consider the new-minted *The Lord of the Rings* but who was also prepared to commit to simultaneously publishing 'The Silmarillion' a project on which he had, by then, been intermittently engaged for some thirty-seven years.

To promote his cause, Tolkien wrote out what he referred to as 'a brief sketch' (although it ran to more than 7,500 words) to serve as a résumé of both 'The Silmarillion' and *The Lord of the Rings* and which took pains to detail the co-dependency of the two projects.

He first outlined the making of Middle-earth – a creation myth of considerable literary power and beauty – followed by opulently crafted histories of its different races and the mighty deeds they wrought and great tragedies that befell them across the generations that comprised what he referred to as the First Age. Then, turning to the events of the Age that followed, Tolkien wrote, 'The next cycle deals (or would deal) with the Second Age. But it is on Earth a dark age, and not very much of its history is (or need be) told.'[3]

This was a curious statement, since Tolkien had already written down much of that history – in many detailed drafts of considerable length – including the origin and rise of Sauron, titular character of *The Lord of the Rings*, the forging of the Rings of Power and of the One Ring to rule them all.

Similarly, from the same span of more than 3,400 years, he had recorded an account of the establishing of the island of Númenor with its geography and nature, its people and their political, social and cultural history and, finally, the events that led to their eventual corruption, decline and catastrophic downfall.

Tolkien's ambitious plan to present readers with the full breadth of the mythology, legend and history of his created world as a prelude to the drama of *The Lord of the Rings* came to naught – publishers being understandably wary of such a costly and uncertain investment – and he was left with no alternative but to accept that the tale of Frodo Baggins and the Company of the Ring would need to stand alone.

Nevertheless, the creation and eventual ruin of Númenor

and the making of the Rings of Power were central events in the chronology of Middle-earth and when, in July and November 1954, the first two volumes of *The Lord of the Rings* – *The Fellowship of the Ring* and *The Two Towers* – were eventually published by George Allen & Unwin, readers had their first tantalizing glimpses of that past history, providing a richly tapestried backdrop to the struggle by the Free Peoples of Middle-earth against Sauron and the forces of Mordor. These potent elements, though peripheral to the main narrative, proved to be – as, indeed, they have remained – an integral part of the book's appeal.

When, in 1955, *The Return of the King* was published as the third and final volume of *The Lord of the Rings*, Tolkien added more than one hundred pages of Appendices that provided many details about Middle-earth: its languages, the lineage of its Kings and Rulers and a chronological timeline of the events of the Second and Third Ages. For many years, these appendices, as amended in 1966 for the second edition of *The Lord of the Rings*, were the only gleanings of information available to the average reader seeking background knowledge to the published adventures of Mr Bilbo Baggins and the later quest undertaken by his nephew, Frodo.

As Tolkien wrote in 1965 in his Foreword to the Second Edition of *The Lord of the Rings*: 'This tale grew in the telling, until it became a history of the Great War of the Ring and included many glimpses of the yet more ancient history that preceded it.' With the author's death on 2 September 1973, it might have seemed that there would be no further insights into that 'yet more ancient history' of Middle-earth; but, in May 1977, Humphrey Carpenter published *J. R. R. Tolkien, A Biography*, which not only revealed more fully than had otherwise been understood the vast scope of the work that Tolkien had created but also offered new and enticing details of specific verse and prose narratives, such as 'The Voyage of Earendel the Evening Star' and 'The Fall of Gondolin': alluring references that would herald the appearance, in September the same year, of *The Silmarillion* as presented for publication by Christopher, a project to which he had tirelessly devoted himself for the preceding four years, as he sought to offer readers the opportunity to revel in his father's grand vision of the First Age of Middle-earth.

Although *The Silmarillion* focused chiefly on the mythology and history of the 'Elder Days' of Middle-earth, it also contained two key works relating to the Second Age: the self-explanatory essay 'Of the Rings of Power and the Third Age' and 'Akallabêth'. This latter text provided an account of the island kingdom of Númenor – gifted to the Men of Middle-earth who had loyally fought alongside the Elves in the War of Wrath at the conclusion of the First Age – and described how, through the corruption of Sauron, its destruction was accomplished. Tolkien's original title for this narrative was 'The Fall of Númenor', later changed to 'The Downfall of Númenor'. In *The Silmarillion* Christopher Tolkien used the title 'Akallabêth', meaning in the language of the Númenóreans 'She that hath Fallen' or 'The Downfallen', noting that whilst no version of the work bore that title, it was the name by which it was referred to by his father.[4]

More Númenórean detail – historic, geographic and genealogical – was revealed when, in 1980, Christopher Tolkien published *Unfinished Tales of Númenor and Middle-earth*, a further selection of narratives, largely incomplete, drawn from his father's writings recounting various moments of high drama during the Three Ages of Middle-earth.

Like *The Silmarillion*, *Unfinished Tales* sprang from Christopher's dedicated study of his father's papers and the book's success, despite its fragmentary nature, initiated a unique endeavour in the sphere of literary research that would result, over a thirteen-year period, in the magisterial 12-volume series, *The History of Middle-earth*.

Mention must be made of two further significant texts by J.R.R. Tolkien relating to Númenor. His fascination with his island

creation and its eventual fate owed its origin, in part, to a recur-
ring nightmare that began in early childhood and continued
into adult life. In a letter, written in 1964, he described this
experience: 'This legend or myth or dim memory of some
ancient history has always troubled me. In sleep I had the
dreadful dream of the ineluctable Wave, either coming up out of
a quiet sea, or coming in towering over the green inlands. It still
occurs occasionally, though now exorcized by writing about it.'[5]

An incentive for Tolkien to attempt such an exorcism arose
in, as seems likely, 1936 as the result of an exchange with
C.S. Lewis, his friend and fellow member of the literary group,
the Inklings. Tolkien later recalled: 'L[ewis] said to me one
day: "Tollers, there is too little of what we really like in stories.
I am afraid we shall have to try and write some ourselves." We
agreed that he should try "space travel", and I should try
"time-travel".'[6]

Lewis would write *Out of the Silent Planet*,[7] the first of a
trilogy using science fiction to allegorically address moral and
theological themes. Tolkien's attempt proved less successful.
'I began,' he wrote, 'an abortive book of time-travel of which the
end was to be the presence of my hero in the drowning of Atlantis. This was to be called *Númenor*, the Land in the West.'[8] The
story was to span many generations of a family beginning with
a father and son, Edwin and Elwin, and would trace their ancestry back through time to key characters at the time of
Númenor's fall. 'My effort,' he subsequently reflected, 'after a
few promising chapters, ran dry: it was too long a way round to
what I really wanted to make, a new version of the Atlantis
legend.'[9]

Although Tolkien wrote of what he referred to as his 'Atlantis
complex' or 'Atlantis-haunting', obviously acknowledging a link
to the fictional island described in Plato's dialogues, he was
more directly attracted by the romance of a civilization overtaken by an Atlantean tragedy, something that has exerted its
hold on the human imagination across many centuries of
popular culture.[10]

In Tolkien's interpretation, the cataclysmic sinking of Númenor beneath the waves is followed by the world being reshaped – or 'bent' – from flat to round and with the lands of the West being 'removed for ever from the circles of the world'. A crucial element of this myth was the continuing existence of a Straight Road to the Ancient West which, though now hidden from view, might be travelled by any who could find it: a concept embodied in the proposed title for the book, *The Lost Road*.

The literal rise and fall of Tolkien's island (for it had been initially raised from the sea as a gift to Men) was informed not just by Plato's philosophical allegory on the politics of statehood but also by the Judeo-Christian narrative of the frailty and fallibility of mankind as related in the Biblical Book of Genesis. This is evident in his description of *The Downfall of Númenor* as 'the Second Fall of Man (or Man rehabilitated but still mortal)'.[11]

It is clear from Christopher Tolkien's detailed study of his father's papers that the tale of the Númenóreans and their fate was conceived in complete harmony with 'The Silmarillion' and the continually developing history of Middle-earth and the natural and supernatural laws to which it was subject. The initial 'contest' with Lewis to write what Tolkien described as 'an excursionary "Thriller" . . . discovering Myth'[12] rapidly acquired far greater importance as a component in his legendarium – indeed Númenor became a keystone in Tolkien's emerging structure for the events of the Second Age.

Although incomplete, Tolkien had shown his publisher the first draft chapters of *The Lost Road* in 1937, but their discouraging response was that, even if completed, the book was unlikely to find commercial success.

In 1945 Tolkien returned to the idea of a separate exploration of a time-travelling Atlantean concept (still linked to Middle-earth) when he began writing *The Notion Club Papers*, a planned novel that was to take the fanciful form of a discovery, in the then-distant year 2012, of assorted papers relating to the meetings of an Oxford literary circle and the attempts of two of their number to experiment with time-travel. The Notion Club is a punning reference to the Inklings, a similarly Oxford university-based club of self-confessed 'amateur' writers of fiction of which Tolkien and Lewis were prime movers. The name Inklings had, of course, been cleverly chosen to suggest both 'ideas' and those who are apt to dabble in ink and Tolkien's choice of the word 'notion' was an obvious synonym for 'inkling'; furthermore, Tolkien toyed with the idea that some of the characters listed as members of 'the Notion Club' were, perhaps, fictional portraits of himself and fellow Inklings.

At the time of its composition, Tolkien had still to complete *The Lord of the Rings* and *The Notion Club Papers*, like *The Lost Road*, was eventually abandoned, although not before a considerable part of the book had been drafted and a further considerable investment of time had been spent in creating a Númenórean language, Adûnayân – or, in its anglicized form, Adûnaic ('Language of the West'). Having returned to and finally completed *The Lord of the Rings*, Tolkien failed to resume work on *The Notion Club Papers* due, doubtlessly, to him increasingly focusing his attention on the Elder Days of Middle-earth.

Although the content of *The Lost Road* and *The Notion Club Papers* as planned and partially completed have an important thematic connection with the Númenórean writings as found in *The Silmarillion*'s 'Akallabêth' and other posthumously published narratives of the Second Age, they are radically individual in their style and tone – especially in their time-travelling concepts involving partial 'real world' (and 'future world') settings.

Readers wishing to further explore these discrete experiments in the chronicling of the Númenórean concept (including its language) are encouraged to read two volumes of Christopher Tolkien's *History of Middle-earth*: *The Lost Road and Other Writings* (1987) and *Sauron Defeated* (1992), though by way of illustration an extensive and particularly significant narrative, which is taken from *The Lost Road* and is referred to by Christopher in *The Lost Road* as 'The Númenórean chapters', is included in this volume in the form of an Appendix.

\* \* \*

Christopher Tolkien died in 2020 aged 95, after a lifetime of intimate involvement with the annals of Middle-earth and a near fifty-year career meticulously curating his father's work. The unparalleled scholarly legacy that remains has immeasurably enriched readers' understanding and appreciation of the book that, in 1997, was voted the best-loved work of fiction of the twentieth century and which now – via a variety of media – holds an unassailable place in the affections of an international audience.

Without Christopher's passion, dedication and skill, the story of the Second Age of Middle-earth would never have been told.

# BEFORE THE SECOND AGE

J.R.R. Tolkien's *The Lord of the Rings* had its foundation in the book we now know as *The Silmarillion*, eventually published in 1977 under the masterful editorship of his son, Christopher. It was a volume that drew together the whole matter of Middle-earth's creation and its passage from an age of myth to a time where stories merge into histories – inspired, as its author would say, by his 'basic passion . . . for myth (not allegory!) and for fairy-story, and above all for heroic legend on the brink of fairy-tale and history, of which there is far too little in the world (accessible to me) for my appetite.'

In 1951, long before the publication of *The Silmarillion* with its tales of the First Age of Middle-earth – and, indeed, before even *The Lord of the Rings* had reached the hands of a reading public, Tolkien wrote to his friend, Milton Waldman, about the scope of his ambition as a teller of tales:[1]

> Do not laugh! But once upon a time (my crest has long since fallen) I had a mind to make a body of more or less connected legend, ranging from the large and cosmogonic, to the level of romantic fairy-story – the larger founded on the lesser in contact with the earth, the lesser drawing splendour from the vast backcloths – which I could dedicate simply to: to England; to my country. It should possess the tone and quality that I desired, somewhat cool and clear, be redolent of our 'air' (the clime and soil of the North West, meaning Britain and the hither parts of Europe: not Italy or the Aegean, still less the

East), and, while possessing (if I could achieve it) the fair elusive beauty that some call Celtic (though it is rarely found in genuine ancient Celtic things), it should be 'high', purged of the gross, and fit for the more adult mind of a land long now steeped in poetry. I would draw some of the great tales in fullness, and leave many only placed in the scheme, and sketched. The cycles should be linked to a majestic whole, and yet leave scope for other minds and hands, wielding paint and music and drama. Absurd.

Ambitious, certainly, but – fortunately for us – not as absurd as Tolkien imagined in his more frustrated and doubtful moments and it was a concept to which he constantly returned and determinedly pursued, even though his mode of pursuit was that of a wandering traveller: picking up languages, making maps and ever ready to leave the highway of his central narrative in order to explore picturesque or dangerous byways, before returning to the road ahead – which explains, no doubt, why the idea of the 'Road' is one that runs, twisting and turning, through so much of his writing.

Commenting on the grand imagined sweep of his 'absurd' scheme, Tolkien readily admitted that it had neither been conceived nor developed 'all at once'; instead it had come together in a way that speaks to the very specific impact that his writing was to have – and still has – on a readership that spans continents and cultures. 'The mere stories,' he wrote, 'were the thing. They arose in my mind as "given" things, and as they came, separately, so too the links grew. An absorbing, though continually interrupted labour (especially since, even apart from the necessities of life, the mind would wing to the other pole and spend itself on the linguistics): yet always I had the sense of recording what was already "there", somewhere: not of "inventing".'

Perhaps the power of all great literature lies in that audacious moment of suspended disbelief. Tolkien's reference to 'linguistics' is, itself, key to that creative process since his love and great knowledge of languages infuses the fictional with antiquity. As he wrote:

> Many children make up, or begin to make up, imaginary languages. I have been at it since I could write. But I have never stopped, and of course, as a professional philologist (especially interested in linguistic aesthetics), I have changed in taste, improved in theory, and probably in craft. Behind my stories is now a nexus of languages (mostly only structurally sketched). But to those creatures which in English I call misleadingly Elves are assigned two related languages more nearly completed, whose history is written, and whose forms (representing two different sides of my own linguistic taste) are deduced scientifically from a common origin. Out of these languages are made nearly all the *names* that appear in my legends. This gives a certain character (a cohesion, a consistency of linguistic style, and an illusion of historicity) to the nomenclature, or so I believe, that is markedly lacking in other comparable things.

The foregoing comments were a preface to his attempt at providing an outline of the events recorded in his complex legendarium, and which take place in the long Age preceding the one chronicled in the present volume.

> The cycles begin [he wrote] with a cosmogonical myth: the *Music of the Ainur*. God and the Valar . . . are revealed. These latter are, as we should say, angelic powers, whose function is to exercise delegated authority in their spheres. . . They are 'divine', that is, were originally 'outside' and existed 'before' the making of the world.

Following the creation story, the narrative of *The Silmarillion* continues as Tolkien outlined in his letter:

It moves then swiftly to the *History of the Elves*, or the *Silmarillion* proper; to the world as we perceive it, but of course transfigured in a still half-mythical mode: that is it deals with rational incarnate creatures of more or less comparable stature with our own. These are the *First-born*, the Elves; and the *Followers* Men. The doom of the Elves is to be immortal, to love the beauty of the world, to bring it to full flower with their gifts of delicacy and perfection, to last while it lasts, never leaving it even when 'slain', but returning – and yet, when the Followers come, to teach them, and make way for them, to 'fade' as the Followers grow and absorb the life from which both proceed. The Doom (or the Gift) of Men is mortality, freedom from the circles of the world.

As I say, the legendary *Silmarillion* is peculiar, and differs from all similar things that I know. . . . Its centre of view and interest is not Men but 'Elves'. Men come in inevitably: after all the author is a man, and if he has an audience they will be Men and Men must come in to our tales, as such, and not merely transfigured or partially represented as Elves, Dwarfs, Hobbits, etc. But they remain peripheral – late comers, and however growingly important, not principals.

The main body of the tale, the *Silmarillion* proper, is about the fall of the most gifted kindred of the Elves, their exile from Valinor (a kind of Paradise, the home of the Gods) in the furthest West, their re-entry into Middle-earth, the land of their birth but long under the rule of the Enemy, and their strife with him, the power of Evil still visibly incarnate. It receives its name because the events are all threaded upon the fate and significance of the *Silmarilli* ('radiance of pure light') or Primeval Jewels . . . but the Silmarilli were more than just beautiful things as such. There was Light. There was the Light of Valinor made visible in the Two Trees of Silver and Gold.[2] These were slain by the Enemy out of malice, and Valinor was darkened, though from them, ere they died utterly, were derived the lights of Sun and Moon. (A marked difference here between these legends and most others is that the Sun is not a divine symbol, but a second-best thing, and the 'light of the Sun' (the world under the sun) become terms for a fallen world, and a dislocated imperfect vision).[3]

But the chief artificer of the Elves (Fëanor) had imprisoned the Light of Valinor in the three supreme jewels, the Silmarilli, before the Trees were sullied or slain. This Light thus lived thereafter only in these gems. The fall of the Elves comes about through the possessive attitude of Fëanor and his seven sons to these gems. They are captured by the Enemy, set in his Iron Crown, and guarded in his impenetrable stronghold. The sons of Fëanor take a terrible and blasphemous oath of enmity and vengeance against all or any, even of the gods, who dares to claim any part or right in the Silmarilli. They pervert the greater part of their kindred, who rebel against the gods, and depart from paradise, and go to make hopeless war upon the Enemy. The first fruit of their fall is war in Paradise, the slaying of Elves by Elves, and this and their evil oath dogs all their later heroism, generating treacheries and undoing all victories. The *Silmarillion* is the history of the War of the Exiled Elves against the Enemy, which all takes place in the North-west of the world (Middle-earth). Several tales of victory and tragedy are caught up in it; but it ends with catastrophe, and the passing of the Ancient World, the world of the long *First Age*. The jewels are recovered (by the final intervention of the gods) only to be lost for ever to the Elves, one in the sea, one in the deeps of earth, and one as a star of heaven. This legendarium ends with a vision of the end of the world, its breaking and remaking, and the recovery of the Silmarilli and the 'light before the Sun'. . . .

As the stories become less mythical, and more like stories and romances, Men are interwoven. For the most part these are 'good Men' – families and their chiefs who rejecting the service of Evil, and hearing rumours of the Gods of the West and the High Elves, flee westward and come into contact with the Exiled Elves in the midst of their war. The Men who appear are mainly those of the Three Houses of the Fathers of Men, whose chieftains become allies of the Elflords. The contact of

Men and Elves already foreshadows the history of the later Ages, and a recurrent theme is the idea that in Men (as they now are) there is a strand of 'blood' and inheritance, derived from the Elves, and that the art and poetry of Men is largely dependent on it, or modified by it.[4] There are thus two marriages of mortal and elf – both later coalescing in the kindred of Eärendil, represented by Elrond the Half-elven who appears in all the stories, even *The Hobbit*. The chief of the stories of *The Silmarillion*, and the one most fully treated is the *Story of Beren and Lúthien the Elfmaiden*. Here we meet, among other things, the first example of the motive (to become dominant in Hobbits) that the great policies of world history, 'the wheels of the world', are often turned not by the Lords and Governors, even gods, but by the seemingly unknown and weak – owing to the secret life in creation, and the part unknowable to all wisdom but One, that resides in the intrusions of the Children of God into the Drama. It is Beren the outlawed mortal who succeeds (with the help of Lúthien, a mere maiden even if an elf of royalty) where all the armies and warriors have failed: he penetrates the stronghold of the Enemy and wrests one of the Silmarilli from the Iron Crown. Thus he wins the hand of Lúthien and the first marriage of mortal and immortal is achieved.

As such the story is (I think a beautiful and powerful) heroic-fairy-romance, receivable in itself with only a very general vague knowledge of the background. But it is also a fundamental link in the cycle, deprived of its full significance out of its place therein. For the capture of the Silmaril, a supreme victory, leads to disaster. The oath of the sons of Fëanor becomes operative, and lust for the Silmaril brings all the kingdoms of the Elves to ruin.

Nevertheless, it was from the union of Beren and Lúthien Tinúviel that came the line of the Half-Elven, later numbering not just Elrond, Master of Rivendell, but also Elros, his twin brother and first King of Númenor and, in a further generation, would be seen in the children from another marriage between Man and Elf in the persons of Aragorn and the Lady Arwen. Tolkien continued:

There are other stories, almost equally full in treatment, and equally independent and yet linked to the general history. There is the *Children of Húrin*, the tragic tale of Túrin Turambar and his sister Níniel – of which Túrin is the hero. . . . There is the *Fall of Gondolin*: the chief Elvish stronghold.[5] And the tale, or tales, of *Eärendil the Wanderer.* He is important as the person who brings the Silmarillion to its end, and as providing in his offspring the main links to and persons in the tales of later Ages. His function, as a representative of both Kindreds, Elves and Men, is to find a sea-passage back to the Land of the Gods, and as ambassador persuade them to take thought again for the Exiles, to pity them, and rescue them from the Enemy. His wife Elwing descends from Lúthien and still possesses the Silmaril. But the curse still works, and Eärendil's home is destroyed by the sons of Fëanor. But this provides the solution: Elwing casting herself into the Sea to save the Jewel comes to Eärendil, and with the power of the great Gem they pass at last to Valinor, and accomplish their errand – at the cost of never being allowed to return or dwell again with Elves or Men. The gods then move again, and great power comes out of the West, and the Stronghold of the Enemy is destroyed; and he himself [is] thrust out of the World into the Void, never to reappear there in incarnate form again. The remaining two Silmarils are regained from the Iron Crown – only to be lost. The last two sons of Fëanor, compelled by their oath, steal them, and are destroyed by them, casting themselves into the sea, and the pits of the earth. The ship of Eärendil adorned with the last Silmaril is set in heaven as the brightest star. So ends *The Silmarillion* and the tales of the First Age.

# THE TALE OF YEARS
*(Chronology of the Westlands)*

# 1 – FOUNDATION OF THE GREY HAVENS AND OF LINDON.

In his 1955 appendices to *The Lord of the Rings*, J.R.R. Tolkien wrote of the Second Age: 'These were the dark years for Men of Middle-earth, but the years of the glory of Númenor.'[1] In what Christopher Tolkien identified as his father's first attempt at establishing a 'Time Scheme' (later to become 'The Tale of Years') the Second Age was described as, 'the "Black Years" or the age between the Great Battle and defeat of Morgoth, and the Fall of Númenor and the overthrow of Sauron.'[2]

These vastly conflicted times and, in particular, the monumental tragedy represented by Númenor – greatness established but then brought low and destroyed – resulted, through the chronicling of the Second Age, in both the shaping of the history of Middle-earth and the physical re-shaping of the whole world: a story that provides a powerful and far-reaching prelude to the great drama of the War of the Ring.

The story begins in the closing days of Year 587 of the First Age:

In the Great Battle and the tumults of the fall of Thangorod-rim there were mighty convulsions in the earth, and Beleriand was broken and laid waste; and northward and westward many lands sank beneath the waters of the Great Sea. In the east, in Ossiriand, the walls of Ered Luin were broken, and a great gap was made in them towards the south, and a gulf of the sea flowed in. Into that gulf the River Lhûn fell by a new course, and it was called therefore the Gulf of Lhûn. That country had of old been named Lindon by the Noldor [those of the second clan of the Elves] and this name it bore thereafter.[3]

At the end of the First Age, the Valar held counsel and the Eldar in Middle-earth were summoned – 'if not commanded, at least sternly counselled' – to return to the West and there to be at peace.[4]

Those that hearkened to the summons dwelt in the Isle of Eressëa;[5] and there is in that land a haven that is named Avallónë,[6] for it is of all cities the nearest to Valinor, and the tower of Avallónë is the first sight that the mariner beholds when at last he draws nigh to the Undying Lands over the leagues of the Sea.[7]

Not all the Elven-kind answered the Valar's call but dwelt still in Middle-earth 'lingering, unwilling yet to forsake Beleriand where they had fought and laboured long'. Gil-galad son of Fingon was their king, and with him was Elrond Half-elven, son of Eärendil the Mariner and brother of Elros first king of Númenor.[8]

Commenting on this, in his 1951 letter to Milton Waldman, Tolkien wrote: 'We see a sort of second fall or at least "error" of the Elves. There was nothing wrong essentially in their lingering against counsel, still sadly with[*] the mortal lands of

---

[*] Some words of the original manuscript were omitted by the typist in this sentence.

their old heroic deeds. But they wanted to have their cake without eating it. They wanted the peace and bliss and perfect memory of "The West", and yet to remain on the ordinary earth where their prestige as the highest people, above wild Elves, dwarves, and Men, was greater than at the bottom of the hierarchy of Valinor. They thus became obsessed with "fading", the mode in which the changes of time (the law of the world under the sun) was perceived by them. They became sad, and their art (shall we say) antiquarian, and their efforts all really a kind of embalming – even though they also retained the old motive of their kind, the adornment of earth, and the healing of its hurts. We hear of a lingering kingdom, in the extreme North-west more or less in what was left in the old lands of *The Silmarillion*, under Gil-galad.'

In the beginning of this age many of the High Elves still remained. Most of these dwelt in Lindon west of the Ered Luin; but before the building of the Barad-dûr many of the Sindar passed eastward, and some established realms in the forests far away, where their people were mostly Silvan Elves. Thranduil, king in the north of Greenwood the Great, was one of these. In Lindon north of the Lune dwelt Gil-galad, last heir of the kings of the Noldor in exile. He was acknowledged as High King of the Elves of the West. In Lindon south of the Lune dwelt for a time Celeborn, kinsman of Thingol; his wife was Galadriel, greatest of Elven women. She was sister of Finrod Felagund, Friend-of-Men, once king of Nargothrond, who gave his life to save Beren son of Barahir.

Later some of the Noldor went to Eregion, upon the west of the Misty Mountains, and near to the West-gate of Moria. This they did because they learned that mithril had been discovered in Moria. The Noldor were great craftsmen and less unfriendly to the Dwarves than the Sindar; but the friendship that grew up between the people of Durin and the Elven-smiths of Eregion was the closest that there has ever been between the two races. Celebrimbor was Lord of Eregion and the greatest of their craftsmen; he was descended from Fëanor.[9]

[Galadriel] did not go West at the Downfall of Melkor [Morgoth], but crossed Ered Lindon with Celeborn and came into Eriador. When they entered that region there were many Noldor in their following, together with Grey-elves and Green-elves; and for a while they dwelt in the country about Lake Nenuial (Evendim, north of the Shire). Celeborn and Galadriel came to be regarded as Lord and Lady of the Eldar in Eriador, including the wandering companies of Nandorin origin who had never passed west over Ered Lindon and come down into Ossiriand.[10]

[Of Galadriel it is said that she] was strong of body, mind, and will, a match for both the loremasters and the athletes of the Eldar in the days of their youth. Even among the Eldar she was accounted beautiful and her [golden] hair was held a marvel unmatched . . . and the Eldar said that the light of the Two Trees, Laurelin and Telperion, had been snared in her tresses. . . . From her earliest years she had a marvellous gift of insight into the minds of others, but judged them with mercy and understanding. . . .[11]

In the account of the visit of the Fellowship of the Ring to Caras Galadhon in the February of year TA 3019, we have a description of Celeborn and Galadriel:

The chamber was filled with a soft light; its walls were green and silver and its roof of gold. Many Elves were seated there. On two chairs beneath the bole of the tree and canopied by a living bough there sat, side by side, Celeborn and Galadriel. They stood up to greet their guests, after the manner of Elves, even those who were accounted mighty kings. Very tall they were, and the Lady no less tall than the Lord; and they were grave and beautiful. They were clad wholly in white; and the hair of the Lady was of deep gold, and the hair of the Lord

Celeborn was of silver long and bright; but no sign of age was upon them, unless it were in the depths of their eyes; for these were keen as lances in the starlight, and yet profound, the wells of deep memory.[12]

> Writing in *Unfinished Tales*, Christopher Tolkien opined: 'There is no part of the history of Middle-earth more full of problems than the story of Galadriel and Celeborn', and readers wishing for a better understanding of that story should consult 'The History of Galadriel and Celeborn', Christopher's lengthy essay on the subject, which is included in Part Two of that work.[13]

Upon the shores of the Gulf of Lhûn the Elves built their havens, and named them Mithlond; and there they held many ships, for the harbourage was good. From the Grey Havens the Eldar ever and anon set sail, fleeing from the darkness of the days of Earth; for by the mercy of the Valar the Firstborn could still follow the Straight Road and return, if they would, to their kindred in Eressëa and Valinor beyond the encircling seas.[14]

> At the end of the First Age, while the Eldar were summoned to take ship for the West, a different fate was presented to Elros and Elrond, the sons of Eärendil, who were descended from a union between the Eldar and Man-kind and known as the Peredhil, or Half-elven. To them the Valar gave 'an irrevocable choice to which kindred they would belong.'[15]

Elrond chose to be of Elven-kind, and became a master of wisdom. To him therefore was granted the same grace as to those of the High Elves that still lingered in Middle-earth: that when weary at last of the mortal lands they could take ship from the Grey Havens and pass into the Uttermost West; and this grace continued after the change of the world. But to the children of Elrond a choice was also appointed: to pass with him from the circles of the world; or if they remained to become mortal and die in Middle-earth. For Elrond, therefore, all chances of the War of the Ring were fraught with sorrow.

Elros chose to be of Man-kind and remain with the Edain; but a great lifespan was granted to him many times that of lesser men.[16]

## 32 – THE EDAIN REACH NÚMENOR.[1]

The Valar, the 'Guardians of the World' who had been delegated by Eru Ilúvatar the All-Powerful transcendent creator, to shape and rule the world, also took thought for the fate of the race of Men, or Edain as they were called in the Sindarin language of the Elves. The tribes of Men who had become friends and noble allies of the Elves, fighting alongside them in the struggles against Morgoth, were of three Houses: the House of Bëor, known as the First House of the Edain; the House of Haleth was the Second House, known by among other names as the Folk of Haleth, the Haladin; and the Third House was the Folk of Marach, later best known as the House of Hador. The history of their lives and deeds during the First Age is told in *The Silmarillion*.[2]

The Valar, having taken counsel, determined to offer the Edain a means of being removed 'from the dangers of Middle-earth'.[3] The Valar, aided by Maiar who were primordial spirit beings 'of the same order as the Valar but of less degree . . . their servants and helpers',[4] brought into existence the island of Númenor.

To the Fathers of Men of the three faithful houses rich reward also was given. Eönwë[5] came among them and taught them; and they were given wisdom and power and life more enduring than any others of mortal race have possessed. A land was made for the Edain to dwell in, neither part of Middle-earth nor of Valinor, for it was sundered from either by a wide sea; yet it was nearer to Valinor. It was raised by Ossë[6] out of the depths of the Great Water, and it was established by Aulë[7] and enriched by Yavanna;[8] and the Eldar brought thither flowers and fountains out of Tol Eressëa. That land the Valar called Andor, the Land of Gift;[9] and the Star of Eärendil shone bright in the West as a token that all was made ready, and as a guide over the sea; and Men marvelled to see that silver flame in the paths of the Sun.[10]

Then the Edain set sail upon the deep waters, following the Star;[11] and the Valar laid a peace upon the sea for many days, and sent sunlight and a sailing wind, so that the waters glittered before the eyes of the Edain like rippling glass, and the foam flew like snow before the stems of their ships. But so bright was Rothinzil that even at morning Men could see it glimmering in the West, and in the cloudless night it shone alone, for no other star could stand beside it. And setting their course towards it the Edain came at last over leagues of sea and saw afar the land that was prepared for them, Andor, the Land of Gift, shimmering in a golden haze. Then they went up out of the sea and found a country fair and fruitful, and they were glad. And they called that land Elenna, which is Starwards; but also Anadûnê, which is Westernesse, Númenórë in the High Eldarin tongue.

This was the beginning of that people that in the Grey-elven speech are called the Dúnedain: the Númenóreans, Kings among Men. But they did not thus escape from the doom of death that Ilúvatar had set upon all Mankind, and they were mortal still, though their years were long, and they knew no sickness, ere the shadow fell upon them. Therefore they grew wise and glorious, and in all things more like to the Firstborn than any other of the kindreds of Men; and they were tall, taller than the tallest of the sons of Middle-earth;

and the light of their eyes was like the bright stars. But their numbers increased only slowly in the land, for though daughters and sons were born to them, fairer than their fathers, yet their children were few.[12]

A more detailed account of the coming of the Men of Middle-earth to the land prepared for them and the length of time taken for the migration is recounted as follows:

The legends of the foundation of Númenor often speak as if all the Edain that accepted the Gift set sail at one time and in one fleet. But this is only due to the brevity of the narrative. In more detailed histories it is related (as might be deduced from the events and the numbers concerned) that after the first expedition, led by Elros, many other ships, alone or in small fleets, came west bearing others of the Edain, either those who were at first reluctant to dare the Great Sea but could not endure to be parted from those who had gone, or some who were far scattered and could not be assembled to go with the first sailing.

Since the boats that were used were of Elvish model, fleet but small, and each steered by one of the Eldar deputed by Círdan, it would have taken a great navy to transport all the people and goods that were eventually brought from Middle-earth to Númenor. The legends make no guess at the numbers, and the histories say little. The fleet of Elros is said to have contained many ships (according to some a hundred and fifty vessels, to others two or three hundred) and to have brought 'thousands' of the men, women, and children of the Edain: probably between five thousand or at the most ten thousand. But the whole process of migration appears in fact to have occupied at least fifty years, possibly longer, and finally ended only when Círdan (no doubt instructed by the Valar) would provide no more ships or guides.[13]

But one command had been laid upon the Númenóreans, the 'Ban of the Valar': they were forbidden to sail west out of sight of their own shores or to attempt to set foot on the Undying Lands. For though a long span of life had been granted to them, in the beginning thrice that of lesser Men, they must remain mortal, since the Valar were not permitted to take from them the Gift of Men (or the Doom of Men, as it was afterwards called).[14]

For many years, the Númenóreans were to accept and observe the ban on their sailing 'so far westward that the coasts of Númenor could no longer be seen' and 'were content though they did not fully understand the purpose of this ban'. Manwë – King of the Valar and brother of the Dark Lord Melkor (Morgoth) – was, in matters of authority (though not in power) the greatest of the Ainur and, as the Lord of the Breath of Arda, was its Ruler.[15]

## 32 – KINGS AND QUEENS OF NÚMENOR I:
### Elros Tar-Minyatur[16]
Born: First Age 532; Died: SA 442 (age 500)
Rule: SA 32-442 (410 years)

The Realm of Númenor is held to have begun in the thirty-second year of the Second Age, when Elros son of Eärendil ascended the throne in the City of Armenelos, being then ninety years of age.[17]

It is written that 'the sceptre was the chief mark of royalty in Númenor'[18] from the reign of the First King to that of the Twenty-Fifth King and that having survived for 3,287 years it was lost with Ar-Pharazôn at the Downfall.

Thereafter [Elros] was known in the Scroll of the Kings by the name of Tar-Minyatur;[19] for it was the custom of the King to take their titles in the forms of the Quenya or High-elven tongue, that being the noblest tongue of the world, and this custom endured until the days of Ar-Adûnakhôr (Tar-Herunúmen).[20]

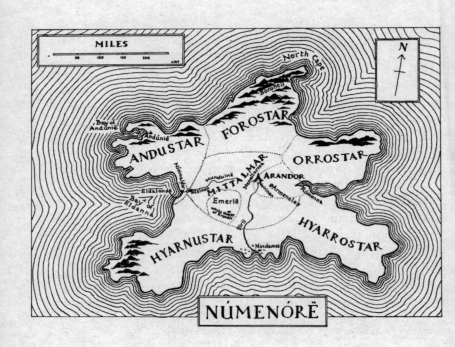

# THE GEOGRAPHY OF NÚMENOR[1]

Accurate charts of Númenor were made at various periods before its downfall; but none of these survived the disaster. They were deposited in the Guildhouse of the Venturers, and this was confiscated by the kings, and removed to the western haven of Andúnië; all its records perished. Maps of Númenor were long preserved in the archives of the Kings of Gondor, in Middle-earth; but these appear to have been derived in part from old drawings made from memory by early settlers; and (the better ones) from a single chart, with little detail beyond sea-soundings along the coast, and descriptions of the ports and their approaches, that was originally in the ship of Elendil, leader of those who escaped the downfall.

Descriptions of the land, and of its flora and fauna, were also preserved in Gondor; but they were not accurate or detailed, nor did they distinguish clearly between the state of the land at different periods, being vague about its condition at the time of the first settlements. Since all such matters were the study of men of lore in Númenor, and many accurate natural histories and geographies must have been composed, it would appear that, like nearly all else of the arts and sciences of Númenor at its high tide, they disappeared in the Downfall.

## *Of the Shape of Númenor*

The land of Númenor resembled in outline a five-pointed star, or pentangle, with a central portion some two hundred and fifty miles across, north and south, and east and west, from which extended five large peninsular promontories. These promontories were regarded as separate regions, and they were named Forostar (Northlands), Andustar (Westlands), Hyarnustar (Southwestlands), Hyarrostar (Southeastlands), and Orrostar (Eastlands). The central portion was called Mittalmar (Inlands), and it had no coast, except the land about Rómenna and the head of its firth. A small part of the Mittalmar was however, separated from the rest, and called Arandor, the Kingsland. In Arandor were the haven of Rómenna, the Meneltarma, and Armenelos, the City of the Kings; and it was at all times the most populous region of Númenor.

The promontories, though these were not all of precisely the same shape or size, were roughly 100 miles across and rather more than 200 miles long. A line drawn from the northernmost point of the Forostar to the southernmost of the Hyarnustar lay more or less directly north and south (at the period of the maps); this line was somewhat more than 700 miles long, and each line drawn from the end of one promontory to the end of another and passing through the land (along the borders of the Mittalmar) was more or less of the same length.

## *Of the Mittalmar*

The Mittalmar was raised above the general level of the promontories, not reckoning the height of any mountain or hills in these; and at the settlement appears to have had few trees and to have consisted mainly of grasslands and low downs. Nearly at its centre, though somewhat nearer the eastern edge, stood the tall mountain, called the Meneltarma, Pillar of the Heavens. It was about 3,000 feet high above the plain. The lower slopes of the Meneltarma were gentle and partly grass-covered, but the mountain grew ever steeper, and the last 500 feet were in places unscalable, save by the climbing road.

The base of the Meneltarma sloped gently into the surrounding plain, but it extended, after the fashion of roots, five long low ridges outwards in the direction of the five promontories of the land; and these were called Tarmasundar, the Roots of the Pillar.

But for the most part the Mittalmar was a region of pastures. In the south-west there were rolling downs of grass; and there, in the Emerië, was the chief region of the Shepherds.

## Of the Forostar

The Forostar was the least fertile part; stony, with few trees, save that on the westward slopes of the high heather-covered moors there were woods of fir and larch. Towards the North Cape the land rose to rocky heights, and there great Sorontil rose sheer from the sea in tremendous cliffs. Here was the abode of many eagles.

## Of the Andustar

The Andustar was also rocky in its northern parts, with high fir-woods looking out upon the sea. Three small bays it had, facing west, cut back into the highlands; but here the cliffs were in many places not at the sea's edge, and there was a shelving land at their feet. . . . But much of the southerly part of the Andustar was fertile, and there also were great woods, of birch and beech upon the upper ground, and in the lower vales of oaks and elms. Between the promontories of the Andustar and the Hyarnustar was the great curved indentation of the Bay that was called Eldanna, because it faced towards Eressëa; and the lands about it, being sheltered from the north and open to the western seas, were warm (almost as warm as the southernmost lands) and the most rain fell there. At the centre of the Bay of Eldanna was the most beautiful of all the havens of Númenor,

Eldalondë the Green; and hither in the earlier days the swift white ships of the Eldar of Eressëa came most often.

The river Nunduinë flowed into the sea at Eldalondë, and on its way made the little lake of Nísinen, that was so named from the abundance of sweet-smelling shrubs and flowers that grew upon its banks.

## Of the Hyarnustar and the Hyarrostar

The Hyarnustar was in its western part a mountainous region, with great cliffs on the western and southern coasts; but eastwards were great vineyards in a warm and fertile land. The promontories of the Hyarnustar and the Hyarrostar were splayed wide apart, and on those long shores sea and land came gently together, as nowhere else in Númenor. Here flowed down Siril, the chief river of the land (for all others, save for the Nunduinë in the west, were short and swift torrents hurrying to the sea), that rose in springs under the Meneltarma in the valley of Noirinan, and running through the Mittalmar southwards became in its lower course a slow and winding stream; for the land was almost flat, and not high above sea level. It issued at last into the sea amid wide marshes and reedy flats, and its many small mouths found their changing paths through great sands; for many miles on either side were wide white beaches and grey shingles, and here the fisherfolk mostly dwelt, in villages upon the hards[2] among the marshes and meres, of which the chief was Nindamos [that lay] upon the east side of the Siril close to the sea. Great seas and high winds hardly ever troubled this region. In later times much of this land was reclaimed, and formed into a region of great fish-haunted pools with outlets to the sea, about which were rich and fertile lands.

In the Hyarrostar grew an abundance of trees of many kinds, and among them the *laurinquë* in which the people delighted for its flowers, for it had no other use . . . From the days of Tar-Aldarion there were great plantations in the Hyarrostar to furnish timber for shipbuilding.

## *Of the Orrostar*

The Orrostar was cooler, but was protected from the north-east (whence came the colder winds) by highlands that rose to a height of 2,100 feet near the north-eastern end of the promontory. In the inner parts, especially in those adjacent to the Kingsland, much grain was grown.

The chief feature of Númenor were the cliffs. . . The whole land was so posed as if it had been thrust upward out of the Sea, but at the same time slightly tilted southward. Except at the southern point, already described, in nearly all places the land fell steeply towards the sea in cliffs, for the most part steep, or sheer. These were at the greatest height in the north and north-west, where they often reached 2,000 feet, at the lowest in the east and south-east.

But these cliffs, except in certain regions such as the North Cape, seldom stood up directly out of the water. At their feet were found shorelands of flat or shelving land, often habitable, that ranged in width (from the water) from about a quarter of a mile to several miles. The fringes of the widest stretches were usually under shallow water even at low tides; but at their seaward edges all these strands plunged down again sheerly into profound water. The great strands and tidal flats of the south also ended in a sheer fall to oceanic depths along a line roughly joining the southernmost ends of the south-west and south-east promontories.

# THE NATURAL LIFE OF NÚMENOR[1]

## *Of Men and Beasts*

It would appear that neither Elves nor Men had dwelt in this island before the coming of the Edain. Beasts and birds had no fear of Men; and the relations of Men and animals remained more friendly in Númenor than anywhere else in the world. It is said that even those that the Númenóreans classed as 'predatory' (by which they meant those that would at need raid their crops and tame cattle) remained on 'honourable terms' with the newcomers, seeking their food so far as they could in the wild, and showing no hostility to Men, save at times of declared war, when after due warning the husbandmen would, as a necessity, hunt the predatory birds and beasts to reduce their numbers within limits.

As has been said, it is not easy to discover what were the beasts and birds and fishes that already inhabited the island before the coming of the Edain, and what were brought in by them. The same is also true of the plants. Neither are the names which the Númenóreans gave to animals and plants always easy to equate with or relate to the names of those found in Middle-earth. Many, though given in apparently Quenya or Sindarin forms, are not found in the Elvish or Human tongues of Middle-earth. This is partly due, no doubt, to the fact that the animals and plants of Númenor, though similar and related to those of the mainlands, were different in variety and seemed to require new names.

As for the major animals, it is clear that there were none of the canine or related kinds. There were certainly no hounds or dogs (all of which were imported). There were no wolves. There were wild cats, the most hostile and untameable of the animals; but no large felines. There were a great number, however, of foxes, or related animals.

Their chief food seems to have been animals which the Númenóreans called *lopoldi*. These existed in large numbers and multiplied swiftly, and were voracious herbivores; so that the foxes were esteemed as the best and most natural way of keeping them in order, and foxes were seldom hunted or molested. In return, or because their food-supply was otherwise abundant, the foxes seem never to have acquired the habit of preying upon the domestic fowl of the Númenóreans. The *lopoldi* would appear to have been rabbits, animals which had been quite unknown before in the north-western regions of Middle-earth. The Númenóreans did not esteem them as food and were content to leave them to the foxes.

### Of Bears and Men

There were bears in considerable numbers, in the mountainous or rocky parts; both of a black and brown variety. The great black bears were found mostly in the Forostar. The relations of the bears and Men were strange. From the first the bears exhibited friendship and curiosity towards the newcomers; and these feelings were returned.

At no time was there any hostility between Men and bears; though at mating times, and during the first youth of their cubs they could be angry and dangerous if disturbed. The Númenóreans did not disturb them except by mischance. Very few Númenóreans were ever killed by bears; and these mishaps were not regarded as reasons for war upon the whole race. Many of the bears were quite tame. They never dwelt in or near the homes of Men, but they would often visit them, in the casual manner of one householder calling upon another. At such times they were often offered honey, to their delight. Only an occasional 'bad bear' ever raided the tame hives. Most strange of all were the bear-dances. The bears, the black bears especially, had curious dances of their own; but these seem to have become improved and elaborated by the instruction of Men. At times the bears would perform dances for the entertainment of their human friends. The most famous was the Great Bear-dance (*ruxoälë*) of Tompollë in the Forostar, to which every year in the autumn many would come from all parts of the island, since it occurred not long after the Eruhantalë, at which a great concourse was assembled. To those not accustomed to the bears the slow (but dignified) motions of the bears, sometimes as many as 50 or more together, appeared astonishing and comic. But it was understood by all admitted to the spectacle that there should be no open laughter. The laughter of Men was a sound that the bears could not understand: it alarmed and angered them.

## Of Beasts of the Woods, Fields and Coasts

The woods of Númenor abounded in squirrels, mostly red, but some dark brown or black. These were all unafraid, and readily tamed. The women of Númenor were specially fond of them. Often they would live in trees near a homestead, and would come when invited into the house. In the short rivers and streams there were otters. Badgers were numerous. There were wild black swine in the woods; and in the west of the Mittalmar at the coming of the Edain were herds of wild kine, some white, some black. Deer were abundant on the grasslands and in and about the forest-eaves, red and fallow; and in the hills were roe-deer. But all seem to have been somewhat smaller of stature than their kin in Middle-earth. In the southern region there were beavers.

The animals named *ekelli* seem to have been urchins or hedgehogs of large size, with long black quills. They were numerous in some parts, and treated with friendship, for they lived mostly upon worms and insects. There seem to have been wild goats in the island, but whether the small horned sheep (which were one of the varieties of sheep-kind that the Númenóreans kept) were native or imported is not known. A small kind of horse, smaller than a donkey, black or dark brown, with flowing mane and tail, and sturdy rather than swift, is said to have been found in the Mittalmar by the settlers. They were soon tamed, but throve and were well-tended and loved. They were much used in the farms; and children used them for riding.

Many other beasts there were no doubt that are seldom named since they did not generally concern Men. All must have been named and described in the books of lore that perished.

About the coasts seals were abundant, especially in the north and west. And there were also many smaller animals, not often mentioned: such as mice and voles, or small preying beasts such as weasels. Hares are named; and other animals of uncertain kind: some that were not squirrels, but lived in trees, and were shy, not of men only; others that ran on the ground and burrowed, small and fat, but were neither rats nor rabbits. In the south there were some land-tortoises, of no great size; and also some small freshwater creatures of turtle-kind.

## Of Seawater and Freshwater Fish

Sea-fish were abundant all about the coasts of the island, and those that were good to eat were much used. Other beasts of the sea there were also off the shores: whales and narwhal, dolphins and porpoises, which the Númenóreans did not confuse with fish (*lingwi*), but classed with fish as *nendili* all those that lived wholly in the water and bred in the sea. Sharks the Númenóreans saw only upon their voyages, for whether by the 'grace of the

Valar' as the Númenóreans said, or for other cause they did not ever come near the shores of the island. Of inland fish we hear little. Of those that live in the sea partly, but enter the rivers at times, there were salmon in the Siril, and also in the Nunduinë, the river that flowed into the sea at Eldalondë, and on its way made the small lake of Nísinen (one of the few in Númenor) about three miles inland: it was so called because of the abundance of sweet-smelling shrubs and flowers that grew on its banks. Eels were abundant in the meres and marshes about the lower course of the Siril.

## Of Birds

The birds of Númenor were beyond count, from the great eagles down to the tiny *kirinki* that were no bigger than wrens, but all scarlet, with high piping voices the sounds of which were on the edge of human hearing. The eagles were of several kinds; but all were held sacred to Manwë, and were never molested nor shot, not until the days of evil and the hatred of the Valar began. Not until then did they on their part molest men or prey on their beasts. From the days of Elros until the time of Tar-Ankalimon [the fourteenth King of Númenor], son of Tar-Atanamir, some two thousand years, there was an eyrie of golden eagles in the summit of the tower of the king's palace in Armenelos. There one pair ever dwelt and lived on the bounty of the king.

The birds that dwell near the sea, and swim or dive in it, and live upon fish, abode in Númenor in multitudes beyond reckoning. They were never killed or molested by intent by the Númenóreans, and were wholly friendly to them. Mariners said that were they blind they would know that their ship was drawing near home because of the great clamour of the shorebirds. When any ship approached the land seabirds in great flocks would arise and fly above it for no purpose but welcome and gladness. Some would accompany the ships on their voyages, even those that went to Middle-earth.

Inland the birds were not so numerous, but were nonetheless abundant. Some beside the eagles were birds of prey, such as the hawks and falcons of many kinds. There were ravens, especially in the north, and about the land other birds of their kin that live in flocks, daws and crows and about the sea-cliffs many choughs. Smaller song-birds with fair voices abounded in the fields, in the reedy meres, and in the woods. Many were little different from those of the lands from which the Edain came; but the birds of finch-kind were more varied and numerous and sweeter-voiced. There were some of small size all white, some all grey; and others all golden, that sang with great joy in long thrilling cadences through the spring and early summer. They had little fear of the Edain, who loved them. The caging of song-birds was thought an unkind deed. Nor was it necessary, for those that were 'tame', that is: who attached themselves of free will to a homestead, would for generations dwell near the same house, singing upon its roof or on the sills, or even in the *solmar* or chambers of those that welcomed them. The birds that dwelt in cages were for the most part reared from young whose parents died by mischance or were slain by birds of prey; but even they were mostly free to go and come if they would. Nightingales were found, though nowhere very abundant, in most parts of Númenor save the north. In the northern parts there were large white owls, but no other birds of this race.

## Of Trees and Plants

Of the native trees and plants little is recorded. Though some trees were brought in seed or scion from Middle-earth, and others (as has been said) came from Eressëa, there seems to have been an abundance of timber when the Edain landed. Of trees already known to them it is said that they missed the horn-beam, the small maple, and the flowering chestnut; but found others that were new to them: the wych-elm, the holm-oak, tall maples, and the sweet chestnut. In the Hyarrostar they found also walnuts; and the *laurinquë* in which they delighted for its flowers, for it had no other use. This name they gave it ('golden rain') because of its long-hanging clusters of yellow flowers; and some who had heard from the Eldar of Laurelin, the Golden Tree of Valinor, believed that it came from that great Tree, being brought in seed thither by the Eldar; but it was not so.[2] Wild apple, cherry, and pear also grew in Númenor; but those that they grew in their orchards came from Middle-earth, gifts from the Eldar. In the Hyarnustar the vine grew wild; but the grape-vines of the Númenóreans seem also to have come from the Eldar.

Of the many plants and flowers of field and wood little is now recorded or remembered; but old songs speak often of the lilies, the many kinds of which, some small, some tall and fair, some single-bloomed, some hung with many bells and trumpets, and all fragrant, were the delight of the Edain.

Of the flora of Eldalondë the Green, the haven at the centre of the Bay of Eldanna, it is recorded:

All about that place, up the seaward slopes and far into the land, grew the evergreen and fragrant trees that they brought out of the West, and so throve there that the Eldar said that almost it was fair as a haven in Eressëa. They were the greatest delight of Númenor, and they were remembered in many songs long after they had perished for ever, for few ever flowered east of the Land of Gift: *oiolairë* and *lairelossë*, *nessamelda*, *vardari-anna*, *taniquelassë*, and *yavannamirë* with its rose-like flowers and globed and scarlet fruits. Flower, leaf, and rind of those trees exuded sweet scents and all that country was full of blended fragrance; therefore it was called Nísimaldar, the Fragrant Trees. Many of them were planted and grew, though far less abundantly, in other region of Númenor; but only here grew the mighty golden tree *malinornë* reaching after five centuries a height scarce less than it achieved in Eressëa itself. Its bark was silver and smooth, and its boughs somewhat upswept after the manner of the beech; but it never grew save with a single trunk. Its leaves, like those of the beech but greater, were pale green above and beneath were silver glistering in the sun; in the autumn they did not fall, but turned to pale gold. In the spring it bore golden blossom in clusters like a cherry, which bloomed on during the summer; and as soon as the flowers opened the leaves fell, so that through spring and summer a grove of *malinornë* was carpeted and roofed with gold, but its pillars were of grey silver.

Long after these times, in the Third Age, Legolas the Elf uses similar words when speaking to the remnant of the Fellowship of the Ring of the Elven-realm of Celeborn and Galadriel.

'There lie the woods of Lothlórien!' said Legolas. 'That is the fairest of all the dwellings of my people. There are no trees like the trees of that land. For in the autumn their leaves fall not, but turn to gold. Not till the spring comes and the new green opens do they fall, and then the boughs are laden with yellow flowers; and the floor of the wood is golden, and golden is the roof, and its pillars are of silver, for the bark of the trees is smooth and grey. So still our songs in Mirkwood say. My heart would be glad if I were beneath the eaves of that wood, and it were springtime!'[3]

The relationship between the trees of the Golden Wood and the *malinornë* of Númenor is chronicled thus:

Its fruit was a nut with a silver shale; and some were given as gift by Tar-Aldarion, the sixth King of Númenor, to King Gil-galad of Lindon. They did not take root in that land; but Gil-galad gave some to his kinswoman Galadriel, and under her power they grew and flourished in the guarded land of Lothlórien beside the River Anduin, until the High Elves at last left Middle-earth; but they did not reach the height or girth of the great groves of Númenor.

## *Of the Beasts and Birds of the Edain*

To the land the Edain brought many things from Middle-earth: sheep, and kine, and horses, and dogs; fruiting trees; and grain. Water-fowl such as birds of duck-kind or geese they found before them; but others they brought also and blended with the native races. Geese and ducks were domestic fowls on their farms; and there also they kept multitudes of doves or pigeons in great houses or dovecotes, mainly for their eggs. Hen-fowl they had not known and found none in the island; though soon after the great voyages began mariners brought back cocks and hens from the southern and eastern lands, and they throve in Númenor, where many of them escaped and lived in the wild, though harried by the foxes.

# THE LIFE OF THE NÚMENÓREANS[1]

### Of Cities

Of old the chief city and haven of Númenor was in the midst of its western coasts, and it was called Andúnië because it faced the sunset . . . with its town beside the shore and many other dwellings climbing up the steep slopes behind.

Hard [by Meneltarma] upon a hill was Armenelos, fairest of cities, and there stood the tower and the citadel that was raised by Elros son of Eärendil, whom the Valar appointed to be the first King of the Dúnedain.[2]

### Of Belief and Worship

Near to the centre of the Mittalmar stood the tall mountain called the Meneltarma, Pillar of the Heavens, sacred to the worship of Eru Ilúvatar. . . . A winding spiral road was made upon it, beginning at its foot upon the south, and ending below the lip of the summit upon the north. For the summit was somewhat flattened and depressed, and could contain a great multitude; but it remained untouched by hands throughout the history of Númenor. No building, no raised altar, not even a pile of undressed stones, ever stood there; and no other likeness of a temple did the Númenóreans possess in all the days of their grace, until the coming of Sauron. There no tool or weapon had ever been borne; and there none might speak any word, save the King only. Thrice only in each year the King spoke, offering prayer for the coming year at the *Erukyermë* in the first days of spring, praise of Eru Ilúvatar at the *Erulaitalë* in midsummer, and thanksgiving to him at the Eruhantalë at the end of autumn. At these times the King ascended the mountain on foot followed by a great concourse of the people, clad in white and garlanded, but silent. At other times the people were free to climb to the summit alone or in company, but it is said that the silence was so great that even a stranger ignorant of Númenor and all its history, if he were transported thither, would not have dared to speak aloud. No bird ever came there, save only eagles. If anyone approached the summit, at once three eagles would appear and alight upon three rocks near to the western edge; but at the times of the Three Prayers they did not descend, remaining in the sky and hovering above the people. They were called the Witnesses of Manwë, and they were believed to be sent by him from Aman to keep watch upon the Holy Mountain and upon all the land.[3]

The Númenóreans thus began a great new good, and as mono-theists; but . . . with only one physical centre of 'worship': the summit of the mountain Meneltarma 'Pillar of Heaven' – literally, for they did not conceive of the sky as a divine residence – in the centre of Númenor; but it had no building and no temple, as all such things had evil associations.[4]

[Between the south-western and south-eastern ridges of the Tarmasundar, the Roots of the Pillar] the land went down into a shallow valley. That was named Noirinan, the Valley of the Tombs; for at its head chambers were cut in the rock at the base of the mountain, in which were the tombs of the Kings and Queens of Númenor.

## Of Language

The Númenórean language was Adûnaic ('language of the West') or, to use its native name, Adûnayân.

The Númenórean language was in the main derived from the speech of the people of [the House of] Hador (much enlarged by additions from the Elven-tongues at different periods).[5] The people of Bëor had in a few generations abandoned their own speech (except in the retention of many personal names of native origin) and adopted the Elven-tongue of Beleriand, the Sindarin. This distinction was still observable in Númenor. Nearly all Númenóreans were bi-lingual. But where the main mass of settlers came from the people of Bëor, as was the case especially in the North-west, Sindarin was the daily tongue of all classes and Númenórean (or Adûnayân) a second language. In most parts of the country Adûnayân was the native language of the people, though Sindarin was known in some degree by all except the stay-at-home and untravelled of the farming folk. In the Royal House, however, and in most of the house of the noble or learned, Sindarin was usually the native tongue, until after the days of Tar-Atanamir [the Thirteenth King of Númenor].

Sindarin used for a long period by mortal Men naturally tended to become divergent and dialectal; but this process was largely checked, at any rate so far as the nobles and learned were concerned, by the constant contact that was maintained with the Eldar in Eressëa, and later with those who remained in Lindon in Middle-earth. The Eldar came mostly to the West regions of the country. Quenya was not a spoken tongue. It was known only to the learned, and to the families of high descent (to whom it was taught in their early youth). It was used in official documents intended for preservation, such as the Laws, and the Scroll and Annals of the Kings, and often in more recondite works of lore. It was also largely used in nomenclature. The official names of all places, regions, and geographical features in the land were of Quenya form (though they usually also had local names, generally of the same meaning, in either Sindarin or Adûnayân). The personal names and especially the official and public names of all members of the Royal House, and of the Line of Elros in general, were given in Quenya form. The same was true of some other families, such as the House of the Lords of Andúnië [who lived in the important city port of the western region of Andustar.][6]

## Of Appearance and Health

The people, tall and strong, were agile, and extremely 'aware': that is they were in control of their bodily actions, and of any tool or material they handled, and seldom made absent-minded or blundering movements; and they were very difficult to take 'off their guard'. Accidents were thus unlikely to occur to them. If any did, they had a power of recovery and self-healing, which if inferior to that of the Eldar, was much greater than that of Men in Middle-earth. Also among the matters of lore that they specially studied was hröangolmë or the lore of the body and the arts of healing.

Sicknesses or other bodily disorders were very rare in Númenor until the latter years. This was due both to the special grace of health and strength given to the race as a whole, but especially due to the blessing of the land itself; and also in some measure no doubt to its situation far out in the Great Sea: animals were also mostly free from disease. But the few cases of sickness provided a practical function, so far as one was needed, for the continued study of hröangolmë (or physiology and medicine) in which the practisers of simple leechcraft among the Edain had received much instruction from the Eldar, and in which they were able still to learn from the Eressëans,[7] so long as they would. In the first days of the coming of Númenórean ships to the shores of Middle-earth [beginning in year 600 of the Second Age] it was indeed their skill in healing, and their willingness to give instruction to all who would receive it, that made the Númenóreans most welcomed and esteemed.

Death untimely, whether by sickness or mischance, seldom occurred in the early centuries. This the Númenóreans recognized as due to the 'grace of the Valar' (which might be withheld in general or in particular cases, if it ceased to be merited): the land was blessed, and all things, including the Sea, were friendly to them.

## Of Ageing and Longevity

Long life and Peace were the two things that the Edain asked for when the Valar offered them reward at the fall of Thangorodrim.

The long life of the Númenóreans was in answer to the actual prayers of the Edain (and Elros). Manwë warned them of its perils. They asked to have more or less the 'life-span of old', because they wanted to learn more.

Of that reward of a longer life-span granted to the Númenóreans, it is written:

The increase of the Númenórean life-span was brought about by assimilating their life-mode to that of the Eldar, up to a limited point. They were however expressly warned that they had not become Eldar, but remained 'mortal Men', and had been granted only an extension of the period of their vigour of mind and body. Thus (as the Eldar) they 'grew' at much the same rate as ordinary Men: gestation, infancy, childhood, and adolescence up to puberty and 'full-growth' proceeded more or less as before; but when they had achieved full-growth they then aged or 'wore out' very much slower. . .

The first approach of 'world-weariness' [or a 'seeking else-wither'] was indeed for them a sign that their period of vigour was nearing its end. When it came to an end, if they persisted in living, then decay would, as growth had done, soon proceed at more or less the same rate as for other Men. Thus, if a Númenórean reached the end of vigour . . . he would then pass quickly, in about ten years, from health and vigour of mind to decrepitude and senility.[8]

Númenórean mental development was also assimilated to some degree to the Eldarin mode. Their mental capacity was greater and developed quicker than that of ordinary Men; and it was dominant. After about seven years they grew up mentally with rapidity, and at 20 years knew and understood far more than a normal human of that age. A consequence of this, reinforced by their expectation of long-lasting vigour which left them with little sense of urgency in the first half of their lives, was that they very often became engrossed in lore, and crafts, and various intellectual or artistic pursuits, to a far greater degree than normal. This was particularly the case with men.

## Of Marriage and Child-raising

Desire for marriage, the begetting, bearing, and rearing of children, thus occupied a smaller place in the lives of Númenóreans, even of the women, than among ordinary Men. Marriage was regarded as natural for all, and once entered into was permanent. . . .

A Númenórean woman might marry when 20 (marriage before full-growth was not permitted); but most usually she married at about 40 to 45 years ('age' 24 to 25). Marriage was considered unduly delayed in her case if postponed much beyond her 95th year ('age' about 35).

Men seldom married before their year 45 (age 25). Their time from the year 15 to 45 was usually engrossed in learning, in apprenticeship to one or more crafts, and (more and more as time went on) in seafaring. Postponement of marriage to about the 95th year (age 35) was very common; and, especially in the case of men of rank, high duty, or great talents, it was not seldom entered into as late as the 120th year (age 40). In the Line of Elros (especially among the children of actual kings), which was somewhat more longeval than the average and also provided many duties and opportunities (both for men and women), marriage was often later than normal: for women 95 (age 35) was frequent; and for men might be as late as the 150th year (age 46) or even later. This had one advantage: that the 'Heir to the Sceptre', even if the king's eldest child, would be able to succeed while still in full vigour, though he would probably have passed through the 'Days of the Children' and be more free to devote himself to public concerns.

Númenóreans, like the Eldar, avoided the begetting of children if they foresaw any separation likely between husband and wife between the conception of the child and at least its very early years.

Númenóreans were strictly monogamous: by law, and by their 'tradition': that is by the tradition of the original Edain concerning conduct, afterwards re-inforced by Eldarin example and teaching. . . .

No one, of whatever rank, could divorce a husband or wife, nor take another spouse in the lifetime of the first.

A second marriage was permitted, by traditional law, if one of the partners died young, leaving the other in vigour and still with a need or desire of children; but the cases were naturally very rare.

Marriage was not entered into by all. There was (it appears from occasional statements in the few surviving tales or annals) a slightly less number of women than men, at any rate in the earlier centuries. But apart from this numerical limitation, there was always a small minority that refused marriage, either because they were engrossed in lore or other pursuits, or because they had failed to obtain the spouse whom they desired and would seek for no other.

Like the Eldar [the Númenóreans] tended to make the period of parenthood (or as the Eldar called it, the 'Days of the Children') a single connected and limited period of their lives. This limitation was regarded as natural. The connexion, the treating of the period of child-bearing as an ordered and unbroken series, was considered proper and desirable, if it could be achieved. That the married pair should dwell together, with as few and short times of separation as possible, between say, the conception of their first child to at least the seventh birthday of the latest, was held to be the ideal arrangement. It was particularly desired by the women, who were naturally (as a rule) less engrossed in lore or crafts; and who had far less desire for moving about.[9]

Thus the Númenóreans, who seldom had more than four children in each marriage, would frequently produce these within a period of about 50 to 75 years (between the first conception and the last birth). The intervals between the children were long as a rule, in ordinary terms: often ten years, sometimes 15 or even as much as 20 years; never less than about five years. But it has to be remembered in this regard that in proportion to their total life-span this period was only equivalent to one of about 10 to 15 years of normal human life. The intervals, if reckoned also according to their degree of approach towards the end of vigour and fertility, were thus equivalent to a (rare) minimum of one year, with a more frequent allowance of two, three, or sometimes four years.

'Vigour', that is primarily bodily health and activity, and the period of fertility and child-bearing in women, were of course not co-extensive. The child-bearing period of women was similar to that of ordinary women, though reckoned in Númenórean terms. That is, it ranged from puberty (reached by Númenórean women not long before full-growth) to an 'age' equivalent to a normal human 45 (with occasional extension towards 50). In years this means from about 18 to about 125 or a little more. But first children were seldom if ever conceived at the end of this time.

Since in matters of growth, which included the conception and bearing of children, the Númenórean development differed little in speed from that of ordinary Men, these intervals seem long. But as has been said their mental interests were dominant; and also they gave great and concentrated attention to any matter that they took up. The matter of children, therefore, being of highest importance, was one that occupied most of the attention of the mother during bearing and infancy, and except in great households cast a great deal of the daily labour upon the father. Both were glad for a while to return to other neglected pursuits. But also (it was said by the Númenóreans themselves) they were in this matter more like the Eldar than other kinds of Men: in the begetting and still more in the bearing of a child far more of their vigour both of body and mind was expended (for the longevity of the later generations was, though a grace or gift, transmitted mediately[10] by the parents). A rest both of body and will was, therefore, needed, especially by the women. After the conception of a child indeed desire for union became dormant for a while, in both men and women, though longer among the mothers.

If the Númenóreans were not lustful, they did not think the love of men and women less important or of less delight than did other Men. On the contrary they were steadfast lovers; and any breaches in the bonds and affection between parents, or between them and their children were thought great evils and sorrows.

## Of Appetites and Behaviours

There were in the early centuries few cases of the breach of the law, or even of desire to break it. The Númenóreans, or Dúnedain, were still in our terms 'fallen Men'; but they were descendants of ancestors who were in general wholly repentant, detesting all the corruptions of the 'Shadow'; and they were specially graced. In general they had little inclination to, and a conscious detestation of lust, greed, hate and cruelty, and tyranny. Not all of course were so noble.

Until the Shadow came, there were in Númenor few gluttons or drunkards. No one ate or drank to excess, or indeed much at any one time. They esteemed good food, which was plentiful, and expended care and art in its cooking and serving. But the distinction between a 'Feast' and an ordinary meal consisted rather in this: in the adornments of the table, in the music, and in the merriment of many eating together, than in the food; though naturally at such feasts food and wines of more rare and choice sorts would sometimes appear.

There were such things as wickedness among them, at first very rarely to be seen. For they were not selected by any test save that of belonging to the Three Houses of the Edain. Among them were no doubt a few of the wild men and renegades of old days, and possibly (though this cannot be asserted) actual conscious servants of the Enemy.

This suspicion would be proved justified by events in the years from c. 2221, see below.

## Of Skills and Crafts

The Edain brought with them much lore, and the knowledge of many crafts, and numerous craftsmen who had learned from the Eldar, directly or through their fathers, besides preserving lore and traditions of their own.

But they could bring with them few materials, save for the tools of their crafts; and for long all metals in Númenor were precious metals. They brought with them many treasures of gold and silver, and gems also; but they did not find these things in Númenor. They loved them for their beauty, and it was this love that first aroused in them cupidity, in later days when they fell under the Shadow and became proud and unjust in their dealings with lesser folk of Middle-earth. Of the Elves of Eressëa in the days of their friendship they had at times gifts of gold and silver and jewels; but such things were rare and prized in all the earlier centuries, until the power of the Kings was spread to the coasts of the East.

Some metals they found in Númenor, and as their cunning in mining and in smelting and smithying swiftly grew things of iron and copper became common. Lead they also had. Iron and steel they needed most for the tools of the craftsmen and for the axes of the woodsmen.

Among the wrights of the Edain were weaponsmiths, and they had with the teaching of the Noldor acquired great skill in the forging of swords, of axe-blades, and of spearheads and knives . . . [and as is observed elsewhere] if they had had the mind they could easily have surpassed the evil kings of Middle-earth in the making of war and the forging of weapons; but they were become men of peace.[11]

Swords the Guild of Weaponsmiths still made, for the preservation of the craft, though most of their labour was spent on the fashioning of tools for the uses of peace. The King and most of the great chieftains possessed swords as heirlooms of their fathers;[12] and at times they would still give a sword as a gift to their heirs. A new sword was made for the King's Heir to be given to him on the day on which this title was conferred. But no man wore a sword in Númenor, not even in the days of the wars in Middle-earth, unless he was actually armed for battle. Thus for long there were practically no weapons of warlike intent made in Númenor. Many things made could of course be so used: axes, and spears, and bows. The bowyers were a great craft. They made bows of many kinds: long bows, and smaller bows, especially those used for shooting from horse-back; and they also devised cross-bows, at first used mainly against predatory birds. Shooting with bows was one of the great sports and pastimes of men; and one in which young women also took part. The Númenórean men, being tall and powerful, could shoot with speed and accuracy upon foot from great long bows, whose shafts would carry to great distance (some 600 yards or more), and at lesser range were of great penetration.

## Of Sports and Pastimes

Númenor was a land of peace; within it there was no war or strife, until the last years. But the people were descended from ancestors of a hardy and warlike kind. The energy of the men was chiefly transferred to the practice of crafts; but they were also much occupied in games and physical sports. Boys and young men loved especially to live, when they could, freely in the open and to journey on foot in the wilder parts of the land. Many exercised themselves in climbing. There were no great mountains in Númenor. The sacred Mountain of the Meneltarma was near the centre of the land; but it was only about 3,000 feet high, and was climbed by a spiral road from its southern base (near where was the Valley of the Tombs, in which the kings were buried) up to its summit. But there were rocky and mountainous regions in the promontories of the North and North-west and South-west, in which some heights were about 2,000 feet. The cliffs, however, were the chief places of climbing for the daring. The cliffs of Númenor were in places of great height, especially along the west-facing coasts, the haunts of innumerable birds.

In the Sea the strong men took their greatest delight: in swimming or in diving; or in small craft for contests of speed in rowing and sailing. The hardiest of the people were engaged in fishing: fish were abundant, and at all times one of the chief sources of food for Númenor. The cities or towns where many people congregated were all by the coast. From the fisher-folk were mostly drawn the special class of mariners, who steadily increased in importance and esteem. At first the Númenórean craft, still largely dependent on Eldarin models, were engaged only in fishing, or in coastwise journeys from port to port. But it was not long before the Númenóreans by their own study and devices improved their art of ship-building, until they could venture far out into the Great Sea.

The women took little part in these things, though they were generally nearer to men than is the case with most races in stature and strength, and were agile and fleet of foot in youth. Their great delight was in dancing (in which many men also took part) at feasts or in leisure time. Many women achieved great fame as dancers, and people would go on long journeys to see displays of their art. They did not, however, greatly love

the Sea. They would journey in need in the coastwise craft
from port to port; but they did not like to be long aboard or to
pass even one night in a ship. Even among the fisher-folk the
women seldom took part in the sailings. But nearly all women
could ride horses, treating them honourably, and housing them
more nobly than any other of their domestic animals. The
stables of a great man were often as large and as fair to look
upon as his own house. Both men and women rode horses for
pleasure. Riding was also the chief means of quick travel from
place to place; and in ceremony of state both men and women
of rank, even queens, would ride, on horseback amid their
escorts or retinues.

The inland roads of Númenor were for the most part 'horse-
roads', unpaved, and made and tended for the purpose of
riding.

Coaches and carriages for journeying were in the earlier
centuries little used; for the heavier transport went largely by
sea. The chief and most ancient road, suitable for wheels, ran
from the greatest port, Rómenna, in the East, north-west to
the royal city of Armenelos (about 40 miles), and thence to the
Valley of Tombs and the Meneltarma. But this road was early
extended to Ondosto within the border of the Forostar (or
Norlands), and thence straight west to Andúnië in the Andustar (or Westlands); it was however little used for wheeled
vehicles of travel, being mainly made and used for the transport by wains of timber, in which the Westlands were rich, or
of stone of the Norlands, which was most esteemed for
building.

Though the Númenóreans used horses for journeys and for
the delight of riding they had little interest in racing them as a
test of speed. In country sports displays of agility, both of horse
and rider, were to be seen; but more esteemed were exhibitions
of understanding between master and beast. The Númenóreans
trained their horses to hear and understand calls (by voice or
whistling) from great distances; and also, where there was great
love between men or women and their favourite steeds, they

could (or so it is said in ancient tales) summon them at need by their thought alone.

So it was also with their dogs. For the Númenóreans kept dogs, especially in the country, partly by ancestral tradition, since they had few useful purposes any longer. The Númenóreans did not hunt for sport or food; and they had only in a few places upon the borders of wild lands any great need of watch-dogs. In the sheep-rearing regions, such as that of Emerië, they had dogs specially trained to help the shepherds. In the earlier centuries country-men also had dogs trained to assist in warding off or tracking down predatory beasts and birds (which to the Númenóreans was only an occasional necessary labour and not an amusement). Dogs were seldom seen in the towns. In the farms they were never chained or tethered; but neither did they dwell in the houses of men; though they were often welcomed to the central solma or hall, where the chief fire burned: especially the old faithful dogs of long service, or at times the puppies. It was men rather than women who had a liking to keep dogs as 'friends'. Women loved more the wild (or 'unowned') birds and beasts, and they were especially fond of squirrels, of which there were great numbers in the wooded country

While obedient [to the Valar ban on sailing to the West], people from the Blessed Realm often visited them, and so their knowledge and arts reached almost an Elvish height.[13]

From Avallónë, the haven of the Eldar upon Eressëa . . . at times the Firstborn still would come sailing to Númenor in oarless boats, as white birds flying from the sunset.[14] For the friendship that was between the peoples . . . they brought to Númenor many gifts: birds of song, and fragrant flowers, and herbs of great virtue. And a seedling they brought of Celeborn, the White Tree that grew in the midst of Eressëa; and that was in its turn a seedling of Galathilion the Tree of Túna, the image of Telperion that Yavanna gave to the Eldar in the

Blessed Realm.[15] And the tree grew and blossomed in the courts of the King in Armenelos; Nimloth it was named, and flowered in the evening, and the shadows of night it filled with its fragrance.

> Nimloth was the ancestor of what would become known as the White Tree of Gondor and memorialised as a symbol of the line of Kings and Stewards of Gondor. The genealogy of the White Tree in its various manifestations is long, dating from the First Age through until the ending of the Third and the beginning of the Fourth Ages.[16] It is recorded that for many years, following the founding of Númenor, the life lived by the Númenóreans was referred to as the 'days of bliss'.

Thus the years passed, and while Middle-earth went backward and light and wisdom faded, the Dúnedain dwelt under the protection of the Valar and in the friendship of the Eldar, and they increased in stature both of mind and body. For though this people used still their own speech, their kings and lords knew and spoke also the Elven tongue, which they had learned in the days of their alliance, and thus they held converse still with the Eldar, whether of Eressëa or of the westlands of Middle-earth. And the loremasters among them learned also the High Eldarin tongue of the Blessed Realm, in which much story and song was preserved from the beginning of the world; and they made letters and scrolls and books, and wrote in them many things of wisdom and wonder in the high tide of their realm, of which all is now forgot.[17]

> These accounts of the first years of life on Númenor end with a reminder that the life of the Númenóreans, for all its excellence, was doomed not to endure.

These things are said for the most part of the days of the bliss of Númenor, which lasted well nigh two thousand years; though the first hints of the later shadows appeared before that. Indeed it was their very arming to take part in the defence of the Eldar and Men of the West of Middle-earth against the wielder of the Shadow (at length revealed as Sauron the Great) that brought about the end of their peace and content. Victory was the herald of their Downfall.[18]

## *c.* 40 – MANY DWARVES LEAVING THEIR OLD CITIES IN ERED LUIN GO TO MORIA AND SWELL ITS NUMBERS.

Durin is the name that the Dwarves used for the eldest of the Seven Fathers of their race, and the ancestor of all the kings of the Longbeards. He slept alone, until in the deeps of time and the awakening of that people he came to Azanulbizar, and in the caves above Kheled-zâram in the east of the Misty Mountains he made his dwelling, where afterwards were the Mines of Moria renowned in song.

There he lived so long that he was known far and wide as Durin the Deathless. Yet in the end he died before the Elder Days had passed, and his tomb was in Khazad-dûm; but his line never failed, and five times an heir was born in his House so like to his Forefather that he received the name of Durin. He was indeed held by the Dwarves to be the Deathless that returned; for they have many strange tales and beliefs concerning themselves and their fate in the world.

After the end of the First Age the power and wealth of Khazad-dûm was much increased; for it was enriched by many people and much lore and craft when the ancient cities of

Nogrod and Belegost in the Blue Mountains were ruined at the breaking of Thangorodrim.[1]

In *The Fellowship of the Ring*, it is told how, at the Council of Elrond in the Third Age, Glóin the Dwarf spoke of that time when, 'amid the splendour of their works of hand the hearts of the Dwarves of the Lonely Mountain were troubled'. He said: 'It is now many years ago . . . that a shadow of disquiet fell upon our people. Whence it came we did not at first perceive. Words began to be whispered in secret: it was said that we were hemmed in a narrow place, and that greater wealth and splendour would be found in a wider world. Some spoke of Moria: the mighty works of our fathers that are called in our own tongue Khazad-dûm; and they declared that now at last we had the power and numbers to return.'[2]

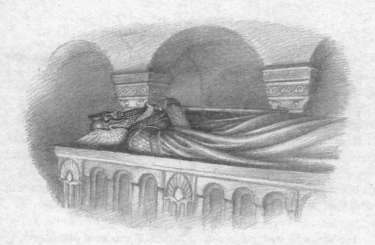

## 442 – DEATH OF ELROS TAR-MINYATUR.

Elros Tar-Minyatur ruled the Númenóreans for four hundred years and ten. For to the Númenóreans long life had been granted, and they remained unwearied for thrice the span of mortal Men in Middle-earth; but to Eärendil's son the longest life of any Man was given, and to his descendants a lesser span and yet one greater than to others even of the Númenóreans; and so it was until the coming of the Shadow, when the years of the Númenóreans began to wane.[1]

Elros had four children: three sons, Vardamir Nólimon, Manwendil, and Atanalcar and one daughter (his second born) Tindómiel.

**442 – KINGS AND QUEENS OF NÚMENOR II:**
**Tar-Vardamir**
Born: SA 61; Died: SA 471 (age 410)
Rule: SA 442

The eldest of Elros Tar-Minyatur's children, Tar-Vardamir was called Nólimon ['Learned One'] for his chief love was for ancient lore, which he gathered from Elves and Men. Upon the departure of Elros, being then 381 years of age, he did not ascend the throne, but gave the sceptre to his son. He is nonetheless accounted the second of the Kings, and is deemed to have reigned one year. It remained the custom thereafter until the days of Tar-Atanamir that the King should yield the sceptre to his successor before he died; and the Kings died of free will while yet in vigour of mind.

Tar-Vardamir had four children: Amandil, Vardilmë (daughter), Aulendil and Nolondil.

### 442 – KINGS AND QUEENS OF NÚMENOR III:
### Tar-Amandil
Born: SA 192; Died: SA 603 (age 411)
Rule: SA 442-590 (148 years)[2]

While chronicled as Númenor's third King, Tar-Amandil was, in truth, the second Ruler of the realm since his father, Vardamir Nólimon, had chosen not to ascend the throne. Amandil was born in the year 192, and the name Amandil comes from the words *Aman* and -(*n*)*dil* meaning, in Quenya, someone who is a 'lover' or 'friend' of Aman, the 'Blessed Realm'.

Tar-Amandil had two sons, Elendil and Eärendur, and a daughter, Mairen.

## *c.* 500 – SAURON BEGINS TO STIR AGAIN
## IN MIDDLE-EARTH.

In the long letter to Milton Waldman outlining the chronology
of events in the first Three Ages of Middle-earth, in all likeli-
hood written in 1951, Tolkien sketched a picture of the world in
the 'dark' days at the beginning of the Second Age:[1] 'In the great
battles against the First Enemy [Morgoth] the lands were broken
and ruined, and the West of Middle-earth became desolate. . . .
Also the Orcs (goblins) and other monsters bred by the First
Enemy are not wholly destroyed. . . .' As was told at the conclusion of the *Quenta Silmarillion*,[2] whilst through the intervention
of the Valar, Morgoth had been 'Thrust through the Door of
Night beyond the Walls of the World, into the Timeless Void. . . .
Yet the lies that Melkor, the mighty and accursed, Morgoth
Bauglir, the Power of Terror and of Hate, sowed in the hearts of
Elves and Men are a seed that does not die and cannot be
destroyed; and ever and anon it sprouts anew, and will bear dark
fruit even unto the latest days.' Those new-sprouting lies and
hatreds were tended and nurtured by Sauron:

Of old there was Sauron the Maia, whom the Sindar in Beleri-
and named Gorthaur. In the beginning of Arda Melkor seduced

47

him to his allegiance, and he became the greatest and most trusted of the servants of the Enemy, and the most perilous, for he could assume many forms, and for long if he willed he could still appear noble and beautiful, so as to deceive all but the most wary.

When Thangorodrim was broken and Morgoth overthrown, Sauron put on his fair hue again and did obeisance to Eönwë, the herald of Manwë, and abjured all his evil deeds. And some hold that this was not at first falsely done, but that Sauron in truth repented, if only out of fear, being dismayed by the fall of Morgoth and the great wrath of the Lords of the West. But it was not within the power of Eönwë to pardon those of his own order, and he commanded Sauron to return to Aman and there receive the judgement of Manwë. Then Sauron was ashamed, and he was unwilling to return in humiliation and to receive from the Valar a sentence, it might be, of long servitude in proof of his good faith; for under Morgoth his power had been great. Therefore when Eönwë departed he hid himself in Middle-earth; and he fell back into evil, for the bonds that Morgoth had laid upon him were very strong.[3]

> In his letter to Milton Waldman, Tolkien would write of Sauron: 'He lingers in Middle-earth. Very slowly, beginning with fair motives: the reorganising and rehabilitation of the ruin of Middle-earth, "neglected by the gods", he becomes a reincarnation of Evil, and a thing lusting for Complete Power – and so consumed ever more fiercely with hate (especially of gods and Elves).'[4]
>
> Among Tolkien's later writings, published posthumously by Christopher Tolkien in his *History of Middle-earth*[5], Tolkien gave consideration to Sauron's motives that indicate a striking subtlety of reflection on the characteristics of his protagonist.

Sauron was 'greater', effectively, in the Second Age than Morgoth at the end of the First. Why? Because, though he was far smaller by natural stature, he had not yet fallen so low.

Eventually he also squandered his power (of being) in the endeavour to gain control of others. But he was not obliged to expend so much of himself. To gain domination over Arda, Morgoth had let most of his being pass into the physical constituents of the Earth – hence all things that were born on Earth and lived on and by it, beasts or plants or incarnate spirits, were liable to be 'stained'. . . .

Sauron, however, inherited the 'corruption' of Arda, and only spent his (much more limited) power on the Rings; for it was the *creatures* of earth, in their *minds and wills*, that he desired to dominate. In this way Sauron was also wiser than Melkor-Morgoth. Sauron was not a beginner of discord; and he probably knew more of the 'Music' [the Music of the Ainur, the great song of creation before the beginning of Time] than did Melkor, whose mind had always been filled with his own plans and devices, and gave little attention to other things. . . .

Sauron had never reached this stage of nihilistic madness. He did not object to the existence of the world, so long as he could do what he liked with it. He still had the relics of positive purposes that descended from the good of the nature in which he began: it had been his virtue (and therefore also the cause of his fall, and of his relapse) that he loved order and coordination, and disliked all confusion and wasteful friction. . . . But like all minds of this cast, Sauron's love (originally) or (later) mere understanding of other individual intelligences was correspondingly weaker; and though the only real good in, or rational motive for, all this ordering and planning and organization was the good of all inhabitants of Arda (even admitting Sauron's right to be their supreme lord), his 'plans', the idea coming from his own isolated mind, became the sole object of his will, and an end, the End, in itself.*

---

* But his capability of corrupting other minds, and even engaging their service, was a residue from the fact that his original desire for 'order' had really envisaged the good estate (especially physical well-being) of his 'subjects'.

Elsewhere in Middle-earth there was peace for many years; yet the lands were for the most part savage and desolate, save only where the people of Beleriand came. Many Elves dwelt there indeed, as they had dwelt through the countless years, wandering free in the wide lands far from the Sea; but they were Avari, to whom the deeds of Beleriand were but a rumour and Valinor only a distant name. And in the south and in the further east Men multiplied; and most of them turned to evil, for Sauron was at work.[6]

Seeing the desolation of the world, Sauron said in his heart that the Valar, having overthrown Morgoth, had again forgotten Middle-earth; and his pride grew apace.[7]

# 521 – BIRTH IN NÚMENOR OF SILMARIËN.

### 590 – KINGS AND QUEENS OF NÚMENOR IV:
**Tar-Elendil**
Born: SA 350; Died: SA 751 (age 401)
Rule: SA 590-740 (150 years)

The name Elendil in Quenya had the meaning of 'Star-lover' (one who loves or studies the stars) from the words *elen* ('star') and -(*n*)*dil* ('friend, lover or devotee') with the additional interpretation of 'Elf-friend', a common appellation among those Edain who had close-friendship with the Eldar, from *Eled* ('star-folk') in referencing the Elves.[1]

[Elendil] was also called Parmaitë,[2] for with his own hand he made many books and legends of the lore gathered by his grandfather [Tar-Vardamir]. He married late in his life, and his eldest child was a daughter, Silmarien, born in the year 521, whose son was Valandil. Of Valandil came the Lords of Andúnië, of whom the last was Amandil father of Elendil the Tall, who came to Middle-earth after the Downfall.

A second daughter, Isilmë, was born in 532 and son, Meneldur in the year 543 who, because of the then law that a female of the line could not succeed, would become the sixth King of Númenor as Tar-Meneldur.

In Tar-Elendil's reign the ships of the Númenóreans first came back to Middle-earth.

## 600 – THE FIRST SHIPS OF THE NÚMENÓREANS APPEAR OFF THE COASTS.

Above all arts they nourished ship-building and sea-craft, and they became mariners whose like shall never be again since the world was diminished; and voyaging upon the wide seas was the chief feat and adventure of their hardy men in the gallant days of their youth.

But the Lords of Valinor forbade them to sail so far westward that the coasts of Númenor could no longer be seen; and for long the Dúnedain were content, though they did not fully understand the purpose of this ban. But the design of Manwë was that the Númenóreans should not be tempted to seek for the Blessed Realm, nor desire to overpass the limits set to their bliss, becoming enamoured of the immortality of the Valar and the Eldar and the lands where all things endure.

For in those days Valinor still remained in the world visible, and there Ilúvatar permitted the Valar to maintain upon Earth an abiding place, a memorial of that which might have been if Morgoth had not cast his shadow on the world. This the Númenóreans knew full well; and at times, when all the air was clear and the sun was in the east, they would look out and descry far off in the west a city white-shining on a distant shore, and a great harbour and a tower. For in those days the Númenóreans were far-sighted; yet even so it was only the keenest eyes among them that could see this vision, from the Meneltarma, maybe, or from some tall ship that lay off their western coast as far as it was lawful for them to go. For they did not dare to break the Ban of the Lords of the West. But the wise among them knew that this distant land was not indeed the Blessed Realm of Valinor, but was Avallónë, the haven of the Eldar upon Eressëa, easternmost of the Undying Lands. . . .

Thus it was that because of the Ban of the Valar the voyages of the Dúnedain in those days went ever eastward and not westward, from the darkness of the North to the heats of the South, and beyond the South to the Nether Darkness; and they came even into the inner seas, and sailed about Middle-earth and glimpsed from their high prows the Gates of Morning in the East.[1]

When six hundred years had passed from the beginning of the Second Age Vëantur, Captain of King's Ships under Tar-Elendil, first achieved the voyage to Middle-earth. He brought his ship *Entulessë* (which signifies 'Return') into Mithlond on the spring winds blowing from the west; and he returned in the autumn of the following year. Thereafter seafaring became the chief enterprise for daring and hardihood among the men of Númenor. . . .[2]

And the Dúnedain came at times to the shores of the Great Lands, and they took pity on the forsaken world of Middle-earth; and the Lords of Númenor set foot again upon the western shores in the Dark Years of Men, and none yet dared to withstand them. For most of the Men of that age that sat under the Shadow were now grown weak and fearful.[3]

But for long the crews of the great Númenórean ships came unarmed among the men of Middle-earth; and though they had axes and bows aboard for the felling of timber and the hunting for food upon wild shores owned by no man, they did not bear these when they sought out the men of the lands.[4]

In a lengthy note in *Unfinished Tales*, Christopher Tolkien quotes from 'a late philological essay' by his father giving 'a description of the first meeting of the Númenóreans with Men of Eriador at that time':

It was six hundred years after the departure of the survivors of the Atani [the Quenya name for the Edain or Men] over the sea to Númenor that a ship first came again out of the West to Middle-earth and passed up the Gulf of Lhûn. Its captain and mariners were welcomed by Gil-galad; and thus was begun the friendship and alliance of Númenor with the Eldar of Lindon. The news spread swiftly and Men in Eriador were filled with wonder. Although in the First Age they had dwelt in the East, rumours of the terrible war 'beyond the Western Mountains' [i.e. Ered Luin] had reached them; but their traditions preserved no clear account of it, and they believed that all the Men who dwelt in the lands beyond had been destroyed or drowned in great tumults of fire and inrushing seas. But since it was still said among them that those Men had in years beyond memory been kinsmen of their own, they sent messages to Gil-galad asking leave to meet the shipmen 'who had returned from death in the deeps of the Sea.' Thus it came about that there was a meeting between them on the Tower Hills; and to that meeting with the Númenóreans came twelve Men only out of Eriador, Men of high heart and courage, for most of their people feared that the newcomers were perilous spirits of the Dead. But when they looked on the shipmen fear left them, though for a while they stood silent in awe; for mighty as they were themselves accounted among their kin, the shipmen resembled rather Elvish lords than mortal Men in bearing and apparel. Nonetheless they felt no doubt of their ancient kinship; and likewise the shipmen looked with glad surprise upon the Men of Middle-earth, for it had been believed in Númenor that the Men left behind were descended from the evil Men who in the last days of the war against Morgoth had been summoned by him out of the East. But now they looked upon faces free from the Shadow and Men who could have walked in Númenor and not been thought aliens save in their clothes and their arms. Then suddenly, after the silence, both the Númenóreans and the Men of Eriador spoke words of welcome and greeting in their own tongues, as if addressing friends and kinsmen after a long parting. At first they were disappointed, for neither side could understand the other; but when they mingled in friendship they found that they shared very many words still clearly recognisable, and others that could be understood with attention, and they were able to converse haltingly about simple matters.[5]

And coming among [the Men of Middle-earth] the Númenóreans taught them many things.[6]

Language they taught them, for the tongues of the Men of Middle-earth, save in the old lands of the Edain, were fallen into brutishness, and they cried like harsh birds, or snarled like savage beasts.[7]

Corn and wine they brought, and they instructed Men in the sowing of seed and the grinding of grain, in the hewing of wood and the shaping of stone, and in the ordering of their life, such as it might be in the lands of swift death and little bliss.

Then the Men of Middle-earth were comforted, and here and there upon the western shores the houseless woods drew back, and Men shook off the yoke of the offspring of Morgoth, and unlearned their terror of the dark. And they revered the memory of the tall Sea-kings, and when they had departed they called them gods, hoping for their return; for at that time the Númenóreans dwelt never long in Middle-earth, nor made there as yet any habitation of their own. Eastward they must sail, but ever west their hearts returned.[8]

During all of this time, Sauron continued to bide his time and wait his moment.

He looked with hatred on the Eldar, and he feared the Men of Númenor who came back at whiles in their ships to the shores of Middle-earth; but for long he dissembled his mind and concealed the dark designs that he shaped in his heart.[9]

## THE VOYAGES OF ALDARION[1]

[Meneldur, son of Tar-Elendil, was wed to] a woman of great beauty, named Almarian. She was the daughter of Vëantur, Captain of the King's Ships under Tar-Elendil; and though she herself loved ships and the sea no more than most women of the land her son followed after Vëantur her father, rather than after Meneldur.

The son of Meneldur and Almarian was Anardil [Lover of the Sun[2]], afterwards renowned among the Kings of Númenor as Tar-Aldarion. He had two sisters, younger than he: Ailinel and Almiel, of whom the elder married Orchaldor, a descendant of the House of Hador, son of Hatholdir, who was close in friendship with Meneldur; and the son of Orchaldor and Ailinel was Soronto, who comes later into the tale.[3]

Aldarion [Son of the Trees[4]], for so he is called in all tales, grew swiftly to a man of great stature, strong and vigorous in mind and body, golden-haired as his mother, ready to mirth and generous, but prouder than his father and ever more bent on his own will. From the first he loved the Sea, and his mind was turned to the craft of shipbuilding. He had little liking for the north country, and spent all the time that his father would grant by the shores of the sea, especially near Rómenna, where was the chief haven of Númenor, the greatest shipyards, and the most skilled shipwrights. His father did little to hinder him for many years, being well-pleased that Aldarion should have exercise for his hardihood and work for thought and hand.

Aldarion was much loved by Vëantur his mother's father, and he dwelt often in Vëantur's house on the southern side of the firth of Rómenna. That house had its own quay, to which many small boats were always moored, for Vëantur would never journey by land if he could by water; and there as a child Aldarion learned to row, and later to manage sail. Before he was full grown he could captain a ship of many men, sailing from haven to haven.

It happened on a time that Vëantur said to his grandson: 'Anardilya,[5] the spring is drawing nigh, and also the day of your full age' (for in that April Aldarion would be twenty-five years old). 'I have in mind a way to mark it fittingly. My own years are far greater, and I do not think that I shall often again have the heart to leave my fair house and the blest shores of Númenor; but once more at least I would ride the Great Sea and face the North wind and the East. This year you shall come with me, and we will go to Mithlond and see the tall blue mountains of Middle-earth and the green land of the Eldar at their feet. Good welcome you will find from Círdan the Shipwright and from King Gil-galad. Speak of this to your father.'

When Aldarion spoke of this venture, and asked leave to go as soon as the spring winds should be favourable, Meneldur was loath to grant it. A chill came upon him, as though his heart guessed that more hung upon this than his mind could foresee. But when he looked upon the eager face of his son he let no sign of this be seen. 'Do as your heart calls, *onya* [*my son*],' he said. 'I shall miss you sorely; but with Vëantur as captain, under the grace of the Valar, I shall live in good hope of your return. But do not become enamoured of the Great Lands, you who one day must be King and Father of this Isle!'

\* \* \*

Thus it came to pass that on a morning of fair sun and white wind, in the bright spring of the seven hundred and twenty-fifth year of the Second Age, the son of the King's Heir of Númenor sailed from the land; and ere day was over he saw it sink shimmering into the sea, and last of all the peak of the Meneltarma as a dark finger against the sunset.

It is said that Aldarion himself wrote records of all his journeys to Middle-earth, and they were long preserved in Rómenna, though all were afterwards lost. Of his first journey little is known, save that he made the friendship of Círdan and Gil-galad, and journeyed far in Lindon and the west of Eriador, and marvelled at all that he saw. He did not return for more than two years, and Meneldur was in great disquiet. It is said that his delay was due to the eagerness he had to learn all that he could of Círdan, both in the making and management of ships, and in the building of walls to withstand the hunger of the sea.

There was joy in Rómenna and Armenelos when men saw the great ship *Númerrámar* (which signifies 'West-wings') coming up from the sea, her golden sails reddened in the sunset. The summer was nearly over and the *Eruhantalë*⁶ was nigh. It seemed to Meneldur when he welcomed his son in the house of Vëantur that he had grown in stature, and his eyes were brighter; but they looked far away.

'What did you see, *onya*, in your far journeys that now lives most in memory?'

But Aldarion, looking east towards the night, was silent. At last he answered, but softly, as one that speaks to himself: 'The fair people of the Elves? The green shores? The mountains wreathed in cloud? The regions of mist and shadow beyond guess? I do not know.' He ceased, and Meneldur knew that he had not spoken his full mind. For Aldarion had become enamoured of the Great Sea, and of a ship riding there alone without sight of land, borne by the winds with foam at its throat to coasts and havens unguessed; and that love and desire never left him until his life's end.

Vëantur did not again voyage from Númenor; but the *Númer-rámar* he gave in gift to Aldarion. Within three years Aldarion begged leave to go again, and he set sail for Lindon. He was three years abroad; and not long after another voyage he made, that lasted for four years, for it is said that he was no longer content to sail to Mithlond, but began to explore the coasts southwards, past the mouths of Baranduin and Gwathló and Angren, and he rounded the dark cape of Ras Morthil and beheld the great Bay of Belfalas, and the mountains of the country of Amroth where the Nandor Elves still dwell.[7]

In the thirty-ninth year of his age Aldarion returned to Númenor, bringing gifts from Gil-galad to his father; for in the following year, as he had long proclaimed, Tar-Elendil relinquished the Sceptre to his son, and Tar-Meneldur became the King. Then Aldarion restrained his desire, and remained at home for a while for the comfort of his father; and in those days he put to use the knowledge he had gained of Círdan concerning the making of ships, devising much anew of his own thought, and he began also to set men to the improvement of the havens and the quays, for he was ever eager to build greater vessels.

The year following Aldarion's return, Tar-Elendil surrendered the sceptre to his son – and Aldarion's father – Meneldur.

### 740 – KINGS AND QUEENS OF NÚMENOR V:
### Tar-Meneldur
Born: SA 543; Died: SA 942 (age 399)
Rule: SA 740-883 (143 years)

[Meneldur was Tar-Elendil's third child] for he had two sisters, named Silmarien and Isilmë. The elder of these was wedded to Elatan of Andúnië, and their son was Valandil, Lord of Andúnië, from whom came long after the lines of the Kings of Gondor and Arnor in Middle-earth.[8]

> His birth-name was Írimon and he took the name Meneldur from 'his love of star-lore', from the Quenya *menel* ('the heavens') and -(*n*)*dur* ('servant').[9]

Meneldur was a man of gentle mood, without pride,[10] whose exercise was rather in thought than in deeds of the body. He loved dearly the land of Númenor and all things in it, but he gave no heed to the Sea that lay all about it; for his mind looked further than Middle-earth: he was enamoured of the stars and the heavens. All that he could gather of the lore of the Eldar and Edain concerning Eä[11] and the deeps that lay about the Kingdom of Arda[12] he studied, and his chief delight was in the watching of the stars. He built a tower in the Forostar (the northernmost region of the island) where the airs were clearest, from which by night he would survey the heavens and observe all the movements of the light of the firmament.[13]

When Meneldur received the Sceptre he removed, as he must, from the Forostar, and dwelt in the great house of the Kings in Armenelos. He proved a good and wise king, though he never ceased to yearn for days in which he might enrich his knowledge of the heavens.

## 750 – EREGION FOUNDED BY THE NOLDOR.

Galadriel became aware that Sauron again, as in the ancient days of the captivity of Melkor [Morgoth],[1] had been left behind. Or rather, since Sauron had as yet no single name, and his operations had not been perceived to proceed from a single evil spirit, prime servant of Melkor, she perceived that there was an evil controlling purpose abroad in the world, and that it seemed to proceed from a source further to the East, beyond Eriador and the Misty Mountains.

Celeborn and Galadriel therefore went eastwards, about the year 700 of the Second Age, and established the (primarily but by no means solely) Noldorin realm of Eregion.[2] It may be that Galadriel chose it because she knew of the Dwarves of Khazad-dûm (Moria). There were and always remained some Dwarves on the eastern side of Ered Lindon, where the very ancient mansions of Nogrod and Belegost had been – not far from Nenuial; but they had transferred most of their strength to Khazad-dûm. Celeborn had no liking for Dwarves of any race (as he showed to Gimli in Lothlórien), and never forgave them for their part in the destruction of Doriath; but it was only the host of Nogrod that took part in that assault, and it was destroyed in the battle of Sarn Athrad. The Dwarves of

Belegost were filled with dismay at the calamity and fear for its outcome, and this hastened their departure eastwards to Khazad-dûm. Thus the Dwarves of Moria may be presumed to have been innocent of the ruin of Doriath and not hostile to the Elves. In any case, Galadriel was more far-sighted in this than Celeborn; and she perceived from the beginning that Middle-earth could not be saved from 'the residue of evil' that Morgoth had left behind him save by a union of all the peoples who were in their way and in their measure opposed to him. She looked upon the Dwarves also with the eye of a commander, seeing in them the finest warriors to pit against the Orcs. Moreover Galadriel was a Noldo, and she had a natural sympathy with their minds and their passionate love of crafts of hand, a sympathy much greater than that found among many of the Eldar; the Dwarves were 'the Children of Aulë', and Galadriel, like others of the Noldor, had been a pupil of Aulë and Yavanna in Valinor.[3]

Galadriel and Celeborn had in their company a Noldorin craftsman named Celebrimbor . . . said to have been one of the survivors of Gondolin, who had been among Turgon's greatest artificers. . . . Celebrimbor had 'an almost "dwarvish" obsession with crafts'; and he soon became the chief artificer of Eregion, entering into a close relationship with the Dwarves of Khazad-dûm, among whom his greatest friend was Narvi. Both Elves and Dwarves had great profit from this association: so that Eregion became far stronger, and Khazad-dûm far more beautiful, than either would have done alone.[4]

The building of the chief city of Eregion, Ost-in-Edhil, ['Fortress of the Eldar'] was begun in about the year 750 of the Second Age [the date that is given in the Tale of Years for the founding of Eregion by the Noldor].[5]

In the year 750, Celebrimbor established in Eregion a brotherhood of Elven master craftsmen called the Gwaith-i-Mírdain, the People of the Jewel-smiths.[6]

It is written in *The Silmarillion* that they 'surpassed in

cunning all that have ever wrought, save only Fëanor himself; and indeed greatest in skill among them was Celebrimbor'.[7]

Narvi was a Dwarvish craftsman whose workmanship, in collaboration with Celebrimbor, would be discovered by the Fellowship of the Ring when they sought a way through Moria. They are confronted by closed and hidden doors whose presence is eventually revealed by the light of the rising moon together with graven emblems of the Houses of Durin and Fëanor, 'wrought of ithildin that mirrors only starlight and moonlight', together with the inscription 'in the elven-tongue of the West of Middle-earth in the Elder Days': *The Doors of Durin, Lord of Moria. Speak, friend, and enter . . . I, Narvi, made them. Celebrimbor of Hollin drew these signs.*[8]

The signs and inscription were evidence of the supreme fortune that had once been possessed by the Dwarves of Khaz-ad-dûm, as Gandalf explained: 'The wealth of Moria was not in gold and jewels, the toys of the Dwarves; nor in iron, their servant. Such things they found here, it is true, especially iron; but they did not need to delve for them: all things that they desired they could obtain in traffic. For here alone in the world was found Moria-silver, or true-silver as some have called it: *mithril* is the Elvish name. The Dwarves have a name which they do not tell. Its worth was ten times that of gold, and now it is beyond price; for little is left above ground, and even the Orcs dare not delve here for it. . . .

'*Mithril!* All folk desired it. It could be beaten like copper, and polished like glass; and the Dwarves could make of it a metal, light and yet harder than tempered steel. Its beauty was like to that of common silver, but the beauty of *mithril* did not tarnish or grow dim. The Elves dearly loved it, and among many uses they made of it *ithildin*, starmoon, which you saw upon the doors.'[9]

## ALDARION AND ERENDIS[1]

[The 'sea-longing' came anew upon Aldarion, son of Tar-Meneldur, fifth king of Númenor] and he departed again and yet again from Númenor; and his mind turned now to ventures that might not be compassed with one vessel's company. Therefore he formed the Guild of Venturers, that afterwards was renowned; to that brotherhood were joined all the hardiest and most eager mariners, and young men sought admission to it even from the inland regions of Númenor, and Aldarion they called the Great Captain. At that time he, having no mind to live upon land in Armenelos, had a ship built that should serve as his dwelling-place; he named it therefore *Eämbar* ['Sea-dwelling'[2]] and at times he would sail in it from haven to haven of Númenor, but for the most part it lay at anchor off Tol Uinen: and that was a little isle in the bay of Rómenna that was set there by Uinen the Lady of the Seas[3]. Upon *Eämbar* was the Guildhouse of the Venturers, and there were kept the records of their great voyages[4]; for Tar-Meneldur looked coldly on the enterprises of his son, and cared not to hear the tale of his journeys, believing that he sowed the seeds of restlessness and the desire of other lands to hold.

In that time Aldarion became estranged from his father, and

ceased to speak openly of his designs and his desires; but Almarian the Queen supported her son in all that he did, and Meneldur perforce let matters go as they must. For the Venturers grew in numbers and in the esteem of men, and they called them *Uinendili*, the lovers of Uinen; and their Captain became the less easy to rebuke or restrain. The ships of the Númenóreans became ever larger and of greater draught in those days, until they could make far voyages, carrying many men and great cargoes; and Aldarion was often long gone from Númenor. Tar-Meneldur ever opposed his son, and he set a curb on the felling of trees in Númenor for the building of vessels; and it came therefore into Aldarion's mind that he would find timber in Middle-earth, and seek there for a haven for the repair of his ships. In his voyages down the coasts he looked with wonder on the great forests; and at the mouth of the river that the Númenóreans called Gwathir, River of Shadow, he established Vinyalondë, the New Haven.[5]

But when nigh on eight hundred years had passed since the beginning of the Second Age, Tar-Meneldur commanded his son to remain now in Númenor and to cease for a time his eastward voyaging; for he desired to proclaim Aldarion the King's Heir, as had been done at that age of the Heir by the Kings before him. Then Meneldur and his son were reconciled, for that time, and there was peace between them; and amid joy and feasting Aldarion was proclaimed Heir in the hundredth year of his age, and received from his father the title and power of Lord of the Ships and Havens of Númenor. To the feasting in Armenelos came one Beregar from his dwelling in the west of the Isle, and with him came Erendis his daughter. There Almarian the Queen observed her beauty, of a kind seldom seen in Númenor; for Beregar came of the House of Bëor by ancient descent, though not of the royal line of Elros, and Erendis was dark-haired and of slender grace, with the clear grey eyes of her kin.[6] But Erendis looked upon Aldarion as he rode by, and for his beauty and splendour of bearing she had eyes for little else. Thereafter Erendis entered the household of the Queen, and found favour also with the King; but little did she see of Aldarion, who busied himself in the tending of the forests, being concerned that in days to come timber should not lack in Númenor. Ere long the mariners of the Guild of Venturers became restless, for they were ill content to voyage more briefly and more rarely under lesser commanders; and when six years had passed since the proclamation of the King's Heir Aldarion determined to sail again to Middle-earth. Of the King he got but grudging leave, for he refused his father's urging that he abide in Númenor and seek a wife; and he set sail in the spring of the year. But coming to bid farewell to his mother he saw Erendis amid the Queen's company; and looking on her beauty he divined the strength that lay concealed in her.

Then Almarian said to him: 'Must you depart again, Aldarion, my son? Is there nothing that will hold you in the fairest of all mortal lands?'

'Not yet,' he answered; 'but there are fairer things in Armenelos than a man could find elsewhere, even in the lands of the Eldar. But mariners are men of two minds, at war with themselves; and the desire of the Sea still holds me.'

Erendis believed that these words were spoken also for her ears; and from that time forth her heart was turned wholly to Aldarion, though not in hope. In those days there was no need, by law or custom, that those of the royal house, not even the King's Heir, should wed only with descendants of Elros Tar-Minyatur; but Erendis deemed that Aldarion was too high. Yet she looked on no man with favour thereafter, and every suitor she dismissed.

Seven years passed before Aldarion came back, bringing with him ore of silver and gold; and he spoke with his father of his voyage and his deeds. But Meneldur said: 'Rather would I have had you beside me, than any news or gifts from the Dark Lands. This is the part of merchants and explorers, not of the King's Heir. What need have we of more silver and gold, unless to use in pride where other things would serve as well? The need of the

King's house is for a man who knows and loves this land and people, which he will rule.'

'Do I not study men all my days?' said Aldarion. 'I can lead and govern them as I will.'

'Say rather, some men, of like mind with yourself,' answered the King. 'There are also women in Númenor, scarce fewer than men; and save your mother, whom indeed you can lead as you will, what do you know of them? Yet one day you must take a wife.'

'One day!' said Aldarion. 'But not before I must; and later, if any try to thrust me towards marriage. Other things I have to do more urgent to me, for my mind is bent on them. "Cold is the life of a mariner's wife"; and the mariner who is single of purpose and not tied to the shore goes further, and learns better how to deal with the sea.'

'Further, but not with more profit,' said Meneldur. 'And you do not "deal with the sea", Aldarion, my son. Do you forget that the Edain dwell here under the grace of the Lords of the West, that Uinen is kind to us, and Ossë is restrained? Our ships are guarded, and other hands guide them than ours. So be not overproud, or the grace may wane; and do not presume that it will extend to those who risk themselves without need upon the rocks of strange shores or in the lands of men of darkness.'

'To what purpose then is the gracing of our ships,' said Aldarion, 'if they are to sail to no shores, and may seek nothing not seen before?'

He spoke no more to his father of such matters, but passed his days upon the ship *Eämbar* in the company of the Venturers, and in the building of a vessel greater than any made before: that ship he named *Palarran*, the Far-Wanderer. Yet now he met Erendis often (and that was by contrivance of the Queen); and the King learning of their meetings felt disquiet, yet he was not displeased. 'It would be more kind to cure Aldarion of his restlessness,' said he, 'before he win the heart of any woman.' 'How else will you cure him, if not by love?' said the Queen. 'Erendis is yet young,' said Meneldur. But Almarian answered: 'The kin of Erendis have not the length of life that is granted to the descendants of Elros; and her heart is already won.'

Now when the great ship *Palarran* was built Aldarion would depart once more. At this Meneldur became wrathful, though by the persuasions of the Queen he would not use the King's power to stay him. Here must be told of the custom that when a ship departed from Númenor over the Great Sea to Middle-earth a woman, most often of the captain's kin, should set upon the vessel's prow the Green Bough of Return; and that was cut from the tree *oiolairë*,[7] that signifies 'Ever-summer', which the Eldar gave to the Númenóreans, saying that they set it upon their own ships in token of friendship with Ossë and Uinen. The leaves of that tree were evergreen, glossy and fragrant; and it throve upon sea-air. But Meneldur forbade the Queen and the sisters of Aldarion to bear the bough of *oiolairë* to Rómenna where lay the *Palarran*, saying that he refused his blessing to his son, who was venturing forth against his will; and Aldarion hearing this said: 'If I must go without blessing or bough, then so I will go.'

Then the Queen was grieved; but Erendis said to her: '*Tarinya* [my Queen], if you will cut the bough from the Elven-tree, I will bear it to the haven, by your leave; for the King has not forbidden it to me.'

The mariners thought it an ill thing that the Captain should depart thus; but when all was made ready and men prepared to weigh anchor Erendis came there, little though she loved the noise and bustle of the great harbour and the crying of the gulls. Aldarion greeted her with amazement and joy; and she said: 'I have brought you the Bough of Return, lord: from the Queen.' 'From the Queen?' said Aldarion, in a changed manner. 'Yes, lord,' said she; 'but I asked for her leave to do so. Others beside your own kin will rejoice at your return, as soon as may be.'

At that time Aldarion first looked on Erendis with love; and he stood long in the stern looking back as the *Palarran* passed out to sea. It is said that he hastened his return, and was gone less time than he had designed; and coming back he brought gifts for the Queen and the ladies of her house, but the richest gift he brought for Erendis, and that was a diamond. Cold now were the greetings between the King and his son; and Meneldur rebuked him, saying that such a gift was unbecoming in the King's Heir unless it were a betrothal gift, and he demanded that Aldarion declare his mind.

'In gratitude I brought it,' said he, 'for a warm heart amid the coldness of others.'

'Cold hearts may not kindle others to give them warmth at their goings and comings,' said Meneldur; and again he urged Aldarion to take thought of marriage, though he did not speak of Erendis. But Aldarion would have none of it, for he was ever and in every course the more opposed as those about him urged it; and treating Erendis now with greater coolness he determined to leave Númenor and further his designs in Vinyalondë.[8] Life on land was irksome to him, for aboard his ship he was subject to no other will, and the Venturers who accompanied him knew only love and admiration for the Great Captain. But now Meneldur forbade his going; and Aldarion, before the winter was fully gone, set sail with a fleet of seven ships and the greater part of the Venturers in defiance of the King. The Queen did not dare incur Meneldur's wrath; but at night a cloaked woman came to the haven bearing a bough, and she gave it into the hands of Aldarion, saying: 'This comes from the Lady of the Westlands' (for so they called Erendis), and went away in the dark.

At the open rebellion of Aldarion the King rescinded his authority as Lord of the Ships and Havens of Númenor; and he caused the Guildhouse of the Venturers on *Eämbar* to be shut, and the shipyards of Rómenna to be closed, and forbade the felling of all trees for shipbuilding. Five years passed; and Aldarion returned with nine ships, for two had been built in Vinyalondë, and they were laden with fine timber from the forests of the coasts of Middle-earth. The anger of Aldarion was great when he found what had been done; and to his father he said: 'If I am to have no welcome in Númenor, and no work for my hands to do, and if my ships may not be repaired in its havens, then I will go again and soon; for the winds have been rough,[9] and I need refitment. Has not a King's son aught to do but study women's faces to find a wife? The work of forestry I took up, and I have been prudent in it; there will be more timber in Númenor ere my day ends than there is under your sceptre.' And true to his word Aldarion left again in the same year with three ships and the hardiest of the Venturers, going without blessing or bough; for Meneldur set a ban on all the women of his house and of the Venturers, and put a guard about Rómenna.

On that voyage Aldarion was away so long that the people feared for him; and Meneldur himself was disquieted, despite the grace of the Valar that had ever protected the ships of Númenor.[10] When ten years were gone since his sailing Erendis at last despaired, and believing that Aldarion had met with disaster, or else that he had determined to dwell in Middle-earth, and also in order to escape the importuning of suitors, she asked the Queen's leave, and departing from Armenelos she returned to her own kindred in the Westlands. But after four years more Aldarion at last returned, and his ships were battered and broken by the seas. He had sailed first to the haven of Vinyalondë, and thence he had made a great coastwise journey southwards, far beyond any place yet reached by the ships of the Númenóreans; but returning northwards he had met contrary winds and great storms, and scarce escaping shipwreck in the Harad found Vinyalondë overthrown by great seas and plundered by hostile men. Three times he was driven back from the crossing of the Great Sea by high winds out of the West, and his own ship was struck by lightning and dismasted; and only with labour and hardship in the deep waters did he come at last to haven in Númenor. Greatly was Meneldur comforted at Aldarion's return; but he rebuked him for his rebellion against king and father, thus forsaking the guardianship of the Valar, and risking the wrath of Ossë not only for himself but for men whom he had bound to himself in devotion. Then Aldarion was chastened in mood, and he received the pardon of Meneldur, who restored to him the Lordship of the Ships and Havens, and added thereto the title of Master of the Forests.

Aldarion was grieved to find Erendis gone from Armenelos, but he was too proud to seek her; and indeed he could not well do so save to ask for her in marriage, and he was still unwilling to be bound. He set himself to the repairing of the neglects of his long absence, for he had been nigh on twenty years away; and at the time great harbour works were put in hand, especially at Rómenna. He found that there had been much felling of trees for building and the making of many things, but all was done without foresight, and little had been planted to replace what was taken; and he journeyed far and wide in Númenor to view the standing woods.

Riding one day in the forests of the Westlands he saw a woman, whose dark hair flowed in the wind, and about her was a green cloak clasped at the throat with a bright jewel; and he took her for one of the Eldar, who came at times to those parts of the Island. But she approached, and he knew her for Erendis, and saw that the jewel was the one that he had given her; then suddenly he knew in himself the love that he bore her, and he felt the emptiness of his days. Erendis seeing him turned pale and would ride off, but he was too quick, and he said: 'Too well have I deserved that you should flee from me, who have fled so often and so far! But forgive me, and stay now.' They rode then together to the house of Beregar her father, and there Aldarion made plain his desire for betrothal to Erendis; but now Erendis was reluctant, though according to custom and the life of her people it was now full time for her marriage. Her love for him was not lessened, nor did she retreat out of guile; but she feared now in her heart that in the war between herself and the Sea for the keeping of Aldarion she would not conquer. Never would Erendis take less, that she might not lose all; and fearing the Sea, and begrudging to all ships the felling of trees which she loved, she determined that she must utterly defeat the Sea and the ships, or else be herself defeated utterly.

But Aldarion wooed Erendis in earnest, and wherever she went he would go; he neglected the havens and the shipyards and all the concerns of the Guild of Venturers, felling no trees but setting himself to their planting only, and he found more contentment in those days than in any others of his life, though he did not know it until he looked back long after when old age was upon him. At length he sought to persuade Erendis to sail with him on a voyage about the Island in the ship *Eämbar*; for one hundred years had now passed since Aldarion founded the Guild of Venturers, and feasts were to be held in all the havens of Númenor. To this Erendis consented, concealing her distaste and fear; and they departed from Rómenna and came to Andúnië in the west of the Isle. There Valandil, Lord of Andúnië and close kin of Aldarion,[11] held a great feast; and at that feast he drank to Erendis, naming her *Uinéniel*, Daughter of Uinen, the new Lady of the Sea. But Erendis, who sat beside the wife of Valandil, said aloud: 'Call me by no such name! I am no daughter of Uinen: rather is she my foe.'

Thereafter for a while doubt again assailed Erendis, for Aldarion turned his thoughts again to the works at Rómenna, and busied himself with the building of great sea-walls, and the raising of a tall tower upon Tol Uinen: *Calmindon*, the Light-tower, was its name. But when these things were done Aldarion returned to Erendis and besought her to be betrothed; yet still she delayed, saying: 'I have journeyed with you by ship, lord. Before I give you my answer, will you not journey with me ashore, to the places that I love? You know too little of this land, for one who shall be its King.' Therefore they departed together, and came to Emerië, where were rolling downs of grass, and it was the chief place of sheep pasturage in Númenor; and they saw the white houses of the farmers and shepherd, and heard the bleating of the flocks.

There Erendis spoke to Aldarion and said: 'Here could I be at ease!'

'You shall dwell where you will, as wife of the King's Heir,' said Aldarion. 'And as Queen in many fair houses, such as you desire.'

'When you are King, I shall be old,' said Erendis. 'Where will the King's Heir dwell meanwhile?'

'With his wife,' said Aldarion, 'when his labours allow, if she cannot share in them.'

'I will not share my husband with the Lady Uinen,' said Erendis.

'That is a twisted saying,' said Aldarion. 'As well might I say that I would not share my wife with the Lord Oromë of Forests, because she loves trees that grow wild.'

'Indeed you would not,' said Erendis; 'for you would fell any wood as a gift to Uinen, if you had a mind.'

'Name any tree that you love and it shall stand till it dies,' said Aldarion.

'I love all that grow in this Isle,' said Erendis.

Then they rode a great while in silence; and after that day they parted, and Erendis returned to her father's house. To him she said nothing, but to her mother Núneth she told the words that had passed between herself and Aldarion.

'All or nothing, Erendis,' said Núneth. 'So you were as a child. But you love this man, and he is a great man, not to speak of his rank; and you will not cast out your love from your heart so easily, nor without great hurt to yourself. A woman must share her husband's love with his work and the fire of his spirit, or make him a thing not loveable. But I doubt that you will ever understand such counsel. Yet I am grieved, for it is full time that you were wed; and having borne a fair child I had hoped to see fair grandchildren; nor if they were cradled in the King's house would that displease me.'

This counsel did not indeed move the mind of Erendis; nevertheless she found that her heart was not under her will, and her days were empty: more empty than in the years when Aldarion had been gone. For he still abode in Númenor, and yet the days passed, and he did not come again into the west.

Now Almarian the Queen, being acquainted by Núneth with

what had passed, and fearing lest Aldarion should seek solace in voyaging again (for he had been long ashore), sent word to Erendis asking that she return to Armenelos; and Erendis being urged by Núneth and by her own heart did as she was bid. There she was reconciled to Aldarion; and in the spring of the year, when the time of the *Erukyermë*[12] was come, they ascended in the retinue of the King to the summit of the Meneltarma, which was the Hallowed Mountain of the Númenóreans. When all had gone down again Aldarion and Erendis remained behind; and they looked out, seeing all the Isle of Westernesse laid green beneath them in the spring, and they saw the glimmer of light in the West where far away was Avallónë, and the shadows in the East upon the Great Sea; and the Menel was blue above them. They did not speak, for no one, save only the King, spoke upon the height of Meneltarma; but as they came down Erendis stood a moment, looking towards Emerië, and beyond, towards the woods of her home.

'Do you not love the Yôzâyan?'[13] she said.

'I love it indeed,' he answered, 'though I think that you doubt it. For I think also of what it may be in time to come, and the hope and splendour of its people; and I believe that a gift should not lie idle in hoard.'

But Erendis denied his words, saying: 'Such gifts as come from the Valar, and through them from the One, are to be loved for themselves now, and in all nows. They are not given for barter, for more or for better. The Edain remain mortal Men, Aldarion, great though they be: and we cannot dwell in the time that is to come, lest we lose our now for a phantom of our own design.' Then taking suddenly the jewel from her throat she asked him: 'Would you have me trade this to buy me other goods that I desire?'

'No!' said he. 'But you do not lock it in hoard. Yet I think you set it too high; for it is dimmed by the light of your eyes.' Then he kissed her on the eyes, and in that moment she put aside fear, and accepted him; and their troth was plighted upon the steep path of the Meneltarma.

They went back then to Armenelos, and Aldarion presented Erendis to Tar-Meneldur as the betrothed of the King's Heir; and the King was rejoiced, and there was merrymaking in the city and in all the Isle. As betrothal gift Meneldur gave to Erendis a fair portion of land in Emerië, and there he had built for her a white house. But Aldarion said to her: 'Other jewels I have in hoard, gifts of kings in far lands to whom the ships of Númenor have brought aid. I have gems as green as the light of the sun in the leaves of trees which you love.'

'No!' said Erendis. 'I have had my betrothal gift, though it came beforehand. It is the only jewel that I have or would have; and I will set it yet higher.' Then he saw that she had caused the white gem to be set as a star in a silver fillet; and at her asking he bound it on her forehead. She wore it so for many years, until sorrow befell; and thus she was known far and wide as Tar-Elestirnë, the Lady of the Star-brow.[14] Thus there was for a time peace and joy in Armenelos in the house of the King, and in all the Isle, and it is recorded in ancient books that there was great fruitfulness in the golden summer of that year, which was the eight hundred and fifty-eighth of the Second Age.

But alone among the people the mariners of the Guild of Venturers were not well content. For fifteen years Aldarion had remained in Númenor, and led no expedition abroad; and though there were gallant captains who had been trained by him, without the wealth and authority of the King's son their voyages were fewer and more brief, and went but seldom further than the land of Gil-galad. Moreover timber was become scarce in the shipyards, for Aldarion neglected the forests; and the Venturers besought him to turn again to this work. At their prayer Aldarion did so, and at first Erendis would go about with him in the woods; but she was saddened by the sight of trees felled in their prime, and afterwards hewn and sawn. Soon therefore Aldarion went alone, and they were less in company.

Now the year came in, in which all looked for the marriage of the King's Heir; for it was not the custom that betrothal should last much longer than three years. One morning in that spring Aldarion rode up from the haven of Andúnië, to take the road to the house of Beregar; for there he was to be guest, and thither Erendis had preceded him, going from Armenelos by the roads of the land. As he came to the top of the great bluff that stood out from the land and sheltered the haven from the north, he turned and looked back over the sea. A west wind was blowing, as often at that season, beloved by those who had a mind to sail to Middle-earth, and white-crested waves marched towards the shore. Then suddenly the sea-longing took him as though a great hand had been laid on his throat, and his heart hammered, and his breath was stopped. He strove for the mastery, and at length turned his back and continued on his journey; and by design he took his way through the wood where he had seen Erendis riding as one of the Eldar, now fifteen years gone. Almost he looked to see her so once more; but she was not there, and desire to see her face again hastened him, so that he came to Beregar's house before evening.

There she welcomed him gladly, and he was merry; but he said nothing touching their wedding, though all had thought that this was a part of his errand to the Westlands. As the days passed Erendis marked that he now often fell silent in company when others were gay; and if she looked towards him suddenly she saw his eyes upon her. Then her heart was shaken; for the blue eyes of Aldarion seemed to her now grey and cold, yet she perceived as it were a hunger in his gaze. That look she had seen too often before, and feared what it boded; but she said nothing. At that Núneth, who marked all that passed, was glad; for 'words may open wounds,' as she said. Ere long Aldarion and Erendis rode away, returning to Armenelos, and as they drew further from the sea he grew merrier again. Still he said nothing to her of his trouble: for indeed he was at war within himself, and irresolute.

So the year drew on, and Aldarion spoke neither of the sea nor of wedding; but he was often in Rómenna, and in the company of the Venturers. At length, when the next year came in, the King called him to his chamber; and they were at ease together, and the love they bore one another was no longer clouded.

'My son,' said Tar-Meneldur, 'when will you give me the daughter that I have so long desired? More than three years have now passed, and that is long enough. I marvel that you could endure so long a delay.'

Then Aldarion was silent, but at length he said: 'It has come upon me again, *Atarinya* [My father]. Eighteen years is a long fast. I can scarce lie still in a bed, or hold myself upon a horse, and the hard ground of stone wounds my feet.'

Then Meneldur was grieved, and pitied his son; but he did not understand his trouble, for he himself had never loved ships, and he said: 'Alas! But you are betrothed. And by the laws of Númenor and the right ways of the Eldar and Edain a man shall not have two wives. You cannot wed the Sea, for you are affianced to Erendis.'

Then Aldarion's heart was hardened, for these words recalled his speech with Erendis as they passed through Emerië; and he thought (but untruly) that she had consulted with his father. It was ever his mood, if he thought that others combined to urge him on some path of their choosing, to turn away from it. 'Smiths may smithy, and horsemen ride, and miners delve, when they are betrothed,' said he. 'Therefore why may not mariners sail?'

'If smiths remained five years at the anvil few would be smiths' wives,' said the King. 'And mariners' wives are few, and they endure what they must, for such is their livelihood and their necessity. The King's Heir is not a mariner by trade, nor is he under necessity.'

'There are other needs than livelihood that drive a man,' said Aldarion. 'And there are yet many years to spare.'

'Nay, nay,' said Meneldur, 'you take your grace for granted: Erendis has shorter hope than you, and her years wane swifter. She is not of the line of Elros; and she has loved you now many years.'

'She held back well nigh twelve years, when I was eager,' said Aldarion. 'I do not ask for a third of such a time.'

'She was not then betrothed,' said Meneldur. 'But neither of you are now free. And if she held back, I doubt not that it was in fear of what now seems likely to befall, if you cannot master yourself. In some way you must have stilled that fear; and though you may have spoken no plain word, yet you are beholden, as I judge.'

Then Aldarion said in anger: 'It were better to speak with my betrothed myself, and not hold parley by proxy.' And he left his father. Not long after he spoke to Erendis of his desire to voyage again upon the great waters, saying that he was robbed of all sleep and rest. But she sat pale and silent. At length she said: 'I thought that you were come to speak of our wedding.'

'I will,' said Aldarion. 'It shall be as soon as I return, if you will wait.' But seeing the grief in her face he was moved, and a thought came to him. 'It shall be now,' he said. 'It shall be before this year is done. And then I will fit out such a ship as the Venturers made never yet, a Queen's house on the water. And you shall sail with me, Erendis, under the grace of the Valar, of Yavanna and of Oromë whom you love; you shall sail to lands where I shall show you such woods as you have never seen, where even now the Eldar sing; or forests wider than Númenor, free and wild since the beginning of days, where still you may hear the great horn of Oromë the Lord.'

But Erendis wept. 'Nay, Aldarion,' she said. 'I rejoice that the world yet holds such things as you tell of; but I shall never see them. For I do not desire it: to the woods of Númenor my heart is given. And, alas! if for love of you I took ship, I should not return. It is beyond my strength to endure; and out of sight of land I should die. The Sea hates me; and now it is revenged that I kept you from it and yet fled from you. Go, my lord! But have pity, and take not so many years as I lost before.'

Then Aldarion was abashed; for as he had spoken in heedless anger to his father, so now she spoke with love. He did not sail that year; but he had little peace or joy. 'Out of sight of land she will die!' he said. 'Soon I shall die, if I see it longer. Then if we are to spend any years together I must go alone, and go soon.' He made ready therefore at last for sailing in the spring; and the Venturers were glad, if none else in the Isle who knew of what was done. Three ships were manned, and in the month of Víressë[15] they departed. Erendis herself set the green bough of *oiolairë* on the prow of the *Palarran*, and hid her tears, until it passed out beyond the great new harbour-walls.

Six years and more passed away before Aldarion returned to Númenor. He found even Almarian the Queen colder in welcome, and the Venturers were fallen out of esteem; for men thought that he had treated Erendis ill. But indeed he was longer gone than he had purposed; for he had found the haven of Vinyalondë now wholly ruined, and great seas had brought to nothing all his labours to restore it. Men near the coasts were growing afraid of the Númenóreans, or were become openly hostile; and Aldarion heard rumours of some lord in Middle-earth who hated the men of the ships. Then when he would turn for home a great wind came out of the south, and he was borne far to the northward. He tarried a while at Mithlond, but when his ships stood out to sea once more they were again swept away north, and driven into wastes perilous with ice, and they suffered cold. At last the sea and wind relented, but even as Aldarion looked out in longing from the prow of the *Palarran* and saw far off the Meneltarma, his glance fell upon the green bough, and he saw that it was withered. Then Aldarion was dismayed, for such a thing had never befallen the bough of *oiolairë*, so long as it was washed with the spray. 'It is frosted, Captain,' said a mariner who stood beside him. 'It has been too cold. Glad am I to see the Pillar.'

When Aldarion sought out Erendis she looked at him keenly but did not come forward to meet him; and he stood for a while at a loss for words, as was not his wont. 'Sit, my lord,' said Erendis, 'and first tell me of all your deeds. Much must you have seen and done in these long years!'

Then Aldarion began haltingly, and she sat silent, listening, while he told all the tale of his trials and delays; and when he ended she said: 'I thank the Valar by whose grace you have returned at last. But I thank them also that I did not come with you; for I should have withered sooner than any green bough.'

'Your green bough did not go into the bitter cold by will,' he answered. 'But dismiss me now, if you will, and I think that men will not blame you. Yet dare I not to hope that your love will prove stronger to endure even than fair *oiolairë*?'

'So it does prove indeed,' said Erendis. 'It is not yet chilled to the death, Aldarion. Alas! How can I dismiss you, when I look on you again, returning as fair as the sun after winter!'

'Then let spring and summer now begin!' he said.

'And let not winter return,' said Erendis.

# THE WEDDING OF ALDARION AND ERENDIS

Then to the joy of Meneldur and Almarian the wedding of the King's Heir was proclaimed for the next spring; and so it came to pass. In the eight hundred and seventieth year of the Second Age Aldarion and Erendis were wedded in Armenelos, and in every house there was music, and in all the streets men and women sang. And afterwards the King's Heir and his bride rode at their leisure through all the Isle, until at midsummer they came to Andúnië, where the last feast was prepared by Valandil its lord; and all the people of the Westlands were gathered there, for love of Erendis and pride that a Queen of Númenor should come from among them.

In the morning before the feast Aldarion gazed out from the window of the bedchamber, which looked west-over-sea. 'See, Erendis!' he cried. 'There is a ship speeding to haven; and it is no ship of Númenor, but one such as neither you nor I shall ever set foot upon, even if we would.' Then Erendis looked forth, and she saw a tall white ship, with white birds turning in the sunlight all about it; and its sails glimmered with silver as with foam at the stem it rode towards the harbour. Thus the Eldar graced the wedding of Erendis, for love of the people of the Westlands, who were closest in their friendship.[1] Their ship was laden with flowers for the adornment of the feast, so that all that sat there, when evening was come, were crowned with *elanor*[2] and sweet *lissuin* whose fragrance brings heart's ease. Minstrels they brought also, singers who remembered songs of Elves and Men in the days of Nargothrond and Gondolin long ago; and many of the Eldar high and fair were seated among Men at the tables. But the people of Andúnië, looking upon the blissful company, said that none were more fair than Erendis; and they said that her eyes were as bright as were the eyes of Morwen Eledhwen of old,[3] or even as those of Avallónë.

Many gifts the Eldar brought also. To Aldarion they gave a sapling tree, whose bark was snow-white, and its stem straight, strong and pliant as it were of steel; but it was not yet in leaf. 'I thank you,' said Aldarion to the Elves. 'The wood of such a tree must be precious indeed.'

'Maybe; we know not,' said they. 'None has ever been hewn. It bears cool leaves in summer, and flowers in winter. It is for this that we prize it.'

To Erendis they gave a pair of birds, grey, with golden beaks and feet. They sang sweetly one to another with many cadences never repeated through a long thrill of song; but if one were separated from the other, at once they flew together, and they would not sing apart.

'How shall I keep them?' said Erendis.

'Let them fly and be free,' answered the Eldar. 'For we have spoken to them and named you; and they will stay wherever you dwell. They mate for their life, and that is long. Maybe there will be many such birds to sing in the gardens of your children.'

That night Erendis awoke, and a sweet fragrance came through the lattice; but the night was light, for the full moon was westering. Then leaving their bed Erendis looked out and saw all the land sleeping in silver; but the two birds sat side by side upon her sill.

When the feasting was ended Aldarion and Erendis went for a while to her home; and the birds again perched upon the sill

of her window. At length they bade Beregar and Núneth farewell, and they rode back at last to Armenelos; for there by the
King's wish his Heir would dwell, and a house was prepared for
them amidst a garden of trees. There the Elven-tree was planted,
and the Elven-birds sang in its boughs.

Two years later Erendis conceived, and in the spring of the
year after she bore to Aldarion a daughter. Even from birth the
child was fair, and grew ever in beauty: the woman most beautiful, as old tales tell, that ever was born in the line of Elros, save
Ar-Zimraphel, the last. When her first naming was due they
called her Ancalimë. In heart Erendis was glad, for she thought:
'Surely now Aldarion will desire a son, to be his heir; and he
will abide with me long yet.' For in secret she still feared the Sea
and its power upon his heart; and though she strove to hide it,
and would talk with him of his old ventures and of his hopes
and designs, she watched jealously if he went to his house-ship
or was much with the Venturers. To *Eämbar* Aldarion once
asked her to come, but seeing swiftly in her eyes that she was
not full-willing he never pressed her again. Not without cause
was Erendis' fear. When Aldarion had been five years ashore he
began to busy again with his Mastership of Forests, and was
often many days away from his house. There was now indeed
sufficient timber in Númenor (and that was chiefly owing to his
prudence); yet since the people were now more numerous there
was ever need of wood for building and for the making of many
things beside. For in those ancient days, though many had great
skill with stone and with metals (since the Edain of old had
learned much of the Noldor), the Númenóreans loved things
fashioned of wood, whether for daily use, or for beauty of
carving. At that time Aldarion again gave most heed to the
future, planting always where there was felling, and he had new
woods set to grow where there was room, a free land that was
suited to trees of different kinds. It was then that he became
most widely known as Aldarion, by which name he is remembered among those who held the sceptre in Númenor. Yet to

many beside Erendis it seemed that he had little love for trees in themselves, caring for them rather as timber that would serve his designs.

Not far otherwise was it with the Sea. For as Núneth had said to Erendis long before: 'Ships he may love, my daughter, for those are made by men's minds and hands; but I think that it is not the winds or the great waters that so burn his heart, nor yet the sight of strange lands, but some heat in his mind, or some dream that pursues him.' And it may be that she struck near the truth; for Aldarion was a man long-sighted, and he looked forward to days when the people would need more room and greater wealth; and whether he himself knew this clearly or no, he dreamed of the glory of Númenor and the power of its kings, and he sought for footholds whence they could step to wider dominion. So it was that ere long he turned again from forestry to the building of ships, and a vision came to him of a mighty vessel like a castle with tall masts and great sails like clouds, bearing men and stores enough for a town. Then in the yards of Rómenna the saws and hammers were busy, while among many lesser craft a great ribbed hull took shape; at which men wondered. *Turuphanto*, the Wooden Whale, they called it, but that was not its name.

Erendis learned of these things, though Aldarion had not spoken to her of them, and she was unquiet. Therefore one day she said to him: 'What is all this busyness with ships. Lord of the Havens? Have we not enough? How many fair trees have been cut short of their lives in this year?' She spoke lightly, and smiled as she spoke.

'A man must have work to do upon land,' he answered, 'even though he have a fair wife. Trees spring and trees fall. I plant more than are felled.' He spoke also in a light tone, but he did not look her in the face; and they did not speak again of these matters.

But when Ancalimë was close on four years old Aldarion at last declared openly to Erendis his desire to sail again from Númenor. She sat silent, for he said nothing that she did not already know; and words were in vain. He tarried until the birthday of Ancalimë, and made much of her that day. She laughed and was merry, though others in that house were not so; and as she went to her bed she said to her father: 'Where will you take me this summer, *tatanya* [my father]? I should like to see the white house in the sheep-land that *mamil* [mother] tells of.' Aldarion did not answer; and the next day he left the house, and was gone for some days. When all was ready he returned, and bade Erendis farewell. Then against her will tears were in her eyes. They grieved him, and yet irked him, for his mind was resolved, and he hardened his heart. 'Come, Erendis!' he said. 'Eight years I have stayed. You cannot bind for ever in soft bonds the son of the King, of the blood of Tuor and Eärendil! And I am not going to my death. I shall soon return.'

'Soon?' she said. 'But the years are unrelenting, and you will not bring them back with you. And mine are briefer than yours. My youth runs away; and where are my children, and where is your heir? Too long and often of late is my bed cold.'[4]

'Often of late I have thought that you preferred it so,' said Aldarion. 'But let us not be wroth, even if we are not of like mind. Look in your mirror, Erendis. You are beautiful, and no shadow of age is there yet. You have time to spare to my deep need. Two years! Two years is all that I ask!'

But Erendis answered: 'Say rather: "Two years I will take, whether you will or no." Take two years, then! But no more. A King's son of the blood of Eärendil should also be a man of his word.'

Next morning Aldarion hastened away. He lifted up Ancalimë and kissed her, but though she clung to him he set her down quickly and rode off. Soon after the great ship set sail from Rómenna. *Hirilondë* he named it, Haven-finder; but it went from Númenor without the blessing of Tar-Meneldur; and Erendis was not at the harbour to set the green Bough of Return, nor did she send. Aldarion's face was dark and troubled as he stood at the prow of *Hirilondë*, where the wife of his captain had set a great branch of *oiolairë*, but he did not look back until the Meneltarma was far off in the twilight.

All that day Erendis sat in her chamber alone, grieving; but deeper in her heart she felt a new pain of cold anger, and her love of Aldarion was wounded to the quick. She hated the Sea; and now even trees, that once she had loved, she desired to look upon no more, for they recalled to her the masts of great ships. Therefore ere long she left Armenelos, and went to Emerië in the midst of the Isle, where ever, far and near, the bleating of sheep was borne upon the wind. 'Sweeter it is to my ears than the mewing of gulls,' she said, as she stood at the doors of her white house, the gift of the King; and that was upon a downside, facing west, with great lawns all about that merged without wall or hedge into the pastures. Thither she took Ancalimë, and they were all the company that either had. For Erendis would have only servants in her household, and they were all women; and she sought ever to mould her daughter to her own mind, and to feed her upon her own bitterness against men. Ancalimë seldom indeed saw any man, for Erendis kept no state, and her few farm-servants and shepherds had a homestead at a distance. Other men did not come there, save rarely some messenger from the King; and he would ride away soon, for to men there seemed a chill in the house that put them to flight, and while there they felt constrained to speak half in whisper.

One morning soon after Erendis came to Emerië she awoke to the song of birds, and there on the sill of her window were the Elven-birds that long had dwelt in her garden in Armenelos, but which she had left behind forgotten. 'Sweet fools, fly away!' she said. 'This is no place for such joy as yours.'

Then their song ceased, and they flew up over the trees; thrice they wheeled above the roofs, and then they went away westwards. That evening they settled upon the sill of the chamber in the house of her father, where she had lain with Aldarion on their way from the feast in Andúnië; and there Núneth and Beregar found them on the morning of the next day. But when Núneth held out her hands to them they flew steeply up and fled away, and she watched them until they were specks in the sunlight, speeding to the sea, back to the land whence they came.

'He has gone again, then, and left her,' said Núneth.

'Then why has she not sent news?' said Beregar. 'Or why has she not come home?'

'She has sent news enough,' said Núneth. 'For she has dismissed the Elven-birds, and that was ill done. It bodes no good. Why, why, my daughter? Surely you knew what you must face? But let her alone, Beregar, wherever she may be. This is her home no longer, and she will not be healed here. He will come back. And then may the Valar send her wisdom – or guile, at the least!'

When the second year after Aldarion's sailing came in, by the King's wish Erendis ordered the house in Armenelos to be arrayed and made ready; but she herself made no preparation for return. To the King she sent answer saying: 'I will come if you command me, *atar aranya* [royal father]. But have I a duty now to hasten? Will it not be time enough when his sail is seen in the East?' And to herself she said: 'Will the King have me wait upon the quays like a sailor's lass? Would that I were, but I am so no longer. I have played that part to the full.'

But that year passed, and no sail was seen; and the next year came, and waned to autumn. Then Erendis grew hard and silent. She ordered that the house in Armenelos be shut, and she went never more than a few hours' journey from her house in Emerië. Such love as she had was all given to her daughter, and she clung to her, and would not have Ancalimë leave her side, not even to visit Núneth and her kin in the Westlands. All Ancalimë's teaching was from her mother; and she learned well to write and to read, and to speak the Elven-tongue with Erendis, after the manner in which high men of Númenor used it. For in the Westlands it was a daily speech in such houses as Beregar's, and Erendis seldom used the Númenórean tongue, which Aldarion loved the better. Much Ancalimë also learned of

Númenor and the ancient days in such books and scrolls as were in the house which she could understand; and lore of other kinds, of the people and the land, she heard at times from the women of the household, though of this Erendis knew nothing. But the women were chary of their speech to the child, fearing their mistress; and there was little enough of laughter for Ancalimë in the white house in Emerië. It was hushed and without music, as if one had died there not long since; for in Númenor in those days it was the part of men to play upon instruments, and the music that Ancalimë heard in childhood was the singing of women at work, out of doors, and away from the hearing of the White Lady of Emerië. But now Ancalimë was seven years old, and as often as she could get leave she would go out of the house and on to the wide downs where she could run free; and at times she would go with a shepherdess, tending the sheep, and eating under the sky.

One day in the summer of that year a young boy, but older than herself, came to the house on an errand from one of the distant farms; and Ancalimë came upon him munching bread and drinking milk in the farm-courtyard at the rear of the house. He looked at her without deference, and went on drinking. Then he set down his mug.

'Stare, if you must, great eyes!' he said. 'You're a pretty girl, but too thin. Will you eat?' He took a loaf out of his bag.

'Be off, Îbal!' cried an old woman, coming from the dairy-door. 'And use your long legs, or you'll forget the message I gave you for your mother before you get home!'

'No need for a watch-dog where you are, mother Zamîn!' cried the boy, and with a bark and a shout he leapt over the gate and went off at a run down the hill. Zamîn was an old country-woman, free-tongued, and not easily daunted, even by the White Lady.

'What noisy thing was that?' said Ancalimë.

'A boy,' said Zamîn, 'if you know what that is. But how should you? They're breakers and eaters, mostly. That one is ever eating – but not to no purpose. A fine lad his father will find when he comes back; but if that is not soon, he'll scarce know him. I might say that of others.'

'Has the boy then a father too?' asked Ancalimë.

'To be sure,' said Zamîn. 'Ulbar, one of the shepherds of the great lord away south: the Sheep-lord we call him, a kinsman of the King.'

'Then why is the boy's father not at home?'

'Why, *hérinkë* [little lady],' said Zamîn, 'because he heard of those Venturers, and took up with them, and went away with your father, the Lord Aldarion: but the Valar know whither, or why.'

That evening Ancalimë said suddenly to her mother: 'Is my father also called the Lord Aldarion?'

'He was,' said Erendis. 'But why do you ask?' Her voice was quiet and cool, but she wondered and was troubled; for no word concerning Aldarion had passed between them before.

Ancalimë did not answer the question. 'When will he come back?' she said.

'Do not ask me!' said Erendis. 'I do not know. Never, perhaps. But do not trouble yourself; for you have a mother, and she will not run away, while you love her.'

Ancalimë did not speak of her father again.

The days passed bringing in another year, and then another; in that spring Ancalimë was nine years old. Lambs were born and grew; shearing came and passed; a hot summer burned the grass. Autumn turned to rain. Then out of the East upon a cloudy wind *Hirilondë* came back over the grey seas, bearing Aldarion to Rómenna; and word was sent to Emerië, but Erendis did not speak of it. There were none to greet Aldarion upon the quays. He rode through the rain to Armenelos; and he found his house shut. He was dismayed, but he would ask news of no man; first he would seek the King, for he thought he had much to say to him.

He found his welcome no warmer than he looked for; and Meneldur spoke to him as King to a captain whose conduct is in question. 'You have been long away,' he said coldly. 'It is more than three years now since the date that you set for your return.'

'Alas!' said Aldarion. 'Even I have become weary of the sea, and for long my heart has yearned westward. But I have been detained against my heart: there is much to do. And all things go backward in my absence.'

'I do not doubt it,' said Meneldur. 'You will find it true here also in your right land, I fear.'

'That I hope to redress,' said Aldarion. 'But the world is changing again. Outside nigh on a thousand years have passed since the Lords of the West sent their power against Angband; and those days are forgotten, or wrapped in dim legend among Men of Middle-earth. They are troubled again, and fear haunts them. I desire greatly to consult with you, to give account of my deeds, and my thought concerning what should be done.'

'You shall do so,' said Meneldur. 'Indeed I expect no less. But there are other matters which I judge more urgent. "Let a King first rule well his own house ere he correct others," it is said. It is true of all men. I will now give you counsel, son of Meneldur. You have also a life of your own. Half of yourself you have ever neglected. To you I say now: Go home!'

Aldarion stood suddenly still, and his face was stern. 'If you know, tell me,' he said. 'Where is my home?'

'Where your wife is,' said Meneldur. 'You have broken your word to her, whether by necessity or no. She dwells now in Emerië, in her own house, far from the sea. Thither you must go at once.'

'Had any word been left for me, whither to go, I would have gone directly from the haven,' said Aldarion. 'But at least I need not now ask tidings of strangers.' He turned then to go, but paused, saying: 'Captain Aldarion has forgotten somewhat that belongs to his other half, which in his waywardness he also thinks urgent. He has a letter that he was charged to deliver to the King of Armenelos.' Presenting it to Meneldur he bowed and left the chamber; and within an hour he took horse and rode away, though night was falling. With him he had but two companions, men from his ship: Henderch of the Westlands, and Ulbar who came from Emerië.

Riding hard they came to Emerië at nightfall of the next day, and men and horses were weary. Cold and white looked the house on the hill in a last gleam of sunset under cloud. He blew a horn-call as soon as he saw it from afar.

As he leapt from his horse in the forecourt he saw Erendis: clad in white she stood upon the steps that went up to the pillars before the door. She held herself high, but as he drew near he saw that she was pale and her eyes over-bright.

'You come late, my lord,' she said. 'I had long ceased to expect you. I fear that there is no such welcome prepared for you as I had made when you were due.'

'Mariners are not hard to please,' he said.

'That is well,' she said; and she turned back into the house and left him. Then two women came forward, and an old crone who went down the steps. As Aldarion went in she said to the men in a loud voice so that he could hear her: 'There is no lodging for you here. Go down to the homestead at the hill's foot!'

'No, Zamîn,' said Ulbar. 'I'll not stay. I am for home, by the Lord Aldarion's leave. Is all well there?'

'Well enough,' said she. 'Your son has eaten himself out of your memory. But go, and find your own answers! You'll be warmer there than your Captain.'

Erendis did not come to the table at his late evening-meal, and Aldarion was served by women in a room apart. But before he was done she entered, and said before the women: 'You will be weary, my lord, after such haste. A guest-room is made ready for you, when you will. My women will wait on you. If you are cold, call for fire.'

Aldarion made no answer. He went early to the bedchamber, and being now weary indeed he cast himself on the bed and forgot soon the shadows of Middle-earth and of Númenor in a heavy sleep. But at cockcrow he awoke to a great disquiet and anger. He rose at once, and thought to go without noise from the house: he would find his man Henderch and the horses, and ride to his kinsman Hallatan, the sheep-lord of Hyarastorni. Later he would summon Erendis to bring his daughter to Armenelos, and not have dealings with her upon her own ground. But as he went out towards the doors Erendis came forward. She had not lain in bed that night, and she stood before him on the threshold.

'You leave more promptly than you came, my lord,' she said. 'I hope that (being a mariner) you have not found this house of women irksome already, to go thus before your business is done. Indeed, what business brought you hither? May I learn it before you leave?'

'I was told in Armenelos that my wife was here, and had removed my daughter hither,' he answered. 'As to the wife I am mistaken, it seems, but have I not a daughter?'

'You had one some years ago,' she said. 'But my daughter has not yet risen.'

'Then let her rise, while I go for my horse,' said Aldarion.

Erendis would have withheld Ancalimë from meeting him at that time; but she feared to go so far as to lose the King's favour, and the Council[5] had long shown their displeasure at the upbringing of the child in the country. Therefore when Aldarion rode back, with Henderch beside him, Ancalimë stood beside her mother on the threshold. She stood erect and stiff as her mother, and made him no courtesy as he dismounted and came up the steps towards her. 'Who are you?' she said. 'And why do you bid me to rise so early, before the house is stirring?'

Aldarion looked at her keenly, and though his face was stern he smiled within: for he saw there a child of his own, rather than of Erendis, for all her schooling.

'You knew me once, Lady Ancalimë,' he said, 'but no matter. Today I am but a messenger from Armenelos, to remind you that you are the daughter of the King's Heir; and (so far as I can now see) you shall be his Heir in your turn. You will not always dwell here. But go back to your bed now, my lady, until your maidservant wakes, if you will. I am in haste to see the King. Farewell!' He kissed the hand of Ancalimë and went down the steps; then he mounted and rode away with a wave of his hand.

Erendis alone at a window watched him riding down the hill, and she marked that he rode towards Hyarastorni and not towards Armenelos. Then she wept, from grief, but still more from anger. She had looked for some penitence, that she might extend after rebuke pardon if prayed for; but he had dealt with her as if she were the offender, and ignored her before her daughter. Too late she remembered the words of Núneth long before, and she saw Aldarion now as something large and not to be tamed, driven by a fierce will, more perilous when chill. She rose, and turned from the window, thinking of her wrongs. 'Perilous!' she said. 'I am steel hard to break. So he would find even were he the King of Númenor.'

Aldarion rode on to Hyarastorni, the house of Hallatan his cousin; for he had a mind to rest there a while and take thought. When he came near, he heard the sound of music, and he found the shepherds making merry for the homecoming of Ulbar, with many marvellous tales and many gifts; and the wife of Ulbar garlanded was dancing with him to the playing of pipes. At first none observed him, and he sat on his horse watching with a smile; but then suddenly Ulbar cried out 'The Great Captain!' and Îbal his son ran forward to Aldarion's stirrup. 'Lord Captain!' he said eagerly.

'What is it? I am in haste,' said Aldarion; for now his mood was changed, and he felt wrathful and bitter.

'I would but ask,' said the boy, 'how old must a man be, before he may go over sea in a ship, like my father?'

'As old as the hills, and with no other hope in life,' said Aldarion. 'Or whenever he has a mind! But your mother, Ulbar's son: will she not greet me?'

When Ulbar's wife came forward Aldarion took her hand.

'Will you receive this of me?' he said. 'It is but little return for six years of good man's aid that you gave me.' Then from a wallet under his tunic he took a jewel red like fire, upon a band of gold, and he pressed it into her hand. 'From the King of the Elves it came,' he said. 'But he will think it well-bestowed, when I tell him.' Then Aldarion bade farewell to the people there, and rode away, having no mind now to stay in that house. When Hallatan heard of his strange coming and going he marvelled, until more news ran through the countryside.

Aldarion rode only a short way from Hyarastorni and then he stayed his horse, and spoke to Henderch his companion. 'Whatever welcome awaits you, friend, out West, I will not keep you from it. Ride now home with my thanks. I have a mind to go alone.'

'It is not fitting. Lord Captain,' said Henderch.

'It is not,' said Aldarion. 'But that is the way of it. Farewell!'

Then he rode on alone to Armenelos, and never again set foot in Emerië.

When Aldarion left the chamber, Meneldur looked at the letter that his son had given him, wondering; for he saw that it came from King Gil-galad in Lindon. It was sealed and bore his device of white stars upon a blue rondure. Upon the outer fold was written:

Given at Mithlond to the hand of the Lord Aldarion King's Heir of Númenórë, to be delivered to the High King at Armenelos in person.

Then Meneldur broke the seal and read:

Ereinion Gil-galad son of Fingon to Tar-Meneldur of the line of Eärendil, greeting: the Valar keep you and may no shadow fall upon the Isle of Kings.

Long I have owed you thanks, for you have so many times sent to me your son Anardil Aldarion: the greatest

Elf-friend that now is among Men, as I deem. At this time I ask your pardon, if I have detained him overlong in my service; for I had great need of the knowledge of Men and their tongues which he alone possesses. He has dared many perils to bring me counsel. Of my need he will speak to you; yet he does not guess how great it is, being young and full of hope. Therefore I write this for the eyes of the King of Númenórë only.

A new shadow arises in the East. It is no tyranny of evil Men, as your son believes; but a servant of Morgoth is stirring, and evil things wake again. Each year it gains in strength, for most Men are ripe to its purpose. Not far off is the day, I judge, when it will become too great for the Eldar unaided to withstand. Therefore, whenever I behold a tall ship of the Kings of Men, my heart is eased. And now I make bold to seek your help. If you have any strength of Men to spare, lend it to me, I beg.

Your son will report to you, if you will, all our reasons. But in fine it is his counsel (and that is ever wise) that when assault comes, as it surely will, we should seek to hold the Westlands, where still the Eldar dwell, and Men of your race, whose hearts are not yet darkened. At the least we must defend Eriador about the long rivers west of the mountains that we name Hithaeglir: our chief defence. But in that mountain-wall there is a great gap southward in the land of Calenardhon;[6] and by that way inroad from the East must come. Already enmity creeps along the coast towards it. It could be defended and assault hindered, did we hold some seat of power upon the nearer shore.

So the Lord Aldarion long has seen. At Vinyalondë by the mouth of Gwathló he has long laboured to establish such a haven, secure against sea and land; but his mighty works have been in vain. He has great knowledge in such matters, for he has learned much of Círdan, and he understands better than any the needs of your great ships. But he has never had men enough; whereas Círdan has no wrights or masons to spare.

The King will know his own needs; but if he will listen with favour to the Lord Aldarion, and support him as he may, then hope will be greater in the world. The memories of the First Age are dim, and all things in Middle-earth grow colder. Let not the ancient friendship of Eldar and Dúnedain wane also.

Behold! The darkness that is to come is filled with hatred for us, but it hates you no less. The Great Sea will not be too wide for its wings, if it is suffered to come to full growth.

Manwë keep you under the One, and send fair wind to your sails.


Meneldur let the parchment fall into his lap. Great clouds borne upon a wind out of the East brought darkness early, and the tall candles at his side seemed to dwindle in the gloom that filled his chamber.

'May Eru call me before such a time comes!' he cried aloud. Then to himself he said: 'Alas! that his pride and my coolness have kept our minds apart so long. But sooner now than I had resolved it will be the course of wisdom to resign the Sceptre to him. For these things are beyond my reach.

'When the Valar gave to us the Land of Gift they did not make us their vice-gerents; we were given the Kingdom of Númenor, not of the world. They are the Lords. Here we were to put away hatred and war; for war was ended, and Morgoth thrust forth from Arda. So I deemed, and so was taught.

'Yet if the world grows again dark, the Lords must know; and they have sent me no sign. Unless this be the sign. What then? Our fathers were rewarded for the aid they gave in the defeat of the Great Shadow. Shall their sons stand aloof, if evil finds a new head?

'I am in too great doubt to rule. To prepare or to let be? To prepare for war, which is yet only guessed: train craftsmen and tillers in the midst of peace for bloodspilling and battle: put iron in the hands of greedy captains who will love only conquest, and count the slain as their glory? Will they say to Eru: *At least your enemies were amongst them?* Or to fold hands, while friends die unjustly: let men live in blind peace, until the ravisher is at the gate? What then will they do: match naked hands against iron and die in vain, or flee leaving the cries of women behind them? Will they say to Eru: *At least I spilled no blood?*

'When either way may lead to evil, of what worth is choice? Let the Valar rule under Eru! I will resign the Sceptre to Aldarion. Yet that also is a choice, for I know well which road he will take. Unless Erendis. . . .'

Then Meneldur's thought turned in disquiet to Erendis in Emerië. 'But there is little hope there (if it should be called hope). He will not bend in such grave matters. I know her choice – even were she to listen long enough to understand. For her heart has no wings beyond Númenor, and she has no guess of the cost. If her choice should lead to death in her own time, she would die bravely. But what will she do with life, and other wills? The Valar themselves, even as I, must wait to discover.'

Aldarion came back to Rómenna on the fourth day after *Hirilondë* had returned to haven. He was way-stained and weary, and he went at once to *Eämbar*, upon which he now intended to dwell. By that time, as he found to his embitterment, many tongues were already wagging in the City. On the next day he gathered men in Rómenna and brought them to Armenelos. There he bade some fell all the trees, save one, in his garden, and take them to the shipyards; others he commanded to raze his house to the ground. The white Elven-tree alone he spared; and when the woodcutters were gone he looked at it, standing amid the desolation, and he saw for the first time that it was in itself beautiful. In its slow Elven growth it was yet but twelve feet high, straight, slender, youthful, now budded with its winter flowers upon upheld branches pointing to the sky. It recalled to him his daughter, and he said: 'I will call you also Ancalimë. May you and she stand so in long life, unbent by wind or will, and unclipped!'

On the third day after his return from Emeriё Aldarion sought the King. Tar-Meneldur sat still in his chair and waited. Looking at his son he was afraid; for Aldarion was changed: his face was become grey, cold, and hostile, as the sea when the sun is suddenly veiled in dull cloud. Standing before his father he spoke slowly with tone of contempt rather than of wrath.

'What part you have played in this you yourself know best,' he said. 'But a King should consider how much a man will endure, though he be a subject, even his son. If you would shackle me to this Island, then you choose your chain ill. I have now neither wife, nor love of this land, left. I will go from this misenchanted isle of daydreams where women in their insolence would have men cringe. I will use my days to some purpose, elsewhere, where I am not scorned, more welcome in honour. Another Heir you may find more fit for a house-servant. Of my inheritance I demand only this: the ship *Hirilondë* and as many men as it will hold. My daughter I would take also, were she older; but I will commend her to my mother. Unless you dote upon sheep, you will not hinder this, and will not suffer the child to be stunted, reared among mute women in cold insolence and contempt of her kin. She is of the Line of Elros, and no other descendant will you have through your son. I have done. I will go now about business more profitable.'

Thus far Meneldur had sat in patience with downcast eyes and made no sign. But now he sighed, and looked up. 'Aldarion, my son,' he said sadly, 'the King would say that you also show cold insolence and contempt of your kin, and yourself condemn others unheard; but your father who loves you and grieves for you will remit that. The fault is not mine only that I have not ere now understood your purposes. But as for what you have suffered (of which, alas! too many now speak): I am guiltless. Erendis I have loved, and since our hearts lean the same way I have thought that she had much to endure that was hard. Your purposes are now become clear to me, though if you are in mood to hear aught but praise I would say that at first your own pleasure also led you. And it may be that things would have been otherwise if you had spoken more openly long ago.'

'The King may have some grievance in this,' cried Aldarion, now more hotly, 'but not the one you speak of! To her at least I spoke long and often: to cold ears uncomprehending. As well might a truant boy talk of tree-climbing to a nurse anxious only about the tearing of clothes and the due time of meals! I love her, or I should care less. The past I will keep in my heart; the future is dead. She does not love me, or aught else. She loves herself with Númenor as a setting, and myself as a tame hound, to drowse by the hearth until she has a mind to walk in her own fields. But since hounds now seem too gross, she will have Ancalimë to pipe in a cage. But enough of this. Have I the King's leave to depart? Or has he some command?'

'The King,' answered Tar-Meneldur, 'has thought much about these matters, in what seem the long days since last you were in Armenelos. He has read the letter of Gil-galad, which is earnest and grave in tone. Alas! To his prayer and your wishes the King of Númenor must say *nay*. He cannot do otherwise, according to his understanding of the perils of either course: to prepare for war, or not to prepare.'

Aldarion shrugged his shoulders, and took a step as if to go. But Meneldur held up his hand commanding attention, and continued: 'Nevertheless, the King, though he has now ruled the land of Númenor for one hundred and forty-two years, has no certainty that his understanding of the matter is sufficient for a just decision in matters of such high import and peril.' He paused, and taking up a parchment written in his own hand he read from it in a clear voice:

Therefore: first for the honour of his well-beloved son; and second for the better direction of the realm in courses which his son more clearly understands, the King has resolved: that he will forthwith resign the Sceptre to his son, who shall now become Tar-Aldarion, the King.

'This,' said Meneldur, 'when it is proclaimed, will make known to all my thought concerning this present pass. It will raise you above scorn; and it will set free your powers so that other losses may seem more easy to endure. The letter of Gil-galad, when you are King, you shall answer as seems fit to the holder of the Sceptre.'

Aldarion stood still for a moment in amaze. He had braced himself to face the King's anger, which wilfully he had endeavoured to kindle. Now he stood confounded. Then, as one swept from his feet by a sudden wind from a quarter unexpected, he fell to his knees before his father; but after a moment he raised his bowed head and laughed – so he always did, when he heard of any deed of great generosity, for it gladdened his heart.

'Father,' he said, 'ask the King to forget my insolence to him. For he is a great King, and his humility sets him far above my pride. I am conquered: I submit myself wholly. That such a King should resign the Sceptre while in vigour and wisdom is not to be thought.'

'Yet so it is resolved,' said Meneldur. 'The Council shall be summoned forthwith.'

When the Council came together, after seven days had passed, Tar-Meneldur acquainted them with his resolve, and laid the scroll before them. Then all were amazed, not yet knowing what were the courses of which the King spoke; and all demurred, begging him to delay his decision, save only Hallatan of Hyarastorni. For he had long held his kinsman Aldarion in esteem, though his own life and likings were far otherwise; and he judged the King's deed to be noble, and timed with shrewdness, if it must be.

But to those others who urged this or that against his resolve Meneldur answered: 'Not without thought did I come to this resolution, and in my thought I have considered all the reasons that you wisely argue. Now and not later is the time most fit for my will to be published, for reasons which though none here has uttered all must guess. Forthwith then let this decree be proclaimed. But if you will, it shall not take effect until the time of the *Erukyermë* in the Spring. Till then, I will hold the Sceptre.'

When news came to Emerië of the proclamation of the decree Erendis was dismayed; for she read therein a rebuke by the King in whose favour she had trusted. In this she saw truly, but that anything else of greater import lay behind she did not conceive. Soon afterwards there came a message from Tar-Meneldur, a command indeed, though graciously worded. She was bidden to come to Armenelos and to bring with her the lady Ancalimë, there to abide at least until the *Erukyermë* and the proclamation of the new King.

'He is swift to strike,' she thought. 'So I should have foreseen. He will strip me of all. But myself he shall not command, though it be by the mouth of his father.'

Therefore she returned answer to Tar-Meneldur: 'King and father, my daughter Ancalimë must come indeed, if you command it. I beg that you will consider her years, and see to it that she is lodged in quiet. For myself, I pray you to excuse me. I learn that my house in Armenelos has been destroyed; and I would not at this time willingly be a guest, least of all upon a house-ship among mariners. Here then permit me to remain in my solitude, unless it be the King's will also to take back this house.'

This letter Tar-Meneldur read with concern, but it missed its mark in his heart. He showed it to Aldarion, to whom it seemed chiefly aimed. Then Aldarion read the letter; and the King, regarding the face of his son, said: 'Doubtless you are grieved. But for what else did you hope?'

'Not for this, at least,' said Aldarion. 'It is far below my hope of her. She has dwindled; and if I have wrought this, then black is my blame. But do the large shrink in adversity? This was not the way, not even in hate or revenge! She should have demanded that a great house be prepared for her, called for a Queen's escort, and come back to Armenelos with her beauty adorned, royally, with the star on her brow; then well nigh all the Isle of Númenor she might have bewitched to her part, and made me seem madman and churl. The Valar be my witness, I would rather have had it so: rather a beautiful Queen to thwart me and flout me, than freedom to rule while the Lady Elestirnë falls down dim into her own twilight.'

Then with a bitter laugh he gave back the letter to the King. 'Well: so it is,' he said. 'But if one has a distaste to dwell on a ship among mariners, another may be excused dislike of a sheep-farm among serving-women. But I will not have my daughter so schooled. At least she shall choose by knowledge.' He rose, and begged leave to go.

# THE ACCESSION OF TAR-ALDARION

## 883 – KINGS AND QUEENS OF NÚMENOR VI:
### Tar-Aldarion
Born: SA 700; Died: SA 1098 (age 398)
Rule: SA 883–1075 (192 years)

As Christopher Tolkien writes in *Unfinished Tales*, p. 205: 'From the point where Aldarion read the letter from Erendis, refusing to return to Armenelos, the story can only be traced in glimpses and snatches, from notes and jottings: and even those do not constitute the fragments of a wholly consistent story, being composed at different times and often at odds with themselves.' Drawing on these disparate sources, Christopher editorially continues and concludes Aldarion's story under the heading:

### *The Further Course of the Narrative*

It seems that when Aldarion became King of Númenor in the year 883 he determined to revisit Middle-earth at once, and departed for Mithlond either in the same year or the next. It is recorded that on the prow of *Hirilondë* he set no bough of *oiolairë*, but the image of an eagle with golden beak and jewelled eyes, which was the gift of Círdan.

It perched there, by the craft of its maker, as if poised for flight unerring to some far mark that it espied. 'This sign shall lead us to our aim,' he said. 'For our return let the Valar care – if our deeds do not displease them.'

It is also stated that 'no records are now left of the later voyages that Aldarion made,' but that 'it is known that he went much on land as well as sea, and went up the River Gwathló as far as Tharbad, and there met Galadriel'. There is no mention elsewhere of this meeting; but at that time Galadriel and Celeborn were dwelling in Eregion, at no great distance from Tharbad.

But all Aldarion's labours were swept away. The works that he began again at Vinyalondë were never completed, and the sea gnawed them. Nevertheless he laid the foundation for the achievement of Tar-Minastir long years after, in the first war with Sauron, and but for his works the fleets of Númenor could not have brought their power in time to the right place – as he foresaw. Already the hostility was growing and dark men out of the mountains were thrusting into Enedwaith. But in Aldarion's day the Númenóreans did not yet desire more room, and his Venturers remained a small people, admired but little emulated.

There is no mention of any further development of the alliance with Gil-galad, or of the sending of the aid that he requested in his letter to Tar-Meneldur; it is said indeed that:

Aldarion was too late, or too early. Too late: for the power that hated Númenor had already waked. Too early: for the time was not yet ripe for Númenor to show its power or to come back into the battle for the world.

There was a stir in Númenor when Tar-Aldarion determined to return to Middle-earth in 883 or 884, for no King had ever before left the Isle, and the Council had no precedent. It seems that Meneldur was offered but refused the regency, and that Hallatan of Hyarastorni became regent, either appointed by the Council or by Tar-Aldarion himself.

Of the history of Ancalimë during those years when she was growing up there is no certain form. There is less doubt concerning her somewhat ambiguous character, and the influence that her mother exerted on her. She was less prim than Erendis, and natively liked display, jewels, music, admiration, and deference; but she liked them at will and not unceasingly, and she made her mother and the white house in Emerië an excuse for escape. She approved, as it were, both Erendis' treatment of Aldarion on his late return, but also Aldarion's anger, impenitence, and subsequent relentless dismissal of Erendis from his heart and concern. She had a profound dislike of obligatory marriage, and in marriage of any constraint on her will. Her mother had spoken unceasingly against men, and indeed a remarkable example of Erendis' teaching in this respect is preserved:

Men in Númenor are half-Elves (said Erendis), especially the high men; they are neither the one nor the other. The long life that they were granted deceives them, and they dally in the world, children in mind, until age finds them – and then many only forsake play out of doors for play in their houses. They turn their play into great matters and great matters into play. They would be craftsmen and loremasters and heroes all at once; and women to them are but fires on the hearth – for others to tend, until they are tired of play in the evening. All things were made for their service: hills are for quarries, river to furnish water or to turn wheels, trees for boards, women for their body's need, or if fair to adorn their table and hearth; and children to be teased when nothing else is to do – but they would as soon play with their hounds' whelps. To all they are gracious and kind, merry as larks in the morning (if the sun shines); for they are never wrathful if they can avoid it. Men should be gay, they hold, generous as the rich, giving away what they do not need. Anger they show only when they become aware, suddenly, that there are other wills in the world beside their own. Then they will be as ruthless as the seawind if anything dare to withstand them.

Thus it is, Ancalimë, and we cannot alter it. For men fashioned Númenor: men, those heroes of old that they sing of – of their women we hear less, save that they wept when their men were slain. Númenor was to be a rest after war. But if they weary of rest and the plays of peace, soon they will go back to their great play, manslaying and war. Thus it is; and we are set here among them. But we need not assent. If we love Númenor also, let us enjoy it before they ruin it. We also are daughters of the great, and we have wills and courage of our own. Therefore do not bend, Ancalimë. Once bend a little, and they will bend you further until you are bowed down. Sink your roots into the rock, and face the wind, though it blow away all your leaves.

Moreover, and more potently, Erendis had made Ancalimë accustomed to the society of women: the cool, quiet, gentle life of Emerië without interruptions or alarms. Boys, like Îbal, shouted. Men rode up blowing horns at strange hours, and were fed with great noise. They begot children and left them in the care of women when they were troublesome. And though childbirth had less of ills and peril, Númenor was not an 'earthly paradise', and the weariness of labour or of all making was not taken away.

Ancalimë, like her father, was resolute in pursuing her

policies; and like him she was obstinate, taking the opposite course to any that was counselled. She had something of her mother's coldness and sense of personal injury; and deep in her heart, almost but not quite forgotten, was the firmness with which Aldarion had unclasped her hand and set her down when he was in haste to be gone. She loved dearly the downlands of her home, and never (as she said) in her life could she sleep at peace far from the sound of sheep. But she did not refuse the Heirship, and determined that when her day came she would be a powerful Ruling Queen; and when so, to live where and how she pleased.

It seems that for some eighteen years after Aldarion became King he was often gone from Númenor; and during that time Ancalimë passed her days both in Emerië and in Armenelos, for Queen Almarian took a great liking to her, and indulged her as she had indulged Aldarion in his youth. In Armenelos she was treated with deference by all, and not least by Aldarion; and though at first she was ill at ease, missing the wide airs of her home, in time she ceased to be abashed, and became aware that men looked with wonder upon her beauty, now come to its full. As she grew older she became ever more wilful, and she found irksome the company of Erendis, who behaved like a widow and would not be Queen; but she continued to return to Emerië, both as a retreat from Armenelos and because she desired thus to vex Aldarion. She was clever, and malicious, and saw promise of sport as the prize for which her mother and her father did battle.

Now in the year 892, when Ancalimë was nineteen years old, she was proclaimed the King's Heir (at a far earlier age than had previously been the case); and at that time Tar-Aldarion caused the law of succession in Númenor to be changed. It is said specifically that Tar-Aldarion did this 'for reasons of private concern, rather than policy', and out of 'his long resolve to defeat Erendis'. The change of the law is referred to in *The Lord of the Rings*, Appendix A (I, i):

The sixth King [Tar-Aldarion] left only one child, a daughter. She became the first Queen [i.e. Ruling Queen]; for it was then made a law of the royal house that the eldest child of the King, whether man or woman, should receive the sceptre.

But elsewhere the new law is formulated differently from this. The fullest and clearest account states in the first place that the 'old law', as it was afterwards called, was not in fact a Númenórean 'law', but an inherited custom which circumstances had not yet called in question; and according to that custom the Ruler's eldest son inherited the Sceptre. It was understood that if there were no son the nearest male kinsman *of male descent* from Elros Tar-Minyatur would be the Heir.[1] But by the 'new law' the (eldest) daughter of the Ruler inherited the Sceptre, if he had no son (this being, of course, in contradiction to what is said in *The Lord of Rings*). By the advice of the Council it was added that she was free to refuse.[2] In such a case, according to the 'new law', the heir of the Ruler was the nearest male kinsman whether by male or female descent.[3]

It was also ordained at the instance of the Council that a female heir must resign, if she remained unwed beyond a certain time; and to these provisions Tar-Aldarion added that the King's Heir should not wed save in the Line of Elros, and that any who did so should cease to be eligible for the Heirship. It is said that this ordinance arose directly from Aldarion's disastrous marriage to Erendis and his reflections upon it; for she was not of the Line of Elros, and had a lesser life-span, and he believed that therein lay the root of all their troubles.

Beyond question these provisions of the 'new law' were recorded in such detail because they were to bear closely on the later history of these reigns; but unhappily very little can now be said of it.

At some later date Tar-Aldarion rescinded the law that a Ruling Queen must marry, or resign (and this was certainly due to Ancalimë's reluctance to countenance either alternative); but the marriage of the Heir to another member of the Line of Elros remained the custom ever after.[4]

At all events, suitors for Ancalimë's hand soon began to appear in Emerië, and not only because of the change in her position, for the fame of her beauty, of her aloofness and disdain, and of the strangeness of her upbringing had run through the land. In that time the people began to speak of her as Emerwen Aranel, the Princess Shepherdess. To escape from importunity Ancalimë, aided by the old woman Zamîn, went into hiding at a farm on the borders of the lands of Hallatan of Hyarastorni, where she lived for a time the life of a shepherdess. The accounts (which are indeed no more than hasty jottings) vary as to how her parents responded to this state of affairs. According to one, Erendis herself knew where Ancalimë was, and approved the reason for her flight, while Aldarion prevented the Council from searching for her, since it was to his mind that his daughter should act thus independently. According to another, however, Erendis was disturbed at Ancalimë's flight and the King was wrathful; and at this time Erendis attempted some reconciliation with him, at least in respect of Ancalimë. But Aldarion was unmoved, declaring that the King had no wife, but that he had a daughter and an heir; and that he did not believe that Erendis was ignorant of her hiding-place.

What is certain is that Ancalimë fell in with a shepherd who was minding flocks in the same region; and to her this man named himself Mámandil. Ancalimë was all unused to such company as his, and she took delight in his singing, in which he was skilled; and he sang to her songs that came out of far-off days, when the Edain pastured their flocks in Eriador long ago, before ever they met the Eldar. They met thus in the pastures often and often, and he altered the songs of the lovers of old and brought into them the names of Emerwen and Mámandil; and Ancalimë feigned not to understand the drift of the words. But at length he declared his love for her openly, and she drew back, and refused him, saying that her fate lay between them, for she was the Heir of the King. But Mámandil was not abashed, and he laughed, and told her that his right name was Hallacar, son of Hallatan of Hyarastorni, of the line of Elros Tar-Minyatur. 'And how else could any wooer find you?' he said.

Then Ancalimë was angry, because he had deceived her, knowing from the first who she was; but he answered: 'That is true in part. I contrived indeed to meet the Lady whose ways were so strange that I was curious to see more of her. But then I loved Emerwen, and I care not now who she may be. Do not think that I pursue your high place; for far rather would I have it that you were Emerwen only. I rejoice but in this, that I also am of the Line of Elros, because otherwise I deem that we could not wed.'

'We could,' said Ancalimë, 'if I had any mind to such a state. I could lay down my royalty, and be free. But if I were to do so, I should be free to wed whom I will; and that would be Úner (which is "Noman"), whom I prefer above all others.'

It was however to Hallacar that Ancalimë was wedded in the end. From one version it appears that the persistence of Hallacar in his suit despite her rejection of him, and the urging of the Council that she choose a husband for the quiet of the realm, led to their marriage not many years after their first meeting among the flocks in Emerië. But elsewhere it is said that she remained unmarried so long that her cousin Soronto, relying on the provision of the new law, called upon her to surrender the Heirship, and that she then married Hallacar in order to spite Soronto. In yet another brief notice it is implied that she wedded Hallacar after Aldarion had rescinded the provision, in order to put an end to Soronto's hopes of becoming King if Ancalimë died childless.

However this may be, the story is clear that Ancalimë did not desire love, nor did she wish for a son; and she said: 'Must I become like Queen Almarian, and dote upon him?' Her life with Hallacar was unhappy, and she begrudged him her son

Anárion, and there was strife between them thereafter. She sought to subject him, claiming to be the owner of his land, and forbidding him to dwell upon it, for she would not, as she said, have her husband a farm-steward. From this time comes the last tale that is recorded of those unhappy things. For Ancalimë would let none of her women wed, and although for fear of her most were restrained, they came from the country about and had lovers whom they wished to marry. But Hallacar in secret arranged for them to be wedded; and he declared that he would give a last feast at his own house, before he left it. To this feast he invited Ancalimë, saying that it was the house of his kindred, and should be given a farewell of courtesy.

Ancalimë came, attended by all her women, for she did not care to be waited on by men. She found the house all lit and arrayed as for a great feast, and men of the household attired in garlands as for their weddings, and each with another garland in his hands for a bride. 'Come!' said Hallacar. 'The weddings are prepared, and the bride-chambers ready. But since it cannot be thought that we should ask the Lady Ancalimë, King's Heir, to lie with a farm-steward, then, alas! she must sleep alone tonight.' And Ancalimë perforce remained there, for it was too far to ride back, nor would she go unattended. Neither men nor women hid their smiles; and Ancalimë would not come to the feast, but lay abed listening to the laughter far off and thinking it aimed at herself. Next day she rode off in a cold rage, and Hallacar sent three men to escort her. Thus he was revenged, for she came never back to Emerië, where the very sheep seemed to make scorn of her. But she pursued Hallacar with hatred afterwards.

Of Erendis it is said that when old age came upon her, neglected by Ancalimë and in bitter loneliness, she longed once more for Aldarion; and learning that he was gone from Númenor on what proved to be his last voyage but that he was soon expected to return, she left Emerië at last and journeyed unrecognised and unknown to the haven of Rómenna. There, it seems, she met her fate; but only the words 'Erendis perished in water in the year 985' remain to suggest how it came to pass.

Of the life-span granted the Númenóreans, Erendis had once said that the women 'became a kind of Imitation Elves; and their Men had so much in their heads and desire of doing that they ever felt the pressure of time, and so seldom rested or rejoiced in the present. Fortunately their wives were cool and busy – but Númenor was no place for great love.'[5]

## *c.* 1000 – SAURON, ALARMED BY THE GROWING POWER OF THE NÚMENÓREANS, CHOOSES MORDOR AS A LAND TO MAKE INTO A STRONGHOLD. HE BEGINS THE BUILDING OF BARAD-DÛR.

News of [the founding of Eregion and the friendship and shared craftsmanship between the Elves who dwelt there and the Dwarves of Khazad-dûm] came to the ears of Sauron, and increased the fears that he felt concerning the coming of the Númenóreans to Lindon and the coasts further south, and their friendship with Gil-galad; and he heard tell also of Aldarion, son of Tar-Meneldur the King of Númenor, now become a great ship-builder who brought his vessels to haven far down into the Harad. Sauron therefore left Eriador alone for a while, and he chose the land of Mordor, as it was afterwards called, for a stronghold as a counter to the threat of the Númenórean landings.[1]

Sauron's choice of Mordor for his stronghold was likely based on its geographic location. It was enclosed within a naturally defensive, three-sided and roughly rectangular wall provided by two great mountain ranges: to the north was the Ered Lithui or Ash Mountains; to west and south was the Ephel Dúath, also known as the Mountains of Shadow or the Outer Fence, within the north-western escarpment of which ran an additional lower ridge 'its edge notched and jagged with crags like fangs that stood out black against the red light behind them: it was the grim Morgai, the inner ring of the fences of the land.'[2] Almost encircled by these mighty barriers in the north and to the east lay a high, desolate plain, the Plateau of Gorgoroth a name derived from the Sindarin word *gorgor* ('horror', 'dread'), and dominated by the towering presence of Mount Doom, or Orodruin ('burning mountain'),[3] 'a huge mass of ash and slag and burned stone, out of which a sheer-sided cone was raised into the clouds.'[4] The lands all about were scarred from its violent volcanic eruptions, 'which were not made by Sauron but were a relic of the devastating works of Melkor in the long First Age.'[5] This frightful prospect was to remain for many years, even until the Third Age:

Ever and anon the furnaces far below [Orodruin's] ashen cone would grow hot and with a great surging and throbbing pour forth rivers of molten rock from chasms in its sides. Some would flow blazing towards Barad-dûr down great channels; some would wind their way into the stony plain, until they cooled and lay like twisted dragon-shapes vomited from the tormented earth.[6]

As a site for the fortress of Barad-dûr, the Dark Tower, Sauron chose the end of a long southern spur of the Ered Lithui that ran down into the northern part of the Plain of Gorgoroth. There, during a period of 600 years and long-hidden from the Eldar and Edain, Sauron raised a mighty structure, a 'vast fortress, armoury, prison, furnace of great power . . . which suffered no rival, and laughed at flattery, biding its time, secure in its pride and its immeasurable strength.'[7] In both the Second and Third Ages, Barad-dûr represented 'the dreadful menace of the Power that waited, brooding in deep thought and sleepless malice behind the dark veil about its Throne . . . like the oncoming of a wall of night at the last end of the world.'[8]

Of the later years of [Númenor's king] Tar-Aldarion nothing can now be said, save that he seems to have continued his voyages to Middle-earth, and more than once left Ancalimë as his regent. His last voyage took place about the end of the first millennium of the Second Age.[9]

# 1075 – TAR-ANCALIMË BECOMES THE FIRST RULING QUEEN OF NÚMENOR.

### KINGS AND QUEENS OF NÚMENOR VII:
Tar-Ancalimë
Born: SA 873; Died: SA 1285 (age 412)
Rule: SA 1075-1280 (205 years)

Tar-Ancalimë reigned for 205 years, longer than any ruler after Elros. . . . She long remained unwed; but when pressed by [her cousin] Soronto to resign, in his despite she married in the year 1000 Hallacar son of Hallatan, a descendant of Vardamir. After the birth of her son Anárion there was strife between Ancalimë and Hallacar. She was proud and wilful. After Aldarion's death she neglected all his policies, and gave no further aid to Gil-galad.

Her son Anárion, who was afterwards the eighth Ruler of Númenor, first had two daughters. They disliked and feared

118

the Queen, and refused the Heirship, remaining unwed, since the Queen would not in revenge allow them to marry.[1] Anárion's son Súrion was born the last, and [would, in his time, become] the ninth Ruler of Númenor.

## 1200 – SAURON ENDEAVOURS TO SEDUCE THE ELDAR. GIL-GALAD REFUSES TO TREAT WITH HIM; BUT THE SMITHS OF EREGION ARE WON OVER. THE NÚMENÓREANS BEGIN TO MAKE PERMANENT HAVENS.

Very great changes came to pass as the Second Age proceeded. The first ships of the Númenóreans appeared off the coasts of Middle-earth about Second Age 600, but no rumour of this portent reached the distant North. At the same time, however, Sauron came out of hiding and revealed himself in fair form. For long he paid little heed to Dwarves or Men and endeavoured to win the friendship and trust of the Eldar. But slowly he reverted again to the allegiance of Morgoth and began to seek power by force, marshalling again and directing the Orks [Orcs] and other evil things of the First Age, and secretly building his great fortress in the mountain-girt land in the South that was afterwards known as Mordor.[1]

Men he found the easiest to sway of all the peoples of the Earth; but long he sought to persuade the Elves to his service, for he knew that the Firstborn had the greater power; and he went far and wide among them, and his hue was still that of one both fair and wise. Only to Lindon he did not come, for Gilgalad and Elrond doubted him and his fair-seeming, and though they knew not who in truth he was they would not admit him to that land.[2]

### 1280 – KINGS AND QUEENS OF NÚMENOR VIII:
### Tar-Anárion
Born: SA 1003; Died: SA 1404 (age 401)
Rule: SA 1280-1394 (114 years)

Tar-Anárion had two daughters whose names are not recorded and a son, Súrion, who acceded to the throne when his sisters refused the sceptre.

### 1394 – KINGS AND QUEENS OF NÚMENOR IX:
### Tar-Súrion
Born: SA 1174; Died: SA 1574 (age 400)
Rule: SA 1394-1556 (162 years)

Tar-Súrion had two children: a daughter, Telperien, and a son, Isilmo.

## *c.* 1500 – THE ELVEN-SMITHS INSTRUCTED BY SAURON REACH THE HEIGHT OF THEIR SKILL. THEY BEGIN THE FORGING OF THE RINGS OF POWER.

But elsewhere the Elves [of Eregion] received [Sauron] gladly, and few among them hearkened to the messengers from Lindon bidding them beware; for Sauron took to himself the name of Annatar, the Lord of Gifts, and they had at first much profit from his friendship. And he said to them [speaking of his rejection by the Elves of Lindon]: 'Alas, for the weakness of the great! For a mighty king is Gil-galad, and wise in all lore is Master Elrond, and yet they will not aid me in my labours. Can it be that they do not desire to see other lands become as blissful as their own? But wherefore should Middle-earth remain for ever desolate and dark, whereas the Elves could make it as fair as Eressëa, nay even as Valinor? And since you have not returned thither, as you might, I perceive that you love this Middle-earth, as do I. Is it not then our task to labour together for its enrichment, and for the raising of all the Elven-kindreds that wander here untaught to the height of that power and knowledge which those have who are beyond the Sea?'[1]

It was in Eregion that the counsels of Sauron were most

gladly received, for in that land the Noldor desired ever to increase the skill and subtlety of their works. Moreover they were not at peace in their hearts, since they had refused to return into the West, and they desired both to stay in Middle-earth, which indeed they loved, and yet to enjoy the bliss of those that had departed. Therefore they hearkened to Sauron, and they learned of him many things, for his knowledge was great. In those days the smiths of Ost-in-Edhil surpassed all that they had contrived before; and they took thought, and they made Rings of Power. But Sauron guided their labours, and he was aware of all that they did; for his desire was to set a bond upon the Elves and to bring them under his vigilance.[2]

Sauron used all his arts upon Celebrimbor and his fellow-smiths, who had formed a society or brotherhood, very powerful in Eregion, the Gwaith-i-Mírdain; but he worked in secret, unknown to Galadriel and Celeborn. Before long Sauron had the Gwaith-i-Mírdain under his influence, for at first they had great profit from his instruction in secret matters of their craft.[3]

In his letter to Milton Waldman, Tolkien wrote: 'Sauron found their weak point in suggesting that, helping one another, they could make Western Middle-earth as beautiful as Valinor. It was really a veiled attack on the gods, an incitement to try and make a separate independent paradise. Gil-galad repulsed all such overtures, as also did Elrond. But at Eregion great work began – and the Elves came their nearest to falling to "magic" and machinery. With the aid of Sauron's lore they made *Rings of Power* ("power" is an ominous and sinister word in all these tales, except as applied to the gods).

'The chief power (of all the rings alike) was the prevention or slowing of *decay* (i.e. "change" viewed as a regrettable thing), the preservation of what is desired or loved, or its semblance – this is more or less an Elvish motive. But also they enhanced the natural powers of a possessor – thus approaching "magic", a motive easily corruptible into evil, a lust for domination. And finally they had other powers, more directly derived from Sauron ("the Necromancer": so he is called as he casts a fleeting shadow and presage on the pages of *The Hobbit*): such as rendering invisible the material body, and making things of the invisible world visible.'

### 1556 – KINGS AND QUEENS OF NÚMENOR X:
#### Tar-Telperien
Born: SA 1320; Died: SA 1731 (age 411)
Rule: SA 1556-1731 (175 years)

She was the second Ruling Queen of Númenor. She was long-lived (for the women of the Númenóreans had the longer life, or laid down their lives less easily), and she would wed with no man.

During the reign of Tar-Telperien momentous events were to unfold in Middle-earth.

## *c.* 1590 – THE THREE RINGS ARE
## COMPLETED IN EREGION.

In conversation with Frodo Baggins about Bilbo's Ring in the spring of Year 3018 of the Third Age, Gandalf the Grey succinctly summarized the history of the forging of the Rings of Power: 'In Eregion long ago many Elven-rings were made, magic rings as you call them, and they were, of course, of various kinds: some more potent and some less. The lesser rings were only essays in the craft before it was full-grown, and to the Elven-smiths they were but trifles – yet still to my mind dangerous for mortals. But the Great Rings, the Rings of Power, they were perilous.'[1]

Of the time when those Rings of Power were forged, 'The History of Galadriel and Celeborn' recounts:

[In the days of the Second Age when Sauron had withdrawn to Mordor and before the time that he began to send emissaries to Eregion[2]] the power of Galadriel and Celeborn had grown, and Galadriel, assisted in this by her friendship with the Dwarves of Moria, had come into contact with the Nandorin realm of Lórinand [afterwards called 'Lórien' and 'Lothlórien'] on the other side of the Misty Mountains.[3] This was peopled by those

Elves who forsook the Great Journey of the Eldar from Cuivié-nen[4] and settled in the woods of the Vale of Anduin;[5] and it extended into the forests on both sides of the Great River, including the region where afterwards was Dol Guldur. These Elves had no princes or rulers, and led their lives free of care while all Morgoth's power was concentrated in the North-west of Middle-earth;[6] Galadriel, striving to counteract the machinations of Sauron, was successful in Lórinand; while in Lindon Gil-galad [had] shut out Sauron's emissaries and even Sauron himself. But Sauron had better fortune with the Noldor of Eregion and especially with Celebrimbor, who desired in his heart to rival the skill and fame of Feanor.[7]

In Eregion Sauron posed as an emissary of the Valar, sent by them to Middle-earth ('thus anticipating the Istari') or ordered by them to remain there to give aid to the Elves. He perceived at once that Galadriel would be his chief adversary and obstacle, and he endeavoured therefore to placate her, bearing her scorn with outward patience and courtesy[8]. . . . So great became his hold on the [Gwaith-i-Mírdain] that at length he persuaded them to revolt against Galadriel and Celeborn and to seize power in Eregion; and that was at some time between 1350 and 1400 of the Second Age. Galadriel thereupon left Eregion and passed through Khazad-dûm to Lórinand taking with her Amroth and Celebrían, but Celeborn would not enter the mansions of the Dwarves, and he remained behind in Eregion, disregarded by Celebrimbor. In Lórinand Galadriel took up rule, and defence against Sauron.[9]

Sauron himself had departed from Eregion about the year 1500, after the [Gwaith-i-Mírdain] had begun the making of the Rings of Power.[10]

## *c.* 1600 – SAURON FORGES THE ONE RING IN ORODRUIN. HE COMPLETES THE BARAD-DÛR. CELEBRIMBOR PERCEIVES THE DESIGNS OF SAURON.

Now the Elves made many rings; but secretly Sauron made One Ring to rule all the others, and their power was bound up with it, to be subject wholly to it and to last only so long as it too should last. And much of the strength and will of Sauron passed into that One Ring; for the power of the Elven-rings was very great, and that which should govern them must be a thing of surpassing potency; and Sauron forged it in the Mountain of Fire in the Land of Shadow. And while he wore the One Ring he could perceive all the things that were done by means of the lesser rings, and he could see and govern the very thoughts of those that wore them.[1]

In writing to Milton Waldman, Tolkien addresses the source and effect of the One Ring's power:

'[Sauron] rules a growing empire from the great dark tower of Barad-dûr in Mordor, near to the Mountain of Fire, wielding the One Ring.

'But to achieve this he had been obliged to let a great part of his own inherent power (a frequent and very significant motive in myth and fairy-story) pass into the One Ring. While he wore it, his power on earth was actually enhanced. But even if he did not wear it, that power existed and was in "rapport" with himself: he was not "diminished". Unless some other seized it and became possessed of it. If that happened, the new possessor could (if sufficiently strong and heroic by nature) challenge Sauron, become master of all that he had learned or done since the making of the One Ring, and so overthrow him and usurp his place. This was the essential weakness he had introduced into his situation in his effort (largely unsuccessful) to enslave the Elves, and in his desire to establish a control over the minds and wills of his servants. There was another weakness: if the One Ring was actually *unmade*, annihilated, then its power would be dissolved, Sauron's own being would be diminished to vanishing point, and he would be reduced to a shadow, a mere memory of malicious will. But that he never contemplated nor feared. The Ring was unbreakable by any smithcraft less than his own. It was indissoluble in any fire, save the undying subterranean fire where it was made – and that was unapproachable, in Mordor. Also so great was the Ring's power of lust, that anyone who used it became mastered by it; it was beyond the strength of any will (even his own) to injure it, cast it away, or neglect it. So he thought. It was in any case on his finger.'

Although only revealed when subjected to fire, the One Ring bore an inscription.[2] The letters were of Elvish, 'of an ancient mode', but the language was that of Mordor, which, rendered in the 'Common Tongue' read:

*One Ring to rule them all, One Ring to find them,*
*One Ring to bring them all and in the darkness bind them.*

This rhyme was 'only two lines of a verse long known in Elven-lore':

*Three Rings for the Elven-kings under the sky,*
  *Seven for the Dwarf-lords in their halls of stone,*
*Nine for Mortal Men doomed to die,*
  *One for the Dark Lord on his dark throne*
*In the Land of Mordor where the Shadows lie.*
  *One Ring to rule them all, One Ring to find them,*
  *One Ring to bring them all and in the darkness bind them*
*In the Land of Mordor where the Shadows lie.*

And this very Ring, towards the close of the Third Age, would be the subject of an alarming revelation made by Gandalf in Bag End: 'This is the Master-ring, the One Ring to rule them all. This is the One Ring that he lost many ages ago, to the great weakening of his power. He greatly desires it – but he must *not* get it.'

Six months later in Rivendell, Master Elrond Half-Elven speaks of the Ring to those representatives of the Free People gathered in Council, telling 'of the Elven-smiths of Eregion and their friendship with Moria, and their eagerness for knowledge, by which Sauron ensnared them. For in that time he was not yet evil to behold, and they received his aid and grew mighty in craft, whereas he learned all their secrets, and betrayed them, and forged secretly in the Mountain of Fire the

One Ring to be their master.'³ But, as is recorded in 'Of the Rings of Power and the Third Age' and 'The History of Galadriel and Celeborn', Sauron underestimated the Elves of Eregion.

But the Elves were not so lightly to be caught. As soon as Sauron set the One Ring upon his finger they were aware of him; and they knew him, and perceived that he would be master of them, and of all that they wrought. Then in anger and fear they took off their rings.⁴

Now Celebrimbor was not corrupted in heart or faith, but had accepted Sauron as what he posed to be; and when at length he discovered the existence of the One Ring he revolted against Sauron, and went to Lórinand to take counsel once more with Galadriel. They should have destroyed all the Rings of Power at this time, 'but they failed to find the strength'. Galadriel counselled him that the Three Rings of the Elves should be hidden, never used, and dispersed, far from Eregion where Sauron believed them to be. It was at that time that she received Nenya, the White Ring, from Celebrimbor, and by its power the realm of Lórinand was strengthened and made beautiful; but its power upon her was great also and unforeseen, for it increased her latent desire for the Sea and for return into the West, so that her joy in Middle-earth was diminished. Celebrimbor followed [Galadriel's] counsel that the Ring of Air and the Ring of Fire should be sent out of Eregion; and he entrusted them to Gil-galad in Lindon.⁵

At this time, after six centuries of labour by those creatures held in Sauron's thrall – and aided by the power of the One Ring – the mighty structure of Barad-dûr reached completion, being the mightiest fortress to be built in Middle-earth since the Fall of Angband, the Iron Prison (or 'Hell of Iron') in the depths of the Iron Mountains that, in the First Age, had served as the fortress of Melkor.⁶ Later, in the Third Age, shortly before the breaking of the Fellowship of the Ring, Frodo sitting on the Seat of Seeing on Amon Hen, and wearing the One Ring, saw a vision of the terrible magnificence of Barad-dûr: '. . .his gaze was held: wall upon wall, battlement upon battlement, black, immeasurably strong, mountain of iron, gate of steel, tower of adamant, he saw it: Barad-dûr, Fortress of Sauron. All hope left him.'[7]

It may be asked why, in the Second Age, Sauron was not assaulted by an alliance of the Elves and the Men of the West as soon as he was divined as assembling and empowering his forces, as opposed to waiting for him to finally instigate war. It is a question Tolkien would later address, in January 1970, in a text headed:

## NOTE ON THE DELAY OF GIL-GALAD AND THE NÚMENÓREANS IN ATTACKING SAURON, BEFORE HE COULD GATHER HIS FORCES.[8]

It is now vain, and indeed unjust, to judge them foolish not to do, as in the end they were obliged to do, to have quickly gathered their forces and assailed Sauron. (See the *Debate of the Loremasters upon the Ban of Manwë* and his conduct as the Lord of Arda.) They could not have any certain knowledge of Sauron's intentions, or his power, and it was one of the successes of his cunning and deceits that they were unaware of his actual weakness, and his need for a long time in which to gather armies sufficient to assail an alliance of the Elves and Western Men. His occupation of Mordor he no doubt would have kept secret if he could, and it would appear from later events that he had secured the allegiance of Men that dwelt in lands adjacent, even those west of Anduin, in those regions where afterwards was Gondor in the Ered Nimrais and Calenardhon. But the Númenóreans occupying the Mouths of Anduin and the shorelands of Lebennin had discovered his devices, and revealed them to Gil-galad. But until [S.A.] 1600 he was still using the disguise of beneficent friend, and often journeyed at will in Eriador with few attendants, and so could not risk any rumour that he was gathering armies. At this time he perforce neglected the East (where Morgoth's ancient power had been) and though his emissaries were busy among the multiplying tribes of eastern Men, he dared not permit any of them to come within sight of the Númenóreans, or of Western Men.[*]

The Orcs of various kind (creatures of Morgoth) were to prove the most numerous and terrible of his soldiers and servants; but great hosts of them had been destroyed in the war against Morgoth, and in the destruction of Beleriand. Some remnant had escaped to hidings in the northern parts of the Misty Mountains and the Grey Mountains, and were now multiplying again. But further East there were more and stronger kinds, descendants of Morgoth's kingship, but long masterless during his occupation of Thangorodrim, they were yet wild and ungovernable, preying upon one another and upon Men (whether good or evil). But not until Mordor and the Barad-dûr were ready could he allow them to come out of hiding, while the Eastern Orcs, who had not experienced the power and terror of the Eldar, or the valour of the Edain, were not subservient to Sauron – while he was obliged for the cozening of Western Men and Elves to wear as fair a form and countenance as he could, they despised him and laughed at him. Thus it was that though, as soon as his disguise was pierced and he was recognized as an enemy, he exerted all his time and strength to gathering and training armies, it took some ninety years

---

[*] That is, of the numerous tribes of Men, whom the Elves called Men of Good Will, who lived in Eriador and Calenardhon and the Vales of Anduin and in the Great Wood and the plains between that and Mordor and the Sea of Rhûn. In Eriador there were actually some of the remnants of the Three Houses of Men that had fought with the Elves against Morgoth. Others were of their kin, who (like the Silvan Elves) had never passed the Ered Luin, and others of remoter kin. But nearly all were descendants of ancient rebels against Morgoth. (Some evil men there were also.)

before he felt ready to open war. And he misjudged this, as we see in his final defeat, when the great host of Minastir from Númenor landed in Middle-earth. His gathering of armies had not been unopposed, and his success had been much less than his hope. . . .

## 1693 – WAR OF THE ELVES AND SAURON BEGINS. THE THREE RINGS ARE HIDDEN.

But [Sauron], finding that he was betrayed and that the Elves were not deceived, was filled with wrath; and he came against them with open war, demanding that all the rings should be delivered to him, since the Elven-smiths could not have attained to their making without his lore and counsel. But the Elves fled from him; and three of their rings they saved, and bore them away, and hid them.

Now these were the Three that had last been made, and they possessed the greatest powers. Narya, Nenya, and Vilya, they were named, the Rings of Fire, and of Water, and of Air, set with ruby and adamant and sapphire; and of all the Elven-rings Sauron most desired to possess them, for those who had them in their keeping could ward off the decays of time and postpone the weariness of the world. But Sauron could not discover [the Three], for they were given into the hands of the Wise, who concealed them and never again used them openly while Sauron kept the Ruling Ring. Therefore the Three remained unsullied, for they were forged by Celebrimbor alone, and the hand of

Sauron had never touched them; yet they also were subject to the One.

From that time war never ceased between Sauron and the Elves. . . .[1]

## 1695 – SAURON'S FORCES INVADE ERIADOR. GIL-GALAD SENDS ELROND TO EREGION.

When Sauron learned of the repentance and revolt of Cele-brimbor his disguise fell and his wrath was revealed; and gathering a great force he moved over Calenardhon (Rohan) to the invasion of Eriador in the year 1695. When news of this reached Gil-galad he sent out a force under Elrond Half-elven; but Elrond had far to go, and Sauron turned north and made at once for Eregion. The scouts and vanguard of Sauron's host were already approaching when Celeborn made a sortie and drove them back; but though he was able to join his force to that of Elrond they could not return to Eregion, for Sauron's host was far greater than theirs, great enough both to hold them off and closely to invest Eregion.[1]

## 1697 – EREGION LAID WASTE. DEATH OF CELEBRIMBOR. THE GATES OF MORIA ARE SHUT. ELROND RETREATS WITH REMNANT OF THE NOLDOR AND FOUNDS THE REFUGE OF IMLADRIS.

At last the attackers broke into Eregion with ruin and devastation, and captured the chief object of Sauron's assault, the House of the Mírdain, where were their smithies and their treasures. Celebrimbor, desperate, himself withstood Sauron on the steps of the great door of the Mírdain; but he was grappled and taken captive, and the House was ransacked. There Sauron took the Nine Rings and other lesser works of the Mírdain; but the Seven and the Three he could not find. Then Celebrimbor was put to torment, and Sauron learned from him where the Seven were bestowed. This Celebrimbor revealed, because neither the Seven nor the Nine did he value as he valued the Three; the Seven and the Nine were made with Sauron's aid, whereas the Three were made by Celebrimbor alone, with a different power and purpose.[1] Concerning the Three Rings Sauron could learn nothing from Celebrimbor; and he had him put to death. But he guessed the truth, that the Three had been committed to Elvish guardians: and that must mean to Galadriel and Gil-galad.

In black anger he turned back to battle; and bearing as a banner Celebrimbor's body hung upon a pole, shot through with Orc-arrows, he turned upon the forces of Elrond. Elrond had gathered such few of the Elves of Eregion as had escaped, but he had no force to withstand the onset. He would indeed have been overwhelmed had not Sauron's host been attacked in the rear; for Durin sent out a force of Dwarves from Khazad-dûm, and with them came Elves of Lórinand led by Amroth. Elrond was able to extricate himself, but he was forced away northwards, and it was at that time that he established a refuge and stronghold at Imladris (Rivendell).[2]

## 1699 – SAURON OVERRUNS ERIADOR.

But now Sauron attempted to gain the mastery of Eriador: Lórinand could wait. But as he ravaged the lands, slaying or drawing off all the small groups of Men and hunting the remaining Elves, many fled to swell Elrond's host to the north-ward. Now Sauron's immediate purpose was to take Lindon, where he believed that he had most chance of seizing one, or more, of the Three Rings; and he called in therefore his scattered forces and marched west towards the land of Gil-galad, ravaging as he went. But his force was weakened by the necessity of leaving a strong detachment to contain Elrond and prevent him coming down upon his rear.

Sauron withdrew the pursuit of Elrond and turned upon the Dwarves and the Elves of Lórinand, whom he drove back; but the Gates of Moria were shut, and he could not enter. Ever afterwards Moria had Sauron's hate, and all Orcs were commanded to harry Dwarves whenever they might.[1]

Although the Dwarves were secure within their Dwarf-hall, their eager delving for *mithril* in the Third Age would arouse a Balrog. With the Dwarves driven out, the great city of

Khazad-dûm would become a dwelling for the Orcs of Sauron. Many years later, at the Council of Elrond, Glóin the Dwarf reflected on this catastrophe: 'Too deep we delved there, and woke the nameless fear. Long have its vast mansions lain empty since the children of Durin fled . . . no dwarf has dared to pass the doors of Khazad-dûm for many lives of kings, save Thrór only, and he perished.'[2] An ancient Dwarvish lament speaks of the lost splendour of Khazad-dûm:

> *The world was young, the mountains green,*
> *No stain yet on the Moon was seen,*
> *No words were laid on stream or stone*
> *When Durin woke and walked alone.*
> *He named the nameless hills and dells;*
> *He drank from yet untasted wells;*
> *He stooped and looked in Mirrormere,*
> *And saw a crown of stars appear,*
> *As gems upon a silver thread,*
> *Above the shadow of his head.*
>
> *The world was fair, the mountains tall,*
> *In Elder Days before the fall*
> *Of mighty kings in Nargothrond*
> *And Gondolin, who now beyond*
> *The Western Seas have passed away:*
> *The world was fair in Durin's Day.*
>
> *A king he was on carven throne*
> *In many-pillared halls of stone*
> *With golden roof and silver floor,*
> *And runes of power upon the door.*
> *The light of sun and star and moon*
> *In shining lamps of crystal hewn*
> *Undimmed by cloud or shade of night*
> *There shone for ever fair and bright.*

*There hammer on the anvil smote,*
*There chisel clove, and graver wrote;*
*There forged was blade, and bound was hilt;*
*The delver mined, the mason built.*
*There beryl, pearl, and opal pale,*
*And metal wrought like fishes' mail,*
*Buckler and corslet, axe and sword,*
*And shining spears were laid in hoard.*

*Unwearied then were Durin's folk;*
*Beneath the mountains music woke:*
*The harpers harped, the minstrels sang,*
*And at the gates the trumpets rang.*

*The world is grey, the mountains old,*
*The forge's fire is ashen-cold;*
*No harp is wrung, no hammer falls:*
*The darkness dwells in Durin's halls;*
*The shadow lies upon his tomb*
*In Moria, in Khazad-dûm.*
*But still the sunken stars appear*
*In dark and windless Mirrormere;*
*There lies his crown in water deep,*
*Till Durin wakes again from sleep.*[3]

## 1700 – TAR-MINASTIR SENDS A GREAT NAVY FROM NÚMENOR TO LINDON. SAURON IS DEFEATED.[1]

Now for long years the Númenóreans had brought in their ships to the Grey Havens, and there they were welcome. As soon as Gil-galad began to fear that Sauron would come with open war into Eriador he sent messages to Númenor; and on the shores of Lindon the Númenóreans began to build up a force and supplies for war. In 1695, when Sauron invaded Eriador, Gil-galad called on Númenor for aid. Then Tar-Minastir the King sent out a great navy; but it was delayed, and did not reach the coasts of Middle-earth until the year 1700. By that time Sauron had mastered all Eriador, save only besieged Imladris, and had reached the line of the River Lhûn. He had summoned more forces, which were approaching from the south-east, and were indeed in Enedwaith at the Crossing of Tharbad, which was only lightly held. Gil-galad and the Númenóreans were holding the Lhûn in desperate defence of the Grey Havens, when in the very nick of time the great armament of Tar-Minastir came in; and Sauron's host was heavily defeated and driven back. The Númenórean admiral Ciryatur ['Ship Master'] sent part of his ships to make a landing further to the south.

Sauron was driven away south-east after great slaughter at Sarn Ford (the crossing of the Baranduin); and though strengthened by his force at Tharbad he suddenly found a host of the Númenóreans again in his rear, for Ciryatur had put a strong force ashore at the mouth of the Gwathló (Greyflood), 'where there was a small Númenórean harbour'. [This was Vinyalondë of Tar-Aldarion, afterwards called Lond Daer.] In the Battle of the Gwathló Sauron was routed utterly and he himself only narrowly escaped.[2]

# 1701 – SAURON IS DRIVEN OUT OF ERIADOR. THE WESTLANDS HAVE PEACE FOR A LONG WHILE.

[Sauron's] small remaining force was assailed in the east of Calenardhon, and he with no more than a bodyguard fled to the region afterwards called Dagorlad (Battle Plain), whence broken and humiliated he returned to Mordor, and vowed vengeance upon Númenor. The army that was besieging Imladris was caught between Elrond and Gil-galad, and utterly destroyed. Eriador was cleared of the enemy, but lay largely in ruins.

At this time the first White Council was held, and it was there determined that an Elvish stronghold in the east of Eriador should be maintained at Imladris rather than in Eregion. At that time also Gil-galad gave Vilya, the Blue Ring, to Elrond, and appointed him to be his vice-regent in Eriador; but the Red Ring he kept, until he gave it to Círdan when he set out from Lindon in the days of the Last Alliance. For many years the Westlands had peace, and time in which to heal their wounds.

It is told of Galadriel that at this time a strong 'sea-longing' grew in her.

(Though [Galadriel] deemed it her duty to remain in Middle-earth while Sauron was still unconquered) she determined to leave Lórinand and to dwell near the sea. She committed Lórinand to Amroth, and passing again through Moria with Celebrían she came to Imladris, seeking Celeborn. There (it seems) she found him, and there they dwelt together for a long time; and it was then that Elrond first saw Celebrían, and loved her, though he said nothing of it.

It was while Galadriel was in Imladris that the Council referred to above was held. But at some later time [there is no indication of the date] Galadriel and Celeborn together with Celebrían departed from Imladris and went to the little-inhabited lands between the mouth of the Gwathló and Ethir Anduin. There they dwelt in Belfalas, at the place that was afterwards called Dol Amroth; there Amroth their son at times visited them, and their company was swelled by Nandorin Elves from Lórinand. It not until far on in the Third Age, when Amroth was lost and Lórinand was in peril, that Galadriel returned there, in the year 1981.[1]

## 1731 – KINGS AND QUEENS OF NÚMENOR XI:
### Tar-Minastir
Born: SA 1474; Died: SA 1873 (age 399)
Rule: SA 1731-1869 (138 years)

This name he had because he built a high tower upon the hill of Oromet, nigh to Andúnië and the west shores, and thence would spend great part of his days gazing westward. For the yearning was grown strong in the hearts of the Númenóreans. He loved the Eldar but envied them. He it was who [had] sent a great fleet to the aid of Gil-galad in the first war against Sauron.

## *c.* 1800 – FROM ABOUT THIS TIME ONWARD THE NÚMENÓREANS BEGIN TO ESTABLISH DOMINIONS ON THE COASTS. SAURON EXTENDS HIS POWER EASTWARDS. THE SHADOW FALLS ON NÚMENOR.

The Númenóreans had tasted power in Middle-earth, and from that time forward they began to make permanent settlements on the western coasts, becoming too powerful for Sauron to attempt to move west out of Mordor for a long time.[1]

The Númenóreans had now become great mariners, exploring all the seas eastward, and they began to yearn for the West and the forbidden waters; and the more joyful was their life, the more they began to long for the immortality of the Eldar.[2]

**1869 – KINGS AND QUEENS OF NÚMENOR XII:**
**Tar-Ciryatan**
Born: SA 1634; Died: SA 2035 (age 401)
Rule: SA 1869-2029 (160 years)

The first sign of the shadow that was to fall upon them [had] appeared in the days of Tar-Minastir, eleventh King. . . .[3]

[His son, Ciryatan,] scorned the yearnings of his father, and eased the restlessness of his heart by voyaging, east, and north, and south, until he took the sceptre. It is said that he constrained his father to yield to him ere of his free will he would. In this way (it is held) might the first coming of the Shadow upon the bliss of Númenor be seen. [Tar-Ciryatan] built a great fleet of royal ships, and his servants brought back great store of metals and gems, and oppressed the men of Middle-earth.[4]

Moreover, after Minastir the Kings became greedy of wealth and power. At first the Númenóreans had come to Middle-earth as teachers and friends of lesser Men afflicted by Sauron; but now their havens became fortresses, holding wide coastlands in subjection.[5]

These things took place in the days of Tar-Ciryatan the Shipbuilder, and of Tar-Atanamir his son; and they were proud men, eager for wealth, and they laid the men of Middle-earth under tribute, taking now rather than giving.[6]

### 2029 – KINGS AND QUEENS OF NÚMENOR XIII:
#### Tar-Atanamir the Great
Born: SA 1800; Died: SA 2221 (age 421)
Rule: SA 2029-2221 (192 years)

Much is said of this King in the Annals, such as now survive the Downfall. For he was like his father proud and greedy of wealth, and the Númenóreans in his service exacted heavy tribute from the men of the coasts of Middle-earth. In his time the Shadow fell upon Númenor; and the King, and those that followed his lore, spoke openly against the ban of the Valar, and their hearts were turned against the Valar and the Eldar. . . .[7]

It was Tar-Atanamir who first spoke openly against the Ban and declared that the life of the Eldar was his by right. Thus the shadow deepened, and the thought of death darkened the hearts of the people.[8]

Now [the yearning of the Númenóreans] grew ever greater with the years; and [they] began to hunger for the undying city that they saw from afar, and the desire of everlasting life, to escape from death and the ending of delight, grew strong upon them; and ever as their power and glory grew greater their unquiet increased. For though the Valar had rewarded the Dúnedain with long life, they could not take from them the weariness of the world that comes at last, and they died, even their kings of the seed of Eärendil; and the span of their lives was brief in the eyes of the Eldar. Thus it was that a shadow fell upon them: in which maybe the will of Morgoth was at work that still moved in the world. And the Númenóreans began to murmur, at first in their hearts, and then in open words, against the doom of Men, and most of all against the Ban which forbade them to sail into the West.

And they said among themselves: 'Why do the Lords of the West sit there in peace unending, while we must die and go we know not whither, leaving our home and all that we have made? And the Eldar die not, even those that rebelled against the Lords. And since we have mastered all seas, and no water is so wild or so wide that our ships cannot overcome it, why should we not go to Avallónë and greet there our friends?'

And some there were who said: 'Why should we not go even to Aman, and taste there, were it but for a day, the bliss of the Powers? Have we not become mighty among the people of Arda?'

The Eldar reported these words to the Valar, and Manwë was grieved, seeing a cloud gather on the noon-tide of Númenor. And he sent messengers to the Dúnedain, who spoke earnestly to the King, and to all who would listen, concerning the fate and fashion of the world.

'The Doom of the World,' they said, 'One alone can change who made it. And were you so to voyage that escaping all deceits and snares you came indeed to Aman, the Blessed Realm, little would it profit you. For it is not the land of Manwë that makes its people deathless, but the Deathless that dwell therein have hallowed the land; and there you would but wither and grow weary the sooner, as moths in a light too strong and steadfast.'

But the King said: 'And does not Eärendil, my forefather, live? Or is he not in the land of Aman?'

To which they answered: 'You know that he has a fate apart, and was adjudged to the Firstborn who die not; yet this also is his doom that he can never return again to mortal lands. Whereas you and your people are not of the Firstborn, but are mortal Men as Ilúvatar made you. Yet it seems that you desire now to have the good of both kindreds, to sail to Valinor when you will, and to return when you please to your homes. That cannot be. Nor can the Valar take away the gifts of Ilúvatar. The Eldar, you say, are unpunished, and even those who rebelled do not die. Yet that is to them neither reward nor punishment, but the fulfilment of their being. They cannot escape, and are bound to this world, never to leave it so long as it lasts, for its life is theirs. And you are punished for the rebellion of Men, you say, in which you had small part, and so it is that you die. But that was not at first appointed for a punishment. Thus you escape, and leave the world, and are not bound to it, in hope or in weariness. Which of us therefore should envy the others?'

And the Númenóreans answered: 'Why should we not envy the Valar, or even the least of the Deathless? For of us is required a blind trust, and a hope without assurance, knowing not what lies before us in a little while. And yet we also love the Earth and would not lose it.'

Then the Messengers said: 'Indeed the mind of Ilúvatar concerning you is not known to the Valar, and he has not revealed all things that are to come. But this we hold to be true, that your home is not here, neither in the Land of Aman nor anywhere within the Circles of the World. And the Doom of Men, that they should depart, was at first a gift of Ilúvatar. It became a grief to them only because coming under the shadow of Morgoth it seemed to them that they were surrounded by a great darkness, of which they were afraid; and some grew wilful and proud and would not yield, until life was reft from them. We who bear the ever-mounting burden of the years do not clearly understand this; but if that grief has returned to trouble you, as you say, then we fear that the Shadow arises once more and grows again in your hearts. Therefore, though you be the Dúnedain, fairest of Men, who escaped from the Shadow of old and fought valiantly against it, we say to you: Beware! The will of Eru may not be gainsaid; and the Valar bid you earnestly not to withhold the trust to which you are called, lest soon it become again a bond by which you are constrained. Hope rather that in the end even the least of your desires shall have fruit. The love of Arda was set in your hearts by Ilúvatar, and he does not plant to no purpose. Nonetheless, many ages of Men unborn may pass ere that purpose is made known; and to you it will be revealed and not to the Valar.'

It was to Tar-Atanamir that the Messengers came; and he was the thirteenth King, and in his day the Realm of Númenor had endured for more than two thousand years, and was come to the zenith of its bliss, if not yet of its power.

But Atanamir was ill pleased with the counsel of the Messengers and gave little heed to it, and the greater part of his people followed him; for they wished still to escape death in their own day, not waiting upon hope. And Atanamir lived to a great age, clinging to his life beyond the end of all joy; and he was the first of the Númenóreans to do this, refusing to depart until he was witless and unmanned, and denying to his son the kingship at the height of his days. For the Lords of Númenor had been wont to wed late in their long lives and to depart and leave the mastery to their sons when these were come to full stature of body and mind.[9]

[Thus Tar-Atanamir] is called also the Unwilling, for he was the first of the Kings to refuse to lay down his life, or to renounce the sceptre; and he lived until death took him perforce in dotage.[10]

In this Age, as is elsewhere told, Sauron arose again in Middle-earth, and grew, and turned back to the evil in which he was nurtured by Morgoth, becoming mighty in his service. Already in the days of Tar-Minastir, the eleventh King of Númenor, he had fortified the land of Mordor and had built there the Tower of Barad-dûr, and thereafter he strove ever for the dominion of Middle-earth, to become a king over all kings and as a god unto Men. And Sauron hated the Númenóreans, because of the deeds of their fathers and their ancient alliance with the Elves and allegiance to the Valar; nor did he forget the aid that Tar-Minastir had rendered to Gil-galad of old, in that time when the One Ring was forged and there was war between Sauron and the Elves in Eriador. Now he learned that the kings of Númenor had increased in power and splendour, and he hated them the more; and he feared them, lest they should invade his lands and wrest from him the dominion of the East. But for a long time he did not dare to challenge the Lords of the Sea, and he withdrew from the coasts.[11]

## 2251 – DEATH OF TAR-ATANAMIR. TAR-ANCALIMON TAKES THE SCEPTRE.[1] REBELLION AND DIVISION OF THE NÚMENÓREANS BEGINS. ABOUT THIS TIME THE NAZGÛL OR RINGWRAITHS, SLAVES OF THE NINE RINGS, FIRST APPEAR.

### KINGS AND QUEENS OF NÚMENOR XIV:
#### Tar-Ancalimon
Born: SA 1986; Died: SA 2386 (age 400)
Rule: SA 2221-2386 (165 years)

Then Tar-Ancalimon, son of Atanamir, became King, and he was of like mind; and in his day the people of Númenor became divided. On the one hand was the greater party, and they were called the King's Men, and they grew proud and were estranged from the Eldar and the Valar. And on the other hand was the lesser party, and they were called the Elendili, the Elf-friends; for though they remained loyal indeed to the King and the House of Elros, they wished to keep the friendship of the Eldar, and they hearkened to the counsel of the Lords of the West. Nonetheless even they, who named themselves the Faithful, did not wholly escape from the affliction of their people, and they were troubled by the thought of death.

Thus the bliss of Westernesse became diminished; but still its might and splendour increased. For the kings and their people had not yet abandoned wisdom, and if they loved the Valar no longer at least they still feared them. They did not dare openly to break the Ban or to sail beyond the limits that had been appointed. Eastwards still they steered their tall ships. But the fear of death grew ever darker upon them, and they delayed it by all means that they could; and they began to build great houses for their dead, while their wise men laboured unceasingly to discover if they might the secret of recalling life, or at the least of the prolonging of Men's days. Yet they achieved only the art of preserving incorrupt the dead flesh of Men, and they filled all the land with silent tombs in which the thought of death was enshrined in the darkness.[2]

And some taught that there was a land of shades filled with the wraiths of the things that they had known and loved upon the mortal earth, and that in shadow the dead should come there bearing with them the shadows of their possessions.[3]

But those that lived turned the more eagerly to pleasure and revelry, desiring ever more goods and more riches; and after the days of Tar-Ancalimon the offering of the first fruits to Eru was neglected, and men went seldom any more to the Hallow upon the heights of Meneltarma in the midst of the land.[4]

Many of the King's Men began to forsake the use of the Elven-tongues, and to teach them no longer to their children. But the royal titles were still given in Quenya, out of ancient custom rather than love, for fear lest the breaking of the old usage should bring ill-fortune.[5]

Sauron gathered into his hands all the remaining Rings of Power; and he dealt them out to the other peoples of Middle-earth, hoping thus to bring under his sway all those that desired secret power beyond the measure of their kind. Seven rings he gave to the Dwarves; but to Men he gave nine, for Men proved in this matter as in others the readiest to his will.[6]

In his letter to Milton Waldman, Tolkien would write: 'All through the twilight of the Second Age the Shadow is growing in the East of Middle-earth, spreading its sway more and more over Men – who multiply as the Elves begin to fade.'[7]

And all those rings that he governed he perverted, the more easily since he had a part in their making, and they were accursed, and they betrayed in the end all those that used them. The Dwarves indeed proved tough and hard to tame; they ill endure the domination of others, and the thoughts of their hearts are hard to fathom, nor can they be turned to shadows. They used their rings only for the getting of wealth; but wrath and an overmastering greed of gold were kindled in their hearts, of which evil enough after came to the profit of Sauron. It is said that the foundation of each of the Seven Hoards of the Dwarf-kings of old was a golden ring; but all those hoards long ago were plundered and the Dragons devoured them, and of the Seven Rings some were consumed in fire and some Sauron recovered.

Men proved easier to ensnare. Those who used the Nine Rings became mighty in their day, kings, sorcerers, and warriors of old. They obtained glory and great wealth, yet it turned to their undoing. They had, as it seemed, unending life, yet life became unendurable to them. They could walk, if they would, unseen by all eyes in this world beneath the sun, and they could see things in worlds invisible to mortal men; but too often they beheld only the phantoms and delusions of Sauron. And one by one, sooner or later, according to their native strength and to the good or evil of their wills in the beginning, they fell under the thraldom of the ring that they bore and under the domination of the One, which was Sauron's. And they became for ever invisible save to him that wore the Ruling Ring, and they entered into the realm of shadows. The Nazgûl were they, the Ringwraiths, the Enemy's most terrible servants; darkness went with them, and they cried with the voices of death.[8]

Yet Sauron was ever guileful, and it is said that among those whom he ensnared with the Nine Rings three were great lords of Númenórean race.[9]

In *The Fellowship of the Ring*, Tolkien creates a vivid image of the Nazgûl as, centuries later in the Third Age, they appeared to Frodo when wearing the One Ring: 'So black were they that they seemed like black holes in the deep shade behind them. [He] thought that he heard a faint hiss as of venomous breath and felt a thin piercing chill . . .

'Though everything else remained as before, dim and dark, the shapes became terribly clear. He was able to see beneath their black wrappings . . . In their white faces burned keen and merciless eyes; under their mantles were long grey robes; upon their grey hairs were helms of silver; in their haggard hands were swords of steel. Their eyes fell on him and pierced him, as they rushed towards him.'[10]

Later, in *The Two Towers*, the author has Faramir speak of the Nazgûl's origins: 'It is said that their lords were men of Númenor who had fallen into dark wickedness; to them the Enemy had given rings of power, and he had devoured them: living ghosts they were become, terrible and evil.'[11]

## 2280 – UMBAR IS MADE INTO A GREAT FORTRESS OF NÚMENOR.

\*

## 2350 – PELARGIR IS BUILT. IT BECOMES THE CHIEF HAVEN OF THE FAITHFUL NÚMENÓREANS.

Thus it came to pass in that time that the Númenóreans first made great settlements upon the west shores of the ancient lands; for their own land seemed to them shrunken, and they had no rest or content therein, and they desired now wealth and dominion in Middle-earth, since the West was denied. Great harbours and strong towers they made, and there many of them took up their abode; but they appeared now rather as lords and masters and gatherers of tribute than as helpers and teachers. And the great ships of the Númenóreans were borne east on the winds and returned ever laden, and the power and majesty of their kings were increased; and they drank and they feasted and they clad themselves in silver and gold.

In all this the Elf-friends had small part. They alone came now ever to the north and the land of Gil-galad, keeping their friendship with the Elves and lending them aid against Sauron. . . . But the King's Men sailed far away to the south, and though the kingdoms and strongholds they made have left many rumours in the legends of Men, the Eldar know naught of them. Only Pelargir they remember, for there was the haven of the Elf-friends above the mouths of Anduin the Great.[1]

> The Númenóreans, who had first gone to Middle-earth 'seeking wealth and dominion', were driven to build fortifications and defences on its coastal regions as a result of Sauron's relentless ambition and the coming of the Úlairi, as the Nazgûl are named in Quenya.

And when the Úlairi arose that were the Ringwraiths, [Sauron's] servants, and the strength of his terror and mastery over Men had grown exceedingly great, he began to assail the strong places of the Númenóreans upon the shores of the sea.[2]

The Elf-friends go chiefly to the North-west, but their strongest place is at Pelargir above the Mouths of Anduin. The King's Folk establish lordships in Umbar and Harad and in many other places on the coasts of the Great Lands.

During the same time Sauron extends his dominion slowly over the great part of Middle-earth; but his power reaches out eastward, since he is withheld from the coasts by the Númenóreans.[3]

> In successive years, the divisions were to deepen between Númenóreans known as 'The King's Folk' or 'The King's Men' and those who were 'Elf-friends' and who retained an unswerving loyalty to the Eldar.

The Kings and their followers little by little abandoned the use of the Eldarin tongues; and at last the twentieth King took his royal name, in Númenórean form, calling himself Ar-Adûnakhôr, 'Lord of the West'. This seemed ill-omened to the Faithful, for hitherto they had given that title only to one of the Valar, or to the Elder King himself.[4]

Now Sauron's lust and pride increased, until he knew no bounds, and he determined to make himself master of all things in Middle-earth, and to destroy the Elves, and to compass, if he might, the downfall of Númenor. He brooked no freedom nor any rivalry, and he named himself Lord of the Earth. A mask he still could wear so that if he wished he might deceive the eyes of Men, seeming to them wise and fair. But he ruled rather by force and fear, if they might avail; and those who perceived his shadow spreading over the world called him the Dark Lord and named him the Enemy; and he gathered again under his government all the evil things of the days of Morgoth that remained on earth or beneath it, and the Orcs were at his command and multiplied like flies. Thus the Black Years began, which the Elves call the Days of Flight. In that time many of the Elves of Middle-earth fled to Lindon and thence over the seas never to return; and many were destroyed by Sauron and his servants. But in Lindon Gil-galad still maintained his power, and Sauron dared not as yet to pass the Mountains of Ered Luin nor to assail the Havens; and Gil-galad was aided by the Númenóreans. Elsewhere Sauron reigned, and those who would be free took refuge in the fastnesses of wood and mountain, and ever fear pursued them. In the east and south well nigh all Men were under his dominion, and they grew strong in those days and built many towns and walls of stone, and they were numerous and fierce in war and armed with iron. To them Sauron was both king and god; and they feared him exceedingly, for he surrounded his abode with fire.[5]

## 2386 – KINGS AND QUEENS OF NÚMENOR XV:
### Tar-Telemmaitë
Born: SA 2136; Died: SA 2526 (age 390)
Rule: SA 2386-2526 (140 years)

Hereafter the Kings ruled in name from the death of their father to their own death, though the actual power passed often to their sons or counsellors; and the days of the descendants of Elros waned under the Shadow. The fifteenth Ruler of Númenor is said to have been called [Telemmaitë] ('silver-handed') because of his love of silver, 'and he bade his servants to seek ever for *mithril*'.[6]

## 2526 – KINGS AND QUEENS OF NÚMENOR XVI:
### Tar-Vanimeldë
Born: SA 2277; Died: SA 2637 (age 360)
Rule: SA 2526-2637 (111 years)

[Tar-Vanimeldë] was the third Ruling Queen. . . . She gave little heed to ruling, loving rather music and dance; and the power was wielded by her husband Herucalmo, younger than she, but a descendant of the same degree from Tar-Atanamir.

## 2637 – KINGS AND QUEENS OF NÚMENOR [USURPER]
### Tar-Anducal (Herucalmo)
Born: SA 2286; Died: SA 2657 (age 371)
Rule: (*illégalement*) SA 2637-2657 (20 years)

Herucalmo took the sceptre upon his wife's death, calling himself Tar-Anducal, and withholding the rule from his son Alcarin; yet some do not reckon him in the Line of Kings as seventeenth, and pass to Alcarin.

### 2657 – KINGS AND QUEENS OF NÚMENOR XVII:
### Tar-Alcarin
Born: SA 2406; Died: SA 2737 (age 331)
Rule: (*de jure*) SA 2637-2737 (100 years)
(*de facto*) SA 2657-2737 (80 years)

Due to the usurpation by his father, Herucalmo (the so called Tar-Anducal) Tar-Alcarin only ruled as King for eighty years.

### 2737 – KINGS AND QUEENS OF NÚMENOR XVIII:
### Tar-Calmacil (Ar-Belzagar)
Born: SA 2516; Died: SA 2825 (age 309)
Rule: SA 2737-2825 (88 years)

He took [the name Tar-Calmacil], for in his youth he was a great captain, and won wide lands along the coasts of Middle-earth. Thus he kindled the hate of Sauron, who nonetheless withdrew, and built his power in the East, far from the shores, biding his time. In the days of Tar-Calmacil the name of the King was first spoken in Adûnaic; and by the King's Men he was called Ar-Belzagar.

## 2825 – KINGS AND QUEENS OF NÚMENOR XIX:
### Tar-Ardamin (Ar-Abattârik)
Born: SA 2618; Died: SA 2899 (age 281)
Rule: SA 2825-2899 (74 years)

Tar-Ardamin was the last of the Númenórean kings to take the sceptre using a Quenya-styled royal name.[7]

# 2899 – AR-ADÛNAKHÔR TAKES THE SCEPTRE.

### 2899 – KINGS AND QUEENS OF NÚMENOR XX:
Ar-Adûnakhôr (Tar-Herunúmen)
Born: SA 2709; Died: SA 2962 (age 253)
Rule: SA 2899-2962 (63 years)

In those days the Shadow grew deeper upon Númenor; and the lives of the Kings of the House of Elros waned because of their rebellion, but they hardened their hearts the more against the Valar. And the twentieth king took the sceptre of his fathers, and he ascended the throne in the name of Adûnakhôr, Lord of the West, forsaking the Elven-tongues and forbidding their use in his hearing. Yet in the Scroll of Kings the name Herunúmen was inscribed in the High-elven speech, because of ancient custom, which the kings feared to break utterly, lest evil befall. Now this title seemed to the Faithful over-proud, being the title of the Valar; and their hearts were sorely tried between their loyalty to the House of Elros and their reverence of the appointed Powers. But worse was yet to come.[1]

In this reign the Elven-tongues were no longer used, nor permitted to be taught, but were maintained in secret by the Faithful; and the ships from Eressëa came seldom and secretly to the west shores of Númenor thereafter.[2]

And indeed Ar-Adûnakhôr began to persecute the Faithful and punished those who used the Elven-tongues openly; and the Eldar came no more to Númenor.

The power and wealth of the Númenóreans nonetheless continued to increase; but their years lessened as their fear of death grew, and their joy departed.[3]

### 2962 – KINGS AND QUEENS OF NÚMENOR XXI:
### Ar-Zimrathôn (Tar-Hostamir)
Born: SA 2798; Died: SA 3033 (age 235)
Rule: SA 2962-3033 (71 years)

### 3033 – KINGS AND QUEENS OF NÚMENOR XXII:
### Ar-Sakalthôr (Tar-Falassion)
Born: SA 2876; Died: SA 3102 (age 226)
Rule: SA 3033-3102 (69 years)

### 3102 – KINGS AND QUEENS OF NÚMENOR XXIII:
### Ar-Gimilzôr (Tar-Telemnar)
Born: SA 2960; Died: SA 3175 (age 215)
Rule: SA 3102-3175 (73 years)[4]

Ar-Gimilzôr the [twenty-third] king was the greatest enemy of the Faithful that had yet arisen. In his day the White Tree was untended and began to decline; and he forbade utterly the use of the Elven-tongues, and punished those that welcomed the ships of Eressëa, that still came secretly to the west-shores of the land.[5]

He revered nothing, and went never to the Hallow of Eru.[6]

Now the Elendili [the Faithful] dwelt mostly in the western regions of Númenor; but Ar-Gimilzôr commanded all that he could discover to be of this party to remove from the west and dwell in the east of the land; and there they were watched. And the chief dwelling of the Faithful in the later days was thus nigh to the harbour of Rómenna; thence many set sail to Middle-earth, seeking the northern coasts where they might speak still with the Eldar in the kingdom of Gil-galad. This was known to the kings, but they hindered it not, so long as the Elendili departed from their land and did not return; for they desired to end all friendship between their people and the Eldar of Eressëa, whom they named the Spies of the Valar, hoping to keep their deeds and their counsels hidden from the Lords of the West. But all that they did was known to Manwë, and the Valar were wroth with the Kings of Númenor, and gave them counsel and protection no more; and the ships of Eressëa came never again out of the sunset, and the havens of Andúnië were forlorn.

Highest in honour after the house of the kings were the Lords of Andúnië; for they were of the line of Elros, being descended from Silmarien, daughter of Tar-Elendil the fourth king of Númenor. And these lords were loyal to the kings, and revered them; and the Lord of Andúnië was ever among the chief councillors of the Sceptre. Yet also from the beginning they bore especial love to the Eldar and reverence for the Valar; and as the Shadow grew they aided the Faithful as they could. But for long they did not declare themselves openly, and sought rather to amend the hearts of the lords of the Sceptre with wiser counsels.

There was a lady Inzilbêth, renowned for her beauty, and her mother was Lindórië, sister of Eärendur, the Lord of Andúnië in the days of Ar-Sakalthôr father of Ar-Gimilzôr. Gimilzôr took her to wife, though this was little to her liking, for she was in heart one of the Faithful, being taught by her mother; but the kings and their sons were grown proud and not to be gainsaid in their wishes. No love was there between Ar-Gimilzôr and his queen, or between their sons. Inziladûn, the elder, was like his mother in mind as in body; but Gimilkhâd, the younger, went with his father, unless he were yet prouder and more wilful. To him Ar-Gimilzôr would have yielded the sceptre rather than to the elder son, if the laws had allowed.[7]

# 3175 – REPENTANCE OF TAR-PALANTIR.
## CIVIL WAR IN NÚMENOR.

### KINGS AND QUEENS OF NÚMENOR XXIV:
Tar-Palantir (Ar-Inziladûn[1])
Born: SA 3035; Died: SA 3255 (age 220)
Rule: SA 3175-3255 (80 years)[2]

When Inziladûn acceded to the sceptre, he took again a title in the Elven-tongue as of old, calling himself Tar-Palantir, for he was far-sighted both in eye and in mind, and even those that hated him feared his words as those of a true-seer.[3]

Tar-Palantir repented of the ways of the Kings before him, and would fain have returned to the friendship of the Eldar and the Lords of the West.[4]

He gave peace for a while to the Faithful; and he went once more at due seasons to the Hallow of Eru upon the Meneltarma, which Ar-Gimilzôr had forsaken. The White Tree he tended again with honour; and he prophesied, saying that when the

Tree perished, then also would the line of the Kings come to its end. But his repentance was too late to appease the anger of the Valar with the insolence of his fathers, of which the greater part of his people did not repent. And Gimilkhâd [the King's brother] was strong and ungentle, and [following the ways of Ar-Gimilzôr], he took the leadership of those that had been called the King's Men and opposed the will of his brother as openly as he dared, and yet more in secret. Thus the days of Tar-Palantir became darkened with grief; and he would spend much of his time in the west, and there ascended often the ancient tower of King Minastir upon the hill of Oromet nigh to Andúnië, whence he gazed westward in yearning, hoping to see, maybe, some sail upon the sea. But no ship came ever again from the West to Númenor, and Avallónë was veiled in cloud.[5]

He also would spend much of his days in Andúnië, since Lindórie his mother's mother was of the kin of the Lords, being sister indeed of Eärendur, the fifteenth Lord and grandfather of Númendil, who was Lord of Andúnië in the days of Tar-Palantir his cousin.[6]

[Tar-Palantir's brother,] Gimilkhâd, died two years before his two hundredth year (which was accounted an early death for one of Elros' line even in its waning), but this brought no peace to the King. For Pharazôn son of Gimilkhâd [and nephew to the King] had become a man yet more restless and eager for wealth and power than his father.[7]

[Ar-Pharazôn] was a man of great beauty and strength/ stature after the image of the first kings, and indeed in his youth was not unlike the Edain of old in mind also, though he had [courage and] strength of will rather than of wisdom as after appeared, when he was corrupted by the counsels of his father and the acclaim of the people. In his earlier days he had a close friendship with Amandil who was afterwards Lord of Andúnië, and he had loved the people of the House of Valandil with whom he had kinship (through Inzilbêth his father's mother). With them he was often a guest, and there came Zimraphel [named Míriel in the Elven-tongue] his cousin, daughter of Inziladûn who was later King Tar-Palantir.[8]

Now Zimraphel . . . was a woman of great beauty, smaller [?in . . . stature] than were most women of that land, with bright eyes. . . . She was older than Pharazôn by one year, but seemed younger. . . .

Elentir the brother of Amandil loved [Míriel], but when first she saw Pharazôn . . . in the splendour of his young manhood . . . and when Pharazôn was greeted upon the steps of the house . . . her eyes and her heart were turned to him, for his beauty, and for his wealth also.
[And Pharazôn] went away and [Míriel] remained unwed.[9]

[Pharazôn] had fared often abroad, as a leader in the wars that the Númenóreans made then in the coastlands of Middle-earth, seeking to extend their dominion over Men; and thus he had won great renown as a captain both by land and by sea. Therefore when he came back to Númenor, hearing of his father's death, the hearts of the people were turned to him; for he brought with him great wealth, and was for the time free in his giving.[10]

And it came to pass that Tar-Palantir grew weary of grief and died. He had [married late and had] no son, but a daughter only [born in the year 3117], whom he named Míriel in the Elven-tongue; and to her now by right and the laws of the Númenóreans came the sceptre. But Pharazôn took her to wife against her will, doing evil in this and evil also in that the laws of Númenor did not permit the marriage, even in the royal house, of those more nearly akin than cousins in the second degree. And when they were wedded, he seized the sceptre into his own hand, taking the title of Ar-Pharazôn (Tar-Calion in the Elven-tongue); and the name of his queen he changed to Ar-Zimraphel.[11]

# 3255 – AR-PHARAZÔN THE GOLDEN SEIZES THE SCEPTRE.

### KINGS AND QUEENS OF NÚMENOR:
### Tar-Míriel (Ar-Zimraphel)
Born: SA 3117; Died in the Downfall: SA 3319 (age 202)
Rule: Although rightfully twenty-fifth ruler of Númenor, she did
not succeed her father due to her having surrendered the sceptre
to Ar-Pharazôn.

She would be Queen Regnant for the brief period in SA 3319
between Ar-Pharazôn embarking for his assault on Valinor and
the final drowning of Númenor.

### 3255 – KINGS AND QUEENS OF NÚMENOR XXV:
### Ar-Pharazôn (Tar-Calion)
Born: SA 3118; Died in the Downfall: SA 3319 (age 201)
Rule (by usurpation): SA 3255-3319 (64 years)

The mightiest and proudest was Ar-Pharazôn the Golden of all those that had wielded the Sceptre of the Sea-Kings since the foundation of Númenor; and four and twenty Kings and Queens had ruled the Númenóreans before, and slept now in their deep tombs under the mount of Meneltarma, lying upon beds of gold.[1]

No less than the kingship of the world was his desire.[2]

The Elendili ['Elf-friends', 'The Faithful'] alone were not subservient to [Ar-Pharazôn], or dared to speak against his wishes, and it became well-known to all in that time that Amandil the Lord of Andúnië was head of their party though not openly declared. Therefore Ar-Pharazôn persecuted the Faithful, stripping them of any wealth that they had, and he deprived the heirs of Valandil of their lordship.[3]

Andúnië he took then and made it the chief harbour of the king's ships, and Amandil the Lord he commanded to dwell in Rómenna. Yet he did not otherwise molest him, nor dismiss him yet from his Council. For in the days of his youth (ere his father corrupted him) Amandil had been his dear friend.[4] And Amandil was well beloved also by many who were not of the Elendili.[5]

Describing the change that had overtaken the Númenóreans, J.R.R. Tolkien wrote in the letter to Milton Waldman, penned in 1951:[6]

*Númenor* has grown in wealth, wisdom, and glory, under its line of great kings of long life, directly descended from Elros, Eärendil's son, brother of Elrond. The *Downfall of Númenor*, the Second Fall of Man (or Man rehabilitated but still mortal), brings on the catastrophic end, not only of the Second Age, but of the Old World, the primeval world of legend (envisaged as flat and bounded). After which the Third Age began, a Twilight Age, a Medium Aevum, the first of the broken and changed world; the last of the lingering dominion of visible fully incarnate Elves, and the last also in which Evil assumes a single dominant incarnate shape.

*The Downfall* [that will follow] is partly the result of an inner weakness in Men – consequent, if you will, upon the first Fall (unrecorded in these tales), repented but not finally healed. Reward on earth is more dangerous for men than punishment! The Fall is achieved by the cunning of Sauron in exploiting this weakness. Its central theme is (inevitably, I think, in a story of Men) a Ban, or Prohibition.

The Númenóreans dwell within far sight of the easternmost 'immortal' land, Eressëa; and as the only men to speak an Elvish tongue (learned in the days of their Alliance) they are in constant communication with their ancient friends and allies, either in the bliss of Eressëa, or in the kingdom of Gil-galad on the shores of Middle-earth. They became thus in appearance, and even in powers of mind, hardly distinguishable from the Elves – but they remained mortal, even though rewarded by a triple, or more than a triple, span of years. Their reward is their undoing – or the means of their temptation. Their long life aids their achievements in art and wisdom, but breeds a possessive attitude to these things, and desire awakes for more *time* for their enjoyment. Foreseeing this in part, the gods laid a Ban on the Númenóreans from the beginning: they must never sail to Eressëa, nor westward out of sight of their own land. In all other directions they could go as they would. They must not set foot on 'immortal' lands, and so become enamoured of an immortality (within the world), which was against their law, the special doom or gift of Ilúvatar (God), and which their nature could not in fact endure.[*]

---

[*] The view is taken (as clearly reappears later in the case of the Hobbits that have the Ring for a while) that each 'Kind' has a natural span, integral to its biological and spiritual nature. This cannot really be *increased* qualitatively or quantitatively; so that prolongation in time is like stretching a wire out ever tauter, or 'spreading butter ever thinner' – it becomes an intolerable torment.

There are three phases in their fall from grace. First acquiescence, obedience that is free and willing, though without complete understanding. Then for long they obey unwillingly, murmuring more and more openly. Finally they rebel – and a rift appears between the King's men and rebels, and the small minority of persecuted Faithful.

In the first stage, being men of peace, their courage is devoted to sea-voyages. As descendants of Eärendil, they became the supreme mariners, and being barred from the West, they sail to the uttermost north, and south, and east. Mostly they come to the west-shores of Middle-earth, where they aid the Elves and Men against Sauron, and incur his undying hatred. In those days they would come amongst Wild Men as almost divine benefactors, bringing gifts of arts and knowledge, and passing away again – leaving many legends behind of kings and gods out of the sunset.

In the second stage, the days of Pride and Glory and grudging of the Ban, they begin to seek wealth rather than bliss. The desire to escape death produced a cult of the dead, and they lavished wealth and art on tombs and memorials. They now made settlements on the west-shores, but these became rather strongholds and 'factories' of lords seeking wealth, and the Númenóreans became tax-gatherers carrying off over the sea ever more and more goods in their great ships. The Númenóreans began the forging of arms and engines.

This phase ended and the last began with the ascent of the throne by the [twenty-fifth] king of the line of Elros, Tar-Calion the Golden [Ar-Pharazôn], the most powerful and proud of all kings.

## 3261 – AR-PHARAZÔN SETS SAIL AND
## LANDS AT UMBAR.

Now Sauron knowing of the dissension in Númenor thought how he might use it to achieve his revenge. He began therefore to assail the havens and forts of the Númenóreans, and invaded the coast-lands under their dominion. As he foresaw this aroused the great wrath of the King, who resolved to challenge Sauron the Great for the lordship of Middle-earth.[1]

Mariners of Númenor brought rumour of him. Some said that he was a king greater than the King of Númenor; some said that he was one of the Gods or their sons set to govern Middle-earth. A few reported that he was an evil spirit, perchance Morgoth himself returned. But this was held to be only a foolish fable of the wild Men. . . . The Lords sent messages to the king and spake through the mouths of wise men and counselled him against this mission; for they said that Sauron would work evil if he came.[2]

And sitting upon his carven throne in the city of Armenelos in the glory of his power, [Ar-Pharazôn] brooded darkly, thinking of war. For he had learned in Middle-earth of the strength of the realm of Sauron, and of his hatred of Westernesse.

And now there came to him the masters of ships and captains returning out of the East, and they reported that Sauron was putting forth his might, since Ar-Pharazôn had gone back from Middle-earth, and he was pressing down upon the cities by the coasts; and he had taken now the title of King of Men, and declared his purpose to drive the Númenóreans into the sea, and destroy even Númenor, if that might be.

Great was the anger of Ar-Pharazôn at these tidings, and as he pondered long in secret, his heart was filled with the desire of power unbounded and the sole dominion of his will. And he determined without counsel of the Valar, or the aid of any wisdom but his own, that the title of King of Men he would himself claim, and would compel Sauron to become his vassal and his servant; for in his pride he deemed that no king should ever arise so mighty as to vie with the Heir of Eärendil. Therefore he began in that time to smithy great hoard of weapons, and many ships of war he built and stored them with his arms; [for five years Ar-Pharazôn prepared] and when all was made ready he himself set sail with his host into the East.

And men saw [Ar-Pharazôn's] sails coming up out of the sunset, dyed as with scarlet and gleaming with red gold, and fear fell upon the dwellers by the coasts, and they fled far away. But the fleet came at last to that place that was called Umbar, where was the mighty haven of the Númenóreans that no hand had wrought.³ Empty and silent were all the lands about when the King of the Sea marched upon Middle-earth. For seven days he journeyed with banner and trumpet, and he came to a hill, and he went up, and he set there his pavilion and his throne; and he sat him down in the midst of the land, and the tents of his host were ranged all about him, blue, golden, and white, as a field of tall flowers. Then he sent forth heralds, and he commanded Sauron to come before him and swear to him fealty.

And Sauron came. Even from his mighty tower of Barad-dûr he came, and made no offer of battle. For he perceived that the power and majesty of the Kings of the Sea surpassed all rumour of them, so that he could not trust even the greatest of his servants to withstand them; and he saw not his time yet to work his will with the Dúnedain. And he was crafty, well skilled to gain what he would by subtlety when force might not avail. Therefore he humbled himself before Ar-Pharazôn and smoothed his tongue; and men wondered, for all that he said seemed fair and wise.

But Ar-Pharazôn was not yet deceived, and it came into his mind that, for the better keeping of Sauron and of his oaths of fealty, he should be brought to Númenor, there to dwell as a hostage for himself and all his servants in Middle-earth. To this Sauron assented as one constrained, yet in his secret thought he received it gladly, for it chimed indeed with his desire.[4]

'This is a hard doom,' said Sauron, 'but great kings must have their will', and he submitted as one under compulsion, concealing his delight; for things had fallen out according to his design.[5]

## 3262 – SAURON IS TAKEN AS PRISONER TO NÚMENOR; 3262–3310 SAURON SEDUCES THE KING AND CORRUPTS THE NÚMENÓREANS.

Hoping to accomplish by cunning what he could not achieve by force[1]. . . . Sauron passed over the sea and looked upon the land of Númenor, and on the city of Armenelos in the days of its glory, and he was astounded; but his heart within was filled the more with envy and hate.

Yet such was the cunning of his mind and mouth, and the strength of his hidden will, that ere three years had passed he had become closest to the secret counsels of the King; for flattery sweet as honey was ever on his tongue, and knowledge he had of many things yet unrevealed to Men.[2]

Now Sauron had great wisdom and knowledge, and could find words of seeming reason for the persuasion of all but the most wary; and he could still assume a fair countenance when he wished. . . .

'Great kings must have their will': this was the burden of all his advice; and whatever the King desired he said was his right, and devised plans whereby he might gain it.[3]

\* \* \*

And seeing the favour that he had of their lord all the councillors began to fawn upon him, save one alone, Amandil lord of Andúnië. Then slowly a change came over the land, and the hearts of the Elf-friends were sorely troubled, and many fell away out of fear; and although those that remained still called themselves the Faithful, their enemies named them rebels. For now, having the ears of men, Sauron with many arguments gainsaid all that the Valar had taught; and he bade men think that in the world, in the east and even in the west, there lay yet many seas and many lands for their winning, wherein was wealth uncounted. And still, if they should at the last come to the end of those lands and seas, beyond all lay the Ancient Darkness. 'And out of it the world was made. For Darkness alone is worshipful, and the Lord thereof may yet make other worlds to be gifts to those that serve him, so that the increase of their power shall find no end.'

And Ar-Pharazôn said: 'Who is the Lord of the Darkness?'

Then behind locked doors Sauron spoke to the King, and he lied, saying: 'It is he whose name is not now spoken; for the Valar have deceived you concerning him, putting forward the name of Eru, a phantom devised in the folly of their hearts, seeking to enchain Men in servitude to themselves. For they are the oracle of this Eru, which speaks only what they will. But he that is their master shall yet prevail, and he will deliver you from this phantom; and his name is Melkor, Lord of All, Giver of Freedom, and he shall make you stronger than they.'

Then Ar-Pharazôn the King turned back to the worship of the Dark, and of Melkor the Lord thereof, at first in secret, but ere long openly and in the face of his people; and they for the most part followed him. Yet there dwelt still a remnant of the Faithful, as has been told, at Rómenna and in the country near, and other few there were here and there in the land. The chief among them, to whom they looked for leading and courage in evil days, was Amandil, councillor of the King, and his son Elendil, whose sons were Isildur and Anárion, then young men by the reckoning of Númenor. Amandil and Elendil were great ship-captains; and they were of the line of Elros Tar-Minyatur, though not of the ruling house to whom belonged the crown and the throne in the city of Armenelos. In the days of their youth together Amandil had been dear to Pharazôn, and though he was of the Elf-friends he remained in his council until the coming of Sauron. Now he was dismissed, for Sauron hated him above all others in Númenor. But he was so noble, and had been so mighty a captain of the sea, that he was still held in honour by many of the people, and neither the King nor Sauron dared to lay hands on him as yet.

Therefore Amandil withdrew to Rómenna, and all that he trusted still to be faithful he summoned to come thither in secret; for he feared that evil would now grow apace, and all the Elf-friends were in peril. And so it soon came to pass. For the Meneltarma was utterly deserted in those days; and though not even Sauron dared to defile the high place, yet the King would let no man, upon pain of death, ascend to it, not even those of the Faithful who kept Ilúvatar in their hearts. And Sauron urged the King to cut down the White Tree, Nimloth the Fair, that grew in his courts, for it was a memorial of the Eldar and of the light of Valinor.

At the first the King would not assent to this, since he believed that the fortunes of his house were bound up with the Tree, as was forespoken by Tar-Palantir. Thus in his folly he who now hated the Eldar and the Valar vainly clung to the shadow of the old allegiance of Númenor. But when Amandil heard rumour of the evil purpose of Sauron he was grieved to the heart, knowing that in the end Sauron would surely have his will. Then he spoke to Elendil and the sons of Elendil, recalling the tale of the Trees of Valinor; and Isildur said no word, but went out by night and did a deed for which he was afterwards renowned. For he passed alone in disguise to Armenelos and to the courts of the King, which were now forbidden to the Faithful; and he came to the place of the Tree, which was forbidden to all by the orders of Sauron, and the Tree was watched day and night by guards in his service. At that time Nimloth was dark and bore no bloom, for it was late in the autumn, and its winter was nigh; and Isildur passed through the guards and took from the Tree a fruit that hung upon it, and turned to go. But the guard was aroused, and he was assailed, and fought his way out, receiving many wounds; and he escaped, and because he was disguised it was not discovered who had laid hands on the Tree. But Isildur came at last hardly back to Rómenna and delivered the fruit to the hands of Amandil, ere his strength failed him. Then the fruit was planted in secret, and it was blessed by Amandil; and a shoot arose from it and sprouted in the spring. But when its first leaf opened then Isildur, who had lain long and come near to death, arose and was troubled no more by his wounds.

None too soon was this done; for after the assault the King yielded to Sauron and felled the White Tree, and turned then wholly away from the allegiance of his fathers. But Sauron caused to be built upon the hill in the midst of the city of the Númenóreans, Armenelos the Golden, a mighty temple; and it was in the form of a circle at the base, and there the walls were fifty feet in thickness, and the width of the base was five hundred feet across the centre, and the walls rose from the ground five hundred feet, and they were crowned with a mighty dome. And that dome was roofed all with silver, and rose glittering in the sun, so that the light of it could be seen afar off; but soon the light was darkened, and the silver became black. For there was an altar of fire in the midst of the temple, and in the topmost of the dome there was a louver, whence there issued a great smoke. And the first fire upon the altar Sauron kindled with the hewn wood of Nimloth, and it crackled and was consumed; but men marvelled at the reek that went up from it, so that the land lay under a cloud for seven days, until slowly it passed into the west.

Thereafter the fire and smoke went up without ceasing; for the power of Sauron daily increased, and in that temple, with spilling of blood and torment and great wickedness, men made sacrifice to Melkor that he should release them from Death.

And most often from among the Faithful they chose their victims; yet never openly on the charge that they would not worship Melkor, the Giver of Freedom, rather was cause sought against them that they hated the King and were his rebels, or that they plotted against their kin, devising lies and poisons. These charges were for the most part false; yet those were bitter days, and hate brings forth hate.

But for all this Death did not depart from the land, rather it came sooner and more often, and in many dreadful guises. For whereas aforetime men had grown slowly old, and had laid them down in the end to sleep, when they were weary at last of the world, now madness and sickness assailed them; and yet they were afraid to die and go out into the dark, the realm of the lord that they had taken; and they cursed themselves in their agony. And men took weapons in those days and slew one another for little cause; for they were become quick to anger, and Sauron, or those whom he had bound to himself, went about the land setting man against man, so that the people murmured against the King and the lords, or against any that had aught that they had not; and the men of power took cruel revenge.

Nonetheless for long it seemed to the Númenóreans that they prospered, and if they were not increased in happiness, yet they grew more strong, and their rich men ever richer. For with the aid and counsel of Sauron they multiplied their possessions, and they devised engines, and they built ever greater ships. And they sailed now with power and armoury to Middle-earth, and they came no longer as bringers of gifts, nor even as rulers, but as fierce men of war. And they hunted the men of Middle-earth and took their goods and enslaved them, and many they slew cruelly upon their altars. For they built in their fortresses temples and great tombs in those days; and men feared them, and the memory of the kindly kings of the ancient days faded from the world and was darkened by many a tale of dread.

Thus Ar-Pharazôn, King of the Land of the Star, grew to the mightiest tyrant that had yet been in the world since the

reign of Morgoth, though in truth Sauron ruled all from behind
the throne.[4]

So great was his power over the hearts of the most of that
people that maybe had he wished he could have taken the
sceptre; but all that he wished was to bring Númenór to ruin.
Therefore he said to the King: 'One thing only now you lack
to make you the greatest King in the world, the undying life
that is withheld from you in fear and jealousy by the lying
Powers in the West. But great kings take what is their right.'
And Ar-Pharazôn pondered these words, but for long fear held
him back.[5]

But the years passed, and the King felt the shadow of death
approach, as his days lengthened; and he was filled with fear
and wrath. Now came the hour that Sauron had prepared and
long had awaited. And Sauron spoke to the King, saying that
his strength was now so great that he might think to have his
will in all things, and be subject to no command or ban.

And he said: 'The Valar have possessed themselves of the
land where there is no death; and they lie to you concerning it,
hiding it as best they may, because of their avarice, and their
fear lest the Kings of Men should wrest from them the deathless
realm and rule the world in their stead. And though, doubtless,
the gift of life unending is not for all, but only for such as are
worthy, being men of might and pride and great lineage, yet
against all justice is it done that this gift, which is his due,
should be withheld from the King of Kings, Ar-Pharazôn,
mightiest of the sons of Earth, to whom Manwë alone can be
compared, if even he. But great kings do not brook denials, and
take what is their due.'

Then Ar-Pharazôn, being besotted, and walking under the
shadow of death, for his span was drawing towards its end,
hearkened to Sauron; and he began to ponder in his heart how
he might make war upon the Valar.[6]

## 3310 – AR-PHARAZÔN BEGINS THE BUILDING
## OF THE GREAT ARMAMENT.[1]

[Ar-Pharazôn] began to prepare a vast armament for the assault upon Valinor, that should surpass the one with which he had come to Umbar even as a great galleon of Númenor surpassed a fisherman's boat.[2]

He was long preparing this design, and he spoke not openly of it, yet it could not be hidden from all. And Amandil, becoming aware of the purposes of the King, was dismayed and filled with a great dread, for he knew that Men could not vanquish the Valar in war, and that ruin must come upon the world, if this war were not stayed. Therefore he called his son, Elendil, and he said to him:

'The days are dark, and there is no hope in Men, for the Faithful are few. Therefore I am minded to try that counsel which our forefather Eärendil took of old, to sail into the West, be there ban or no, and to speak to the Valar, even to Manwë himself, if may be, and beseech his aid ere all is lost.'[3]

'Would you then betray the King?' said Elendil. 'For you know well the charge that they make against us, that we are traitors and spies, and that until this day it has been false.'

'If I thought that Manwë needed such a messenger,' said Amandil, 'I would betray the King. For there is but one loyalty from which no man can be absolved in heart for any cause. But it is for mercy upon Men and their deliverance from Sauron the Deceiver that I would plead, since some at least have remained faithful. And as for the Ban, I will suffer in myself the penalty, lest all my people should become guilty.'

'But what think you, my father, is like to befall those of your house whom you leave behind, when your deed becomes known?'

'It must not become known,' said Amandil. 'I will prepare my going in secret, and I will set sail into the east, whither daily the ships depart from our havens; and thereafter, as wind and chance may allow, I will go about, through south or north, back into the west, and seek what I may find. But for you and your folk, my son, I counsel that you should prepare yourselves other ships, and put aboard all such things as your hearts cannot bear to part with; and when the ships are ready, you should lie in the haven of Rómenna, and give out among men that you purpose, when you see your time, to follow me into the east. Amandil is no longer so dear to our kinsman upon the throne that he will grieve over much, if we seek to depart, for a season or for good. But let it not be seen that you intend to take many men, or he will be troubled, because of the war that he now plots, for which he will need all the force that he may gather. Seek out the Faithful that are known still to be true, and let them join you in secret, if they are willing to go with you, and share in your design.'

'And what shall that design be?' said Elendil.

'To meddle not in the war, and to watch,' answered Amandil. 'Until I return I can say no more. But it is most like that you shall fly from the Land of the Star with no star to guide you; for that land is defiled. Then you shall lose all that you have loved, foretasting death in life, seeking a land of exile elsewhere. But east or west the Valar alone can say.'

Then Amandil said farewell to all his household, as one that is about to die. 'For,' said he, 'it may well prove that you will see me never again; and that I shall show you no such sign as Eärendil showed long ago. But hold you ever in readiness, for the end of the world that we have known is now at hand.'

It is said that Amandil set sail in a small ship at night, and steered first eastward, and then went about and passed into the west. And he took with him three servants, dear to his heart, and never again were they heard of by word or sign in this world, nor is there any tale or guess of their fate. Men could not a second time be saved by any such embassy, and for the treason of Númenor there was no easy absolving.

But Elendil did all that his father had bidden, and his ships lay off the east coast of the land; and the Faithful put aboard their wives and their children, and their heirlooms, and great store of goods. Many things there were of beauty and power, such as the Númenóreans had contrived in the days of their wisdom, vessels and jewels, and scrolls of lore written in scarlet and black. And Seven Stones they had, the gift of the Eldar; but in the ship of Isildur was guarded the young tree, the scion of Nimloth the Fair. Thus Elendil held himself in readiness, and did not meddle in the evil deeds of those days; and ever he looked for a sign that did not come. Then he journeyed in secret to the western shores and gazed out over the sea, for sorrow and yearning were upon him, and he greatly loved his father. But naught could he descry save the fleets of Ar-Pharazôn gathering in the havens of the west.

Now aforetime in the isle of Númenor the weather was ever apt to the needs and liking of Men: rain in due season and ever in measure; and sunshine, now warmer, now cooler, and winds from the sea. And when the wind was in the west, it seemed to many that it was filled with a fragrance, fleeting but sweet, heart-stirring, as of flowers that bloom for ever in undying meads and have no names on mortal shores. But all this was now changed; for the sky itself was darkened, and there were storms of rain and hail in those days, and violent winds; and ever and anon a great ship of the Númenóreans would founder and return not to haven, though such a grief had not till then befallen them since the rising of the Star. And out of the west there would come at times a great cloud in the evening, shaped as it were an eagle, with pinions spread to the north and the south; and slowly it would loom up, blotting out the sunset, and then uttermost night would fall upon Númenor. And some of the eagles bore lightning beneath their wings, and thunder echoed between sea and cloud.

Then men grew afraid. 'Behold the Eagles of the Lords of the West!' they cried. 'The Eagles of Manwë are come upon Númenor!' And they fell upon their faces.

Then some few would repent for a season, but others hardened their hearts, and they shook their fists at heaven, saying: 'The Lords of the West have plotted against us. They strike first. The next blow shall be ours!' These words the King himself spoke, but they were devised by Sauron.

Now the lightnings increased and slew men upon the hills, and in the fields, and in the streets of the city; and a fiery bolt smote the dome of the Temple and shore it asunder, and it was wreathed in flame. But the Temple itself was unshaken, and Sauron stood there upon the pinnacle and defied the lightning and was unharmed; and in that hour men called him a god and did all that he would. When therefore the last portent came they heeded it little. For the land shook under them, and a groaning as of thunder underground was mingled with the roaring of the sea, and smoke issued from the peak of the Meneltarma. But all the more did Ar-Pharazôn press on with his armament.

### 3319 – AR-PHARAZÔN ASSAILS VALINOR. DOWNFALL OF NÚMENOR. ELENDIL AND HIS SONS ESCAPE.[1]

In that time the fleets of the Númenóreans darkened the sea upon the west of the land, and they were like an archipelago of a thousand isles; their masts were as a forest upon the mountains, and their sails like a brooding cloud; and their banners were golden and black. And all things waited upon the word of Ar-Pharazôn; and Sauron withdrew into the inmost circle of the Temple, and men brought him victims to be burned.

Then the Eagles of the Lords of the West came up out of the dayfall, and they were arrayed as for battle, advancing in a line the end of which diminished beyond sight; and as they came their wings spread ever wider, grasping the sky. But the West burned red behind them, and they glowed beneath, as though they were lit with a flame of great anger, so that all Númenor was illumined as with a smouldering fire; and men looked upon the faces of their fellows, and it seemed to them that they were red with wrath.

Then Ar-Pharazôn hardened his heart, and he went aboard his mighty ship, *Alcarondas*, Castle of the Sea. Many-oared it was and many-masted, golden and sable; and upon it the throne of Ar-Pharazôn was set. Then he did on his panoply and his crown, and let raise his standard, and he gave the signal for the raising of the anchors; and in that hour the trumpets of Númenor outrang the thunder.

Thus the fleets of the Númenóreans moved against the menace of the West; and there was little wind, but they had many oars and many strong slaves to row beneath the lash. The sun went down, and there came a great silence. Darkness fell upon the land, and the sea was still, while the world waited for what should betide. Slowly the fleets passed out of the sight of the watchers in the havens, and their lights faded, and night took them; and in the morning they were gone. For a wind arose in the east and it wafted them away; and they broke the Ban of the Valar, and sailed into forbidden seas, going up with war against the Deathless, to wrest from them everlasting life within the Circles of the World.

But the fleets of Ar-Pharazôn came up out of the deeps of the sea and encompassed Avallónë and all the isle of Eressëa, and the Eldar mourned, for the light of the setting sun was cut off by the cloud of the Númenóreans. And at last Ar-Pharazôn came even to Aman, the Blessed Realm, and the coasts of Valinor; and still all was silent, and doom hung by a thread. For Ar-Pharazôn wavered at the end, and almost he turned back. His heart misgave him when he looked upon the sound-less shores and saw Taniquetil shining, whiter than snow, colder than death, silent, immutable, terrible as the shadow of the light of Ilúvatar. But pride was now his master, and at last he left his ship and strode upon the shore, claiming the land for his own, if none should do battle for it. And a host of the Númenóreans encamped in might about Túna, whence all the Eldar had fled.

Then Manwë upon the Mountain called upon Ilúvatar, and for that time the Valar laid down their government of Arda. But Ilúvatar showed forth his power, and he changed the fashion of the world; and a great chasm opened in the sea between

Númenor and the Deathless Lands, and the waters flowed down into it, and the noise and smoke of the cataracts went up to heaven, and the world was shaken. And all the fleets of the Númenóreans were drawn down into the abyss, and they were drowned and swallowed up for ever. But Ar-Pharazôn the King and the mortal warriors that had set foot upon the land of Aman were buried under falling hills: there it is said that they lie imprisoned in the Caves of the Forgotten, until the Last Battle and the Day of Doom.

But the land of Aman and Eressëa of the Eldar were taken away and removed beyond the reach of Men for ever. And Andor, the Land of Gift, Númenor of the Kings, Elenna of the Star of Eärendil, was utterly destroyed. For it was nigh to the east of the great rift, and its foundations were overturned, and it fell and went down into darkness, and is no more. And there is not now upon Earth any place abiding where the memory of a time without evil is preserved. For Ilúvatar cast back the Great Seas west of Middle-earth, and the Empty Lands east of it, and new lands and new seas were made; and the world was diminished, for Valinor and Eressëa were taken from it into the realm of hidden things.

In an hour unlooked for by Men this doom befell, on the nine and thirtieth day since the passing of the fleets. Then suddenly fire burst from the Meneltarma, and there came a mighty wind and a tumult of the earth, and the sky reeled, and the hills slid, and Númenor went down into the sea, with all its children and its wives and its maidens and its ladies proud; and all its gardens and its halls and its towers, its tombs and its riches, and its jewels and its webs and its things painted and carven, and its laughter and its mirth and its music, its wisdom and its lore: they vanished for ever. And last of all the mounting wave, green and cold and plumed with foam, climbing over the land, took to its bosom Tar-Míriel the Queen, fairer than silver or ivory or pearls. Too late she strove to ascend the steep ways of the Meneltarma to the holy place; for the waters overtook her, and her cry was lost in the roaring of the wind.

But whether or no it were that Amandil came indeed to Valinor and Manwë hearkened to his prayer, by grace of the Valar Elendil and his sons and their people were spared from the ruin of that day. For Elendil had remained in Rómenna, refusing the summons of the King when he set forth to war; and avoiding the soldiers of Sauron that came to seize him and drag him to the fires of the Temple, he went aboard his ship and stood off from the shore, waiting on the time. There he was protected by the land from the great draught of the sea that drew all towards the abyss, and afterwards he was sheltered from the first fury of the storm. But when the devouring wave rolled over the land and Númenor toppled to its fall, then he would have been overwhelmed and would have deemed it the lesser grief to perish, for no wrench of death could be more bitter than the loss and agony of that day; but the great wind took him, wilder than any wind that Men had known, roaring from the west, and it swept his ships far away; and it rent their sails and snapped their masts, hunting the unhappy men like straws upon the water.

Nine ships there were: four for Elendil, and for Isildur three, and for Anárion two; and they fled before the black gale out of the twilight of doom into the darkness of the world. And the deeps rose beneath them in towering anger, and waves like unto mountains moving with great caps of writhen snow bore them up amid the wreckage of the clouds, and after many days cast them away upon the shores of Middle-earth. And all the coasts and seaward regions of the western world suffered great change and ruin in that time; for the seas invaded the lands, and shores foundered, and ancient isles were drowned, and new isles were uplifted; and hills crumbled and rivers were turned into strange courses.

Of the changes brought about in 'the tumult of the winds and seas that followed the Downfall' it is written in 'The Tale of Years of the Second Age', but nowhere else:

189

. . .in some places the sea rode in upon the land, and in others it piled up new coasts. Thus while Lindon suffered great loss, the Bay of Belfalas was much filled at the east and south, so that Pelargir which had been only a few miles from the sea was left far inland, and Anduin carved a new path by many mouths to the Bay. But the Isle of Tolfalas was almost destroyed, and was left at last like a barren and lonely mountain in the water not far from the issue of the River.[2]

Sauron himself was filled with great fear at the wrath of the Valar, and the doom that Eru laid upon sea and land. It was greater far than aught he had looked for, hoping only for the death of the Númenóreans and the defeat of their proud king. And Sauron, sitting in his black seat in the midst of the Temple, had laughed when he heard the trumpets of Ar-Pharazôn sounding for battle; and again he had laughed when he heard the thunder of the storm; and a third time, even as he laughed at his own thought, thinking what he would do now in the world, being rid of the Edain for ever, he was taken in the midst of his mirth, and his seat and his temple fell into the abyss. But Sauron was not of mortal flesh, and though he was robbed now of that shape in which he had wrought so great an evil, so that he could never again appear fair to the eyes of Men, yet his spirit arose out of the deep and passed as a shadow and a black wind over the sea. . . .

But these things come not into the tale of the Drowning of Númenor, of which now all is told. And even the name of that land perished, and Men spoke thereafter not of Elenna, nor of Andor the Gift that was taken away, nor of Númenórë on the confines of the world; but the exiles on the shores of the sea, if they turned towards the West in the desire of their hearts, spoke of Mar-nu Falmar that was whelmed in the waves, Akallabêth the Downfallen, Atalantë in the Eldarin tongue.[3]

So ended the Glory of Númenor.[4]

Among the Exiles many believed that the summit of the Meneltarma, the Pillar of Heaven, was not drowned for ever, but rose again above the waves, a lonely island lost in the great waters; for it had been a hallowed place, and even in the days of Sauron none had defiled it. And some there were of the seed of Eärendil that afterwards sought for it, because it was said among loremasters that the farsighted men of old could see from the Meneltarma a glimmer of the Deathless Land. For even after the ruin the hearts of the Dúnedain were still set westwards; and though they knew indeed that the world was changed, they said: 'Avallónë is vanished from the Earth and the Land of Aman is taken away, and in the world of this present darkness they cannot be found. Yet once they were, and therefore they still are, in true being and in the whole shape of the world as at first it was devised.'

For the Dúnedain held that even mortal Men, if so blessed, might look upon other times than those of their bodies' life; and they longed ever to escape from the shadows of their exile and to see in some fashion the light that dies not; for the sorrow of the thought of death had pursued them over the deeps of the sea. Thus it was that great mariners among them would still search the empty seas, hoping to come upon the Isle of Meneltarma, and there to see a vision of things that were. But they found it not. And those that sailed far came only to the new lands, and found them like to the old lands, and subject to death. And those that sailed furthest set but a girdle about the Earth and returned weary at last to the place of their beginning; and they said: 'All roads are now bent.'

Thus in after days, what by the voyages of ships, what by lore and star-craft, the kings of Men knew that the world was indeed made round, and yet the Eldar were permitted still to depart and to come to the Ancient West and to Avallónë, if they would. Therefore the loremasters of Men said that a Straight Road must still be, for those that were permitted to find it. And they taught that, while the new world fell away, the old road and the path of the memory of the West still went on, as it were a mighty bridge invisible that passed through the air of breath and of flight (which were bent now as the world was bent), and traversed Ilmen which flesh unaided cannot endure, until it came to Tol Eressëa, the Lonely Isle, and maybe even beyond, to Valinor, where the Valar still dwell and watch the unfolding of the story of the world. And tales and rumours arose along the shores of the sea concerning mariners and men forlorn upon the water who, by some fate or grace or favour of the Valar, had entered in upon the Straight Way and seen the face of the world sink below them, and so had come to the lamplit quays of Avallónë, or verily to the last beaches on the margin of Aman, and there had looked upon the White Mountain, dreadful and beautiful, before they died.[5]

In his letter to Milton Waldman, written three years before the publication of *The Fellowship of the Ring*, the author wrote of the disaster: 'Númenor itself on the edge of the rift topples and vanishes for ever with all its glory in the abyss. Thereafter there is no visible dwelling of the divine or immortal on earth. Valinor (or Paradise) and even Eressëa are removed, remaining only in the memory of the earth. Men may sail now West, if they will, as far as they may, and come no nearer to Valinor or the Blessed Realm, but return only into the east and so back again; for the world is round, and finite, and a circle inescapable – save by death. Only the "immortals", the lingering Elves, may still if they will, wearying of the circle of the world, take ship and find the "straight way", and come to the ancient or True West, and be at peace.'[6]

The flight of Elendil and the Exiles following the Downfall was memorialized in a song about the tall kings and their nine tall ships. It was a rhyme that came into the mind of Gandalf as he and Pippin rode on Shadowfax towards Minas Tirith:

*Tall ships and tall kings*
*Three times three,*
*What brought they from the foundered land*
*Over the flowing sea?*
*Seven stars and seven stones*
*And one white tree.*[7]

The calamitous events of the Downfall would live long in the memories of the peoples of Middle-earth. In the Third Age, as all awaited the final outcome to the War of the Ring, Faramir and Éowyn stood upon the walls of Minas Tirith, the City of Gondor, looking toward the east and Mordor:

It seemed to them that above the ridges of the distant mountains another vast mountain of darkness rose, towering up like a wave that should engulf the world, and about it lightnings flickered; and then a tremor ran through the earth, and they felt the walls of the City quiver. A sound like a sigh went up from all the lands about them; and their hearts beat suddenly again.

'It reminds me of Númenor,' said Faramir, and wondered to hear himself speak.

'Of Númenor?' said Éowyn.

'Yes,' said Faramir, 'of the land of Westernesse that foundered, and of the great dark wave climbing over the green lands and above the hills, and coming on, darkness unescapable. I often dream of it.'[8]

## 3320 – FOUNDATIONS OF THE REALMS IN EXILE: ARNOR AND GONDOR. THE STONES ARE DIVIDED. SAURON RETURNS TO MORDOR.

So the end of the Second Age draws on in a major catastrophe; but it is not yet quite concluded. From the cataclysm there are survivors. . . .[1]

The last leaders of the Faithful, Elendil and his sons, escaped from the Downfall with nine ships, bearing a seedling of Nimloth, and the Seven Seeing-stones (gifts of the Eldar to their House); and they were borne on the wind of a great storm and cast upon the shores of Middle-earth.[2]

*Et Eärello Endorenna utúlien. Sinome maruvan ar Hildinyar tenn' Ambar-metta!*

And those were the words that Elendil spoke when he came up out of the Sea on the wings of the wind: 'Out of the Great Sea to Middle-earth I am come. In this place will I abide, and my heirs, unto the ending of the world.'[3]

## THE NÚMENÓREAN KINGS IN EXILE:
Elendil of Númenor, High King of Gondor and Arnor[4]
Born: SA 3119; Died: SA 3441 (age 322)
Rule: SA 3320-3441 (121 years)

In that time those of the Númenóreans who were saved from destruction fled eastward, as is told in the *Akallabêth*. The chief of these were Elendil the Tall and his sons, Isildur and Anárion. Kinsmen of the King they were, descendants of Elros, but they had been unwilling to listen to Sauron, and had refused to make war on the Lords of the West. Manning their ships with all who remained faithful they forsook the land of Númenor ere ruin came upon it. They were mighty men and their ships were strong and tall, but the tempests overtook them, and they were borne aloft on hills of water even to the clouds, and they descended upon Middle-earth like birds of the storm.

Elendil was cast up by the waves in the land of Lindon, and he was befriended by Gil-galad. Thence he passed up the River Lhûn, and beyond Ered Luin he established his realm, and his people dwelt in many places in Eriador about the courses of the Lhûn and the Baranduin; but his chief city was at Annúminas beside the water of Lake Nenuial. At Fornost upon the North Downs also the Númenóreans dwelt, and in Cardolan, and in the hills of Rhudaur; and towers they raised upon Emyn Beraid and upon Amon Sûl; and there remain many barrows and ruined works in those places, but the towers of Emyn Beraid still look towards the sea.

Isildur and Anárion were borne away southwards, and at the last they brought their ships up the Great River Anduin, that flows out of Rhovanion into the western sea in the Bay of Belfalas; and they established a realm in those lands that were after called Gondor, whereas the Northern Kingdom was named Arnor. Long before in the days of their power the mariners of Númenor had established a haven and strong places about the mouths of Anduin, in despite of Sauron in the Black Land that lay nigh upon the east. In the later days to this haven came only the Faithful of Númenor, and many therefore of the folk of the coastlands in that region were in whole or in part akin to the Elf-friends and the people of Elendil, and they welcomed his sons. The chief city of this southern realm was Osgiliath, through the midst of which the Great River flowed; and the Númenóreans built there a great bridge, upon which there were towers and houses of stone wonderful to behold, and tall ships came up out of the sea to the quays of the city. Other strong places they built also upon either hand: Minas Ithil, the Tower of the Rising Moon, eastward upon a shoulder of the Mountains of Shadow as a threat to Mordor; and to the westward Minas Anor, the Tower of the Setting Sun, at the feet of Mount Mindolluin, as a shield against the wild men of the dales. In Minas Ithil was the house of Isildur, and in Minas Anor the house of Anárion, but they shared the realm between them and their thrones were set side by side in the Great Hall of Osgiliath. These were the chief dwellings of the Númenóreans in Gondor, but other works marvellous and strong they built in the land in the days of their power, at the Argonath, and at Aglarond, and at Erech; and in the circle of Angrenost, which Men called Isengard, they made the Pinnacle of Orthanc of unbreakable stone.

Many treasures and great heirlooms[5] of virtue and wonder the Exiles had brought from Númenor; and of these the most renowned were the Seven Stones and the White Tree. The White Tree was grown from the fruit of Nimloth the Fair that stood in the courts of the King at Armenelos in Númenor, ere Sauron burned it; and Nimloth was in its turn descended from the Tree of Tirion, that was an image of the Eldest of Trees, White Telperion which Yavanna caused to grow in the land of the Valar. The Tree, memorial of the Eldar and of the light of

Valinor, was planted in Minas Ithil before the house of Isildur, since he it was that had saved the fruit from destruction[6]; but the Stones were divided.

Elendil, Isildur and Anárion divided among them the seven Seeing-stones:

Three Elendil took, and his sons each two. Those of Elendil were set in towers upon Emyn Beraid, and upon Amon Sûl, and in the city of Annúminas. But those of his sons were at Minas Ithil and Minas Anor, and at Orthanc and in Osgiliath. Now these Stones had this virtue that those who looked therein might perceive in them things far off, whether in place or in time. For the most part they revealed only things near to another kindred Stone, for the Stones each called to each; but those who possessed great strength of will and of mind might learn to direct their gaze whither they would. Thus the Númenóreans were aware of many things that their enemies wished to conceal, and little escaped their vigilance in the days of their might.

It is said that the towers of Emyn Beraid were not built indeed by the Exiles of Númenor, but were raised by Gil-galad for Elendil, his friend; and the Seeing Stone of Emyn Beraid was set in Elostirion, the tallest of the towers. Thither Elendil would repair, and thence he would gaze out over the sundering seas, when the yearning of exile was upon him; and it is believed that thus he would at whiles see far away even the Tower of Avallónë upon Eressëa, where the Master-stone abode, and yet abides. These stones were gifts of the Eldar to Amandil, father of Elendil, for the comfort of the Faithful of Númenor in their dark days, when the Elves might come no longer to that land under the shadow of Sauron. They were called the Palantíri, those that watch from afar; but all those that were brought to Middle-earth long ago were lost.[7]

Speaking of the Seeing-stones, Gandalf said: 'The *palantíri* came from beyond Westernesse, from Eldamar. The Noldor made them. Fëanor himself, maybe, wrought them, in days so long ago that the time cannot be measured in years. But there is nothing that Sauron cannot turn to evil uses. . . . Perilous to us all are the devices of an art deeper than we possess ourselves. . . .'[8]

In the last days of the Second Age 'the Exiles of Númenor established their realms in Arnor and in Gondor; but ere many years had passed it became manifest that their enemy, Sauron, had also returned'.[9]

[The ruin of Númenor] was more terrible than Sauron had foreseen, for he had forgotten the might of the Lords of the West in their anger.[10]

This good at least [the Exiles] believed had come out of ruin, that Sauron also had perished.

But it was not so. Sauron was indeed caught in the wreck of Númenor, so that the bodily form in which he long had walked perished; but he fled back to Middle-earth, a spirit of hatred borne upon a dark wind. He was unable ever again to assume a form that seemed fair to men, but became black and hideous, and his power thereafter was through terror alone.[11]

He came in secret, as has been told, to his ancient kingdom of Mordor beyond the Ephel Dúath, the Mountains of Shadow, and that country marched with Gondor upon the east. There above the valley of Gorgoroth was built his fortress vast and strong, Barad-dûr, the Dark Tower; and there was a fiery mountain in that land that the Elves named Orodruin. Indeed for that reason Sauron had set there his dwelling long before, for he used the fire that welled there from the heart of the earth in his sorceries and in his forging; and in the midst of the Land of Mordor he had fashioned the Ruling Ring. There now he brooded in the dark, until he had wrought for himself a new shape; and it was terrible, for his fair semblance had departed for ever when he was cast into the abyss at the drowning of Númenor. He took up again the great Ring and clothed himself in power; and the malice of the Eye of Sauron few even of the great among Elves and Men could endure.[12]

[Sauron's] anger was great when he learned that Elendil, whom he most hated, had escaped him, and was now ordering a realm upon his borders.[13]

Now Sauron prepared war against the Eldar and the Men of Westernesse, and the fires of the Mountain were wakened again. Wherefore seeing the smoke of Orodruin from afar, and perceiving that Sauron had returned, the Númenóreans named that mountain anew Amon Amarth, which is Mount Doom. And Sauron gathered to him great strength of his servants out of the east and the south; and among them were not a few of the high race of Númenor. For in the days of the sojourn of Sauron in that land the hearts of well nigh all its people had been turned towards darkness. Therefore many of those who sailed east in that time and made fortresses and dwellings upon the coasts were already bent to his will, and they served him still gladly in Middle-earth. But because of the power of Gil-galad these renegades, lords both mighty and evil, for the most part took up their abodes in the southlands far away; yet two there were, Herumor and Fuinur, who rose to power among the Haradrim, a great and cruel people that dwelt in the wide lands south of Mordor beyond the mouths of Anduin.[14]

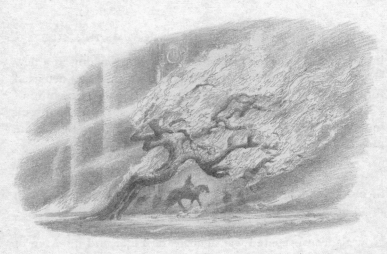

## 3429 – SAURON ATTACKS GONDOR, TAKES MINAS ITHIL AND BURNS THE WHITE TREE. ISILDUR ESCAPES DOWN ANDUIN AND GOES TO ELENDIL IN THE NORTH. ANÁRION DEFENDS MINAS ANOR AND OSGILIATH.

When therefore Sauron saw his time he came with great force against the new realm of Gondor, and he took Minas Ithil, and he destroyed the White Tree of Isildur that grew there. But Isildur escaped, and taking with him a seedling of the Tree he went with his wife and his sons by ship down the River, and they sailed from the mouths of Anduin seeking Elendil. Meanwhile Anárion held Osgiliath against the Enemy, and for that time drove him back to the mountains; but Sauron gathered his strength again, and Anárion knew that unless help should come his kingdom would not long stand.[1]

As Gandalf would later tell Frodo: 'The strength of the Elves to resist him was greater long ago; and not all Men were estranged from them. The Men of Westernesse came to their aid. That is a chapter of ancient history which it might be good to recall; for there was sorrow then too, and gathering dark, but great valour, and great deeds that were not wholly vain.'[2]

## 3430 – THE LAST ALLIANCE OF ELVES AND MEN IS FORMED.

Now Elendil and Gil-galad took counsel together, for they perceived that Sauron would grow too strong and would overcome all his enemies one by one, if they did not unite against him. Therefore they made that League which is called the Last Alliance.[1]

During the hobbits' journey towards Rivendell, Strider alludes briefly to Elendil, Gil-galad and their Alliance with reference to Weathertop, the highest and most southerly of the Weather Hills of Northern Eriador overlooking the dwarven-made Great East Road:

'In the first days of the North Kingdom, they built a great watch-tower on Weathertop, Amon Sûl they called it. It was burned and broken, and nothing remains of it now but a tumbled ring, like a rough crown on the old hill's head. Yet once it was tall and fair. It is told that Elendil stood there watching for the coming of Gil-galad out of the West, in the days of the Last Alliance.'[2]

201

## 3431 – GIL-GALAD AND ELENDIL MARCH
## EAST TO IMLADRIS.

Gil-galad and Elendil marched east into Middle-earth gathering a great host of Elves and Men; and they halted for a while at Imladris. It is said that the host that was there assembled was fairer and more splendid in arms than any that has since been seen in Middle-earth, and none greater has been mustered since the host of the Valar went against Thangorodrim.[1]

Years later, during the Council of Elrond, the Master of Rivendell would recall that muster:

"'Then Elendil the Tall and his mighty sons, Isildur and Anárion, became great lords; and the North-realm they made in Arnor, and the South-realm in Gondor above the mouths of Anduin. But Sauron of Mordor assailed them, and they made the Last Alliance of Elves and Men, and the hosts of Gil-galad and Elendil were mustered in Arnor."

'Thereupon Elrond paused a while and sighed. "I remember well the splendour of their banners," he said. "It recalled to me the glory of the Elder Days and the hosts of Beleriand,

so many great princes and captains were assembled. And yet
not so many, nor so fair, as when Thangorodrim was broken,
and the Elves deemed that evil was ended for ever, and it was
not so."[2]

## 3434 – THE HOST OF THE ALLIANCE CROSSES THE MISTY MOUNTAINS. BATTLE OF DAGORLAD AND DEFEAT OF SAURON. SIEGE OF BARAD-DÛR BEGINS.

Sauron readied himself for an onslaught. One of the outcomes of Sauron's preparations for war was the disappearance from Middle-earth of the Entwives, mates to the Ents, 'Shepherds of the Trees', who, in the Third Age would play a significant role in the taking of Isengard. In a letter from 1954, J.R.R. Tolkien wrote:

I think that in fact the Entwives had disappeared for good, being destroyed with their gardens in the War of the Last Alliance (Second Age 3429-3441) when Sauron pursued a scorched earth policy and burned their land against the advance of the Allies down the Anduin. Some, of course, may have fled east, or even have become enslaved: tyrants even in such tales must have an economic and agricultural background to their soldiers and metal-workers. If any survived so, they would indeed be far estranged from the Ents, and any rapprochement would be difficult – unless experience of industrialized and militarized agriculture had made them a little more anarchic. I hope so. I don't know.[1]

The forces of the Alliance stayed three years at Imladris, doubtless formulating battle plans and equipping themselves for the conflict to come.

From Imladris they crossed the Misty Mountains by many passes and marched down the River Anduin, and so came at last upon the host of Sauron on Dagorlad, the Battle Plain, which lies before the gate of the Black Land.[2]

The Battle of Dagorlad was fought on a vast, dusty, featureless plain and was to be the greatest conflict of the Second Age, involving forces representing most of the races of Middle-earth.

All living things were divided in that day, and some of every kind, even of beasts and birds, were found in either host, save the Elves only. They alone were undivided and followed Gilgalad. Of the Dwarves few fought upon either side; but the kindred of Durin of Moria fought against Sauron.[3]

Among the forces that were numbered with the Alliance were two armies of Elves that had long chosen to keep themselves apart and had, as a result, enjoyed 'long years of peace and obscurity . . . until the Downfall of Númenor and the sudden return of Sauron': the Elves of Lórien and the Silvan Elves north of Greenwood the Great.[4]

[The Silvan Elves'] realm is said to have extended into the woods surrounding the Lonely Mountain and growing along the west shores of the Long Lake, before the coming of the Dwarves exiled from Moria and the invasion of the Dragon. The Elvish folk of this realm had migrated from the south, being the kin and neighbours of the Elves of Lórien; but they had dwelt in Greenwood the Great east of Anduin. In the Second Age their king, Oropher [the father of Thranduil, father of Legolas], had withdrawn northward beyond the Gladden

Fields. This he did to be free from the power and encroachments of the Dwarves of Moria, which had grown to be the greatest of the mansions of the Dwarves recorded in history; and also he resented the intrusions of Celeborn and Galadriel into Lórien. But as yet there was little to fear between the Greenwood and the Mountains and there was constant intercourse between his people and their kin across the river, until the War of the Last Alliance.

Despite the desire of the Silvan Elves to meddle as little as might be in the affairs of the Noldor and Sindar, or of any other peoples, Dwarves, Men, or Orcs, Oropher had the wisdom to foresee that peace would not return unless Sauron was overcome. He therefore assembled a great army of his now numerous people, and joining with the lesser army of Malgalad [Amdír] of Lórien he led the host of the Silvan Elves to battle. The Silvan Elves were hardy and valiant, but ill-equipped with armour or weapons in comparison with the Eldar of the West; also they were independent, and not disposed to place themselves under the supreme command of Gil-galad. Their losses were thus more grievous than they need have been, even in that terrible war. Malgalad [Amdír] and more than half his following perished in the great battle of the Dagorlad, being cut off from the main host and driven into the Dead Marshes. Oropher was slain in the first assault upon Mordor, rushing forward at the head of his most doughty warriors before Gil-galad had given the signal for the advance. Thranduil his son survived, but when the war ended and Sauron was slain (as it seemed) he led back home barely a third of the army that had marched to war.[5]

So it is told, that the Battle of Dagorlad was long and hard fought and the number of fallen whose remains were subsumed into the Dead Marshes was legion. Over three thousand years later, the Marshes were still a haunted burial site of those slain in battle, as Frodo and Sam discovered when Gollum led them through the Marshes on their journey towards Mordor and they were bewitched by flickering lights, as of candles, hovering over stagnant pools: 'They lie in all the pools,' [said Frodo] 'pale faces, deep deep under the dark water. I saw them: grim faces and evil, and noble faces and sad. Many faces proud and fair, and weeds in their silver hair. But all foul, all rotting, all dead. A fell light is in them.'

[To which Gollum responded:] 'Yes, yes. . . . It was a great battle. Tall Men with long swords, and terrible Elves, and Orcses shrieking. They fought on the plain for days and months at the Black Gates. But the Marshes have grown since then, swallowed up the graves; always creeping, creeping.'[6]

Although the Battle of Dagorlad was long waged and at the cost of many fatalities, the Alliance triumphed at the last:

The host of Gil-galad and Elendil had the victory, for the might of the Elves was still great in those days, and the Númenóreans were strong and tall, and terrible in their wrath. Against Aeglos the spear of Gil-galad none could stand; and the sword of Elendil filled Orcs and Men with fear, for it shone with the light of the sun and of the moon, and it was named Narsil.[7]

Later, Elrond would recollect: 'I was the herald of Gil-galad and marched with his host. I was at the Battle of Dagorlad before the Black Gate of Mordor, where we had the mastery: for the Spear of Gil-galad and the Sword of Elendil, Aeglos and Narsil, none could withstand.'[8]

With the battle won, the Alliance entered the Plateau of Gorgoroth, encircled by the mountain walls of Ered Lithui and Ephel Dúath, with intent to bring final defeat to Sauron by laying siege to his mighty fortress-tower of Barad-dûr.

Then Gil-galad and Elendil passed into Mordor and encompassed the stronghold of Sauron; and they laid siege to it for seven years, and suffered grievous loss by fire and by the darts and bolts of the Enemy, and Sauron sent many sorties against them.[9]

## 3440 – ANÁRION SLAIN.

There in the valley of Gorgoroth Anárion son of Elendil was slain, and many others.[1]

Elsewhere it is recorded:

The crown of Gondor [in later times] was derived from the form of a Númenórean war-helm. In the beginning it was indeed a plain helm; and it is said to have been the one that Isildur wore in the Battle of Dagorlad (for the helm of Anárion was crushed by the stone-cast from Barad-dûr that slew him).[2]

## 3441 – SAURON OVERTHROWN BY ELENDIL AND GIL-GALAD, WHO PERISH. ISILDUR TAKES THE ONE RING. SAURON PASSES AWAY AND THE RINGWRAITHS GO INTO THE SHADOWS. THE SECOND AGE ENDS.

But at the last, the siege was so strait that Sauron himself came forth; and he wrestled with Gil-galad and Elendil, and they both were slain, and the sword of Elendil broke under him as he fell.[1]

The fall of Gil-galad the Elven-king would long be remembered in legend and rhyme:

> *Gil-galad was an Elven-king.*
> *Of him the harpers sadly sing:*
> *the last whose realm was fair and free*
> *between the Mountains and the Sea.*
>
> *His sword was long, his lance was keen,*
> *his shining helm afar was seen;*
> *the countless stars of heaven's field*
> *were mirrored in his silver shield.*

*But long ago he rode away,*
*and where he dwelleth none can say;*
*for into darkness fell his star*
*in Mordor where the shadows are.*[2]

Many of the Elves and many of the Númenóreans and Men who were their allies had perished in the Battle and the Siege; and Elendil the Tall and Gil-galad the High King were no more. Never again was such a host assembled, nor was there any such league of Elves and Men; for after Elendil's day the two kindreds became estranged.[3]

The loss of both Gil-galad and Elendil in their struggle with Sauron on the slopes of Orodruin was a tragic blow to the armies of the Alliance, but for their enemy, his triumph was short-lived:

But Sauron also was thrown down, and with the hilt-shard of Narsil Isildur cut the Ruling Ring from the hand of Sauron and took it for his own. Then Sauron was for that time vanquished, and he forsook his body, and his spirit fled far away and hid in waste places; and he took no visible shape again for many long years.[4]

As is told in *The Fellowship of the Ring*, long after the battle that saw not just the fall of Sauron but also that of Gil-galad and Elendil, Elrond Half-Elven would speak of those days at the Council at Rivendell: 'Fruitless did I call the victory of the Last Alliance? Not wholly so, yet it did not achieve its end. Sauron was diminished, but not destroyed. His Ring was lost but not unmade. The Dark Tower was broken, but its foundations were not removed; for they were made with the power of the Ring, and while it remains they will endure. Many Elves and many mighty Men, and many of their friends, had perished in the war. Anárion was slain, and Isildur was slain; and Gil-galad and Elendil were no more. Never again shall there be any such league of Elves and Men; for Men multiply and the Firstborn decrease, and the two kindreds are estranged. And ever since that day the race of Númenor has decayed, and the span of their years has lessened.'⁵

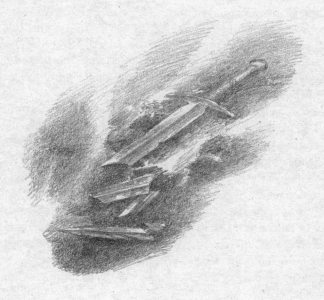

# EPILOGUE

**THE NÚMENÓREAN KINGS IN EXILE:**
**Isildur, High King of Gondor and Arnor**
Born: SA 3209; Died: TA 2 (age 234)
Rule: SA 3441–TA 2 (2 years)

The Ruling Ring passed out of the knowledge even of the Wise in that age; yet it was not unmade. For Isildur would not surrender it to Elrond and Círdan who stood by. They counselled him to cast it into the fire of Orodruin nigh at hand, in which it had been forged, so that it should perish, and the power of Sauron be for ever diminished, and he should remain only as a shadow of malice in the wilderness. But Isildur refused this counsel, saying: 'This I will have as weregild for my father's death, and my brother's. Was it not I that dealt the Enemy his death-blow?' And the Ring that he held seemed to him exceedingly fair to look on; and he would not suffer it to be destroyed. Taking it therefore he returned at first to Minas Anor, and there planted the White Tree in memory of his brother Anárion.[1]

213

Among the 'hoarded scrolls and books' within the archives of lore kept in the City of Gondor, were 'many records of ancient days' that 'few even of the lore-masters' could read, 'for their scripts and tongues' had become 'dark to later men'. Among these documents in Minas Tirith lay a scroll concerning the One Ring, made by Isildur following the war in Mordor and prior to his going North:

*The Great Ring shall go now to be an heirloom of the North Kingdom; but records of it shall be left in Gondor, where also dwell the heirs of Elendil, lest a time come when the memory of these great matters shall grow dim.*

And after these words Isildur described the Ring, such as he found it.

*It was hot when I first took it, hot as a glede, and my hand was scorched, so that I doubt if ever again I shall be free of the pain of it. Yet even as I write it is cooled, and it seemeth to shrink, though it loseth neither its beauty nor its shape. Already the writing upon it, which at first was as clear as red flame, fadeth and is now only barely to be read. It is fashioned in an elven-script of Eregion, for they have no letters in Mordor for such subtle work; but the language is unknown to me. I deem it to be a tongue of the Black Land, since it is foul and uncouth. What evil it saith I do not know; but I trace here a copy of it, lest it fade beyond recall. The Ring misseth, maybe, the heat of Sauron's hand, which was black and yet burned like fire, and so Gil-galad was destroyed; and maybe were the gold made hot again, the writing would be refreshed. But for my part I will risk no hurt to this thing: of all the works of Sauron the only fair. It is precious to me, though I buy it with great pain.* [2]

But soon [Isildur] departed, and after he had given counsel to Meneldil, his brother's son, and had committed to him the realm of the south, he bore away the Ring, to be an heirloom of his house, and marched north from Gondor by the way that

Elendil had come; and he forsook the South Kingdom, for he purposed to take up his father's realm in Eriador, far from the shadow of the Black Land.

But Isildur was overwhelmed by a host of Orcs that lay in wait in the Misty Mountains; and they descended upon him at unawares in his camp between the Greenwood and the Great River, nigh to Loeg Ningloron, the Gladden Fields, for he was heedless and set no guard, deeming that all his foes were overthrown. There well nigh all his people were slain, and among them were his three elder sons, Elendur, Aratan, and Ciryon; but his wife and his youngest son, Valandil, he had left in Imladris when he went to the war. Isildur himself escaped by means of the Ring, for when he wore it he was invisible to all eyes; but the Orcs hunted him by scent and slot, until he came to the River and plunged in. There the Ring betrayed him and avenged its maker, for it slipped from his finger as he swam, and it was lost in the water. Then the Orcs saw him as he laboured in the stream, and they shot him with many arrows, and that was his end.[3]

# APPENDICES

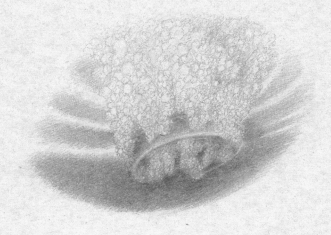

# APPENDIX A

## A BRIEF CHRONICLE OF THE THIRD AGE
## OF MIDDLE-EARTH[1]

Only three of [Isildur's] people came ever back over the mountains after long wandering; and of these one was Ohtar his esquire, to whose keeping he had given the shards of the sword of Elendil.

Thus Narsil came in due time to the hand of Valandil, Isildur's heir, in Imladris; but the blade was broken and its light was extinguished, and it was not forged anew. And Master Elrond foretold that this would not be done until the Ruling Ring should be found again and Sauron should return; but the hope of Elves and Men was that these things might never come to pass.

Valandil took up his abode in Annúminas, but his folk were diminished, and of the Númenóreans and of the Men of Eriador there remained now too few to people the land or to maintain all the places that Elendil had built; in Dagorlad, and in Mordor, and upon the Gladden Fields many had fallen. And it came to pass after the days of Eärendur [TA 640-861], the seventh king that followed Valandil, that the Men of Westernesse, the Dúnedain of the North, became divided into petty realms and lordships, and their foes devoured them one by one. Ever they dwindled with the years, until their glory passed, leaving only green mounds in the grass. At length naught was left of them but a strange people wandering secretly in the wild, and other men knew not their homes nor the purpose of their journeys, and save in Imladris, in the house of Elrond, their ancestry was forgotten. Yet the shards of the sword were cherished during many lives of Men by the heirs of Isildur; and their line, from father to son, remained unbroken.

In the south the realm of Gondor endured, and for a time its splendour grew, until it recalled the wealth and majesty of Númenor ere it fell. High towers the people of Gondor built, and strong places, and havens of many ships; and the Winged Crown of the Kings of Men was held in awe by people of many lands and tongues. For many a year the White Tree grew before the King's house in Minas Anor, the seed of that tree which Isildur brought out of the deeps of the sea from Númenor; and the seed before that came from Avallónë, and before that from Valinor in the Day before days when the world was young.

Yet at the last, in the wearing of the swift years of Middle-earth, Gondor waned, and the line of Meneldil son of Anárion failed. For the blood of the Númenóreans became much mingled with that of other men, and their power and wisdom was diminished, and their life-span was shortened, and the watch upon Mordor slumbered. And in the days of Telemnar [Ruled: TA 1634-36], the third and twentieth of the line of Meneldil, a plague came upon dark winds out of the east, and it smote the King and his children, and many of the people of Gondor perished. Then the forts on the borders of Mordor were deserted, and Minas Ithil was emptied of its people; and evil entered again into the Black Land secretly, and the ashes of Gorgoroth were stirred as by a cold wind, for dark shapes gathered there. It is said that these were indeed the Úlairi, whom Sauron called the Nazgûl, the Nine Ringwraiths that had long remained hidden, but returned now to prepare the ways of their Master, for he had begun to grow again.

And in the days of Eärnil [TA 1945-2043] they made their first stroke, and they came by night out of Mordor over the passes of the Mountains of Shadow, and took Minas Ithil for their abode; and they made it a place of such dread that none dared to look upon it. Thereafter it was called Minas Morgul, the Tower of Sorcery; and Minas Morgul was ever at war with Minas Anor in the west. Then Osgiliath, which in the waning of the people had long been deserted, became a place of ruins and a city of ghosts. But Minas Anor endured, and it was named anew Minas Tirith, the Tower of Guard; for there the kings caused to be built in the citadel a white tower, very tall and fair, and its eye was upon many lands. Proud still and strong was that city, and in it the White Tree still flowered for a while before the house of the Kings; and there the remnant of the Númenóreans still defended the passage of the River against the terrors of Minas Morgul and against all the enemies of the West, Orcs and monsters and evil Men; and thus the lands behind them, west of Anduin, were protected from war and destruction.

Still Minas Tirith endured after the days of Eärnur [TA 2043-2050], son of Eärnil, and the last King of Gondor. He it was that rode alone to the gates of Minas Morgul to meet the challenge of the Morgul-lord; and he met him in single combat, but he was betrayed by the Nazgûl and taken alive into the city of torment, and no living man saw him ever again. Now Eärnur left no heir, but when the line of the Kings failed the Stewards of the house of Mardil the Faithful ruled the city and its ever-shrinking realm; and the Rohirrim, the Horsemen of the North, came and dwelt in the green land of Rohan, which before was named Calenardhon and was a part of the kingdom of Gondor; and the Rohirrim aided the Lords of the City in their wars. And northward, beyond the Falls of Rauros and the Gates of Argonath, there were as yet other defences, powers more ancient of which Men knew little, against whom the things of evil did not dare to move, until in the ripening of time their dark lord, Sauron, should come forth again.

And until that time was come, never again after the days of Eärnil did the Nazgûl dare to cross the River or to come forth from their city in shape visible to Men.

* * *

In all the days of the Third Age, after the fall of Gil-galad, Master Elrond abode in Imladris, and he gathered there many Elves, and other folk of wisdom and power from among all the kindreds of Middle-earth, and he preserved through many lives of Men the memory of all that had been fair; and the house of Elrond was a refuge for the weary and the oppressed, and a treasury of good counsel and wise lore. In that house were harboured the Heirs of Isildur, in childhood and old age, because of the kinship of their blood with Elrond himself, and because he knew in his wisdom that one should come of their line to whom a great part was appointed in the last deeds of that Age. And until that time came the shards of Elendil's sword were given into the keeping of Elrond, when the days of the Dúnedain darkened and they became a wandering people.

In Eriador Imladris was the chief dwelling of the High Elves; but at the Grey Havens of Lindon there abode also a remnant of the people of Gil-galad the Elvenking. At times they would wander into the lands of Eriador, but for the most part they dwelt near the shores of the sea, building and tending the elven-ships wherein those of the Firstborn who grew weary of the world set sail into the uttermost West. Círdan the Shipwright was lord of the Havens and mighty among the Wise.

Of the Three Rings that the Elves had preserved unsullied no open word was ever spoken among the Wise, and few even of the Eldar knew where they were bestowed. Yet after the fall of Sauron their power was ever at work, and where they abode there mirth also dwelt and all things were unstained by the griefs of time. Therefore ere the Third Age was ended the Elves perceived that the Ring of Sapphire was with Elrond, in the fair valley of Rivendell, upon whose house the stars of heaven most brightly shone; whereas the Ring of Adamant was in the Land of Lórien where dwelt the Lady Galadriel. A queen she was of the woodland Elves, the wife of Celeborn of Doriath, yet she herself was of the Noldor and remembered the Day before days in Valinor, and she was the mightiest and fairest of all the Elves that remained in Middle-earth. But the Red Ring remained hidden until the end, and none save Elrond and Galadriel and Círdan knew to whom it had been committed.

Thus it was that in two domains the bliss and beauty of the Elves remained still undiminished while that Age endured: in Imladris; and in Lothlórien, the hidden land between Celebrant and Anduin, where the trees bore flowers of gold and no Orc or evil thing dared ever come. Yet many voices were heard among the Elves foreboding that, if Sauron should come again, then either he would find the Ruling Ring that was lost, or at the best his enemies would discover it and destroy it; but in either chance the powers of the Three must then fail and all things maintained by them must fade, and so the Elves should pass into the twilight and the Dominion of Men begin.

. . . In that time the Noldor walked still in the Hither Lands, mightiest and fairest of the children of the world, and their tongues were still heard by mortal ears. Many things of beauty and wonder remained on earth in that time, and many things also of evil and dread: Orcs there were and trolls and dragons and fell beasts, and strange creatures old and wise in the woods whose names are forgotten; Dwarves still laboured in the hills and wrought with patient craft works of metal and stone that none now can rival. But the Dominion of Men was preparing and all things were changing, until at last the Dark Lord arose in Mirkwood again.

Now of old the name of that forest was Greenwood the Great, and its wide halls and aisles were the haunt of many beasts and of birds of bright song; and there was the realm of King Thranduil under the oak and the beech. But after many years, when well nigh a third of that age of the world had passed, a darkness crept slowly through the wood from the southward, and fear walked there in shadowy glades; fell beasts came hunting, and cruel and evil creatures laid there their snares.

Then the name of the forest was changed and Mirkwood it was called, for the nightshade lay deep there, and few dared to pass through, save only in the north where Thranduil's people still held the evil at bay. Whence it came few could tell, and it was long ere even the Wise could discover it. It was the shadow of Sauron and the sign of his return. For coming out of the wastes of the East he took up his abode in the south of the forest, and slowly he grew and took shape there again; in a dark hill he made his dwelling and wrought there his sorcery, and all folk feared the Sorcerer of Dol Guldur, and yet they knew not at first how great was their peril.

Even as the first shadows were felt in Mirkwood there appeared in the west of Middle-earth the Istari, whom Men called the Wizards. None knew at that time whence they were, save Círdan of the Havens, and only to Elrond and to Galadriel did he reveal that they came over the Sea. But afterwards it was said among the Elves that they were messengers sent by the Lords of the West to contest the power of Sauron, if he should arise again, and to move Elves and Men and all living things of good will to valiant deeds. In the likeness of Men they appeared, old but vigorous, and they changed little with the years, and aged but slowly, though great cares lay on them; great wisdom they had, and many powers of mind and hand. Long they journeyed far and wide among Elves and Men, and held converse also with beasts and with birds; and the peoples of Middle-earth gave to them many names, for their true names they did not reveal. Chief among them were those whom the Elves called Mithrandir and Curunír, but Men in the North named Gandalf and Saruman. Of these Curunír was the eldest and came first, and after him came Mithrandir and Radagast, and others of the Istari who went into the east of Middle-earth, and do not come into these tales. Radagast was the friend of all beasts and birds; but Curunír went most among Men, and he was subtle in speech and skilled in all the devices of smithcraft. Mithrandir was closest in counsel with Elrond and the Elves. He wandered far in the North and West and made never in any land any lasting abode; but Curunír journeyed into the East, and when he returned he dwelt at Orthanc in the Ring of Isengard, which the Númenóreans made in the days of their power.

Ever most vigilant was Mithrandir, and he it was that most

doubted the darkness in Mirkwood, for though many deemed that it was wrought by the Ringwraiths, he feared that it was indeed the first shadow of Sauron returning; and he went to Dol Guldur, and the Sorcerer fled from him, and there was a watchful peace for a long while. But at length the Shadow returned and its power increased; and in that time was first made the Council of the Wise that is called the White Council, and therein were Elrond and Galadriel and Círdan, and other lords of the Eldar, and with them were Mithrandir and Curunír. And Curunír (that was Saruman the White) was chosen to be their chief, for he had most studied the devices of Sauron of old. Galadriel indeed had wished that Mithrandir should be the head of the Council, and Saruman begrudged them that, for his pride and desire of mastery was grown great; but Mithrandir refused the office, since he would have no ties and no allegiance, save to those who sent him, and he would abide in no place nor be subject to any summons. But Saruman now began to study the lore of the Rings of Power, their making and their history.

Now the Shadow grew ever greater, and the hearts of Elrond and Mithrandir darkened. Therefore on a time Mithrandir at great peril went again to Dol Guldur and the pits of the Sorcerer, and he discovered the truth of his fears, and escaped. And returning to Elrond he said:

'True, alas, is our guess. This is not one of the Úlairi, as many have long supposed. It is Sauron himself who has taken shape again and now grows apace; and he is gathering again all the Rings to his hand; and he seeks ever for news of the One, and of the Heirs of Isildur, if they live still on earth.'

And Elrond answered: 'In the hour that Isildur took the Ring and would not surrender it, this doom was wrought, that Sauron should return.'

'Yet the One was lost,' said Mithrandir, 'and while it still lies hid, we can master the Enemy, if we gather our strength and tarry not too long.'

Then the White Council was summoned; and Mithrandir

urged them to swift deeds, but Curunír spoke against him, and counselled them to wait yet and to watch.

'For I believe not,' said he, 'that the One will ever be found again in Middle-earth. Into Anduin it fell, and long ago, I deem, it was rolled to the Sea. There it shall lie until the end, when all this world is broken and the deeps are removed.'

Therefore naught was done at that time, though Elrond's heart misgave him, and he said to Mithrandir: 'Nonetheless I forebode that the One will yet be found, and then war will arise again, and in that war this Age will be ended. Indeed in a second darkness it will end, unless some strange chance deliver us that my eyes cannot see.'

'Many are the strange chances of the world,' said Mithrandir, 'and help oft shall come from the hands of the weak when the Wise falter.'

Thus the Wise were troubled, but none as yet perceived that Curunír had turned to dark thoughts and was already a traitor in heart: for he desired that he and no other should find the Great Ring, so that he might wield it himself and order all the world to his will. Too long he had studied the ways of Sauron in hope to defeat him, and now he envied him as a rival rather than hated his works. And he deemed that the Ring, which was Sauron's, would seek for its master as he became manifest once more; but if he were driven out again, then it would lie hid. Therefore he was willing to play with peril and let Sauron be for a time, hoping by his craft to forestall both his friends and the Enemy, when the Ring should appear.

He set a watch upon the Gladden Fields; but soon he discovered that the servants of Dol Guldur were searching all the ways of the River in that region. Then he perceived that Sauron also had learned of the manner of Isildur's end, and he grew afraid and withdrew to Isengard and fortified it; and ever he probed deeper into the lore of the Rings of Power and the art of their forging. But he spoke of none of this to the Council, hoping still that he might be the first to hear news of the Ring. He gathered a great host of spies, and many of these were birds; for Radagast lent him his aid, divining naught of his treachery, and deeming that this was but part of the watch upon the Enemy.

But ever the shadow in Mirkwood grew deeper, and to Dol Guldur evil things repaired out of all the dark places of the world; and they were united again under one will, and their malice was directed against the Elves and the survivors of Númenor. Therefore at last the Council was again summoned and the lore of the Rings was much debated; but Mithrandir spoke to the Council, saying:

'It is not needed that the Ring should be found, for while it abides on earth and is not unmade, still the power that it holds will live, and Sauron will grow and have hope. The might of the Elves and the Elf-friends is less now than of old. Soon he will be too strong for you, even without the Great Ring; for he rules the Nine, and of the Seven he has recovered three. We must strike.'

To this Curunír now assented, desiring that Sauron should be thrust from Dol Guldur, which was nigh to the River, and should have leisure to search there no longer. Therefore, for the last time, he aided the Council, and they put forth their strength; and they assailed Dol Guldur, and drove Sauron from his hold, and Mirkwood for a brief while was made wholesome again.

But their stroke was too late. For the Dark Lord had foreseen it, and he had long prepared all his movements; and the Úlairi, his Nine Servants, had gone before him to make ready for his coming. Therefore his flight was but a feint, and he soon returned, and ere the Wise could prevent him he re-entered his kingdom in Mordor and reared once again the dark towers of Barad-dûr. And in that year the White Council met for the last time, and Curunír withdrew to Isengard, and took counsel with none save himself.

Orcs were mustering, and far to the east and the south the wild peoples were arming. Then in the midst of gathering fear and the rumour of war the foreboding of Elrond was proved true, and the One Ring was indeed found again, by a chance more strange than even Mithrandir had foreseen; and it was hidden from Curunír and from Sauron. For it had been taken from Anduin long ere they sought for it, being found by one of the small fisher-folk that dwelt by the River, ere the Kings failed in Gondor; and by its finder it was brought beyond search into dark hiding under the roots of the mountains. There it dwelt, until even in the year of the assault upon Dol Guldur it was found again, by a wayfarer, fleeing into the depths of the earth from the pursuit of the Orcs, and passed into a far distant country, even to the land of the Periannath, the Little People, the Halflings, who dwelt in the west of Eriador. And ere that day they had been held of small account by Elves and by Men, and neither Sauron nor any of the Wise save Mithrandir had in all their counsels given thought to them.

Now by fortune and his vigilance Mithrandir first learned of the Ring, ere Sauron had news of it; yet he was dismayed and in doubt. For too great was the evil power of this thing for any of the Wise to wield, unless like Curunír he wished himself to become a tyrant and a dark lord in his turn; but neither could it be concealed from Sauron for ever, nor could it be unmade by the craft of the Elves. Therefore with the help of the Dúnedain of the North Mithrandir set a watch upon the land of the Periannath and bided his time. But Sauron had many ears, and soon he heard rumour of the One Ring, which above all things he desired, and he sent forth the Nazgûl to take it. Then war was kindled, and in battle with Sauron the Third Age ended even as it had begun.

### THE TALE CONTINUES IN
### *THE LORD OF THE RINGS*

## APPENDIX B

### THE NÚMENÓREAN CHAPTERS FROM
### *THE LOST ROAD*

Within the manuscripts of J.R.R. Tolkien's unfinished novel, *The Lost Road*, begun some time prior to 1937, there are many foreshadowings of themes later realised in his writings concerning the Fall of Númenor. In the second chapter there is a verse, in translation from Anglo-Saxon, which clearly describes places akin to the lands of Númenor and the Blessed Realm and the yearning of Men for the West:

'There is many a thing in the West-regions unknown to men, marvels and strange beings, a land fair and lovely, the homeland of the Elves, and the bliss of the Gods. Little doth any man know what longing is his whom old age cutteth off from return.'

And, elsewhere, appear the names 'Númenor', 'Sauron', 'Morgoth', 'Melko' [Melkor] and 'Eärendel' [Eärendil]. The many-layered 'time travel' device is complex and was, doubtless, the reason for the novel being abandoned, proving, as Tolkien was to later express it, 'too long a way round to what I really wanted to make, a new version of the Atlantis legend'.

When, in 1987, Christopher Tolkien published the surviving elements of his father's manuscript in *The Lost Road and Other Writings*, he singled out what he referred to as 'The

Númenórean Chapters' as a discrete section to be given appropriate prominence in consideration of the text.

Whilst not easily incorporated into the chronological form used in this volume, these chapters merit inclusion here by virtue of their containing a masterly summary of the First Age, the creation of Númenor, the Rise of Sauron and the coming of the Shadow, presented as a Socratic dialogue richly embellished in Tolkien's most majestic and epic style.

In terms of where in the chronology it might be notionally located, it would seem to sit most easily at that point in the Akallabêth where Ar-Pharazôn is promulgating his plans for assaulting the Blessed Realm and Amandil, the loyal counsellor to the King, has left his home in Rómenna and set sail into the West in order to appeal to the Valar for assistance, leaving his son, Elendil, waiting and looking for his father's return.

In this version it is Orontor, not Amandil, who has embarked on that mission. Elendil's son is here named 'Herendil' (as opposed to Tolkien's later choice of Isildur), while Elendil himself is said to be the son of 'Valandil' rather than 'Amandil'; Tolkien later giving the name Valandil to the youngest of Isildur's sons. Ar-Pharazôn is here referred to as 'Tarkalion', an earlier iteration of the Elvish version of his name, Tar-Calion.

## The Númenórean chapters

Christopher Tolkien provides the following introduction:

My father said in his letter of 1964 on the subject that 'in my tale *we were to come at last* to Amandil and Elendil leaders of the loyal party in Númenor, when it fell under the domination of Sauron.' It is nonetheless plain that he did not reach this conception until *after* the extant narrative had been mostly written, or even brought to the point where it was abandoned. At the end of Chapter II the Númenórean story is obviously just about to begin, and the Númenórean chapters were originally numbered continuously with the opening ones. On the other hand the decision to postpone Númenor and make it the conclusion and climax to the book had already been taken when *The Lost Road* went to Allen and Unwin in November 1937.

Since the Númenórean episode was left unfinished, this is a convenient point to mention an interesting note that my father presumably wrote while it was in progress. This says that when the first 'adventure' (i.e. Númenor) is over 'Alboin is still precisely in his chair and Audoin just shutting the door.' [This refers to the foregoing chapters as published in *The Lost Road and Other Writings*.]

With the postponement of Númenor the chapter-numbers were changed, but this has no importance and I therefore number these 'III' and 'IV'; they have no titles. In this case I have found it most convenient to annotate the text by numbered notes.

## Chapter III

Elendil was walking in his garden, but not to look upon its beauty in the evening light. He was troubled and his mind was turned inward. His house with its white tower and golden roof glowed behind him in the sunset, but his eyes were on the path before his feet. He was going down to the shore, to bathe in the blue pools of the cove beyond his garden's end, as was his custom at this hour. And he looked also to find his son Herendil there. The time had come when he must speak to him.

He came at length to the great hedge of *lavaralda*[1] that fenced the garden at its lower, western, end. It was a familiar sight, though the years could not dim its beauty. It was seven twelves of years[2] or more since he had planted it himself when planning his garden before his marriage; and he had blessed his good fortune. For the seeds had come from Eressëa far westward, whence ships came seldom already in those days, and now they came no more. But the spirit of that blessed land and its fair people remained still in the trees that had grown from those seeds: their long green leaves were golden on the undersides, and as a breeze off the water stirred them they whispered with a sound of many soft voices, and glistened like sunbeams on rippling waves. The flowers were pale with a yellow flush, and laid thickly on the branches like a sunlit snow; and their odour filled all the lower garden, faint but clear. Mariners in the old days said that the scent of *lavaralda* could be felt on the air long ere the land of Eressëa could be seen, and that it brought a desire of rest and great content. He had seen the trees in flower day after day, for they rested from flowering only at rare intervals. But now, suddenly, as he passed, the scent struck him with a keen fragrance, at once known and utterly strange. He seemed for a moment never to have smelled it before: it pierced the troubles of his mind, bewildering, bringing no familiar content, but a new disquiet.

'Eressëa, Eressëa!' he said. 'I wish I were there; and had not been fated to dwell in Númenor[3] half-way between the worlds. And least of all in these days of perplexity!'

He passed under an arch of shining leaves, and walked swiftly down rock-hewn steps to the white beach. Elendil looked about him, but he could not see his son. A picture rose in his mind of Herendil's white body, strong and beautiful upon the threshold of early manhood, cleaving the water, or lying on the sand glistening in the sun. But Herendil was not there, and the beach seemed oddly empty.

Elendil stood and surveyed the cove and its rocky walls once more; and as he looked, his eyes rose by chance to his own house among trees and flowers upon the slopes above the shore, white and golden, shining in the sunset. And he stopped and gazed: for suddenly the house stood there, as a thing at once real and visionary, as a thing in some other time and story, beautiful, beloved, but strange, awaking desire as if it were part of a mystery that was still hidden. He could not interpret the feeling.

He sighed. 'I suppose it is the threat of war that maketh me look upon fair things with such disquiet,' he thought. 'The shadow of fear is between us and the sun, and all things look as if they were already lost. Yet they are strangely beautiful thus seen. I do not know. I wonder. A Númenórë! I hope the trees will blossom on your hills in years to come as they do now; and your towers will stand white in the Moon and yellow in the Sun. I wish it were not hope, but assurance – that assurance we used to have before the Shadow. But where is Herendil? I must see him and speak to him, more clearly than we have spoken yet. Ere it is too late. The time is getting short.'

'Herendil!' he called, and his voice echoed along the hollow shore above the soft sound of the light-falling waves. 'Herendil!'

And even as he called, he seemed to hear his own voice, and to mark that it was strong and curiously melodious. 'Herendil!' he called again.

At length there was an answering call: a young voice very clear came from some distance away – like a bell out of a deep cave.

'*Man-ie, atto, man-ie?*'

For a brief moment it seemed to Elendil that the words were strange. '*Man-ie, atto?* What is it, father?' Then the feeling passed.

'Where art thou?'

'Here!'

'I cannot see thee.'

'I am upon the wall, looking down on thee.'

Elendil looked up; and then swiftly climbed another flight of stone steps at the northern end of the cove. He came out upon a flat space smoothed and levelled on the top of the projecting spur of rock. Here there was room to lie in the sun, or sit upon a wide stone seat with its back against the cliff, down the face of which there fell a cascade of trailing stems rich with garlands of blue and silver flowers. Flat upon the stone with his chin in his hands lay a youth. He was looking out to sea, and did not turn his head as his father came up and sat down on the seat.

'Of what art thou dreaming, Herendil, that thy ears hear not?'

'I am thinking; I am not dreaming. I am a child no longer.'

'I know thou art not,' said Elendil; 'and for that reason I wished to find thee and speak with thee. Thou art so often out and away, and so seldom at home these days.'

He looked down on the white body before him. It was dear to him, and beautiful. Herendil was naked, for he had been diving from the high point, being a daring diver and proud of his skill. It seemed suddenly to Elendil that the lad had grown over night, almost out of knowledge.

'How thou dost grow!' he said. 'Thou hast the makings of a mighty man, and have nearly finished the making.'

'Why dost thou mock me?' said the boy. 'Thou knowest I am dark, and smaller than most others of my year. And that is a trouble to me. I stand barely to the shoulder of Almáriel, whose hair is of shining gold, and she is a maiden, and of my own age. We hold that we are of the blood of kings, but I tell thee thy friends' sons make a jest of me and call me *Terendul*[4] – slender and dark; and they say I have Eressëan blood, or that I am half-Noldo. And that is not said with love in these days. It is but a step from being called half a Gnome to being called Godfearing; and that is dangerous.'[5]

Elendil sighed. 'Then it must have become perilous to be the son of him that is named *elendil*; for that leads to Valandil, Godfriend, who was thy father's father.'[6]

There was a silence. At length Herendil spoke again: 'Of whom dost thou say that our king, Tarkalion, is descended?'

'From Eärendel the mariner, son of Tuor the mighty who was lost in these seas.'[7]

'Why then may not the king do as Eärendel from whom he is come? They say that he should follow him, and complete his work.'

'What dost thou think that they mean? Whither should he go, and fulfil what work?'

'Thou knowest. Did not Eärendel voyage to the uttermost West, and set foot in that land that is forbidden to us? He doth not die, or so songs say.'

'What callest thou Death? He did not return. He forsook all

whom he loved, ere he stepped on that shore.[8] He saved his kindred by losing them.'

'Were the Gods wroth with him?'

'Who knoweth? For he came not back. But he did not dare that deed to serve Melko, but to defeat him; to free men from Melko, not from the Lords; to win us the earth, not the land of the Lords. And the Lords heard his prayer and arose against Melko. And the earth is ours.'

'They say now that the tale was altered by the Eressëans, who are slaves of the Lords: that in truth Eärendel was an adventurer, and showed us the way, and that the Lords took him captive for that reason; and his work is perforce unfinished. Therefore the son of Eärendel, our king, should complete it. They wish to do what has been long left undone.'

'What is that?'

'Thou knowest: to set foot in the far West, and not withdraw it. To conquer new realms for our race, and ease the pressure of this peopled island, where every road is trodden hard, and every tree and grass-blade counted. To be free, and masters of the world. To escape the shadow of sameness, and of ending. We would make our king Lord of the West: *Nuaran Númenóren*.[9] Death comes here slow and seldom; yet it cometh. The land is only a cage gilded to look like Paradise.'

'Yea, so I have heard others say,' said Elendil. 'But what knowest thou of Paradise? Behold, our wandering words have come unguided to the point of my purpose. But I am grieved to find thy mood is of this sort, though I feared it might be so. Thou art my only son, and my dearest child, and I would have us at one in all our choices. But choose we must, thou as well as I – for at thy last birthday thou became subject to arms and the king's service. We must choose between Sauron and the Lords (or One Higher). Thou knowest, I suppose, that all hearts in Númenor are not drawn to Sauron?'

'Yes. There are fools even in Númenor,' said Herendil, in a lowered voice. 'But why speak of such things in this open place? Do you wish to bring evil on me?'

'I bring no evil,' said Elendil. 'That is thrust upon us: the choice between evils: the first fruits of war. But look, Herendil! Our house is one of wisdom and guarded learning; and was long revered for it. I followed my father, as I was able. Dost thou follow me? What dost thou know of the history of the world or Númenor? Thou art but four twelves,[10] and wert but a small child when Sauron came. Thou dost not understand what days were like before then. Thou canst not choose in ignorance.'

'But others of greater age and knowledge than mine – or thine – have chosen,' said Herendil. 'And they say that history confirmeth them, and that Sauron hath thrown a new light on history. Sauron knoweth history, all history.'

'Sauron knoweth, verily; but he twisteth knowledge. Sauron is a liar!' Growing anger caused Elendil to raise his voice as he spoke. The words rang out as a challenge.

'Thou art mad,' said his son, turning at last upon his side and facing Elendil, with dread and fear in his eyes. 'Do not say such things to me! They might, they might. . . .'

'Who are *they*, and what might they do?' said Elendil, but a chill fear passed from his son's eyes to his own heart.

'Do not ask! And do not speak – so loud!' Herendil turned away, and lay prone with his face buried in his hands. 'Thou knowest it is dangerous – to us all. Whatever he be, Sauron is mighty, and hath ears. I fear the dungeons. And I love thee, I love thee. *Atarinya tye-meláne.*'

*Atarinya tye-meláne*, my father, I love thee: the words sounded strange, but sweet: they smote Elendil's heart. '*A yonya inye tye-méla*: and I too, my son, I love thee,' he said, feeling each syllable strange but vivid as he spoke it. 'But let us go within! It is too late to bathe. The sun is all but gone. It is bright there westwards in the gardens of the Gods. But twilight and the dark are coming here, and the dark is no longer wholesome in this land. Let us go home. I must tell and ask thee much this evening – behind closed doors, where maybe thou wilt feel safer.' He looked towards the sea, which he loved, longing to bathe his body in it, as though to wash away weariness and care. But night was coming.

The sun had dipped, and was fast sinking in the sea.

There was fire upon far waves, but it faded almost as it was kindled. A chill wind came suddenly out of the West ruffling the yellow water off shore. Up over the fire-lit rim dark clouds reared; they stretched out great wings, south and north, and seemed to threaten the land.

Elendil shivered. 'Behold, the eagles of the Lord of the West are coming with threat to Númenor,' he murmured.

'What dost thou say?' said Herendil. 'Is it not decreed that the king of Númenor shall be called Lord of the West?'

'It is decreed by the king; but that does not make it so,' answered Elendil. 'But I meant not to speak aloud my heart's foreboding. Let us go!'

The light was fading swiftly as they passed up the paths of the garden amid flowers pale and luminous in the twilight. The trees were shedding sweet night-scents. A *lómelindë* [nightingale] began its thrilling bird-song by a pool.

Above them rose the house. Its white walls gleamed as if moonlight was imprisoned in their substance; but there was no moon yet, only a cool light, diffused and shadowless. Through the clear sky like fragile glass small stars stabbed their white flames. A voice from a high window came falling down like silver into the pool of twilight where they walked. Elendil knew the voice: it was the voice of Fíriel, a maiden of his household, daughter of Orontor. His heart sank, for Fíriel was dwelling in his house because Orontor had departed. Men said he was on a long voyage. Others said that he had fled the displeasure of the king. Elendil knew that he was on a mission from which he might never return, or return too late.[11] And he loved Orontor, and Fíriel was fair.

Now her voice sang an even-song in the Eressëan tongue, but made by men, long ago. The nightingale ceased. Elendil stood still to listen; and the words came to him, far off and strange, as some melody in archaic speech sung sadly in a forgotten twilight in the beginning of man's journey in the world.

> *Ilu Ilúvatar en káre eldain a firimoin*
> *ar antaróta mannar Valion: númessier . . .*

The Father made the World for elves and mortals, and he gave it into the hands of the Lords, who are in the West.

So sang Fíriel on high, until her voice fell sadly to the question with which that song ends: *man táre antáva nin Ilúvatar, Ilúvatar, enyáre tar i tyel íre Anarinya qeluva?* What will Ilúvatar, O Ilúvatar, give me in that day beyond the end, when my Sun faileth?'[12]

'*E man antaváro?* What will he give indeed?' said Elendil; and stood in sombre thought.

'She should not sing that song out of a window,' said Herendil, breaking the silence. 'They sing it otherwise now. Melko cometh back, they say, and the king shall give us the Sun forever.'

'I know what they say,' said Elendil. 'Do not say it to thy father, nor in his house.' He passed in at a dark door, and Herendil, shrugging his shoulders, followed him.

## Chapter IV

Herendil lay on the floor, stretched at his father's feet upon a carpet woven in a design of golden birds and twining plants with blue flowers. His head was propped upon his hands. His father sat upon his carved chair, his hands laid motionless upon either arm of it, his eyes looking into the fire that burned bright upon the hearth. It was not cold, but the fire that was named 'the heart of the house' (*hon-maren*)[13] burned ever in that room. It was moreover a protection against the night, which already men had begun to fear.

But cool air came in through the window, sweet and flower-scented. Through it could be seen, beyond the dark spires of still trees, the western ocean, silver under the Moon, that was now swiftly following the Sun to the gardens of the Gods. In the night-silence Elendil's words fell softly. As he spoke he listened, as if to another that told a tale long forgotten.[14]

'There[15] is Ilúvatar, the One; and there are the Powers, of whom the eldest in the thought of Ilúvatar was Alkar the Radiant;[16] and there are the Firstborn of Earth, the Eldar, who perish not while the World lasts; and there are also the After-born, mortal Men, who are the children of Ilúvatar, and yet under the rule of the Lords. Ilúvatar designed the World, and revealed his design to the Powers; and of these some he set to be Valar, Lords of the World and governors of the things that are therein. But Alkar, who had journeyed alone in the Void before the World, seeking to be free, desired the World to be a kingdom unto himself. Therefore he descended into it like a falling fire; and he made war upon the Lords, his brethren. But they established their mansions in the West, in Valinor, and shut him out; and they gave battle to him in the North, and they bound him, and the World had peace and grew exceeding fair.

'After a great age it came to pass that Alkar sued for pardon; and he made submission unto Manwë, lord of the Powers, and was set free. But he plotted against his brethren, and he deceived the Firstborn that dwelt in Valinor, so that many rebelled and were exiled from the Blessed Realm. And Alkar destroyed the lights of Valinor and fled into the night; and he became a spirit dark and terrible, and was called Morgoth, and he established his dominion in Middle-earth. But the Valar made the Moon for the Firstborn and the Sun for Men to confound the Darkness of the Enemy. And in that time at the rising of the Sun the Afterborn, who are Men, came forth in the East of the world; but they fell under the shadow of the Enemy. In those days the exiles of the Firstborn made war upon Morgoth; and three houses of the Fathers of Men were joined unto the Firstborn: the house of Bëor, and the house of Haleth, and the house of Hador. For these houses were not subject to Morgoth. But Morgoth had the victory, and brought all to ruin.

'Eärendel was son of Tuor, son of Huor, son of Gumlin, son of Hador; and his mother was of the Firstborn, daughter of Turgon, last king of the Exiles. He set forth upon the Great Sea, and he came at last unto the realm of the Lords, and the mountains of the West. And he renounced there all whom he loved, his wife and his child, and all his kindred, whether of the Firstborn or of Men; and he stripped himself.[17] And he surrendered himself unto Manwë, Lord of the West; and he made submission and supplication to him. And he was taken and came never again among Men. But the Lords had pity, and they sent forth their power, and war was renewed in the North, and the earth was broken; but Morgoth was overthrown. And the Lords put him forth into the Void without.

'And they recalled the Exiles of the Firstborn and pardoned them; and such as returned dwell since in bliss in Eressëa, the Lonely Isle, which is Avallon, for it is within sight of Valinor and the light of the Blessed Realm. And for the men of the Three Houses they made Vinya, the New Land, west of Middle-earth in the midst of the Great Sea, and named it Andor, the Land of Gift; and they endowed the land and all that lived thereon with good beyond other lands of mortals. But in Middle-earth dwelt lesser men, who knew not the Lords nor the Firstborn save by rumour; and among them were some who had served Morgoth of old, and were accursed. And there were evil things also upon earth, made by Morgoth in the days of his dominion, demons and dragons and mockeries of the creatures of Ilúvatar.[18] And there too lay hid many of his servants, spirits of evil, whom his will governed still though his presence was not among them. And of these Sauron was the chief, and his power grew. Wherefore the lot of men in Middle-earth was evil, for the Firstborn that remained among them faded or departed into the West, and their kindred, the men of Númenor, were afar and came only to their coasts in ships that crossed the Great Sea. But Sauron learned of the ships of Andor, and he feared them, lest free men should become lords of Middle-earth and deliver their kindred; and moved by the will of Morgoth he plotted to destroy Andor, and ruin (if he might) Avallon and Valinor.[19]

'But why should we be deceived, and become the tools of his will? It was not he, but Manwë the fair, Lord of the West, that endowed us with our riches. Our wisdom cometh from the Lords, and from the Firstborn that see them face to face; and we have grown to be higher and greater than others of our race – those who served Morgoth of old. We have knowledge, power, and life stronger than they. We are not yet fallen. Wherefore the dominion of the world is ours, or shall be, from Eressëa to the East. More can no mortals have.'

'Save to escape from Death,' said Herendil, lifting his face to his father's. 'And from sameness. They say that Valinor, where the Lords dwell, has no further bounds.'

'They say not truly. For all things in the world have an end, since the world itself is bounded, that it may not be Void. But Death is not decreed by the Lords: it is the gift of the One, and a gift which in the wearing of time even the Lords of the West shall envy.[20] So the wise of old have said. And though we can perhaps no longer understand that word, at least we have wisdom enough to know that we cannot escape, unless to a worse fate.'

'But the decree that we of Númenor shall not set foot upon the shores of the Immortal, or walk in their land – that is only a decree of Manwë and his brethren. Why should we not? The air there giveth enduring life, they say.'

'Maybe it doth,' said Elendil; 'and maybe it is but the air which those need who already have enduring life. To us perhaps it is death, or madness.'

'But why should we not essay it? The Eressëans go thither, and yet our mariners in the old days used to sojourn in Eressëa without hurt.'

'The Eressëans are not as we. They have not the gift of death. But what doth it profit to debate the governance of the world? All certainty is lost. Is it not sung that the earth was made for us, but we cannot unmake it, and if we like it not we may remember that we shall leave it. Do not the Firstborn call us the Guests? See what this spirit of unquiet has already wrought. Here when I was young there was no evil of mind. Death came late and without other pain than weariness. From Eressëans we obtained so many things of beauty that our land became well nigh as fair as theirs; and maybe fairer to mortal hearts. It is said that of old the Lords themselves would walk at times in the gardens that we named for them. There we set their images, fashioned by Eressëans who had beheld them, as the pictures of friends beloved.

'There were no temples in this land. But on the Mountain we spoke to the One, who hath no image. It was a holy place, untouched by mortal art. Then Sauron came. We had long heard rumour of him from seamen returned from the East. The tales differed: some said he was a king greater than the king of Númenor; some said that he was one of the Powers, or their offspring set to govern Middle-earth. A few reported that he was an evil spirit, perchance Morgoth returned; but at these we laughed.[21]

'It seems that rumour came also to him of us. It is not many years – three twelves and eight[22] – but it seems many, since he came hither. Thou wert a small child, and knew not then what was happening in the east of this land, far from our western house. Tarkalion the king was moved by rumours of Sauron, and sent forth a mission to discover what truth was in the mariners' tales. Many counsellors dissuaded him. My father told me, and he was one of them, that those who were wisest and had most knowledge of the West had messages from the Lords warning them to beware. For the Lords said that Sauron would work evil; but he could not come hither unless he were summoned.[23] Tarkalion was grown proud, and brooked no power in Middle-earth greater than his own. Therefore the ships were sent, and Sauron was summoned to do homage.

'Guards were set at the haven of Moriondë in the east of the land,[24] where the rocks are dark, watching at the king's command without ceasing for the ships' return. It was night, but there was a bright Moon. They descried ships far off, and they seemed to be sailing west at a speed greater than the storm, though there was little wind. Suddenly the sea became unquiet; it rose until it became like a mountain, and it rolled upon the land. The ships were lifted up, and cast far inland, and lay in the fields. Upon that ship which was cast highest and stood dry upon a hill there was a man, or one in man's shape, but greater than any even of the race of Númenor in stature.

'He stood upon the rock[25] and said: "This is done as a sign of power. For I am Sauron the mighty, servant of the Strong" (wherein he spoke darkly). "I have come. Be glad, men of Númenor, for I will take thy king to be my king, and the world shall be given into his hand."

'And it seemed to men that Sauron was great; though they feared the light of his eyes. To many he appeared fair, to others terrible; but to some evil. But they led him to the king, and he was humble before Tarkalion.

'And behold what hath happened since, step by step. At first he revealed only secrets of craft, and taught the making of many things powerful and wonderful; and they seemed good. Our ships go now without the wind, and many are made of metal that sheareth hidden rocks, and they sink not in calm or storm; but they are no longer fair to look upon. Our towers grow ever stronger and climb ever higher, but beauty they leave behind upon earth. We who have no foes are embattled with impregnable fortresses – and mostly on the West. Our arms are multiplied as if for an agelong war, and men are ceasing to give love or care to the making of other things for use or delight. But our shields are impenetrable, our swords cannot be withstood, our darts are like thunder and pass over leagues unerring. Where are our enemies? We have begun to slay one another. For Númenor now seems narrow, that was so large. Men covet, therefore, the lands that other families have long possessed. They fret as men in chains.

'Wherefore Sauron hath preached deliverance; he has bidden

our king to stretch forth his hand to Empire. Yesterday it was over the East. To-morrow – it will be over the West.

'We had no temples. But now the Mountain is despoiled. Its trees are felled, and it stands naked; and upon its summit there is a Temple. It is of marble, and of gold, and of glass and steel, and is wonderful, but terrible. No man prayeth there. It waiteth. For long Sauron did not name his master by the name that from old is accursed here. He spoke at first of the Strong One, of the Eldest Power, of the Master. But now he speaketh openly of Alkar,[26] of Morgoth. He hath prophesied his return. The Temple is to be his house. Númenor is to be the seat of the world's dominion. Meanwhile Sauron dwelleth there. He surveys our land from the Mountain, and is risen above the king, even proud Tarkalion, of the line chosen by the Lords, the seed of Eärendel.

'Yet Morgoth cometh not. But his shadow hath come; it lieth upon the hearts and minds of men. It is between them and the Sun, and all that is beneath it.'

'Is there a shadow?' said Herendil. 'I have not seen it. But I have heard others speak of it; and they say it is the shadow of Death. But Sauron did not bring that; he promiseth that he will save us from it.'

'There is a shadow, but it is the shadow of the fear of Death, and the shadow of greed. But there is also a shadow of darker evil. We no longer see our king. His displeasure falleth on men, and they go out; they are in the evening, and in the morning they are not. The open is insecure; walls are dangerous. Even by the heart of the house spies may sit. And there are prisons, and chambers underground. There are torments; and there are evil rites. The woods at night, that once were fair – men would roam and sleep there for delight, when thou wert a babe – are filled now with horror. Even our gardens are not wholly clean, after the sun has fallen. And now even by day smoke riseth from the temple: flowers and grass are withered where it falleth. The old songs are forgotten or altered; twisted into other meanings.'

'Yea: that one learneth day by day,' said Herendil. 'But some of the new songs are strong and heartening. Yet now I hear that some counsel us to abandon the old tongue. They say we should leave Eressëan, and revive the ancestral speech of Men. Sauron teacheth it. In this at least I think he doth not well.'

'Sauron deceiveth us doubly. For men learned speech of the Firstborn, and therefore if we should verily go back to the beginnings we should find not the broken dialects of the wild men, nor the simple speech of our fathers, but a tongue of the Firstborn. But the Eressëan is of all the tongues of the First-born the fairest, and they use it in converse with the Lords, and it linketh their varied kindreds one to another, and them to us. If we forsake it, we should be sundered from them, and be impoverished.[27] Doubtless that is what he intendeth. But there is no end to his malice. Listen now, Herendil, and mark well. The time is nigh when all this evil shall bear bitter fruit, if it be not cut down. Shall we wait until the fruit be ripe, or hew the tree and cast it into the fire?'

Herendil got suddenly to his feet, and went to the window. 'It is cold, father,' he said; 'and the Moon is gone. I trust the garden is empty. The trees grow too near the house.' He drew a heavy embroidered cloth across the window, and then returned, crouching by the fire, as if smitten by a sudden chill.

Elendil leant forward in his chair, and continued in a lowered voice. 'The king and queen grow old, though all know it not, for they are seldom seen. They ask where is the undying life that Sauron promised them if they would build the Temple for Morgoth. The Temple is built, but they are grown old. But Sauron foresaw this, and I hear (already the whisper is gone forth) that he declareth that Morgoth's bounty is restrained by the Lords, and cannot be fulfilled while they bar the way. To win life Tarkalion must win the West.[28] We see now the purpose of the towers and weapons. War is already being talked of – though they do not name the enemy. But I tell thee: it is known to many that the war will go west to Eressëa: and beyond. Dost thou perceive the extremity of our peril, and the madness of the king? Yet this doom draws swiftly near. Our ships are recalled from the [?corners] of the earth. Hast thou not marked and wondered that so many are absent, especially of the younger folk, and in the South and West of our land both works and pastimes languish? In a secret haven to the North there is a building and forging that hath been reported to me by trusty messengers.'

'Reported to thee? What dost thou mean, father?' asked Herendil as if in fear.

'Even what I say. Why dost thou look on me so strangely? Didst thou think the son of Valandil, chief of the wise men of Númenor, would be deceived by the lies of a servant of Morgoth? I would not break faith with the king, nor do I purpose anything to his hurt. The house of Eärendel hath my allegiance while I live. But if I must choose between Sauron and Manwë, then all else must come after. I will not bow unto Sauron, nor to his master.'

'But thou speakest as if thou wert a leader in this matter – woe is me, for I love thee; and though thou swearest allegiance, it will not save thee from the peril of treason. Even to dispraise Sauron is held rebellious.'

'I am a leader, my son. And I have counted the peril both for myself and for thee and all whom I love. I do what is right and my right to do, but I cannot conceal it longer from thee. Thou must choose between thy father and Sauron. But I give thee freedom of choice and lay on thee no obedience as to a father, if I have not convinced thy mind and heart. Thou shalt be free to stay or go, yea even to report as may seem good to thee all that I have said. But if thou stayest and learnest more, which will involve closer counsels and other [?names] than mine, then thou wilt be bound in honour to hold thy peace, come what may. Wilt thou stay?'

'*Atarinya tye-meláne*,' said Herendil suddenly, and clasping his father's knees he laid his [?head there] and wept. 'It is an evil hour that [?putteth] such a choice on thee,' said his father, laying a hand on his head. 'But fate calleth some to be men betimes. What dost thou say?'

'I stay, father.'

Christopher Tolkien notes: 'The narrative ends here. There is no reason to think that any more was ever written. The manuscript, which becomes increasingly rapid towards the end, peters out in a scrawl.' He then continues with his appraisal of what, at the time, were his father's plans for continuing the story:

There are several pages of notes that give some idea of my father's thoughts – at a certain stage – for the continuation of the story beyond the point where he abandoned it. These are in places quite illegible, and in any case were the concomitant of rapidly changing ideas: they are the vestiges of thoughts, not statements of formulated conceptions. More important, some at least of these notes clearly preceded the actual narrative that was written and were taken up into it, or replaced by something different, and it may very well be that this is true of them all, even those that refer to the latter part of the story which was never written. But they make it very clear that my father was concerned above all with the relation between the father and the son, which was cardinal. In Númenor he had engendered a situation in which there was the potentiality of anguishing conflict between them, totally incommensurate with the quiet harmony in which the Errols began – or ended. [The Errol family – ancestors and descendants – are the central protagonists of the intended narrative in *The Lost Road*.] The relationship of Elendil and Herendil was subjected to a profound menace. This conflict could have many narrative issues within the framework of the known event, the attack on Valinor and the Downfall of Númenor, and in these notes my father was merely sketching out some solutions, none of which did he develop or return to again.

An apparently minor question was the words 'the Eagles of the Lord of the West': what did they mean, and how were they placed within the story? It seems that he was as puzzled by them as was Alboin Errol when he used them ([*Road*], pp. 38, 47). He queries whether 'Lord of the West' means the King of

Númenor, or Manwë, or whether it is the title properly of Manwë but taken in his despite by the King; and concludes 'probably the latter'. There follows a 'scenario' in which Sorontur King of Eagles is sent by Manwë, and Sorontur flying against the sun casts a great shadow on the ground. It was then that Elendil spoke the phrase, but he was overheard, informed upon, and taken before Tarkalion, who declared that the title was his. In the story as actually written Elendil speaks the words to Herendil ([*Road*] p. 62 [This volume, p. 237]), when he sees clouds rising out of the West in the evening sky and stretching out 'great wings' – the same spectacle as made Alboin Errol utter them, and the men of Númenor in the *Akallabêth* (p. 277 [This volume p. 185]); and Herendil replies that the title has been decreed to belong to the King. The outcome of Elendil's arrest is not made clear in the notes, but it is said that Herendil was given command of one of the ships, that Elendil himself joined in the great expedition because he followed Herendil, that when they reached Valinor Tarkalion set Elendil as a hostage in his son's ship, and that when they landed on the shores Herendil was struck down. Elendil rescued him and set him on shipboard, and 'pursued by the bolts of Tarkalion' they sailed back east. 'As they approach Númenor the world bends; they see the land slipping towards them'; and Elendil falls into the deep and is drowned.* This group of notes ends with references to the coming of the Númenóreans to Middle-earth, and to the 'later stories'; 'the flying ships', 'the painted caves', 'how Elf-friend walked on the Straight Road'.

Other notes refer to plans laid by the 'anti-Saurians' for an assault on the Temple, plans betrayed by Herendil 'on condition that Elendil is spared'; the assault is defeated and Elendil

---

* It would be interesting to know if a tantalisingly obscure note, scribbled down in isolation, refers to this dimly-glimpsed story: 'If either fails the other they perish and do not return. Thus at the last moment Elendil must prevail on Herendil to hold back, otherwise they would have perished. At that moment he sees himself as Alboin: and realises that Elendil and Herendil had perished.'

captured. Either associated with this or distinct from it is a suggestion that Herendil is arrested and imprisoned in the dungeons of Sauron, and that Elendil renounces the Gods to save his son.

My guess is that all this had been rejected when the actual narrative was written, and that the words of Herendil that conclude it show that my father had then in mind some quite distinct solution, in which Elendil and his son remained united in the face of whatever events overtook them.*

In the early narratives there is no indication of the duration of the realm of Númenor from its foundation to its ruin; and there is only one named king. In his conversation with Herendil, Elendil attributes all the evils that have befallen to the coming of Sauron: they have arisen therefore in a quite brief time (forty-four years, p. 242); whereas in the *Akallabêth*, when a great extension of Númenórean history had taken place, those evils began long before, and are indeed traced back as far as the twelfth ruler, Tar-Ciryatan the Shipbuilder, who took the sceptre nearly a millennium and a half before the Downfall (*Akallabêth* p. 265, *Unfinished Tales* p. 221 [This volume p. 146]).

From Elendil's words at the end of *The Lost Road* there emerges a sinister picture: the withdrawal of the besotted and aging king from the public view, the unexplained disappearance of people unpopular with the 'government', informers, prisons, torture, secrecy, fear of the night; propaganda in the form of the 'rewriting of history' (as exemplified by Herendil's words concerning what was now said about Eärendel, p. 235); the multiplication of weapons of war, the purpose of which is

---

* I have suggested ([*Road*] p. 31) that since Elendil of Númenor appears in FN II (§14 [*Road*, p. 28]) as king in Beleriand he must have been among those who took no part in the expedition of Tar-kalion, but 'sat in their ships upon the east coast of the land' (FN §9 [*Road*, pp. 27–28]).

concealed but guessed at; and behind all the dreadful figure of Sauron, the real power, surveying the whole land from the Mountain of Númenor. The teaching of Sauron has led to the invention of ships of metal that traverse the seas without sails, but which are hideous in the eyes of those who have not abandoned or forgotten Tol-eressëa; to the building of grim fortresses and unlovely towers; and to missiles that pass with a noise like thunder to strike their targets many miles away. Moreover, Númenor is seen by the young as over-populous, boring, 'over-known': 'every tree and grass-blade is counted', in Herendil's words; and this cause of discontent is used, it seems, by Sauron to further the policy of 'imperial' expansion and ambition that he presses on the king. When at this time my father reached back to the world of the first man to bear the name 'Elf-friend' he found there an image of what he most condemned and feared in his own.

# NOTES

## INTRODUCTION

1   *The Letters of J. R. R. Tolkien* [*Letters*], No. 131, p. 143
2   ibid., No. 91, p. 104
3   *Letters*, No. 131, p. 150. Tolkien wrote this letter to Milton Waldman, an editor with William Collins, Sons & Co Ltd, seeking to interest him in *The Silmarillion* and *The Lord of the Rings* because his existing publisher, George Allen and Unwin (despite having had considerable success with *The Hobbit*), were nervous about commissioning two large books at a time when the publishing industry was hampered by post-war paper shortages. For accounts of this difficult period in the birthing of a literary masterpiece, see Humphrey Carpenter, *J. R. R. Tolkien: a biography* (1977) pp. 207–18 and Rayner Unwin, *George Allen & Unwin: A Remembrancer* (2021) pp. 71–104
4   *The Peoples of Middle-earth* [*Peoples*], p. 142
5   *Letters*, No. 257, p. 347
6   ibid., No. 294, p. 378
7   *Out of the Silent Planet* was published in 1938, the first of C.S. Lewis' 'Space Trilogy' (or 'Cosmic Trilogy') followed in 1943 by *Perelandra* (a.k.a. *Voyage to Venus*) and *That Hideous Strength* in 1945.
8   *Letters*, No. 257, p. 347
9   ibid., No. 294, p. 378
10  In January 1961, Tolkien wrote (*Letters*, No. 227, p. 303): 'Númenor, shortened form of Númenórë, is my own invention, compounded from *numē-n*, 'going down' ($\sqrt{}$ndū, nu), sunset, West, and *nōrë* 'land, country' = *Westernesse*. The legends of *Númenórë* are only in the background of *The Lord of the Rings*, though (of course) they were written first, and are only summarised in Appendix A. They are my own use for my own purposes of the *Atlantis* legend, but not based on special *knowledge*, but on a special personal concern with this tradition of the culture-bearing men of the Sea, which so profoundly affected the imagination of peoples of Europe with westward-shores.'

11   ibid., No. 131, p. 154
12   ibid., No. 24, p. 29

## BEFORE THE SECOND AGE

1   The quotations in this chapter are all taken from *Letters*, No 131, pp. 143 ff.

2   Tolkien adds in a footnote: 'As far as all this has symbolical or allegorical significance, Light is such a primeval symbol in the nature of the Universe, that it can hardly be analysed. The Light of Valinor (derived from light before any fall) is the light of art undivorced from reason, that sees things both scientifically (or philosophically) and imaginatively (or sub-creatively) and says that they are good – as beautiful. The Light of Sun (or Moon) is derived from the Trees only after they were sullied by Evil.'

3   Elsewhere in his letter to Milton Waldman Tolkien addressed what he saw as the primary themes in his writings about Middle-earth, one of which was the concept of 'the Fall', most usually associated with Judeo-Christian beliefs arising from the Biblical narrative of Adam and Eve (Genesis: Chapter 3), but given by Tolkien a far wider applicability:

'In the cosmogony there is a fall: a fall of Angels we should say. Though quite different in form, of course, to that of Christian myth. These tales are "new", they are not directly derived from other myths and legends, but they must inevitably contain a large measure of ancient wide-spread motives or elements. After all, I believe that legends and myths are largely made of "truth", and indeed present aspects of it that can only be received in this mode; and long ago certain truths and modes of this kind were discovered and must always reappear. There cannot be any "story" without a fall – all stories are ultimately about the fall – at least not for human minds as we know them and have them.

'So, proceeding, the Elves have a fall, before their "history" can become storial. (The first fall of Man, for reasons explained, nowhere appears – Men do not come on the stage until all that is long past, and there is only a rumour that for a while they fell under the domination of the Enemy and that some repented.)'

4   Tolkien adds, as a note: 'Of course in reality this only means that my "elves" are only a representation or an apprehension of a part of human nature, but that is not the legendary mode of talking.'

5   *The Children of Húrin* and *The Fall of Gondolin*, edited by Christopher Tolkien as independent works were published, respectively, in 2007 and 2018.

## 1 – FOUNDATION OF THE GREY HAVENS, AND OF LINDON

1  *The Lord of the Rings*, Appendix B [Appendix B], p. 1082
2  *Peoples*, p. 166
3  *The Silmarillion*, 'Of the Rings of Power' [Rings of Power], p. 285
4  *Letters*, No. 131, p. 150. To understand the evolution of the narrative that is included in *The Silmarillion* as Akallabêth, readers should consult *The Peoples of Middle-earth*, Part One: The Prologue and Appendices to *The Lord of the Rings*, V 'The History of the Akallabêth', pp. 140 ff.
5  Tol Eressëa, also known as the Lonely Isle, was situated east of Aman ('blessed realm') containing Valinor, home of the Valar. Its history is told in Chapter 5 of *The Silmarillion*.
6  The etymology of the name Avallónë is addressed in *The Lost Road and Other Writings*, 'The Etymologies', p. 349 and p. 370, but it is clear that this provided Tolkien with a happy coincidence of linking the island in the Middle-earth legendarium with the isle of Avalon featured in the Arthurian legends and which Tolkien cited as a literary influence, paralleling the dying King Arthur's passing by barge with the Ring-bearer's departure to the Undying Lands: 'To Bilbo and Frodo the special grace is granted to go with the Elves they loved – an Arthurian ending, in which it is, of course, not made explicit whether this is an "allegory" of death, or a mode of healing and restoration leading to a return.' (*Sauron Defeated*, Part One – 'The End of the Third Age', 'The Epilogue', p. 132)
7  *The Silmarillion*, Akallabêth [Akallabêth], p. 260. See note 4, above. Also of interest are Tolkien's earlier versions of his Atlantean concept: *The Lost Road and Other Writings*, I 'The Early History of the Legend', pp. 7–10 and II 'The Fall of Númenor' pp. 11 ff.; and *Sauron Defeated*, Part Three: 'The Drowning of Anadûnê', pp. 331 ff.
8  Rings of Power, p. 286
9  Appendix B, p. 1082. In Tolkien's writings, various ancestry is ascribed to Gil-galad, but in editing *The Silmarillion* Christopher Tolkien settled on using his father's option: 'Gil-galad son of Fingon'. His parentage is briefly discussed in *Peoples*, Part Two: Late Writings, XI 'The Shibboleth of Fëanor' [Shibboleth], p. 347. Gil-galad, whose later story is inextricably linked with the fate of the Second Age, was named thus, in Quenya, 'star of radiance . . . because his helm and mail, and his shield overlaid with silver and set with a device of white stars, shone from afar like a star in sunlight or moonlight and could be seen by Elvish eyes at a great distance if he stood upon a height.'
10  *Unfinished Tales*, [UT], pp. 234–5

11  *UT*, pp. 229–30. Part of a much longer description given in 'a very late and largely philological essay' cited by Christopher Tolkien in *UT*, see also note 14 below.

12  *Fellowship*, Book Two, VII 'The Mirror of Galadriel', pp. 354–5. In *The Nature of Middle-earth* [*Nature*] p. 352 note 8, with Tolkien's further etymological comments on the name of Galadriel, it says: 'The name *Galadriel* is in this form Sindarin. Its original meaning was "lady of the glittering coronal", referring to the brilliant sheen of her golden hair, which in her youth she wore in three long braids, the middle one being wound about her head. *Celeborn* is also in this form Sindarin, but originally meant "silver-tall".'

13  In full, Christopher Tolkien wrote: 'There is no part of the history of Middle-earth more full of problems than the story of Galadriel and Celeborn, and it must be admitted that there are severe inconsistencies "embedded in the traditions"; or, to look at the matter from another point of view, that the role and importance of Galadriel only emerged slowly, and that her story underwent continual refashionings.' See *UT*, Part Two: The Second Age, IV 'The History of Galadriel and Celeborn' pp. 288 ff; see also *Nature,* Part Three: The World, its Lands, and its Inhabitants, XVI 'Galadriel and Celeborn', pp. 346 ff.

14  Rings of Power, pp. 286

15  *The Lord of the Rings*, Appendix A [Appendix A], p. 1034

16  Appendix A, pp. 1034–5

## 32 – THE EDAIN REACH NÚMENOR

1  In Tolkien's earlier drafts for 'Of the Tale of Years', he had chronicled 'The Foundation of Númenor' as being dated in the year Second Age 50 (see *Peoples*, Part One, VI p. 168); this date was subsequently amended to SA 32, but in preparing 'The Tale of Years' for inclusion in *Return*, Appendix B, the year 32 is given as being the date when 'The Edain reach Númenór'. It is assumed that the author considered these two events – the Foundation of Númenor and the arrival of the Edain – as taking place within the same time frame.

2  See *The Silmarillion*: XII 'Of Men'; XVII 'Of the Coming of Men into the West'; the Genealogies (III 'The House of Bëor'; IV and V 'The House of Hador and The People of Haleth')

3  Appendix A, p. 1035

4  *The Silmarillion*, Valaquenta [Valaquenta], p. 30

5  A chief of the Maiar described in Valaquenta, p. 30 as 'the banner-bearer and herald of Manwë, whose might in arms is surpassed by none in Arda.'

6 A Maia described in Valaquenta, p. 30 as 'master of the seas that wash the shores of Middle-earth'.

7 A Vala described in Valaquenta, p. 27 as having lordship 'over all the substances of which Arda is made . . . the fashioning of all lands was his labour . . . a smith and master of all crafts.'

8 A Vala and the spouse of Aulë, described in Valaquenta, p. 27 as 'the Giver of Fruits . . . lover of all things that grow in the earth, and all their countless forms she holds in her mind.'

9 From the Quenya *anna* ('gift') and Sindarin *dôr* ('land')

10 Akallabêth, p. 260

11 As noted by Christopher Tolkien, in *Peoples*, p. 144 §5 the original passage in 'The Drowning of Anadûnê' as given in *Sauron Defeated*, p. 360 reads: 'Then the Edain gathered all the ships, great and small, that they had built with the help of the Elves, and those that were willing to depart took their wives and their children and all such wealth as they possessed, and they set sail upon the deep waters, following the Star.'

12 Akallabêth, pp. 260–1

13 First published in *Peoples*, p. 144 §5 continued on p. 145, not having been included among the extracts given in *UT*. Círdan the Shipwright was said to have 'seen further and deeper into the future than anyone else in Middle-earth' (*Peoples*, pp. 385 ff) and it was he to whom Celebrimbor had entrusted the Elven-ring Narya, the Ring of Fire. Círdan subsequently passed Narya to Gandalf on his arrival in Middle-earth, saying: 'Take this ring, Master . . . for your labours will be heavy; but it will support you in the weariness that you have taken upon yourself. For this is the Ring of Fire, and with it you may rekindle hearts in a world that grows chill. But as for me, my heart is with the Sea, and I will dwell by the grey shores until the last ship sails. I will await you.' (*Return*, Appendix B, p. 1085) Círdan fought in the Last Alliance of Elves and Men and, later, as Master of the Grey Havens, welcomed Galadriel, Celeborn, Elrond, Gandalf, Frodo and Bilbo when the Ring-bearers prepared to embark for the Undying Lands on the ship that he had built for their final voyage.

14 Appendix A, p. 1035. Elsewhere it is recorded: 'To the Númenórean people as a whole is ascribed a life-span some five times the length of that of other Men'; see Christopher Tolkien commentary, *UT*, p. 224 note 1.

15 The source of the extracts quoted in this editorial note is Akallabêth, p. 262. Elsewhere (*Letters*, No. 156, pp. 204–5) Tolkien wrote: 'For the point of view of this mythology is that "mortality" or a short span, and "immortality" or an indefinite span was part of what we might call the biological and spiritual *nature* of the Children of God,

Men and Elves (the firstborn) respectively, and could *not* be altered by anyone (even a Power or god), and would not be altered by the One, except perhaps by one of those strange exceptions to all rules and ordinances which seem to crop up in the history of the Universe, and show the Finger of God, as the one wholly free Will and Agent.'

Adding in a note: 'The story of Beren and Lúthien is the one great exception, as it is the way by which "Elvishness" becomes wound in as a thread in human history.'

Tolkien then continues: '[The Edain] were forbidden to sail *west* beyond their own land because they were not allowed to be or try to be "immortal"; and in this myth the Blessed Realm is represented as still having an actual physical existence as a region of the real world, one which they could have reached by ship, being very great mariners.'

16  In a draft letter to a reader Tolkien wrote (*Letters*, No. 244, p. 324): 'A Númenórean King was *monarch*, with the power of unquestioned decision in debate; but he governed the realm with the frame of ancient law, of which he was administrator (and interpreter) but not the maker.' The genealogy of the Kings and Queens of Númenor (there were three of the latter) followed in this book is drawn from *UT* Part Two: The Second Age, III 'The Line of Elros: Kings of Númenor' pp. 218–27. An abbreviated listing appears in *The Lord of the Rings*, Appendix A Annals of the Kings and Rulers I 'The Númenórean Kings' pp. 1033–1037 including (pp. 1035–6) the following notation:

> *These are the names of the Kings and Queens of Númenor:* Elros Tar-Minyatur, Vardamir, Tar-Amandil, Tar-Elendil, Tar-Meneldur, Tar-Aldarion, Tar-Ancalimë (the first Ruling Queen), Tar-Anárion, Tar-Súrion, Tar-Telperiën (the second Queen), Tar-Minastir, Tar-Ciryatan, Tar-Atanamir the Great, Tar-Ancalimon, Tar-Telemmaitë, Tar-Vanimeldë (the third Queen), Tar-Alcarin, Tar-Calmacil, Tar-Ardamin.
>
> After Ardamin the Kings took the sceptre in names of the Númenórean (or Adûnaic) tongue: Ar-Adûnakhôr, Ar-Zimrathôn, Ar-Sakalthôr, Ar-Gimilzôr, Ar-Inziladûn. Inziladûn repented of the ways of the Kings and changed his name to Tar-Palantir 'The Farsighted'. His daughter should have been the fourth Queen, Tar-Míriel, but the King's nephew usurped the sceptre and became Ar-Pharazôn the Golden, last King of the Númenóreans.
>
> In the days of Tar-Elendil the first ships of the Númenóreans came back to Middle-earth. His elder child was a daughter, Silmariën. Her son was Valandil, first of the Lords of Andúnië in the

west of the land, renowned for their friendship with the Eldar. From him were descended Amandil, the last lord, and his son Elendil the Tall.

The sixth King left only one child, a daughter. She became the first Queen; for it was then made a law of the royal house that the eldest child of the King, whether man or woman, should receive the sceptre.

17 Elros (in Elvish, the name means 'Star-foam') and his twin brother Elrond ('Star-dome') were born in the year 532 of the First Age, children of Eärendil and his wife Elwing. Six years later, the boys were taken captive by Maglor and Maedhros (two of the Sons of Fëanor) in the third and cruellest of the Elven Kinslayings resulting from their attempt to recover the Silmaril held by Elwing. Despite much bloodletting, Maglor and Maedhros spared the children's lives and Maglor raised them in his own household.

Following the Third Kinslaying, Eärendil and Elwing voyaged to Valinor in order to entreat the Valar to aid the Men and Elves of Middle-earth in their struggles against the rebel Vala, Morgoth ('Black Foe of the World'), the first Dark Lord and root of all evil in Middle-earth. Although breaking the Valar's ban on a mortal entering upon the sacred soil of the Undying Lands, Eärendil was spared death because his plea had been made on behalf of the Elves and Men of Middle-earth. As a Half-elven, he and Elwing were given the choice of whether to be numbered with the race of Elves or that of Mankind, a choice that was further promised to their children. Eärendil followed the choice of his wife and was numbered with the Elven-kind. Of their children, Elrond made the same choice, while Elros chose to live as a Man and became the first king of Númenor. The full tale of these events is told in *The Silmarillion*, XXIV 'Of the Voyage of Eärendil and the War of Wrath', pp. 246 ff. The end of Eärendil's story is one told in verse by Bilbo in Rivendell and heard by Frodo as he 'wandered long in a dream of music that turned into running water, and then into a voice.' *Fellowship*, Book Two, I 'Many Meetings' pp. 233–6

18 Appendix A, I (iii), p. 1043 note 1

19 Elros took the name Tar-Minyatur meaning in Quenya, 'High First-ruler', from the words *tar* ('king'), *minya* ('first') and *ture* ('lord' or 'master'). By convention subsequent rulers of Númenor adopted the prefix 'Tar-' for their royal title until, as noted, the reign of the twentieth king, Ar-Adûnakhôr (Tar-Herunúmen), who took a title in the Adûnaic, the language of the men of Númenor.

20 *UT*, p. 222

## THE GEOGRAPHY OF NÚMENOR

1  The geographic descriptions of the island Númenor are drawn from
   *UT* (Part Two: The Second Age, I: A Description of Númenor,
   pp. 165 ff) and *Nature* (Part Three: The World, its Lands, and its
   Inhabitants, XIII 'Of the Land and Beasts of Númenor', pp. 328 ff)
   but for the purposes of this book are arranged to best describe the
   island's physical geography. To avoid a surfeit of footnotes, unless
   otherwise stated, these passages are drawn from these two sources.
   Some details relating to specific periods or the reigns of particular
   rulers have been relocated within the relevant time frames where their
   sources are noted.
2  Hards = a firm or solid beach or foreshore

## THE NATURAL LIFE OF NÚMENOR

1  The accounts that follow relating to the flora and fauna on Númenor,
   are again drawn from *UT* (Part Two: The Second Age, I: A Description of Númenor, pp. 165 ff) and *Nature* (Part Three: The World, its
   Lands, and its Inhabitants, XIII 'Of the Land and Beasts of Númenor',
   pp. 328 ff), but arranged in a form to best serve the narrative; and, as
   in 'The Geography of Númenor' above, footnotes are only added
   where material is included from additional sources.
2  Laurelin (The Golden Tree) with Telperion (The Silver Tree) were
   the Two Trees of Valinor that gave light to that realm. Accounts of
   their creation and destruction are to be found in *The Silmarillion*
   (*Quenta Silmarillion* I 'Of the Beginning of Days', VIII 'Of the Dark-
   ening of Valinor' and elsewhere. While successors to Telperion endured
   into the Third Age (as with the White Tree of Gondor) 'no likeness
   remained in Middle-earth of Laurelin the Golden.' (*Return*, Appendix
   A (i) Númenor, p.1034)
3  *Fellowship*, Book Two, VI 'Lothlorien', p. 335

## THE LIFE OF THE NÚMENÓREANS

1  The accounts of the life and culture of the Edain, the Men of Númenor
   are once more drawn from *UT* (Part Two: The Second Age, I: A
   Description of Númenor, pp. 165 ff), Akallabêth p. 261 and *Nature*
   (Part Three: The World, its Lands, and its Inhabitants, XI 'Lives of
   the Númenóreans', pp. 316 ff; XII 'The Aging of the Númenóreans'
   pp. 329 ff), but arranged in a form to best serve the narrative; and, as
   noted above, endnotes are only added where material is included from
   additional sources.

2 From the Sindarin meaning 'west-men' or 'westerner' a name used of Númenóreans who had friendship with the Elves.

3 For Tolkien, the spiritual significance of the religious faith and observances of the Númenóreans was not only ideologically central to *The Lord of the Rings* (and, more broadly, to his entire legendarium), but also had an applicability to the writer's own world. In a note intended as a personal comment on W. H. Auden's review of *The Return of the King* in *The New York Times Book Review* of 22 January 1956 (*Letters*, No. 183, pp. 243–4) Tolkien wrote:

> In *The Lord of the Rings* the conflict is not basically about 'freedom', though that is naturally involved. It is about God, and His sole right to divine honour. The Eldar and the Númenóreans believed in The One, the true God, and held worship of any other person an abomination. Sauron desired to be a God-King, and was held to be this by his servants; if he had been victorious he would have demanded divine honour from all rational creatures and absolute temporal power over the whole world. So even if in desperation 'the West' had bred or hired hordes of orcs and had cruelly ravaged the lands of other Men as allies of Sauron, or merely to prevent them from aiding him, their Cause would have remained indefeasibly right. As does the Cause of those who oppose now the State-God and Marshal This or That as its High Priest, even if it is true (as it unfortunately is) that many of their deeds are wrong, even if it were true (as it is not) that the inhabitants of 'The West', except for a minority of wealthy bosses, live in fear and squalor, while the worshippers of the State-God live in peace and abundance and in mutual esteem and trust.

4 *Letters*, No. 156, p. 204

5 Tolkien devised Adûnaic as part of his unrealized work *The Notion Club Papers* (1945) in which one of the protagonists, Alwin Lowdham, compiles an (unfinished) report on the Númenórean language. An astonishing piece of work, running to many pages, it can be found in *Sauron Defeated*, pp. 413 ff.

For the later use of the language of Númenor, following the end of the Second Age, and its relationship with the other languages of Middle-earth, see *The Lord of the Rings* Appendix F, The Languages and Peoples of the Third Age, 'Of Men' (pp. 1128 ff).

6 The line of the Lords of Andúnië was founded by Valandil whose mother, Silmariën, was wife to Elatan of Andúnië and the eldest child of Tar-Elendil, Fourth King of Númenor. Since, under the laws of Númenor at that time, Silmariën was not allowed to inherit and rule as queen, Valandil and subsequent Lords of Andúnië were not in line

for royal succession. Nevertheless, by the end of the Second Age, Valandil's descendants were to become kings in Middle-earth, beginning with Elendil, the last Lord of Andúnië and first High King of Arnor and Gondor.

See also Appendix A, I (iii), p. 1043, for a note discussing the silver rod of the Lords of Andúnië (the sceptre of Annúminas) that survived the Downfall of Númenor to become the mark of the kings of Arnor and was 'more than five thousand years old when Elrond surrendered it to Aragorn', as is described in *Return*, p. 973.

7 Eressëans = elves of Tol Eressëa

8 Tolkien wrote further on the topic of the Númenorean's longevity in 'Elvish Ages & Númenóreans' (*Nature*, Part One XVIII, p. 151) and, at greater length and with additional reference to the subject of marriage, in 'The Ageing of Númenóreans' (*Nature*, Part Three, XII, pp. 328–30); he also provided (*Nature*, p. 318) the following formula for calculating at 'what "age" a Númenórean was in ordinary human terms of vigour and aptitude':

(1) Deduct 20: since at 20 years a Númenórean would be at about the same stage of development as an ordinary person.
(2) Add to this 20 the remainder divided by 5. Thus a Númenórean man or woman of years:

25 50 75 100 125 150 175 200 225 250 275 300 325 350 375 400 425
would be approximately of the 'age':
21 26 31 36 41 46 51 56 61 66 71 76 81 86 91 96 101

9 In an author's note, Tolkien explained that Númenóreans 'were not of uniform racial descent'; an explanation of these differences can be found in *Nature*, p. 323

10 Mediately = indirectly

11 Akallabêth, p. 262

12 'The King's sword was indeed Aranrúth, the sword of Elu Thingol of Doriath in Beleriand that had descended to Elros from Elwing his mother.' *UT*, pp. 171–2 note 2, which also contains details of 'other heirlooms' including the Ring of Barahir, the great Axe of Tuor and the Bow of Bregor of the House of Bëor.

13 *Letters*, No. 156, pp. 204–5

14 Akallabêth, p. 263

15 With reference to the Two Trees of Valinor, see p. 260, note 2. For the history and names of the White Trees, see Christopher Tolkien's notes in 'The History of the Akallabêth', *Peoples*, pp. 147–9.

16 Akallabêth, p. 263 and *Peoples*, p. 147. The history of the White Tree is spoken of in *The Lord of the Rings*, as in Elrond's description of the

City of Arnor (later Minas Tirith): '. . .Westward at the feet of the White Mountains Minas Anor they made, Tower of the Setting Sun. There in the courts of the King grew a white tree, from the seed of that tree which Isildur brought over the deep waters, and the seed of that tree before came from Eressëa, and before that out of the Uttermost West in the Day before days when the world was young.' (*Fellowship*, pp. 244–5)

By the time of the War of the Ring, the Third White Tree that had been planted in the Court of the Fountain in Minas Tirith was dead, having died in SA 2872 and, as no seedling could be found, was left standing 'until the King come[s]' ('The Heirs of Elendil', *Peoples*, p. 206). That prophecy would be fulfilled, at the closing of the Third Age, with the crowning of Aragorn King Elessar Telcontar, the 26th King of Arnor, 35th King of Gondor and first High King of Gondor and Arnor since the short reign of Isildur. As is told in *The Lord of the Rings* (*Return*, Book Six, V 'The Steward and the King', pp. 972–3) on the eve of the coronation, Gandalf took Aragorn up onto Mount Mindolluin, the easternmost peak of the Ered Nimrais (the White Mountains) to a high hallow high above the city where the Kings of Gondor were wont to go. There, at dawn, Aragorn saw

a stony slope behind him running down from the skirts of the snow; and as he looked he was aware that alone there in the waste a growing thing stood. And he climbed to it, and saw that out of the very edge of the snow there sprang a sapling tree no more than three foot high. Already it had put forth young leaves long and shapely, dark above and silver beneath, and upon its slender crown it bore one small cluster of flowers whose white petals shone like the sunlit snow. . .

Then Aragorn laid his hand gently to the sapling, and lo! it seemed to hold only lightly to the earth, and it was removed without hurt; and Aragorn bore it back to the Citadel. Then the withered tree was uprooted, but with reverence; and they did not burn it, but laid it to rest in the silence of Rath Dínen*. And Aragorn planted the new tree in the court by the fountain, and swiftly and gladly it began to grow; and when the month of June entered in it was laden with blossom.

* Rath Dínen, the way through the Hallows of Minas Tirith – accessed through the gate of Fen Hollen on the sixth level of the city – where, after death, the Kings and Stewards of Gondor were laid to rest.

17  Akallabêth, pp. 261–2
18  *Nature*, p. 340

### c. 40 – MANY DWARVES LEAVING THEIR OLD CITIES IN ERED LUIN GO TO MORIA AND SWELL ITS NUMBERS

1 Appendix A, 'Annals of the Kings and Rulers, III Durin's Folk' p. 1071
2 *Fellowship*, Book Two, II 'The Council of Elrond', pp. 240–1

### 442 – DEATH OF ELROS TAR-MINYATUR

1 *UT*, p. 218
2 *UT*, p. 225 note 3. Christopher Tolkien comments on the rule of Tar-Amandil as follows: 'The figure of 148 (rather than 147) must represent the years of Tar-Amandil's actual rule, and not take the notional year of Vardamir's reign into account.'

### c. 500 – SAURON BEGINS TO STIR AGAIN IN MIDDLE-EARTH

1 *Letters*, No. 131, pp. 150–1
2 *Silmarillion*, XXIV, 'Of the Voyage of Earendil and the War of Wrath', pp. 254–5. Sauron's crimes during the First Age are recounted in *The Silmarillion*, and in particular in chapters XVIII, 'Of the Ruin of Beleriand and the Fall of Fingolfin', and XIX, 'Of Beren and Lúthien'.
3 Rings of Power, p. 285. In a draft letter written by Tolkien in September 1954 (*Letters*, No. 153, p. 190) he writes: 'Sauron was of course not "evil" in origin. He was a "spirit" corrupted by the Prime Dark Lord (the Prime sub-creative Rebel) Morgoth. He was given an opportunity of repentance, when Morgoth was overcome, but could not face the humiliation of recantation, and suing for pardon; and so his temporary turn to good and "benevolence" ended in a greater relapse, until he became the main representative of Evil of later ages. But at the beginning of the Second Age he was . . . not indeed wholly evil, not unless all "reformers" who want to hurry up with "reconstruction" and "reorganization" are wholly evil, even before pride and the lust to exert their will eat them up.'
4 *Letters*, No. 131, p. 151
5 *Morgoth's Ring*, Part Five, 'Myths Transformed', pp. 394–7
6 Rings of Power, p. 286. With reference to the Avari in the *Quenta Silmarillion*, Tolkien writes of those Elves who refused the call of the Valar to sail to West: 'But many refused the summons, preferring the starlight and the wide spaces of Middle-earth to the rumour of the

Trees; and these are the Avari, the Unwilling, and they were sundered in that time from the Eldar, and met never again until many ages were past.' *Silmarillion*, III, 'Of the Coming of the Elves', p. 52.

7 Rings of Power, p. 286

## 521 – BIRTH IN NÚMENOR OF SILMARIËN

1 *The Lost Road*, 'The Etymologies' p. 356
2 From the Quenya *parma* ('book') and *-maitë* ('-handed') meaning 'handy' or 'skilful', *UT*, Index p. 460

## 600 – THE FIRST SHIPS OF THE NÚMENÓREANS APPEAR OFF THE COASTS

1 Akallabêth, pp. 262–3
2 *UT*, p. 221. A later footnote (p. 274) states: 'As is told . . . it was Vëantur who first achieved the voyage to Middle-earth in the year 600 of the Second Age (he was born in 451).'
3 Akallabêth, p. 263
4 *UT*, p. 220. It is added here: 'It was indeed [the Númenóreans'] grievance, when the Shadow crept along the coasts and men whom they had befriended became afraid or hostile, that iron was used against them by those to whom they had revealed it.' And in an earlier passage at this reference it is noted: 'In later days, in the wars upon Middle-earth, it was the bows of the Númenóreans that were most greatly feared. "The Men of the Sea," it was said, "send before them a great cloud, as a rain turned to serpents, or a black hail tipped with steel"; and in those days the great cohorts of the King's Archers used bows made of hollow steel, with black-feathered arrows a full ell long from point to notch.'
5 Footnote 3 to 'Aldarion and Erendis', *UT*, pp. 274–5. Christopher Tolkien adds (pp. 275–6): 'Elsewhere in this essay it is explained that these Men dwelt about Lake Evendim, in the North Downs and the Weather Hills, and in the lands between as far as the Brandywine, west of which they often wandered though they did not dwell there. They were friendly with the Elves, though they held them in awe; and they feared the Sea and would not look upon it. It appears that they were in origin Men of the same stock as the Peoples of Bëor and Hador who had not crossed the Blue Mountains into Beleriand during the First Age.'

A strikingly variant representation of the coming of the Númenóreans to Middle-earth is given in Tolkien's incomplete tale, 'Tal-Elmar', which tells of a young man who lives in 'a fenced town

. . . in the green hills of Agar' and who is the first person to witness Númenórean ships approaching from the Great Sea. There is no indication of the time period in which this tale is set other than that Tolkien surmised it to date from '*before the Downfall*'. Either it portrays the Númenóreans from the fearful perspective of Men or, more likely, suggests a later time when Númenor was in thrall to Sauron (c. 3262–3310). The story is markedly different in style from most of Tolkien's 'Middle-earth' writings and appears in *Peoples*, Part Four: Unfinished Tales, XVII 'Tal-Elmar'.

Whilst not included in this volume, the following short extract conveys the tone of this depiction:

> These [High Men of the Sea] indeed we may dread as Death. For Death they worship and slay men cruelly in honour of the Dark. Out of the Sea they came, and if they ever had any land of their own, ere they came to the west-shores, we know not where it may be. Black tales come to us out of the coast-lands, north and south, where they have now long time established their dark fortresses and their tombs. But hither they have not come since my father's days, and then only to raid and catch men and depart. Now this was the manner of their coming. They came in boats . . . wafted by the winds; for the Sea-men spread great cloths like wings to catch the airs, and bind them to tall poles like trees of the forest. Thus they will come to the shore, where there is shelter, or as nigh as they may; and then they will send forth smaller boats laden with goods, and strange things both beautiful and useful such as our folk covet. These they will sell to us for small price, or give as gifts, feigning friendship, and pity for our need; and they will dwell a while, and spy out the land and the numbers of the folk, and then go. And if they do not return, men should be thankful. For if they come again it is in other guise. In greater numbers they come then: two ships or more together, stuffed with men and not goods, and ever one of the accursed ships hath black wings. For that is the Ship of the Dark, and in it they bear away evil booty, captives packed like beasts, the fairest women and children, or young men unblemished, and that is their end. Some say that they are eaten for meat; and others that they are slain with torment on the black stones in the worship of the Dark. Both maybe are true.

6  Akallabêth, p. 263
7  *Peoples*, p. 149 § 13
8  Akallabêth, p. 263
9  Rings of Power, pp. 286–7. In *UT*, p. 253 note 7, Christopher Tolkien

writes: 'In an isolated and undateable note it is said that although the name *Sauron* is used earlier than this in the Tale of Years, his name, implying identity with the great lieutenant of Morgoth in *The Silmarillion*, was not actually known until about the year 1600 of the Second Age, the time of the forging of the One Ring. The mysterious power of hostility, to Elves and Edain, was perceived soon after the year 500, and among the Númenóreans first by Aldarion towards the end of the eighth century. . . . But it had no known centre.'

## THE VOYAGES OF ALDARION

1  Unless otherwise noted, the chief part of the narrative in this and the chapters 'Aldarion and Erendis', 'The Wedding of Aldarion and Erendis' and 'The Accession of Tar-Aldarion' that follow is to be found (in uninterrupted form) in *UT*, Part Two: The Second Age, II 'Aldarion and Erendis: The Mariner's Wife' [Aldarion] pp. 173–217.

2  From the Quenya *anar* ('sun') and *-(n)dil* ('lover, friend').

3  Christopher Tolkien notes (*UT*, p. 213 note 2): 'Soronto's part in the story can now only be glimpsed'; see pp. 112, 118 and also p. 271 notes 1–3.

4  From the Quenya *aldar* ('trees') and *ion* ('son'), see *The Silmarillion*, Appendix: Elements in Quenya and Sindarin names. The name reflects Aldarion's reputation as a tree steward and a forester, a task he would take seriously since, as a mariner, it was important to ensure that the trees remained plentiful in order to meet the demands of his programme of shipbuilding. Whilst Anardil only took the name on his ascending the throne (in SA 883) it is the name by which he is called from this point going forward in the narrative of 'Aldarion and Erendis'.

5  An endearment based on the name Anardil (see note 2 above).

6  A prayer of thanksgiving made at the close of autumn; the third of the Númenóreans' three annual prayer ceremonies undertaken by the King on behalf of the people on the summit of Meneltarma.

7  Christopher Tolkien notes: '(Sîr) Angren was the Elvish name of the river Isen. Ras Morthil, a name not otherwise found, must be the great headland at the end of the northern arm of the Bay of Belfalas, which was also called Andrast (Long Cape).

'The reference to "the country of Amroth where the Nandor Elves still dwell" can be taken to imply that the tale of Aldarion and Erendis was written down in Gondor before the departure of the last ship from the haven of the Silvan Elves near Dol Amroth in the year 1981 of the Third Age; see *UT*, pp. 240 ff.'

8  As the third child but only son of Tar-Elendil, Tar-Meneldur

succeeded to the throne because, at that time, in Númenórean history female children were not legally eligible to inherit the title.

9   *UT*, p. 219. Although the name Írimon is Quenya, neither J.R.R. Tolkien nor Christopher Tolkien propose a specific Anglicization. Meneldur is also given the name 'Elentirmo' for which the Index to *Unfinished Tales* translates from Quenya as 'Star-watcher'.

10  Elsewhere (*UT*, p. 219) it is said of him: 'He was wise, but gentle and patient.'

11  In Quenya *Eä* means 'to be'; so 'the World that is' or the material universe as summoned into being by Eru Ilúvatar with the one word 'Eä' and shaped by the Music of the Ainur.

12  The story of the creation of Arda (Quenya = 'realm', the Earth as the kingdom of Manwë), at its origin a flat Earth cosmology, is recounted in the first part of *The Silmarillion* ('Ainulindalë', 'Valaquenta' and *Quenta Silmarillion* I: 'Of the Beginning of Days').

13  In 'A Description of Númenor' (*UT*, p. 167) it is recounted how Tar-Meneldur 'built a tall tower, from which he could observe the motions of the stars' in the region of the mountain Sorontil, near to the Northern Cape of Forostar, the eastern flank of which 'rose sheer from the sea in tremendous cliffs'.

## 750 – EREGION FOUNDED BY THE NOLDOR

1   *UT*, p. 234; regarding the 'captivity of Melkor', see *The Silmarillion*, p. 51

2   With reference to the date year 700 being at variance with the date of 750 given in Appendix B, 'The Tale of Years', for the Foundation of Eregion, as is noted on p. 256 note 13 above, caution is needed with regard to the complexities of the histories of Galadriel and Celeborn.

Eregion, 'which Men called Hollin', was situated east of the river Bruinen ('Loudwater') and within the shadow of the Misty Mountains and, in particular, the mighty peak of Caradhras, one of the three great mountains beneath which the Dwarvish clan of Durin's Folk had built their great city of Khazad-dûm.

3   The tragic events concerning Doriath in the history of the First Age are written of in *Quenta Silmarillion*, XXII 'Of the Ruin of Doriath', pp. 227 ff.

4   Concerning the identity of Celebrimbor, Christopher Tolkien further notes that the text referenced in *Unfinished Tales* 'is emended to the later story that made him a descendant of Fëanor as is mentioned in Appendix B to *The Lord of the Rings* (in the revised edition only), and more fully detailed in *The Silmarillion* (pp. 176, 286), where he is said to have been the son of Curufin, the fifth son of Fëanor, who was

estranged from his father and remained in Nargothrond when Celegorm and Curufin were driven forth.'

5  *UT*, p. 235

6  Sindarin, from *gwaith* ('people, host') and *mírdain* ('jewel-smiths').

7  Born in Valinor, Fëanor was the firstborn child of Finwë, High King of the Noldor. A craftsman and jewel-smith he was the maker of the Silmarils and inventor of the Tengwar script with which the Elven tongues of Quenya and Telerin were written down. He likely also created the *palantíri*, the Seeing-stones that figure in the history of the War of the Ring. Fëanor's story is told primarily in *Quenta Silmarillion*, chapters VI–IX and XIII.

8  *Fellowship*, Book Two, IV 'A Journey in the Dark' pp. 304–6 where the *doors*, their signs and inscription are translated and explained by Gandalf.

9  *Fellowship*, Book Two IV 'A Journey in the Dark' p. 317. Gandalf goes on (pp. 317–18) to reveal that 'Bilbo had a corslet of mithril-rings that Thorin gave him' (see *The Hobbit*, Chapter XIII: 'Not At Home'); a gift later passed on by Bilbo to Frodo, (*Fellowship*, Book Two III 'The Ring Goes South' pp. 277–8).

## ALDARION AND ERENDIS

1  See p. 267 note 1

2  *UT*, Index p. 430

3  Uinen was a Maia of the Vala Ulmo, Lord of Waters and Dweller of the Deep. She was the wife of Ossë, Maia of the Inner Seas. It is said (*The Silmarillion* p. 30) that 'the Númenóreans lived long in her protection, and held her in reverence equal to the Valar.'

4  It is stated that the Guildhouse of the Venturers 'was confiscated by the Kings, and removed to the western haven of Andúnië; all its records perished' (i.e. in the Downfall), including all the accurate charts of Númenor. But it is not said when this confiscation of *Eämbar* took place.

5  The river was afterwards called Gwathló or Greyflood, and the haven Lond Daer. (*UT*, p. 214 note 9); for detail, see *UT*, Part Two IV 'The History of Galadriel and Celeborn', Appendix D 'The Port of Lond Daer' pp. 261 ff.

6  Cf. *The Silmarillion* p. 148: 'The Men of that House [i.e. of Bëor] were dark or brown of hair, with grey eyes.' According to a genealogical table of the House of Bëor Erendis was descended from Bereth, who was the sister of Baragund and Belegund, and thus the aunt of Morwen mother of Túrin Turambar and of Rían the mother of Tuor.

7  See p. 24

8 Vinyalondë was a harbour founded by Aldarion and the Venturers on the west coast of Middle-earth at the mouth of the Gwathló (Grey-flood), shown on the map on pp. x–xi by its later name Lond Daer.

9 This is to be understood as a portent.

10 Cf. Akallabêth p. 277, where it is told that in the days of Ar-Pharazôn 'ever and anon a great ship of the Númenóreans would founder and return not to haven, though such a grief had not till then befallen them since the rising of the Star [of Eärendil].'

11 Valandil was Aldarion's cousin, for he was the son of Silmariën, daughter of Tar-Elendil and sister of Tar-Meneldur. Valandil, first of the Lords of Andúnië, was the ancestor of Elendil the Tall, father of Isildur and Anárion.

12 'Prayer to Eru', the feast of the Spring; the first of the Númenóreans' three annual prayer ceremonies undertaken by the King on behalf of the people on the summit of Meneltarma.

13 In Adûnaic, the Númenórean language, the name given to Andor, the 'Land of Gift'.

14 In an 'Author's note' (UT, p. 215 note 18) it is noted: 'Thus came, it is said, the manner of the Kings and Queens afterward to wear as a star a white jewel upon the brow, and they had no crown.'

15 The fourth month of the year in the reckoning of the Second Age.


## THE WEDDING OF ALDARION AND ERENDIS

1 In UT (pp. 215–6) it is noted by the author: 'In the Westlands and in Andúnië the Elven-tongue [Sindarin] was spoken by high and low. In that tongue Erendis was nurtured; but Aldarion spoke the Númenórean speech, although as all high men of Númenor he knew also the tongue of Beleriand.' To this is appended a fuller explication by Christopher Tolkien of the languages used by the Númenóreans.

2 *Elanor* was a small golden star-shaped flower; it grew also upon the mound of Cerin Amroth in Lothlórien:

> At the hill's foot Frodo found Aragorn, standing still and silent as a tree; but in his hand was a small golden bloom of *elanor*, and a light was in his eyes. He was wrapped in some fair memory: and as Frodo looked at him he knew that he beheld things as they once had been in this same place. For the grim years were removed from the face of Aragorn, and he seemed clothed in white, a young lord tall and fair; and he spoke words in the Elvish tongue to one whom Frodo could not see. *Arwen vanimelda, namárië!* he said, and then he drew a breath, and returning out of his thought he looked at Frodo and smiled.

"Here is the heart of Elvendom on earth," he said, "and here my heart dwells ever, unless there be a light beyond the dark roads that we still must tread, you and I. Come with me!" And taking Frodo's hand in his, he left the hill of Cerin Amroth and came there never again as living man. (*Fellowship*, Book Two VI 'Lothlórien' p. 352)

Sam Gamgee gave the name of this flower to his daughter, on Frodo's suggestion.(*Return*, Book Six IX, 'The Grey Havens' p. 1026)

3   See p. 269, note 6 above for Erendis's descent from Bereth, the sister of Morwen's father Baragund.

4   It is stated that the Númenóreans, like the Eldar, avoided the begetting of children if they foresaw any separation likely between husband and wife between the conception of the child and at least its very early years. Aldarion stayed in his house for a very brief time after the birth of his daughter, according to the Númenóreans' idea of the fitness of things.

5   ChristopherTolkien writes (*UT*, pp. 216–7 note 23): 'In a note on the "Council of the Sceptre" at this time in the history of Númenor it is said that this Council had no powers to govern the King save by advice; and no such powers had yet been desired or dreamed of as needful. The Council was composed of members from each of the divisions of Númenor; but the King's Heir when proclaimed was also a member, so that he might learn of the government of the land, and others also the King might summon, or ask to be chosen, if they had special knowledge of matters at any time in debate. At this time there were only two members of the Council (other than Aldarion) who were of the Line of Elros: Valandil of Andúnië for the Andustar, and Hallatan of Hyarastorni for the Mittalmar; but they owed their place not to their descent or their wealth, but to the esteem and love in which they were held in their countries. (In the *Akallabêth* p. 268, it is said that "the Lord of Andúnië was ever among the chief councillors of the Sceptre".)'

6   Calenardhon, in Sindarin, means 'the Green Region' or 'Green Province' and later was known as the Plains of Rohan.

## THE ACCESSION OF TAR-ALDARION

1   ChristopherTolkien here provides an example: 'Thus if Tar-Meneldur had had no son the Heir would not have been Valandil his nephew (son of his sister Silmarien), but Malantur his cousin (grandson of Tar-Elendil's younger brother Eärendur).'

2  A legitimate male heir, on the other hand, could not refuse; but since a King could always resign the Sceptre, a male heir could in fact immediately resign to *his* natural heir. He was then himself deemed also to have reigned for at least one year; and this was the case (the only case) with Vardamir, the son of Elros, who did not ascend the throne but gave the Sceptre to his son Amandil.

3  Again Christopher Tolkien gives an example: 'Thus if Ancalimë had refused the Sceptre Tar-Aldarion's heir would have been Soronto, the son of his sister Ailinel; and if Ancalimë had resigned the Sceptre or died childless Soronto would likewise have been her heir.'

4  It is said elsewhere that this rule of 'royal marriage' was never a matter of law, but it became a custom of pride: 'a symptom of the growth of the Shadow, since it only became rigid when the distinction between the Line of Elros and other families, in life-span, vigour, or ability, had diminished or altogether disappeared.'

5  *Nature*, XII 'The Ageing of the Númenóreans' p. 330

## *c.* 1000 – SAURON, ALARMED BY THE GROWING POWER OF THE NÚMENÓREANS, CHOOSES MORDOR AS A LAND TO MAKE INTO A STRONGHOLD. HE BEGINS THE BUILDING OF BARAD-DÛR

1  *UT*, p. 236

2  *Return*, Book Six I 'The Tower of Cirith Ungol' p. 899

3  Mount Doom is a translation from the Sindarin *amon* ('hill') and *amarth* ('doom'), see *The Silmarillion*, Appendix Elements in Quenya and Sindarin names, p. 355; for Orodruin, literally 'burning mountain', see *The Lord of the Rings*, 'Appendix F II 'On Translation' p. 1134.

4  *Return*, Book Six III, 'Mount Doom', p. 940

5  Christopher Tolkien in *Peoples*, p. 390 note 14

6  *Return*, Book Six I 'The Tower of Cirith Ungol' pp. 899–900

7  *Towers*, Book Three VIII 'The Road to Isengard' p. 555

8  *Return*, Book Six III, 'Mount Doom', p. 935

9  *UT*, p. 212

## 1075 – TAR-ANCALIMË BECOMES THE FIRST RULING QUEEN OF NÚMENOR

1  In his notes to the narrative of Aldarion and Erendis (*UT* p. 217), Christopher Tolkien comments: 'This is strange, because Anárion was the Heir in Ancalimë's life-time. In "The Line of Elros" (*UT*, p. 220) it is said only that Anárion's daughters "refused the sceptre".'

# 1200 – SAURON ENDEAVOURS TO SEDUCE THE ELDAR. GIL-GALAD REFUSES TO TREAT WITH HIM; BUT THE SMITHS OF EREGION ARE WON OVER. THE NÚMENÓREANS BEGIN TO MAKE PERMANENT HAVENS

1  From a 'long essay' by J.R.R. Tolkien included in *Peoples*, Part Two: Late Writings X 'Of Dwarves and Men' pp. 304–5.

2  Rings of Power, p. 287. In 'Concerning Galadriel and Celeborn' (*UT*, Part Two: The Second Age, IV 'The History of Galadriel and Celeborn', p. 236), an account is given of Sauron's overtures to the Elves of Lindon: 'When he felt himself to be secure he sent emissaries to Eriador, and finally, in about the year 1200 of the Second Age, came himself, wearing the fairest form that he could contrive.'

   Christopher Tolkien writing of Sauron's 'fair form', *UT*, pp. 253–4 note 7, states: 'Sauron endeavoured to keep distinct his two sides: *enemy* and *tempter*. When he came among the Noldor he adopted a specious fair form (a kind of simulated anticipation of the later Istari).'

# c. 1500 – THE ELVEN-SMITHS INSTRUCTED BY SAURON REACH THE HEIGHT OF THEIR SKILL. THEY BEGIN THE FORGING OF THE RINGS OF POWER

1  In a draft letter written by Tolkien in September 1954 (*Letters*, No. 153, p. 190) he writes: 'The particular branch of the High-Elves concerned, the Noldor or Loremasters, were always on the side of "science and technology", as we should call it: they wanted to have the knowledge that Sauron genuinely had, and those of Eregion refused the warnings of Gil-galad and Elrond. The particular "desire" of the Eregion Elves – an "allegory" if you like of a love of machinery, and technical devices – is also symbolised by their special friendship with the Dwarves of Moria.'

   With reference to Sauron taking the 'fair name' of Annatar, Christopher Tolkien identifies (in 'The History of Galadriel and Celeborn', *UT*, pp. 253–4 note 7) alternative 'fair names': '*Artano* "high-smith", or *Aulendil*, meaning one who is devoted to the service of the Vala Aulë.'

2  Rings of Power, 287

3  *UT*, p. 237

# c.1590 – THE THREE RINGS ARE COMPLETED IN EREGION.

1  *Fellowship*, Book One II 'The Shadow of the Past', p. 47

2  What follows is taken from 'The History of Galadriel and Celeborn' in *UT*, pp. 236–7.

3 For Christopher Tolkien's extensive note on this matter see *UT*, pp. 252–3 note 5.

4 'Water of Awakening', the lake in Middle-earth where the first Elves awoke, *Quenta Silmarillion*, pp. 48, 50–3, 55, 83, 99, 233

5 *Quenta Silmarillion* p. 94

6 It is noted: 'but many Sindar and Noldor came to dwell among them, and their "Sindarizing" under the impact of Beleriandic culture began'. It is not made clear when this movement into Lórinand took place; it may be that they came from Eregion by way of Khazad-dûm and under the auspices of Galadriel.

7 Christopher Tolkien notes that this is more fully reported in Rings of Power, p. 287. The cozening of the smiths of Eregion by Sauron, and his giving himself the name Annatar, Lord of Gifts, is also told in Rings of Power, but of Galadriel there is no mention.

8 Christopher Tolkien notes within the body of this passage: 'No explanation is offered in this rapid outline of why Galadriel scorned Sauron, unless she saw through his disguise, or of why, if she did perceive his true nature, she permitted him to remain in Eregion.'

9 Celebrían was the daughter of Galadriel and Celeborn and, at the point in the creation of Tolkien's legendarium from which this narrative thread dates, Amroth was named as her brother. However, as Christopher Tolkien notes (*UT*, p. 240), this kinship was likely introduced as part of subsequent emendations made after the completion of *The Lord of the Rings*: 'If Amroth were indeed thought of as the son of Galadriel and Celeborn when *The Lord of the Rings* was written, so important a connection could hardly have escaped mention.' In a variant narrative, Amroth would become the last King of Lórien, inheriting the kingship on the death of his father, Amdír (also called Malgalad), in the Battle of Dagorlad (see year SA 3434). In *Unfinished Tales*, Christopher Tolkien included 'a short tale' (dating from 1969 or later) entitled 'Part of the Legend of Amroth and Nimrodel recounted in brief' (*UT*, pp. 240–2). With regard to Celeborn's refusal to pass through Khazad-dûm, the assumption must be that either he eventually crossed into the east by way of one of the passes over the Misty Mountains or via the Gap of Calenardhon, later known as the Gap of Rohan.

10 *UT*, p. 237

## c. 1600 – SAURON FORGES THE ONE RING IN ORODRUIN. HE COMPLETES THE BARAD-DÛR. CELEBRIMBOR PERCEIVES THE DESIGNS OF SAURON

1 Rings of Power, pp. 287–8

2 The descriptions given and the extracts quoted here are from

*Fellowship*, Book One II 'The Shadow of the Past', pp. 50–1.

3 ibid., Book Two II 'The Council of Elrond' p. 242

4 Rings of Power, p. 288

5 *UT*, p. 237. Christopher Tolkien writes (*UT*, p. 254 note 9): 'Galadriel cannot have made use of the powers of Nenya until a much later time, after the loss of the Ruling Ring; but it must be admitted that the text does not at all suggest this (although she is said just above to have advised Celebrimbor that the Elven Rings should never be used).'

6 Quenta Silmarillion, passim

7 *Fellowship*, Book Two X 'The Breaking of the Fellowship' p. 401

8 *Nature*, Part Three XVIII, pp 369–70. For the Debate of the Loremasters, see *Nature* VIII, 'Manwë's Ban', pp. 306 ff.


## 1693 – WAR OF THE ELVES AND SAURON BEGINS. THE THREE RINGS ARE HIDDEN

1 Rings of Power, p. 288


## 1695 – SAURON'S FORCES INVADE ERIADOR. GIL-GALAD SENDS ELROND TO EREGION

1 *UT*, pp. 237–8


## 1697 – EREGION LAID WASTE. DEATH OF CELEBRIMBOR. THE GATES OF MORIA ARE SHUT. ELROND RETREATS WITH REMNANT OF THE NOLDOR AND FOUNDS THE REFUGE OF IMLADRIS

1 Christopher Tolkien notes (*UT*, p. 238): 'It is not actually said here that Sauron at this time took possession of the Seven Rings, though the implication seems clear that he did so. In Appendix A (III) to *The Lord of the Rings* it is said that there was a belief among the Dwarves of Durin's Folk that the Ring of Durin III, King of Khazad-dûm, was given to him by the Elven-smiths themselves, and not by Sauron; but nothing is said in the present text about the way in which the Seven Rings came into the possession of the Dwarves.'

2 *UT*, p. 238


## 1699 – SAURON OVERRUNS ERIADOR

1 *UT* pp. 238–9

2 *Fellowship*, Book Two, II 'The Council of Elrond', p. 241

3 *Fellowship*, Book Two, IV 'A Journey in the Dark', pp. 316–17

## 1700 – TAR-MINASTIR SENDS A GREAT NAVY FROM NÚMENOR TO LINDON. SAURON IS DEFEATED

1 Although the date of SA 1700 given for this intervention by Tar-Minastir is clearly established in the legendarium, it is at variance with the dates given for the reign of his aunt, Queen Tar-Telperien (S.A. 1556–1731). Christopher Tolkien wrote (*UT*, p. 226 note 9): 'I cannot in any way account for this discrepancy.' It has been suggested that, at the time, Minastir might have been acting on behalf of Queen Tar-Telperien, either as Regent or, possibly, as designated Captain of the Queen's [King's] Ships. His being given the title 'King' in accounts of the sending of the Númenórean fleet to aid the Elves against Sauron might therefore be a case of the chronicler retrospectively acknowledging Minastir's later kingship even though, at that point, he had not taken up the Sceptre.

2 *UT*, p. 239

## 1701 – SAURON IS DRIVEN OUT OF ERIADOR. THE WESTLANDS HAVE PEACE FOR ALONG WHILE

1 *UT*, p. 240, with reference to Amroth and Celebrían, see p. 274 note 9 above.

## c. 1800 – FROM ABOUT THIS TIME ONWARD THE NÚMENÓREANS BEGIN TO ESTABLISH DOMINIONS ON THE COASTS. SAURON EXTENDS HIS POWER EASTWARDS. THE SHADOW FALLS ON NÚMENOR

1 *UT*, p. 239
2 Appendix A, p. 1036
3 ibid.
4 *UT*, p. 221
5 Appendix A, p. 1036
6 Akallabêth, p. 265
7 In the complex development of Tolkien's text for Akallabêth (as presented by Christopher Tolkien in *Peoples*, p. 150) it is further stated that 'To [Tar-Atanamir] came messages from the Valar, which he rejected. He clung to life for an extra 50 years.'
8 Appendix A, p. 1036
9 Akallabêth, pp. 263–6
10 *UT*, p. 221
11 Akallabêth, p. 267

## 2251 – DEATH OF TAR-ATANAMIR. TAR-ANCALIMON TAKES THE SCEPTRE. REBELLION AND DIVISION OF THE NÚMENÓREANS BEGINS. ABOUT THIS TIME THE NAZGÛL OR RINGWRAITHS, SLAVES OF THE NINE RINGS, FIRST APPEAR

1  Christopher Tolkien writes (*UT*, p. 226 note 10): 'In the Tale of Years (Appendix B to *The Lord of the Rings*) occurs the entry: "2251 Tar-Atanamir takes the sceptre. Rebellion and division of the Númenoreans begins." This is altogether discrepant with ['The Line of Elros', p. 221], according to which Tar-Atanamir died in 2221. This date 2221 is, however, itself an emendation from 2251; and his death is given elsewhere as 2251. Thus the same year appears in different texts as both the date of his accession and the date of his death; and the whole structure of the chronology shows clearly that the former must be wrong. Moreover, in the Akallabêth (*The Silmarillion* p. 266) it is said that it was in the time of Atanamir's son Ancalimon that the people of Númenor became divided. I have little doubt therefore that the entry in the Tale of Years is in error for a correct reading: "2251 Death of Tar-Atanamir. Tar-Ancalimon takes the sceptre. Rebellion and division of the Númenoreans begins." But if so, it remains strange that the date of Atanamir's death should have been altered in "The Line of Elros" if it were fixed by an entry in the Tale of Years.' In this volume the dating follows Christopher Tolkien's 'correct reading'.
2  Akallabêth, p. 266
3  Draft passage, not taken into the Akallabêth, given by Christopher Tolkien in *Peoples* p. 152.
4  Akallabêth, p. 266
5  *UT*, p. 221
6  Rings of Power, p. 288
7  *Letters*, No. 131, p. 151
8  Rings of Power, pp. 288–9
9  Akallabêth, p. 267
10  *Fellowship*, Book One, XI 'A Knife in the Dark' p. 196
11  *Towers*, Book Four, VI 'The Forbidden Pool' p. 692

## 2350 – PELARGIR IS BUILT. IT BECOMES THE CHIEF HAVEN OF THE FAITHFUL NÚMENÓREANS

1  Akallabêth, pp. 266–7. The latter part of this passage (after 'lending them aid against Sauron') is taken from 'the authentic text' as given by Christopher Tolkien in *Peoples*, p. 152. The version as given in Akallabêth reads: '. . .and their haven was Pelargir above the mouths

of Anduin the Great. But the King's Men sailed far away to the south; and the lordships and strongholds that they made have left many rumours in the legends of Men.'

2 *Akallabêth*, p. 267

3 *Peoples*, p. 175. Of the importance of Umbar and Pelargir in the Third Age and the role played by the Corsairs of Umbar in the War of the Ring, see *The Lord of the Rings* Books Five and Six.

4 Appendix A, p. 1036. Tolkien notes a reference to the 'Elder King' in 'The Song of Eärendil', or 'Eärendil was a mariner', written by Bilbo Baggins (with, as the poet admits, a contribution to its content from Aragorn) and sung to the assembled company at Rivendell on the evening prior to the Council of Elrond.

The reference appears in the sixth verse which speaks of Eärendil's visit to Valinor before setting out to 'sail the shoreless skies and come / behind the Sun and light of Moon':

> *He came unto the timeless halls*
> *where shining fall the countless years,*
> *and endless reigns the Elder King*
> *in Ilmarin on Mountain sheer;*
> *and words unheard were spoken then*
> *of folk of Men and Elven-kin,*
> *beyond the world were visions showed*
> *forbid to those that dwell therein.*

5 Rings of Power, pp. 289–90

6 *UT*, p. 221; see also *UT* p. 284 note 31.

7 An anomaly exists in the chronicling of Tar-Ardamin's place in the list of rulers that was later addressed by Christopher Tolkien in his notes to The Line of Elros', where he writes (*UT*, pp. 226–7 note 11):

In the list of the Kings and Queens of Númenor in Appendix A (I, i) to *The Lord of the Rings* the ruler following Tar-Calmacil (the eighteenth) was Ar-Adûnakhôr (the nineteenth). In the Tale of Years in Appendix B, Ar-Adûnakhôr is said to have taken the sceptre in the year 2899; and on this basis Mr Robert Foster in *The Complete Guide to Middle-earth* gives the death-date of Tar-Calmacil as 2899. On the other hand, at a later point in the account of the rulers of Númenor in Appendix A, Ar-Adûnakhôr is called the twentieth king; and in 1964 my father replied to a correspondent who had enquired about this: 'As the genealogy stands he should be called the sixteenth king and nineteenth ruler. Nineteen should possibly be read for twenty; but it is also possible that a name has been left out.' He explained that he could not be certain because at the time of writing this letter his papers on the subject were not available to him.

When editing the *Akallabêth* I changed the actual reading 'And the twentieth king took the sceptre of his fathers, and he ascended the throne in the name of Adûnakhôr' to 'And the nineteenth king. . .' (*The Silmarillion* p. 267), and similarly 'four and twenty' to 'three and twenty' (ibid. p. 270). At that time I had not observed that in 'The Line of Elros' the ruler following Tar-Calmacil was not Ar-Adûnakhôr but Tar-Ardamin; but it now seems perfectly clear, from the fact alone that Tar-Ardamin's death-date is here given as 2899, that he was omitted in error from the list in *The Lord of the Rings*.

On the other hand, it is a certainty of the tradition (stated in Appendix A, in the *Akallabêth*, and in 'The Line of Elros') that Ar-Adûnakhôr was the first King to take the sceptre in a name of the Adûnaic tongue. On the assumption that Tar-Ardamin dropped out of the list in Appendix A by a mere oversight, it is surprising that the change in the style of the royal names should there be attributed to the first ruler after Tar-Calmacil. It may be that a more complex textual situation underlies the passage than a mere error of omission.

## 2899 – AR-ADÛNAKHÔR TAKES THE SCEPTRE

1 Akallabêth, pp. 267–8
2 *UT*, p. 222
3 Appendix A, p. 1036
4 In 'The Line of Elros', *UT*, p. 287, the death-date for Ar-Gimilzôr is given as '3177'; however, in 'The Tale of Years' (Appendix B, p. 1084) the 'Repentance of Tar-Palantir' is dated as '3175', which suggests that date being the year in which Tar-Palantir took up the sceptre. Solely for the chronology as set out in this volume, the length of Ar-Gimilzôr's reign and his death-date have been amended accordingly. See Christopher Tolkien's observations in p. 280 note 2, below.
5 Akallabêth, p. 268
6 *UT*, p. 221
7 Akallabêth, pp. 268–9

## 3175 – REPENTANCE OF TAR-PALANTIR. CIVIL WAR IN NÚMENOR

1 Christopher Tolkien notes (*UT*, p. 227 note 13): 'There is a highly formalised floral design of my father's, similar in style to that shown

in *Pictures by J. R. R. Tolkien*, 1979, no. 45, bottom right, which bears the title *Inziladûn*, and beneath it is written both in Fëanorian script and transliterated *Númellótë* ["Flower of the West"].'

2  Christopher Tolkien writes (*UT*, p. 227 note 15): 'A final discrepancy between "The Line of Elros" and the Tale of Years arises in the dates of Tar-Palantir. It is said in the *Akallabêth* (p. 269) that "when Inziladûn acceded to the sceptre, he took again a title in the Elven-tongue as of old, calling himself Tar-Palantir"; and in the Tale of Years occurs the entry: "3175 Repentance of Tar-Palantir. Civil war in Númenor." It would seem almost certain from these statements that "3175" was the year of his accession; and this is borne out by the fact that in "The Line of Elros" the death-date of his father Ar-Gimilzôr was originally given as "3175", and only later emended to "3177". As with the death-date of Tar-Atanamir [see p. 277 note 1 to '2251' above] it is hard to understand why this small change was made, in contradiction to the Tale of Years.'

Solely for the chronology as set out in this volume (as with the dates relating to Ar-Gimilzôr, see p. 279 note 4) an amendment has been made to the date of Tar-Palantir's accession and the length of his reign.

3  Akallabêth, p. 269

4  *UT* p. 223

5  Akallabêth, p. 269

6  *UT*, p. 223

7  Akallabêth, p. 269

8  *Peoples*, pp. 159–62. These three passages appear in a section that Christopher Tolkien titles, '*Note on the marriage of Míriel and Pharazôn*' about which he comments that his father did 'much work' on this story but that the surviving manuscript is both 'very rough' and 'extraordinarily difficult to decipher'. The name 'Zimraphil' in these passages has here been amended to its later version, 'Zimraphel'. In a note on the reference to Amandil, he notes that his father had added, in the margin of the manuscript: '3rd in line from Eärendur and 18th from Valandil the First Lord of Andúnië'. The addition of the words [courage and] are taken from *Peoples*, p. 162.

9  These three passages incorporate material from *Peoples*, pp. 160–62 Bracketed words preceded by a question mark indicate words where Christopher Tolkien found difficulty in deciphering his father's hasty handwriting. In another sentence on p. 161, Tolkien refers to Míriel not just being loved by Elentir, but to the couple being 'betrothed'.

10  Akallabêth, p. 269

11  Akallabêth, pp. 269–70

## 3255 – AR-PHARAZÔN THE GOLDEN SEIZES THE SCEPTRE

1 Akallabêth, p. 270. Further to p. 278 note 7 above, 'three' in the source text has been emended to 'four'.
2 Appendix A, p. 1036
3 *Peoples* p. 160
4 *Peoples*, p. 162
5 *Peoples*, p. 160
6 *Letters*, No. 131, pp. 154–5. Tar-Calion is an early name for Ar-Pharazôn.

## 3261 – AR-PHARAZÔN SETS SAIL AND LANDS AT UMBAR

1 *Peoples*, pp. 181–2
2 *Lost Road*, p. 26 §5
3 The phrase 'gleaming with red gold' is an amendment to that published in *The Silmarillion* 'gleaming with red and gold'; this follows Christopher Tolkien's correction in *Peoples*, p. 155 §41.
4 Akallabêth, pp. 270–1
5 *Peoples*, p. 182

## 3262 – SAURON IS TAKEN AS PRISONER TO NÚMENOR; 3262–3310 SAURON SEDUCES THE KING AND CORRUPTS THE NÚMENÓREANS

1 Rings of Power, p. 290
2 Akallabêth, p. 271
3 *Peoples*, p. 182
4 Akallabêth, pp. 271–4
5 *Peoples*, p. 183
6 Akallabêth, pp. 274–5

## 3310 – AR-PHARAZÔN BEGINS THE BUILDING OF THE GREAT ARMAMENT

1 Unless otherwise indicated the narrative which follows is from Akallabêth, pp. 275–81.
2 *Peoples*, p. 183
3 The phrase 'there is no hope in Men' is an amendment to the wording 'no hope for Men' as published in *The Silmarillion*; this follows Christopher Tolkien's correction in *Peoples*, p. 156 §57.

### 3319 – AR-PHARAZÔN ASSAILS VALINOR. DOWNFALL OF NÚMENOR. ELENDIL AND HIS SONS ESCAPE

1   Unless otherwise indicated, the narrative which follows is from *Akallabêth*, pp. 277–82.

2   *Peoples*, p. 183. Christopher Tolkien notes, immediately following this: 'No such statement is found elsewhere. In the *Akallabêth* (*The Silmarillion* p. 280), in a passage taken virtually without change from *The Drowning of Anadûnê* ([*Sauron*], p. 374, §52), there is no reference to any named region or river.' He further adds (*Peoples*, p. 187 note 23): 'This appears to be the sole reference in any text to Tolfalas, apart from a mention of its capture by Men of the South in an outline made in the course of the writing of *The Two Towers* ([*The Treason of Isengard*], p. 435). The isle and its name appeared already on the First Map of Middle-earth ([*Treason*] pp. 298, 308), but on all maps its extent appears much greater than in the description of it here.'

3   As noted elsewhere, other tellings of the Downfall and the reshaping of the world are to be found in *Sauron Defeated* Part Three: 'The Drowning of Anadûnê' (i)–(iv) and *The Lost Road and Other Writings*, 'Part One: The Fall of Númenor and The Lost Road' I 'The Early History of the Legend', and II 'The Fall of Númenor' (i)–(iv).

In the latter volume (pp. 11–12), Christopher Tolkien includes what he refers to as 'The text of the original "scheme" of the legend . . . written at such speed that here and there words cannot be certainly interpreted. Near the beginning it is interrupted by a very rough and hasty sketch, which shows a central globe, marked *Ambar* ['the inhabited world'], with two circles around it; the inner area thus described is marked *Ilmen* ['the region above the air where the stars are'] and the outer *Vaiya* ['the sky' or 'the air enfolding the world']. Across the top of *Ambar* and cutting through the zones of *Ilmen* and *Vaiya* is a straight line extending to the outer circle in both directions.' It is most likely that this is Tolkien's first diagrammatic attempt at depicting the concept of the World Made Round and the Straight Path.

As Christopher Tolkien further notes: '. . .this remarkable text documents the beginning of the legend of Númenor, and the extension of "The Silmarillion" into a Second Age of the World.'

The passage reads, in part, as follows:

> . . .The Atalanteans [Númenóreans] fall, and rebel. . . . They build an armament and assail the shores of the Gods with thunder.
>
> The Gods therefore sundered Valinor from the earth, and an awful rift appeared down which the water poured and the armament of Atalantë [Númenor] was drowned. They globed the whole earth so that however far a man sailed he could never again

reach the West, but came back to his starting-point. Thus new lands came into being beneath the Old World; and the East and West were bent back and [?water flowed all over the round] earth's surface and there was a time of flood. But Atalantë being near the rift was utter[ly] thrown down and submerged. The remnant of . . . the Númenóreans in their ships flee East and land upon Middle-earth. . . .

The old line of the lands remained as a plain of air upon which only the Gods could walk, and the Eldar who faded as Men usurped the sun. But many of the Númenórië could see it or faintly see it; and tried to devise ships to sail on it. But they achieved only ships that would sail in Wilwa or lower air. Whereas the Plain of the Gods cut through and traversed Ilmen [in] which even birds cannot fly, save the eagles and hawks of Manwë. But the fleets of the Númenórië sailed round the world; and Men took them for gods. Some were content that this should be so.

For further discussion on the physical formation of Middle-earth, as created and as changed following the cataclysms at the end of the First and Second Ages, see Christopher Tolkien's *The Shaping of Middle-earth* (Volume IV of *The History of Middle-earth*).

4 Appendix A, p. 1037
5 The account in the Akallabêth of Númenor's fall was the result of many earlier texts, the complexities of which are addressed at length, and can be referred to, in those volumes of *The History of Middle-earth* cited on p. 282 note 3. Included here, however, for comparison with the 'Epilogue', is an extract from 'The Drowning of Anadûnê' (*Sauron* pp. 392–3) that contains a notably different account of the way in which the exiles viewed the reshaping of the world that had taken place after the Fall.

For even after their ruin the hearts of the Adûnâim were still set westward; and though they knew that the world was changed, they said: 'Avallôni is vanished from the Earth, and the Land of Gift is taken away, and in the world of this present darkness they cannot be found; yet once they were, and therefore they still are in true being and in the whole shape of the world.' And the Adûnâim held that men so blessed might look upon other times than those of the body's life; and they longed ever to escape from the shadows of their exile and to see in some fashion the light that was of old. Therefore some among them would still search the empty seas, hoping to come upon the Lonely Isle, and there to see a vision of things that were.

But they found it not, and they said: 'All the ways are bent that once were straight.' For in the youth of the world it was a hard saying to men that the Earth was not plain* as it seemed to be, and few even of the Faithful of Anadûnê had believed in their hearts this teaching; and when in after days, what by star-craft, what by the voyages of ships that sought out all the ways and waters of the Earth, the Kings of Men knew that the world was indeed round, then the belief arose among them that it had so been made only in the time of the great Downfall, and was not thus before. Therefore they thought that, while the new world fell away, the old road and the path of the memory of the Earth went on towards heaven, as it were a mighty bridge invisible. And many were the rumours and tales among them concerning mariners and men forlorn upon the sea, who by some grace or fate had entered in upon the ancient way and seen the face of the world sink below them, and so had come to the Lonely Isle, or verily to the Land of Amân that was, and had looked upon the White Mountain, dreadful and beautiful, ere they died.

* [The word] *plain* is used in the lost sense 'flat'; but cf. the later spelling *plane* of the same word, and the noun *plain*.

6 *Letters*, No. 131, p. 156. A few years later, in 1954, Tolkien wrote (*Letters*, No. 154, p. 197) about the transformation of the world from flat to round: 'In the imagination of this story we are now living on a physically round Earth. But the whole "legendarium" contains a transition from a flat world (or at least an οἰκουμένη* with borders all about it) to a globe: an inevitable transition, I suppose, to a modern "myth-maker" with a mind subjected to the same "appearances" as ancient men, and partly fed on their myths, but taught that the Earth was round from the earliest years. So deep was the impression made by "astronomy" on me that I do not think I could deal with or imaginatively conceive a flat world, though a world of static Earth with a Sun going round it seems easier (to fancy if not to reason).'

* *ecumene* or *oecumene*, an ancient Greek term for the known, inhabited, or habitable world.

7 *Towers*, Book Three XI 'The Palantír' p. 597. Referencing this rhyme, Christopher Tolkien notes elsewhere (*Peoples*, p. 157 §80): 'All the texts [of the Akallabêth] have "Twelve ships there were: six for Elendil, and for Isildur four, and for Anárion two", but on the amanuensis typescript C my father changed the numbers to "nine: four, three, two", noting in the margin: "Nine, unless the rhyme in LR [*The Lord of the Rings*] is altered to *Four times three*."' The rhyme was not changed, and Christopher Tolkien appropriately emended the 'Twelve ships' to 'Nine' when editing *The Silmarillion*.

8 *Return*, Book Six, V 'The Steward and the King' p. 963. In this strikingly autobiographical passage, Tolkien gives to Faramir his own repeated experience of an 'Atlantean dream' in which a mighty wave descends upon a landscape, see 'Introduction' pp. xx–xxiii above.

### 3320 – FOUNDATIONS OF THE REALMS IN EXILE: ARNOR AND GONDOR. THE STONES ARE DIVIDED. SAURON RETURNS TO MORDOR

1 *Letters*, No. 131, p. 156. In this letter, Tolkien wrote: 'Elendil, a Noachian figure, who has held off from the rebellion, and kept ships manned and furnished off the east coast of Númenor, flees before the overwhelming storm of the wrath of the West, and is borne high upon the towering waves that bring ruin to the west of the Middle-earth. He and his folk are cast away as exiles upon the shores.' 'Noachian' references the patriarch Noah, who appears in the Biblical story of the Deluge (Genesis 6:11–9:19), both being faithful to their beliefs and prepared for what might befall.

2 Appendix A, p. 1037

3 *Return*, Book Six, V 'The Steward and the King' p. 968

4 Accounts of these rulers will be found in *The Lord of the Rings*, Appendices A and B; and in *The Peoples of Middle-earth*, Part One: The Prologue and Appendices to *The Lord of the Rings*, VII 'The Heirs of Elendil' and IX 'The Making of Appendix A'. The narrative that follows is from Rings of Power, pp. 290–2.

5 Also among those heirlooms was the sceptre that, on Númenor, had been the symbol of office of the Lords of Andúnië, of which was later written (Appendix A, p. 1043 footnote): 'The silver rod of the Lords of Andúnie . . . is now perhaps the most ancient work of Men's hands preserved in Middle-earth.'

  The sceptre of Númenor having perished with Ar-Pharazôn in the Fall, it now became the Sceptre of Annúminas, signifying the authority of the line of Númenórean kings in Middle-earth. Many years later it was among the heirlooms in the safekeeping of Elrond in Imladris, as is written in 'The Tale of Aragorn and Arwen' [Appendix A, (v) pp. 1057 ff.].

6 See p. 179

7 Rings of Power, p. 292. By the Third Age, knowledge of the stones' continued existence would have been limited to a very few. Saruman had one in his possession at Orthanc and Denethor, the last Steward of Gondor, had another in Minas Tirith, while Sauron's all-seeing Eye observed activity on those stones using a third held in Barad-dûr.

Although the Orthanc stone played a significant role in the War of the Ring, the ultimate fate of most of the Palantíri would have been unknown at the time of this text.

8  *Towers*, Book Three, XI 'The Palantír' pp. 597–8. For a history of the Seeing-stones, see *UT*, Part Four, III 'The Palantíri' pp. 403 ff.
9  Rings of Power, p. 292
10  Rings of Power, p. 290
11  Appendix A, p. 1037
12  Rings of Power, pp. 292–3
13  Appendix A, p. 1037
14  Rings of Power, p. 293. Herumor and Fuinur were among the Númenóreans who, during Sauron's sojourn on the island, sailed east to establish fortresses and dwellings along the coast of Middle-earth and whose will was already subject to Sauron's influence. These so-called 'Black Númenóreans' may have been among those Men whom Sauron conscripted when he prepared to attack Gondor in SA 3429.

### 3429 – SAURON ATTACKS GONDOR, TAKES MINAS ITHIL AND BURNS THE WHITE TREE. ISILDUR ESCAPES DOWN ANDUIN AND GOES TO ELENDIL IN THE NORTH. ANÁRION DEFENDS MINAS ANOR AND OSGILIATH

1  Rings of Power, p. 293
2  *Fellowship*, Book One, II 'The Shadow of the Past' p. 52

### 3430 – THE LAST ALLIANCE OF ELVES AND MEN IS FORMED

1  Rings of Power, p. 293
2  *Fellowship*, Book One, XI 'A Knife in the Dark', p. 186

### 3431 – GIL-GALAD AND ELENDIL MARCH EAST TO IMLADRIS

1  Rings of Power, p. 293. Thangorodrim was the site of the War of Wrath fought in the First Age by the Host of Valinor, the Eldar and Men of the Three Houses of the Edain against the forces of Morgoth. It was for the valour of the Edain in aiding in the overthrow and defeat of Morgoth that they were given Andor, 'The Land of Gift', on which to dwell and which Men later named Númenor. See *The Silmarillion*, *Quenta Silmarillion*, XXIV 'Of the Voyage of Eärendil and the War of Wrath' pp. 246 ff.
2  *Fellowship*, Book Two, II 'The Council of Elrond', p. 243

## 3434 – THE HOST OF THE ALLIANCE CROSSES THE MISTY MOUNTAINS. BATTLE OF DAGORLAD AND DEFEAT OF SAURON. SIEGE OF BARAD-DÛR BEGINS

1 *Letters*, No. 144, p. 179; see also *Towers*, p. 476
2 Rings of Power, pp. 293–4
3 Rings of Power, p. 294
4 *UT*, Part Two IV 'The History of Galadriel and Celeborn' p. 243
5 *UT*, Part Two IV, Appendix B 'The Sindarin Princes of the Silvan Elves' p. 258. Christopher Tolkien notes here: 'Malgalad of Lórien occurs nowhere else, and is not said here to be the father of Amroth. On the other hand, Amdír father of Amroth is twice (*UT*, pp. 240 and 243) said to have been slain in the Battle of Dagorlad, and it seems therefore that Malgalad can be simply equated with Amdír. But which name replaced the other I cannot say.'
6 *Towers*, Book Four, II 'The Passage of the Dead Marshes', p. 628
7 Rings of Power, p. 294
8 *Fellowship*, Book Two, II 'The Council of Elrond', p. 243
9 Rings of Power, p. 294

### 3440 – ANÁRION SLAIN

1 Rings of Power, p. 294
2 Appendix A, p. 1043 footnote 1, which continues: 'But in the days of Atanatar Alcarin this was replaced by the jewelled helm that was used in the crowning of Aragorn.'

## 3441 – SAURON OVERTHROWN BY ELENDIL AND GIL-GALAD, WHO PERISH. ISILDUR TAKES THE ONE RING. SAURON PASSES AWAY AND THE RINGWRAITHS GO INTO THE SHADOWS. THE SECOND AGE ENDS

1 Rings of Power, p. 294
2 As recited by Sam Gamgee, as the hobbits and Strider make their way towards Weathertop in *Fellowship*, Book One, XI 'A Knife in the Dark', pp. 186–7.
3 Rings of Power, p. 294
4 Rings of Power, p. 294
5 *Fellowship*, Book Two, II, 'The Council of Elrond' p. 244

### EPILOGUE

1 Rings of Power, p. 295. *Weregild* is 'man price' or 'blood money'

established in ancient codes of law as putting a monetary value on a person's life, imposed as a fine on a killer and forming a restitution payment to the family of the victim. Tolkien would have been aware of the word, which appears in *Beowulf*, the *Völsungasaga*, the thirteenth-century Icelandic *Egil's Saga* and elsewhere. An example of this law is also referenced by Tolkien concerning Túrin II, in Appendix A, 'The Stewards', p. 1054.

2 *Fellowship*, Book Two, II 'The Council of Elrond' pp. 252–3. The content of Isildur's scroll is revealed to the Council of Elrond in the Third Age by Gandalf, who tells the company that he surmised it to have remained unread by any – since the line of kings failed – 'save Saruman and myself'. Meaning of 'glede' = a live coal or an ember.

3 Rings of Power, p. 295. A substantial, variant account of the fall of Isildur can be found in Tolkien's narrative, 'The Disaster of the Gladden Fields'. Being both an extensive text and a Third Age event (the Second Age having ended with the defeat of Sauron), it is not included in this volume, but can be read in *UT* pp. 271–85.

## APPENDIX A

1 The narrative that follows is from Rings of Power, pp. 295–303.

## APPENDIX B

1 *Lavaralda* (replacing *lavarin*) is not mentioned in *A Description of Númenor* (*UT*, p. 165 [nor, as a consequence, in this volume]) among the trees brought by the Eldar from Tol-eressëa.

2 *seven twelves of years* is an emendation of *four score of years* (first written *three score of years*); see note 10.

3 *Vinya* is written above *Númenor* in the manuscript; it occurs again in a part of the text that was rewritten (p. 240), rendered 'the New Land'. The name first appeared in an emendation to FN ['Fall of Númenor'] I [*Road*] p. 19, §2.

4 For *Terendul* see the *Etymologies* [*Road*, p. 392], stem TER, TERES.

5 As the text was originally written there followed here:

> 'Poldor called me *Eärendel* yesterday.'
>
> Elendil sighed. 'But that is a fair name. I love the story above others; indeed I chose thy name because it recalleth his. But I did not presume to give his name even to thee, nor to liken myself to Tuor the mighty, who first of Men sailed these seas. At least thou canst answer thy foolish friends that Eärendel was the chief of mariners, and surely that is still held worthy of honour in Númenor?'

'But they care not for Eärendel. And neither do I. We wish to do what he left undone.'

'What dost thou mean?'

'Thou knowest: to set foot in the far West. . . .' (&c. as on p. 235).

6 This is the earliest appearance of a Númenórean named *Valandil*. In later rewriting. . . Valandil is Elendil's brother, and they are the founders of the Númenórean kingdoms in Middle-earth ([*Road*] pp. 33–4). The name was afterwards given to both an earlier Númenórean (the first Lord of Andúnië) and a later (the youngest son of Isildur and third King of Arnor): Index to *Unfinished Tales*, entries Valandil and references.

7 In the *Quenta* ([*The Shaping of Middle-earth*] p. 151) it is not told that Tuor was 'lost'. When he felt old age creeping on him 'he built a great ship *Eärámë*, 'Eagle's Pinion', and with Idril he set sail into the sunset and the West, and came no more into any tale or song.' Later the following was added ([*Shaping*] p. 155): 'But Tuor alone of mortal Men was numbered among the elder race, and joined with the Noldoli whom he loved, and in after time dwelt still, or so it hath been said, ever upon his ship voyaging the seas of the Elvenlands, or resting a while in the harbours of the Gnomes of Tol Eressëa; and his fate is sundered from the fate of Men.'

8 This is the final form in the *Quenta* of the story of Eärendel's landing in Valinor, where in emendations made to the second text Q II ([*Shaping*] p. 156) Eärendel 'bade farewell to all whom he loved upon the last shore, and was taken from them for ever,' and 'Elwing mourned for Eärendel yet found him never again, and they are sundered till the world endeth.' Later Elendil returns more fully to the subject ([*Road*] p. 64). In QS the story is further changed, in that Elwing entered Valinor (see [*Road*] pp. 324–5 §§1–2, and commentary).

9 *Nuaran Númenóren*: the letters *ór* were scratched out in the typescript (only).

10 *Thou art but four twelves* replaced *Thou art scarce two score and ten*. As in the change recorded in note 2, a duodecimal counting replaces a decimal; but the number of years is in either case very strange. For Herendil has been called a 'boy', a 'lad', and a 'youth', and he is 'upon the threshold of early manhood' (p. 232); how then can he be forty-eight years old? But his age is unequivocally stated, and moreover Elendil says later (p. 242) that it is 44 years since Sauron came and that Herendil was then a small child; it can only be concluded there-fore that at this time the longevity of the Númenóreans implied that they grew and aged at a different rate from other men, and were not fully adult until about fifty years old. Cf. *UT*, p. 174.

11  Orontor's mission, from which he might never return, seems like a premonition of the voyage of Amandil into the West, from which he never returned (*Akallabêth* pp. 275–6 [This volume pp. 182–3]).

12  The manuscript (followed by the typescript) is here confused, since in addition to the text as printed the whole song that Fíriel sang is given as well, with translation; thus the two opening and the two closing lines and their translations are repeated. It is clear however from pencilled markings on the manuscript that my father moved at once to a second version (omitting the greater part of the song) without striking out the first. The text of the song was emended in three stages. Changes made probably very near the time of writing were *Valion númenyaron* (translated 'of the Lords of the West') > *Valion: númessier* in line 2, and *hondo-ninya* > *indo-ninya* in line 9; *Vinya* was written above Númenor as an alternative in line 8 (cf. note 3). Before the later emendations the text ran thus:

> Ilu Ilúvatar en kárę eldain a fírimoin
> ar antaróta mannar Valion: númessier.
> Toi aina, mána, meldielto – enga morion:
> talantie. Mardello Melko lende: márie.
> Eldain en kárier Isil, nan hildin Úr-anar.
> Toi írimar. Ilqainen antar annar lestanen
> Ilúvatáren. Ilu vanya, fanya, eari,
> i-mar, ar ilqa ímen. Írima ye Númenor.
> Nan úye sére indo-ninya símen, ullume;
> ten sí ye tyelma, yéva tyel ar i-narqelion,
> írę ilqa yéva nótina, hostainiéva, yallume:
> ananta úva táre fárea, ufárea!
> Man táre antáva nin Ilúvatar, Ilúvatar
> enyárę tar i tyel, írę Anarinya qeluva?

The Father made the World for Elves and Mortals, and he gave it into the hands of the Lords. They are in the West. They are holy, blessed, and beloved: save the dark one. He is fallen. Melko has gone from Earth: it is good. For Elves they made the Moon, but for Men the red Sun; which are beautiful. To all they gave in measure the gifts of Ilúvatar. The World is fair, the sky, the seas, the earth, and all that is in them. Lovely is Númenor. But my heart resteth not here for ever; for here is ending, and there will be an end and the Fading, when all is counted, and all numbered at last, but yet it will not be enough, not enough. What will the Father, O Father, give me in that day beyond the end when my Sun faileth?

Subsequently *Mardello Melko* in line 4 was changed to *Melko Mardello*, and lines 5–6 became

> En kárielto eldain Isil, hildin Úr-anar.
> Toi írimar. Ilyain antalto annar lestanen

Then, after the typescript was made, *Melko* was changed to *Alkar* in text and translation; see note 15.

The thought of lines 5–6 of the song reappears in Elendil's words to Herendil later (p. 239): 'But the Valar made the Moon for the Firstborn and the Sun for Men to confound the Darkness of the Enemy.' Cf. QS §75 (*The Silmarillion* p. 99): 'For the Sun was set as a sign for the awakening of Men and the waning of the Elves; but the Moon cherishes their memory.'

13  For *hon-maren* 'heart of the house' see the *Etymologies* [*Road*, p. 364], stem KHO-N.

14  Here the typescript made at Allen and Unwin ([*Road*] p. 8, footnote) ends. The publishers' reader (see [*Road*] p. 97) said that 'only the preliminary two chapters . . . and one of the last chapters . . . are written.' It might be supposed that the typescript ended where it does because no more had been written at that time, but I do not think that this was the reason. At the point where the typescript breaks off (in the middle of a manuscript page) there is no suggestion at all of any interruption in the writing, and it seems far more likely that the typist simply gave up, for the manuscript here becomes confused and difficult through rewriting and substitutions.

In the previous parts of *The Lost Road* I have taken up all corrections to the manuscript, however quickly and lightly made, since they all appear in the typescript. From this point there is no external evidence to show when the pencilled emendations were made; but I continue to take these up into the text as before.

15  Elendil's long tale to Herendil of the ancient history, from 'There is Ilúvatar, the One' to 'and ruin (if he might) Avallon and Valinor' on p. 241, is a replacement of the original much briefer passage. This replacement must be later than the submission of *The Lost Road* to Allen and Unwin, for Morgoth is here called *Alkar* as the text was first written, not *Melko*, whereas in the song sung by Fíriel in the previous chapter *Melko* was only changed in pencil to *Alkar*, and this was not taken up into the typescript. The original passage read thus:

> He spoke of the rebellion of Melko [later > *Alkar and subsequently*], mightiest of the Powers, that began at the making of the World; and of his rejection by the Lords of the West after he

had wrought evil in the Blessed Realm and caused the exile of the Eldar, the firstborn of the earth, who dwelt now in Eressëa. He told of Melko's tyranny in Middle-earth, and how he had enslaved Men; of the wars which the Eldar waged with him, and were defeated, and of the Fathers of Men that had aided them; how Eärendel brought their prayer to the Lords, and Melko was overthrown and thrust forth beyond the confines of the World.

Elendil paused and looked down on Herendil. He did not move or make a sign. Therefore Elendil went on. 'Dost thou not perceive then, Herendil, that Morgoth is a begetter of evil, and brought sorrow upon our fathers? We owe him no allegiance except by fear. For his share of the governance of the World was forfeit long ago. Nor need we hope in him: the fathers of our race were his enemies; wherefore we can look for no love from him or any of his servants. Morgoth doth not forgive. But he cannot return into the World in present power and form while the Lords are enthroned. He is in the Void, though his Will remaineth and guideth his servants. And his will is to overthrow the Lords, and return, and wield dominion, and have vengeance on those who obey the Lords.

'But why should we be deceived. . .' (&c. as on p. 241).

The closing sentences ('But he cannot return into the World. . .') closely echo, or perhaps rather are closely echoed by (see note 25) a passage in FN ['Fall of Númenor'] II (§1) [*Road*, p. 29].

16  In QS [Quenta Silmarillion] §10 [*Road*, pp. 206–7] it is said that Melko was 'coëval with Manwë'. The name *Alkar* 'the Radiant' of Melko occurs, I believe, nowhere outside this text.

17  See note 8. The reference to Eärendel's *child* shows that Elros had not yet emerged, as he had not in FN II ([*Road*] p. 34).

18  'mockeries of the creatures of Ilúvatar': cf. FN II §1 [*Road*, pp. 24–5] and commentary. [*Road*, p. 29]

19  Here the long replacement passage ends (see note 15), though as written it continued in much the same words as did the earlier form ('For Morgoth cannot return into the World while the Lords are enthroned. . .'); this passage was afterwards struck out.

20  The words 'a gift which in the wearing of time even the Lords of the West shall envy' were a pencilled addition to the text, and are the first appearance of this idea: a closely similar phrase is found in a text of the *Ainulindalë* written years later (cf. *The Silmarillion* p. 42: 'Death is their fate, the gift of Ilúvatar, which as Time wears even the Powers shall envy.')

21  Cf. FN II §5 [*Road*, p. 26]: 'Some said that he was a king greater than

the King of Númenor; some said that he was one of the Gods or their sons set to govern Middle-earth. A few reported that he was an evil spirit, perchance Morgoth himself returned. But this was held to be only a foolish fable of the wild Men.'

22    This duodecimal computation is found in the text as written; see note 10.

23    Cf. FN II §5 [*Road*, p. 26]: 'for [the Lords] said that Sauron would work evil if he came; but he could not come to Númenor unless he was summoned and guided by the king's messengers.'

24    The name *Moriondë* occurs, I think, nowhere else. This eastern haven is no doubt the forerunner of Rómenna.

25    This is the story of the coming of Sauron to Númenor found in FN II §5 [*Road*, pp. 26–7], which was replaced soon after by a version in which the lifting up of the ships by a great wave and the casting of them far inland was removed; see [*Road*] pp. 9, 26–7. In the first FN II version the sea rose like a *mountain*, the ship that carried Sauron was set upon a *hill*, and Sauron stood upon the hill to preach his message to the Númenóreans. In *The Lost Road* the sea rose like a *hill*, changed in pencil to *mountain*, Sauron's ship was cast upon a *high rock*, changed in pencil to *hill*, and Sauron spoke standing on the rock (left unchanged). This is the best evidence I can see that of these two companion works (see notes 15, 21, 23) *The Lost Road* was written first.

26    *Alkar*: pencilled alteration of *Melko*: see note 15.

27    On Eressëan ('Elf-latin', Qenya), the common speech of all Elves, see [*Road*] p. 56. The present passage is the first appearance of the idea of a linguistic component in the attack by the Númenórean 'government' on Eressëan culture and influence; cf. *The Line of Elros* in *Unfinished Tales* (p. 222 [This volume pp. 162–3]), of Ar-Adûnakhôr, the twentieth ruler of Númenor: 'He was the first King to take the sceptre with a title in the Adûnaic tongue. . . In this reign the Elven-tongues were no longer used, nor permitted to be taught, but were maintained in secret by the Faithful'; and of Ar-Gimilzôr, the twenty-third ruler: 'he forbade utterly the use of the Eldarin tongues' (very similarly in the *Akallabêth*, pp. 267–8 [This volume p. 165]). But of course at the time of *The Lost Road* the idea of Adûnaic as one of the languages of Númenor had not emerged, and the proposal is only that 'the ancestral speech of Men' should be 'revived'.

28    This goes back to FN I §6 [*Road*, p. 15]: 'Sûr said that the gifts of Morgoth were withheld by the Gods, and that to obtain plenitude of power and undying life he [the king Angor] must be master of the West.'

## MAP OF MIDDLE-EARTH

1 For the publication of *The Lord of the Rings: The Fellowship of the Ring* (1954), Christopher Tolkien drew a large, general map of Middle-earth. Unnamed, the map was inked in black and red and presented as a fold-out feature at the back of the volume. Although based on his father's original, much-amended and worked-over pencil map, Christopher's rendition was made in some haste due to pressure from the publishers anxious to meet a deadline for completion of the book. When, in 1980, Christopher Tolkien published his late father's writings in *Unfinished Tales*, he created a map of Númenor, facing p. 168 (and in this volume, see p. 12) and re-drew the map of Middle-earth, explaining:

> My first intention was to include in this book the map that accompanies *The Lord of the Rings* with the addition to it of further names; but it seemed to me on reflection that it would be better to copy my original map and take the opportunity to remedy some of its minor defects (to remedy the major ones being beyond my powers). I have therefore redrawn it fairly exactly, on a scale half as large again (that is to say, the new map as drawn is half as large again as the old map in its published dimensions). The area shown is smaller, but the only features lost are the Havens of Umbar and the Cape of Forochel. (*UT*, p.13)

Since Umbar is referenced in this current presentation of Tolkien's Second Age writings, Christopher's original 'unnamed' map is reproduced here (p. 298), while the later *Unfinished Tales* map, titled 'The West of Middle-earth at the End of the Third Age' (now used in all editions of *The Lord of the Rings*), is included at the beginning of this volume on pp. x–xi.

# ACKNOWLEDGEMENTS

As is always the case when closely studying the writings of J.R.R. Tolkien, one is unavoidably reminded that here is an author who was not just gifted with an extraordinary imagination, but who was also a learned academic who was able to bring to his literary creativity (or, as Tolkien would prefer to call it, 'sub-creativity') the rigour and scholarly discipline of a philologist and a student of the rich worlds of myth, legend and folk-tale.

Since the majority of the published texts from which this book has been assembled were the product of Christopher Tolkien's almost lifelong role of understanding, curating and ordering the Tolkien legendarium, it is also a reminder of Christopher's unique talent as an assiduous editor: blessed as he was with a deft and elegant writing style that is his own but which perfectly complements that of his father.

These two – Tolkien, father and son – stand first and centre as the 'onlie begetter' and amanuensis of the tales collected in this volume. Nevertheless, there are a number of others who must also be acknowledged for their generous assistance.

I am deeply indebted to the Directors of the Tolkien Estate and to Christopher Tolkien's estate, not just for giving their approval to this project, but also for their positivity and their active involvement in the form of detailed and constructive comments that significantly helped with the book's development from concept to finished volume. During the book's journey to press, the Tolkien family, Trustees and the wider Tolkien community lost Priscilla Tolkien, the last of the Professor's children.

She was a passionate advocate for her father's work and an untiring friend to those who journeyed in Middle-earth, which is why this volume is fondly dedicated to her memory.

At HarperCollins, appreciation and gratitude go to David Brawn, Publisher of Estates, for suggesting this project and for trusting me to accomplish it; to Hannah Stamp, Editorial and Pub Ops Executive, for her attentive assistance and eye for detail; Designer Terence Caven, whose sympathetic and elegant layouts belie the many versions we went through to get here; and Production Manager Simon Moore, for helping us all to work against the clock and get these books printed and delivered to every corner of the world at a time when such logistics are proving more complicated than ever.

In making revisions and corrections to the text of this paperback edition, I wish to acknowledge the assistance of Ivy Schaapman, Jonathan Hunt and John Garth.

This is at least the twelfth project (books and calendars) on which I have been fortunate to work with HarperCollins' Publishing Director for Tolkien, Chris Smith, as my editor. As ever, Chris has been a paragon of patience and, most importantly, an ever-supportive dispenser of wise, calming and encouraging words to the extent that the resulting book is truly as much his as it is mine.

Although Alan Lee and I have been friends for over twenty years, we've never previously had the opportunity to collaborate on a project, so *The Fall of Númenor* is a special milestone and, as always with Alan's masterly work, I am in awe of the beauty and dynamism of the visions of Middle-earth and Númenor that are captured in his evocative new colour illustrations and the proliferation of pencil decorations found within these pages.

Final thanks go to my agent, Philip Patterson; and, for above-and-beyond loyalty, my long-suffering husband, David Weeks, who – uncomplainingly – shared many months of our joint life living through the tumultuous days of the Second Age of Middle-earth.

*Brian Sibley*

# MAP OF MIDDLE-EARTH